BLOOD AND BULLETS

A FIRESTICK WESTERN

BLOOD AND BULLETS

WILLIAM W. JOHNSTONE
AND J. A. JOHNSTONE

THORNDIKE PRESS
A part of Gale, a Cengage Company

GALE
A Cengage Company

LIBRARY OF CONGRESS CIP DATA ON FILE.
CATALOGUING IN PUBLICATION FOR THIS BOOK
IS AVAILABLE FROM THE LIBRARY OF CONGRESS.

ISBN-13: 978-1-4328-9420-7 (hardcover alk. paper)

Published in 2022 by arrangement with Pinnacle Books, an imprint of Kensington Publishing Corp.

Printed in Mexico
Print Number: 01   Print Year: 2022

BLOOD AND BULLETS

CHAPTER 1

For eleven months out of the year, anyone who found themselves passing through Jepperd's Ford might look around and wonder what needed to be "forded" in this godforsaken, sun-blistered corner of West Texas.

The answer could be found only during the handful of days when the spring rains came hard and every gully and low-lying pocket of land for miles around was awash in muddy torrents except for the hump of rocky ground where the meager collection of ramshackle buildings stood.

It was late on such a day when Charlie Gannon and Josh Stallworth rode into Jepperd's Ford. With a black, boiling sky overhead and sheet after sheet of rain slicing into them, the sight of the gray, sodden structure that bore a faded SALOON sign above its entrance was a thing of beauty to the eyes of the two drifting cowpokes. After tying their horses to the hitch rail out front, they slogged hurriedly inside.

"Close the damn door and skin outta them drippin'-wet slickers before you swamp the place! Why don't you just carry in a couple bucketfuls of water and pour 'em all over while you're at it!"

This warm welcome came from a diminutive old crone behind the plank bar. She couldn't have stood more than five feet tall, her chin only a few inches above the warped, cigarette-scorched planks nailed down over the tops of three wooden barrels. She had iron-gray hair pulled tightly back into a bun, eyes as black as two polished marbles set in a doughy face with a cruel slash of a mouth from which a corncob pipe poked out of one corner.

She wore a faded blue man's work shirt (or a boy's, considering her small frame), tucked into tan corduroy trousers held up by red suspenders and in turn tucked into wine-colored cowboy boots. There was nothing feminine about the shape filling out these clothes; they could have been hung on a cedar log for the same effect.

A gunbelt was buckled around her middle, with a black-handled Schofield revolver riding prominently in the holster.

"There are wooden pegs on the wall there for hangin' up your gear," the crone pointed out, her tone mellowing somewhat. "Then come on over here and belly up. I expect you'll be wantin' a slug of something to warm your innards."

"Likely more than just a slug, Grandma," said Charlie. "But you are definitely on the right track."

"I got rye, corn squeezin's, tequila, and beer," came the response. "And if you call me Grandma again, you pup, I got a wheelful of .45 caliber you can get a slug out of for free."

"Take it easy, take it easy," Charlie said, holding up his hands, palms out, as he and Josh strode up to the bar. "I didn't mean nothing by it."

"State your business then, and no sass."

"We'll have rye. And you can leave the bottle," said Josh.

"A shot I'll pour on trust. To put up a bottle, I'll need to see some money."

Josh pulled a wad of damp bills from his pocket and laid them on the bar. "There you go. Take what you need." He was a bandy-legged specimen, medium height, with a potbelly pushing the front of his shirt taut, a bulbous nose, and an unruly thatch of brown hair, some of which was always spilled out from under the front brim of his hat. He was quick to flash a big, toothy

9

smile, and the laugh crinkles around his deep-set blue eyes were testimony to this and to his generally good nature.

The wad of bills on the bar top produced a smile of sorts from the crone, too, but hers was short-lived and neither bright nor toothy. After withdrawing proper payment, she set a bottle of rye whiskey and two glasses in front of the new arrivals.

"There ya be. Wet your gullets. But don't let that popskull cause you to go rowdy on me."

Charlie reached eagerly for the bottle and began filling the glasses, saying, "Gettin' rowdy is the farthest thing from our minds."

Charlie was half a head taller than Josh, elongated and narrow all over — from his beanpole frame to his blade of a face dominated by a hatchet-sharp nose. He had suspicious little eyes, a weak chin, and limp blond hair that hung in greasy strands down the back of his neck and over his ears. When he tipped back his head to toss down a shot of red-eye, the oversized lump of his Adam's apple bobbed up and down in his stringy throat like there was some kind of frantic bug or small wild animal running back and forth under the whisker-stubbled skin, trying to escape.

The two cowpokes slapped their emptied

glasses back down on the bar top in unison. This time it was Josh who reached for the bottle to pour some more.

"If you don't mind me askin'," he said, filling each glass to the brim, "you got a name you'd rather be called than just 'barkeep'?"

The crone frowned, considering. "I can live with 'barkeep.' But, if you're gonna hang around a spell, reckon you might as well make it what most folks hereabouts call me. Ma. Ma Speckler."

Charlie paused with his drink raised partway to his mouth. "Wait a minute. I called you 'Grandma' a minute ago and you threatened to plant a slug in me. But now you're sayin' it's okay for us — along with everybody else — to go ahead and call you 'Ma'?"

"I reckon that skinny head of yours don't have room for a lot of thinkin' before you run off at the mouth, is that your problem?" Ma said sharply. "In the first place, I *might* be old enough to be a mother to some of your kind who come through here. But that damn sure don't make me old enough to be no grandmaw! In the second place, your pard there was courteous enough to *ask* before he started bein' too forward. That makes a difference, if it ain't too hard for

11

that skinny head of yours to understand."

"He understands, Ma," Josh was quick to assure her, throwing in one of his most charming smiles for good measure. "Ain't that right, Charlie?"

Charlie, who spent a lot of time being self-conscious about his narrow face and head and didn't like being reminded of it by others, replied somewhat sullenly, "Like I said, we ain't here to start no rowdiness."

"Well, see to it you don't, then."

"I'll tell you what *is* rowdy, though," said Josh after tossing down his second drink, "and that's the doggone weather out there. How long does a storm like this usually last hereabouts?"

"This is the spring," said Ma. "Could last the rest of the night, could last another day or two. Even if this one lets up, you can bet there'll be another toad-strangler right on its heels. Then, after a couple, three weeks, it'll all be over and everything will turn dryer than a fried coyote turd. A drop of rain, except for maybe during a little piece of winter, will be scarce as hen's teeth until next spring again."

"In other words," said Charlie, "ain't much hope for us ridin' outta here before tomorrow unless we can grow fins and teach our horses to swim."

12

"I wouldn't even count too strong on tomorrow," said Ma.

"Damn the luck," Charlie grumbled.

"Hey, it could be a whole lot worse," Josh reminded him. "Leastways we're somewhere warm and dry. Wasn't only an hour or so ago we were out there in the middle of nothing with no sign of shelter in sight and water rushin' through every gully and low spot in any direction we looked."

"Where you fellas from, to allow yourselves to get caught in these empty parts in the middle of the rainy season?"

"We been workin' for a rancher up Oklahoma way for the past couple years," Josh told her. "Nice-sized spread. Not too big, room to grow. But then, right after Christmas, the rancher got stomped powerful bad by an ornery ol' bull. Left him ridin' a bed for the rest of his days, which probably won't be many. With him out of commission, his wife and kids wanted nothing to do with keepin' the ranch goin'. So they sold it off in pieces to some surroundin' ranchers who already had full crews of their own, leavin' me and Charlie and a few other fellas all of a sudden out of jobs with no, whatyacall, prospects in the area. So that put us on the drift, lookin' for a new spot to settle."

13

Ma's expression soured. "Even through the rain, I expect you saw that there ain't much in the way of decent ranchin' to be found in these parts."

"To tell the truth, we wasn't really payin' attention," Charlie told her. "You see, we've lately come to agreement on a particular destination we're aimin' for."

"Place about three days' ride from here. We came through there one time in the past, back before we landed in Oklahoma," Josh explained. "Peaceful little valley stretched out below the Vieja Mountains. A sprawl of good grassland with ranchin' outfits that are growin' bigger all the time. And they got a nice, quiet little town there, too, called Buffalo Peak . . ."

CHAPTER 2

It was storming in Buffalo Peak. Hard. It had been, on and off — mostly on — for the past three days. People used to clear skies, wide-open spaces, and plenty of elbow room were starting to feel hemmed in. Cramped and irritable. Nerves were raw and getting rawer.

"I say it's mostly on account of this blasted rain," declared Malachi "Beartooth" Skinner as he tramped down Trail Street, the town's main drag, keeping to the boardwalks as much as possible, covering the open, sloppy alleyways in long, hopping strides.

"The rain sure as hell ain't helpin', I won't argue that," responded Elwood "Firestick" McQueen, striding along beside him.

Both men wore black, shiny wet rain slickers and wide-brimmed, flat-crowned hats. Firestick was a powerfully built individual in his early fifties, a shade over six feet, square-jawed, with pale blue eyes and streaks of gray at his temples. On his feet he wore high moccasin boots with fringed cuffs. Beartooth was equally tall, a year or two younger, leaner of frame, with a wedge-shaped face, intense dark eyes, and a dimpled chin that served to somewhat offset the harder angles of his features.

"But ever since Sterling brought in soiled doves and started makin' 'em available at his place," Firestick continued, "the outbreaks of trouble there have been steadily on the rise, rain or no rain. And his latest girl, especially — that strawberry blonde — is a trouble-causin' little teaser who's ratcheted everything up another notch strictly on her own."

"So you figure we're gonna find she's behind the trouble goin' on there again tonight?" said Beartooth.

Firestick grunted. "She'll factor in somehow. I'd bet on it."

"A troublemakin' tease and this damn endless rain," muttered Beartooth as a low, lonely rumble of thunder rolled across the nighttime sky. "Not a good combination."

By this point they had stepped up onto the stretch of boardwalk that ran in front of a large two-story building with a tall sign that proclaimed in red-trimmed gold lettering: THE LONE STAR PALACE SALOON. The sign was propped on the lip of a narrow strip of shingled awning that jutted out over the entrance and extended across the front of the building. Huddled under this slice of protection, bunched to either side of the batwing doors, were half a dozen men wearing anxious expressions. A couple of them clenched half-empty mugs of beer in their fists.

"You're none too soon, Marshal," said one of the mug holders. "There's trouble brewin' in there and it's primed to bust wide open any second."

"Those High Point wranglers are drunk and riled and takin' turns eggin' each other on," warned another.

"Drunk and riled ain't all those young rannies are," somebody else added snidely. "They're hump-backed for that new gal Sterling's got in there, and they ain't ready to back away without gettin' a turn at what they came for."

"Well I ain't drunk or hump-backed, neither one," grumbled Firestick, "but I'm damn well riled at bein' drug out in this rotten weather. So you fellas stay here out of the way and we'll have this tamed down in short order."

Before pushing through the batwings,

17

Firestick took a second to peel open his slicker, revealing the town marshal's star pinned prominently to the front of his shirt. Beartooth did the same, revealing a deputy's tin, as well as the fact he was carrying a double-barreled Greener twelve-gauge shotgun.

The two lawmen entered the Palace in the same long, quick strides that had carried them down the street. Once in, they promptly fanned out, Firestick taking a couple steps toward the side of the room along which ran a rather ornate bar, Beartooth angling a little wider the other way, over toward where some round-topped gaming tables were spaced out.

The scene froze for a moment as all eyes swept toward them. In that instant, Firestick and Beartooth were able to grasp the situation.

Two of the gaming tables had card players seated at them, apprehension and varying degrees of concern showing on their faces. Behind the bar, Earl Sterling, the unflappable, always precisely groomed owner-proprietor of the Palace, stood with his hair uncharacteristically mussed and a trickle of blood leaking from one corner of his mouth.

Also behind the bar, though a few steps down from Sterling, was Frenchy Fontaine, the cool French beauty who served as hostess/entertainer for the establishment and was generally presumed to be Sterling's lover.

At the far end of the room, near the bottom of the stairs that led up to the second floor, a man sprawled unconscious. His cleanly shaven bullet head and blocky build identified him as Arthur, the Palace's main bartender and bouncer. Lying on the floor beside him was the thick-barreled billy club — its many dents and nicks signifying frequent use — that Arthur resorted to when things started to get out of hand. It looked like this time he hadn't resorted to it quite soon enough.

The source of the trouble was as obvious as the bright red blood dribbling from the corner of Sterling's mouth. It was three liquored-up cowboys, drunk enough and riled enough to feel ready to take on anybody in the saloon or the town or, hell, the whole world.

Two of these *hombres* were leaning insolently against the bar, one positioned in a way that allowed him to keep an eye on Sterling, the other facing outward toward the men seated at the gaming tables and wearing a sneer that silently challenged them to try and do something if they didn't like what was going on.

The third troublemaker, a tall, slab-shouldered specimen with a neck like a young bull, stood in the middle of a roughly defined aisle that ran between the bar and the gaming tables. In his right hand he held a drawn revolver, in his left he gripped a sawed-off shotgun similar to the one Beartooth was brandishing. Above and slightly ahead of where the man stood, a thinning haze of powder smoke hung in the air.

When Firestick and Beartooth first came in, the third man had been facing the stairway where Arthur lay crumpled. At the lawmen's arrival, he cranked his head and upper torso around and raked them with an angry glare.

"Everybody stay just like you are!" barked Firestick, sweeping his slicker open wider and dropping his right hand to hang claw-like above the .44-caliber Frontier Colt holstered on his hip. "You with the guns — drop 'em! The rest of you keep your hands where we can see 'em plain."

Nobody said or did anything . . . except the apparent leader of the troublemakers. His eyes locked on the marshal, and though he remained very still in his half-turned pose, he didn't hold back from working his mouth.

"What if I don't *feel* like droppin' my irons, law dog?"

"Then you can die with 'em in your hands. All the same to me," Firestick replied.

The sneerer at the bar said, "Don't let him bluff you, Orval. Me and Willis will back your play."

"That's a real encouragin' thing for you to say," said Beartooth. "Encouragin' but awful dumb. From where I stand I can cut loose with both barrels and blow you two to mincemeat before you ever clear leather. The spread of this baby might even catch a piece of Orval in the process."

"That's mighty big talk," grated Orval. "But in case you didn't notice, yours ain't the only scattergun here. So far I only used this one I took away from the barkeep to club ol' baldy there when he tried to get in my way. That means I still got a pair of fully loaded barrels, and I'm thinkin' I got a chance to spin and blast at least one of you meddlin' bastards before you're able to cut me down."

"Thinkin' it and doin' it are real different things," Beartooth cautioned him. "But feel free to find out for yourself."

Out of the corner of his mouth, never taking his eyes off Orval and keeping the other two in his peripheral vision, Firestick said to Sterling, "What the hell's this all about, anyway?"

Chalky-faced, his voice trembling a little, Sterling said, "One of my girls, Miss Cleo . . . These fellas showed up lookin' for a turn with her. But she's already booked with a client who paid for a whole night's worth of her services. They're not willing to accept that."

Firestick's expression soured. Miss Cleo. The strawberry blonde he'd had a hunch about.

"You damned right we ain't willin' to accept that," proclaimed Orval. "It plumb ain't right! It's greedy and wrong! Me and my pards rode an hour and a half through the rain for a turn with Miss Cleo, only to be told some money-flasher has claimed her for the whole stinkin' night and we'll have to wait until another day!"

"There are other girls available," Sterling wailed. "I offered them their choice — at a bargain price even, due to the inconvenience."

"We don't want no other choice. We came to see Miss Cleo," insisted the sneerer at the bar.

"Let me do the talkin', Sully," Orval told him. "You and Willis just stay focused on those law dogs; don't get distracted."

"Don't make no difference who does the talkin', or how much of it you do! I wouldn't lay with any of you three ruffians now, even if you had gold coins pourin' out your ears!"

This declaration came from a new voice, a female one, speaking from the second floor. A young woman stood on the landing at the top of the stairs, leaning on the top rail of the waist-high banister. She was thirtyish, still pretty, though starting to show some wear from the hard life she led. Thick reddish-blond hair spilled around her face and the flimsy gown she wore — scooped low enough in front to reveal the upper swells of her generous breasts.

"Cleo!" Sterling shouted. "Get back in your room. You coming out here won't do anything to help."

"Don't look like anybody else is doing a damn thing to help . . . why should I be any different?" the girl responded. "You let that ape blast the hell out of my door. What if one of those slugs had come through and killed somebody?"

For the first time, Firestick noticed the bullet holes in the partly open door of a room overlooking the saloon from the balcony. That explained the wisps of powder smoke still hanging in the air above Orval;

that and the six-gun still in his hand pretty clearly indicated he was the one who'd fired the shots that put the holes there.

Before the marshal could say anything, Orval turned back around and glared up at Cleo, saying, "If those bullets were such a bother, why don't you have Mr. Moneybags hisself step out here and complain to my face about 'em?"

This gave Firestick the opening he needed. Orval's obsession with and anger toward the girl, combined with his drunken state, caused him to cap off the series of foolish decisions he'd already made by taking his attention off the lawmen — the very thing he'd warned Sully against only a minute ago.

Without hesitation and all in one smooth motion, Firestick drew his Colt and fired from the waist. The .44 slug expelled by a tongue of red flame smashed into the heel of Orval's gun hand, just above where he was holding the hogleg down at his side. He yelped in surprise and pain, his bullet-stricken hand jerking involuntarily out in front of him, the gun flying from its grasp.

Perfectly timed to Firestick's draw, Beartooth elevated his Greener slightly and, also firing from the waist, triggered a single barrel. Smoke and flame belched from the muzzle, releasing a twelve-gauge load that went screaming over the heads of Willis and Sully, destroying a wide section of liquor bottles on a high row above the bar. Amidst the gush of booze and pulverized glass that exploded outward as a result — much of it also drenching Sterling and Frenchy — the two startled cowpokes made frantic dives to the floor, covering their heads with their hands and making no attempt to go for their guns in order to try and "back" Orval.

Following his shot, Firestick moved quickly toward Orval. On the way, as he was passing where Sully had dropped to his hands and knees, the marshal swung a well-timed foot and slammed the heel of his moccasin boot hard to the side of the cowpoke's head. He did this without breaking stride, leaving Sully knocked cold and flat in his wake, as Firestick continued toward Orval.

The latter was still on his feet, hunched forward, making mewling noises as he pressed his damaged hand to his chest. But the sawed-off remained gripped in his other hand, making him still too unpredictable and dangerous for Firestick to take any chances.

With this in mind, the marshal stepped up behind the big man and clubbed him across the back of his head with the Colt. He had to do this a second time before Orval finally dropped to his knees. As he teetered there, the sawed-off slipped from his grip and thumped to the floor. And then, at last, Orval tipped slowly forward until he dropped face-first and lay still.

When Firestick looked around, he saw that the remaining troublemaker — the one called Willis, the only one of the three still conscious and uninjured — remained on the floor, pushing himself crablike back against the base of the bar, while Beartooth hovered over him with the business end of the Greener practically shoved up his nose.

Over his shoulder, Beartooth asked casually, "This jasper here look to you like he might be thinkin' about tryin' to resist arrest?"

"Could be," Firestick said. "He's got a kinda shifty look to him. Might be capable of about anything."

"For God's sake no!" Willis gasped. "I ain't gonna try nothing. With a shotgun jammed in my face, you think I'm loco?"

Firestick sighed wearily. "Maybe not. But that sure as hell don't make you smart."

CHAPTER 3

"Buffalo Peak, you say?"

The question was posed by a deep, well-modulated male voice from across the room. Its tone was one of simple curiosity, but it caused Josh and Charlie to both turn with a bit of a start. In their haste to get in out of the rain and throw down some belly-warming red-eye, they'd entered Jepperd's Ford's nameless, dimly lighted little saloon without either of them noticing there was anyone else besides them and the barkeep present.

They saw now that four people sat at a rough-hewn table positioned back near the far wall. They were outside the pool of pale yellow light cast by the oil lamp hanging from a ceiling beam in the middle of the room. This left them largely in shadow, and, if not for a squat candle burning in the center of their table, it would have been difficult to discern their features even once it was known they were there.

"That's right . . . Buffalo Peak," Josh said in answer to the question. He couldn't tell which of the murky faces had asked it, though one of them appeared to be a woman so he was pretty sure it wasn't her. Letting one side of his mouth lift into an easy, lopsided grin, he added, "That's where we're headed, even though we didn't reckon on needin' a boat to make it there and then hopin' it won't be washed away once we do."

One of the faces, a gent of about fifty or so with a long, thin nose, pencil mustache, and fleshy pouches under heavy-lidded eyes, returned something akin to Josh's grin. On him it was so brief it was more like just the hint of a smile.

"You'll make your destination okay," he said, the same voice that had spoken before. "You just need a little patience is all. This rain's bound to let up before too much longer. When it does, the relentlessly thirsty land around here will suck it up and turn dry again practically in an eyeblink. And then, by the time you get to Buffalo Peak, you'll find it waiting for you just fine."

Charlie edged up beside Josh and said, "You familiar with Buffalo Peak, are you?"

"I know *of* it, yes," the man with the pencil mustache replied. "Can't say I've ever been there myself, though I've met some folks who are familiar with the place and they've all spoken highly of it."

"Good. That's the way we remember it, too. Hope it ain't changed none," said Josh.

"Tell you what, why don't you fellas take a load off? Bring your bottle, pull up a chair, and sit for a while. Join us," Pencil Mustache invited. "Don't let Ma throw too much of a scare into you. It might be hard to believe, but once you get used to her you'll find she's actually more human than she-wolf."

"That might be," Ma said from her side of the bar, "but I still got fangs enough to tear the bark off your hide, Pierce Torrence."

Torrence, the man with the pencil mustache, chuckled tolerantly. "Don't doubt it for a minute, Ma. But put your hackles down. All I'm trying to do is spread a little hospitality and maybe make you some money at the same time. After all, this *is* a business you're running here, right? Serving customers and so forth?"

"I get enough customers to suit me," grumbled Ma.

"Yes, I'm sure you do. But most of them are desert rats barely able to squeeze out a few cents for a splash or two of rotgut. But here" — Torrence made a gesture toward Charlie and Josh — "you have two wage earners who can actually afford, like me and my group, to pay for an assortment of services. If, that is, you take the time to let them know what's available."

Ma frowned. "They got mouths and tongues, ain't they? All they got to do is ask."

Torrence sighed. "What I'm trying to get at, gents," he said, addressing Josh and Charlie again, "is that there are some amenities besides liquor that are also available in this out-of-the way little paradise. If you're interested, that is. And at a reasonable price, I might add."

"Such as food and a place to put us up and our horses for the night?" asked Charlie, looking hopeful.

"Exactly," said Torrence. "Much like her liquor supply, Ma's menu isn't big on variety — usually either venison or rabbit stew — but it's tasty and the portions are generous. There's a barn out back for your horses, and I'm sure sleeping accommodations can be arranged. There's a loft upstairs, but I have to warn you that's already spoken for by me and my group."

Charlie turned to Ma. "How about it,

ma'am? We'd like to arrange all those things."

Ma rolled her eyes. "Jesus, are we gonna have to go through that again? I ain't no damn ma'am or I ain't no grandma. I'm Ma — can you get that through your head?" Then, jutting her chin out, she added, "Yeah, you can get vittles and a place for you and your horses to spend the night. Like the man said, there's a barn out back. If you put up your horses there and pay for hay and grain, it'd be no extra charge for you to sleep out there, too. It ain't exactly leak free but there's more dry spots than wet ones. If you want to pay some for stayin' under the roof here, I can put down a couple straw mats on the floor and you can bring in your bedrolls to use with 'em."

Charlie and Josh exchanged glances and then, turning once more to Ma, Charlie said, "We'll take the straw mats and some grub for ourselves, hay and grain for our horses. It sounds just fine . . . er, Ma."

"No need to butter me up. The prices are the same, sweet talk or no."

"Sure. Okay. You want us to take our horses around back while you're dishin' up a couple bowls of that stew? If there's a lantern out there, we oughta be able to see well enough to —"

"No need for that, either. Breed!" This last part the old woman turned and bellowed over her shoulder at full voice. A moment later, some curtains on the wall behind the bar parted and a man stepped through them. He was obviously an Indian of some sort — a Yaqui maybe — well over six feet tall and with shoulders wide as an ox. Reaching down to those shoulders was a mane of glossy black hair held in place by a leather headband. His face was flat, dark, expressionless.

"These gents have got horses hitched outside," Ma told him. "Bring in their bedrolls and saddlebags, then put the horses in the barn. Give 'em hay and grain."

Without acknowledgment of any sort, the Indian giant moved past Josh and Charlie — who quickly stepped back to give him plenty of room — and glided silently out the door into the rainy night.

From the table across the room, Torrence said matter-of-factly, "That was Breed. What Ma can't take care of around here with her bark or her six-gun . . . he does."

Ignoring him, Ma made a shooing-away gesture to Josh and Charlie, saying, "Go on and sit down if you're gonna. I'll be bringin' your stew out to you in a minute. When Breed fetches in your gear, tell him where you want it put. And mind you if it leaves puddles all over, that's what you'll be sleepin' in."

After Ma disappeared through the curtain, Josh and Charlie picked up their bottle and glasses and went over to Torrence's table where those already seated shifted around to make room for them.

"Well. Now that we've made it this far," said Torrence once the cowpokes were settled in their own chairs, "I guess further introductions are in order. We all know that you're Charlie and Josh from Oklahoma on your way to Buffalo Peak, and you know I'm Pierce Torrence.

"Here on my right, please make the acquaintance of Miss Leticia Beauregard. Don't let her beauty fool you, she's almost as mean and ornery as Ma Speckler. To my left is Black Hills Buckner. He doesn't say more than a dozen or so words a day, not to anybody, so don't take his silence personally. On the other side of Black Hills is Romo Perlison. He has no shyness when it comes to talking, but he saves his best and smoothest lines for the ladies; his name might have more appropriately been Rome-o."

As Torrence introduced each person, they made eye contact and gave nods of acknowledgment, not much more. No handshakes were offered.

Leticia Beauregard, as Torrence indicated, was quite attractive. She had an almost perfectly oval face set with wide, dark eyes and full, sensuous lips, all surrounded by a thick mass of curly black hair. What showed of her figure was trim and full busted, the latter proudly displayed by a low-cut, cleavage-baring blouse. The shadowy, flickering candlelight added a kind of mysterious, smoldering quality to her appearance.

Black Hills Buckner was a muscular slab, massive through the shoulders and chest, with huge, thick-fingered hands. His eyes were a shade too close together and had a cold, vacant quality to them that gave an immediate impression of no emotion ever showing there. Romo Perlison was of average size, solid looking, with a wide, expressive mouth surrounded by black whiskers that contrasted with a close-cropped cap of dirty blond hair.

"We appreciate you folks bein' so friendly, invitin' us over and all," said Josh once the introductions were complete. "What with me and Charlie havin' nobody but each other to yap at for the past few weeks, it'll be right nice to visit with some others for a change."

"That's right," Charlie agreed. "Hadn't been for you fillin' us in on what all was available here we might have headed back out into the rain again without ever knowin'. I got a hunch Ma likely never would have said." He paused to scrunch up his face distastefully. "Especially after she took a plumb dislike to me right off the bat."

Torrence chuckled. "Nah, don't take it personal. Can't you tell? It's her nature; she treats everybody like that."

"That's right," affirmed Romo. "She's got a rotten disposition toward everything and everybody. Comes from not havin' a man in her life is my opinion. Women get that way when they ain't got a man around to take care of 'em proper. Why do you think all the nuns you ever see look so somber and gloomy faced all the time?"

"What do you know about nuns? You haven't been near a church since they kicked you out of Sunday school for short-changing the collection plate," Leticia responded. "Besides, Ma does have a man in her life. She's got her husband."

"Yeah, but he ain't amounted to nothing since that mule kicked him in the head a couple years back," argued Romo. "All he does is lay in bed starin' at the ceiling, like a block of wood with eyeballs. My point, you'll remember, was about a woman havin' a man around to take care of her proper."

Leticia gave him a disgusted look. "Yeah, and we all know what you mean by that. It's the only direction your mind ever goes."

"Alright you two, that's enough," Torrence said sharply. "I didn't invite these fellas over here to listen to the pair of you bicker."

Josh shifted in his chair uncomfortably. "Listen, Mr. Torrence, if we're gettin' in the way of —"

"Nonsense," Torrence cut him off. "I just said I invited you over, didn't I? I didn't do that to have you bounce right back up and leave again. This is an example of why we need some fresh blood, so to speak, in the mix. You said that you and Charlie have had no one else to talk to for a while? Well, that goes for our group, too."

"Okay." Josh cleared his throat. "How long have you folks been travelin' together?"

"Better part of a year. But, unlike you, we have no particular destination in mind. Not at this point, anyway." Torrence paused to smile his thin, brief smile once again. "Let's just say that wherever we end up will be somewhere we haven't been before."

A remark like that could be taken a couple different ways. But the main message seemed clear enough: Never mind, don't bother asking more. In the West, it was common — and commonly accepted — to run into folks who'd left behind a past they didn't want to talk about. When even the hint of such an attitude was encountered, it was smartest to just leave it be.

"That's why I envy you two fellas," Torrence went on. "You've got a clear-cut goal, a determination to reach it, and a partner to share it with. That makes you pretty lucky, I'd say."

"I don't know that we ever felt like we had a lot of luck runnin' on our side," said Charlie. "Seems like whatever good came our way, we had to work our tails off for. But, then again, I reckon we've met our share of those who had it worse."

"See what I mean?"

Josh nodded. "Even havin' that Oklahoma job fall apart on us might turn out to be a better thing than we first thought. Leastways, that's how we're tryin' to look at it. It put the spurs to us to move on and try for something better down in Buffalo Peak."

"What are you aiming for that 'something better' to take the shape of ?" asked Leticia offhandedly.

Josh squirmed a little uncomfortably under her smoldering gaze. "Well, we ain't sure exactly. Something different than ranch work, we're thinkin'. We ain't fussy, we'll do any honest job, but it'd be nice to get out of the saddle for a spell and do something besides push around stupid, stubborn cows." He paused, a shade of color rising in his cheeks, then added, "Most of all, we're lookin' to settle down, find a couple o' good women, and get married."

"Married?" squawked Romo. "What in blazes you want to go and do something like that for?"

"We figure it's time," said Charlie, setting his jaw firmly. "We ain't gettin' no younger and we figure we been knockin' around loose long enough. We've rode the river a time or two, drank more than our share of liquor, paid for it now and then with knots on our heads and even a taste of jail. Dallied with a good many, er . . . well, not to speak vulgar, ma'am" — here he tossed a quick, nervous glance at Leticia — "but the kind of gals you don't think about marryin'. We reckon it's time to put that kind of stuff behind us and, like Josh said, settle down to something more permanent."

"Those are sad words, my friends. Sad words indeed," said Romo, wagging his head. "I hope I never see the day when I'm done chasin' — and I don't mean cows — and feel ready to quit runnin' loose."

"Don't worry. No decent woman would ever consent to settling down with the likes of you anyway," remarked Leticia.

Speaking before the two of them could start up again, Torrence said to Josh and Charlie, "If that's what suits you fellas, then I say good for you. Not a doggone thing wrong with the way you're thinking. I'm curious, though. Why are you so set on Buffalo Peak as the place where you think all of this can happen for you?"

Josh appeared a little surprised by the question. "Well, like we told you — and like you said some friends of yours even mentioned — it just seems like the perfect spot for plans like we're makin'. It stuck in both our minds as bein' that from just passin' through the one time. A nice, friendly place where we'd have a good chance to meet the right kind of gal so's we could commence to courtin', then marry and settle in."

"I must say, you seem to have thought it through very thoroughly," allowed Torrence. Then, his brow creasing, he added, "But this whole 'courting' thing . . . are you sure that's the best way to go about it?"

"Ain't quite sure I follow you," Josh said, his expression turning a bit puzzled. "I mean, that's how it's done, ain't it?"

"In some cases, yes, I suppose that's a

method that works. That's what the story-books would have you believe. And, back East, in prim and proper settings, I imagine that may even be how it's done a good deal of the time." Torrence leaned forward over the table and regarded the two cowpokes closely. "But this is the West, boys. Surely you've seen how hard life is out here and how fast it can go by. If you waste time for all the niceties and delicate manners like they put in those storybooks and suppos-edly practice in other places, why, you might find everything passing by you like a stam-pede leaving you in the dust.

"Just look at what happened to that Okla-homa rancher where you just left. What if he'd tarried when it came to finding a wife and starting a family and a ranch? He might have wasted time looking for just the right girl and the right circumstances and the right piece of land . . . Then boom! That same old bull could have tore him up and he would have suffered and died a lonely man with his last thoughts being nothing but regrets for not making his move on what he wanted out of life quicker and sooner than he did."

By the time he finished speaking, Charlie and Josh were leaning over the table, too, leaning right into his words. Charlie gulped and said, "So what are you sayin', exactly? About us, I mean — about how you think we maybe oughta proceed different to go after what we're lookin' for?"

CHAPTER 4

"I don't know where he is, I tell you. If I did, I'd certainly cooperate." Earl Sterling stood behind the bar in his saloon, palms planted flat on the polished surface, his expression very earnest. "Believe me, with all the problems I've got piling up, the last thing I want is to lose Arthur on top of everything else."

"What do you mean by 'lose' him?" asked Firestick from where he stood with his elbow resting on the bar from the opposite side.

It was still fairly early in the morning and the two men had the place to themselves. The Lone Star Palace Saloon wasn't yet officially open for business, but Firestick had spotted Sterling inside through the front window and had rapped on the glass to gain admittance.

"Oh, come on, Marshal," replied Sterling. "You know how talk travels around this town. You think I can't figure out why you're here looking for Arthur in the first place? Everybody's heard by now that you're letting those three troublemaking cowboys loose today, turning them over to the custody of Clint Harvey, owner of the High Point Ranch — a highly questionable decision, if you ask me."

"Nobody did," Firestick pointed out tersely.

"Uh-huh. And nobody asked me about the rumors going around about Arthur claiming he'll be waiting to get even with big Orval Retlock as soon as he's out from behind bars, either — at least not until now. But I heard the talk all the same."

"You hear it from Arthur himself?"

Sterling shook his head. "No, he never said anything like that to me. I do know, however, he was pretty upset by what happened the other night — getting coldcocked by Retlock the way he did. A matter of pride. It embarrassed him, I guess you could say. He even offered to resign because he failed to keep things under control that night, to do his job as bouncer. I refused, of course. He's too good a man, a competent bartender *and* a good bouncer. Hell, he's quelled twenty times more signs of trouble than he ever let get out of hand. You know that, from all the times you *haven't* been called to tame things down."

"That used to be the case," Firestick said pointedly. "But here lately, since you've made certain changes, that's starting to hold true less and less of the time."

Sterling cocked a brow. "By 'certain changes' you of course mean the gals I brought in and made available for interested men. Do I sense a note of prudishness, Marshal? I must say that surprises me, coming from a big, rugged former mountain man like you. Surely, coming down after months up in the high, lonely mountains, you must have let the wolf howl now and then at one of those famous rendezvous I've heard tell of. Didn't you?"

"Whether I did or didn't ain't none of your damn business." Firestick scowled. "And I ain't no prude. What goes on up in those second-floor rooms between a fella and a willing gal don't make no never mind to me. Long as no trouble comes out of it, that is. Like I said, that ain't exactly been the case lately and you know it. And a big increase in the trouble has come since you brought that gal Cleo aboard."

"You can't blame Cleo for being good looking and popular. She can't help it if a bunch of hump-backed cowboys are unable to control their urges and act like a pack of rutting dogs," protested Sterling.

"I'll put blame where and when I see fit. All I'm sayin' for right now is that when there's been trouble in here lately, it often as not turns out to have Cleo somewhere in the middle of it." Firestick made a slashing motion with one hand. "But that ain't what I came to talk about. Let's get back to the subject of Arthur."

"Fine by me."

"I don't have no beef with him. Like you said, he's helped stop a lot more trouble in here than he ever started. I appreciate that. But this talk about Arthur layin' for Orval Retlock when I let Orval out of jail . . . I can't hold with that. If you see him before I do, you make sure he understands."

"I will . . . *if* I see him."

Firestick gestured toward the wall of bottles behind the saloon owner. The section of shelving and the bottles on it that had been destroyed by Beartooth's shotgun blast the other night had all been replaced. "Clint Harvey sent word that he'll go ahead and cover your costs for repairin' the damage from the other night. Since neither you nor Arthur are willin' to file charges outside of that, there ain't a whole lot more I can do. If you don't like the idea of me lettin'

Orval out of jail, you had your chance to do otherwise."

Sterling glowered at him. "Let's just say I have my reasons. But that still don't mean I like it."

Leaving the Lone Star Palace, Firestick headed in the direction of the jail building at the west end of Trail Street. After three days of drenching rain and battering winds, the sky overhead was clear and Buffalo Peak was bustling with activity, even this early in the day. The marshal spotted several buckboards and wagons carrying folks he recognized as being from outlying farms and ranches, taking advantage of the break in weather to make it in for supplies.

As he strode along the boardwalk, pinching his hat to the ladies and nodding to the men he passed, Firestick reflected on how comfortable he'd grown in his role here. He guessed maybe it was Sterling's remark about his mountain-man days that had set his thoughts stirring. It was true he'd spent a big chunk of his life up in the high reaches, hunting and trapping from one end of the Rockies to the other and even some points farther west. In the course of leading that life, he'd formed solid friendships with two other men cut from bolts of rawhide

46

similar to the one he came out of.

It was over their years of sticking together that they earned, from the Indians with whom they frequently skirmished, the colorful nicknames they carried with them to this day. Elwood McQueen was called "Firestick" due to his unerring accuracy with a rifle; Malachi Skinner became "Beartooth" due to his knife-fighting prowess with a blade as sharp and deadly as a grizzly tooth; and Jim Hendricks was "Moosejaw" as the result of an incident where he fought off a handful of braves armed with tomahawks and war clubs by snatching up the jawbone from a moose skeleton lying on the floor of the gully where they'd jumped him.

During that time, if anybody had tried telling Firestick he would not only eventually settle in a little West Texas border town but would end up also wearing a marshal's badge for the place, he would have given them the biggest horse laugh you ever heard.

Yet here he was, doing exactly that. What was more, his two close pals who had traipsed the mountains at his side were right here with him. When the freedoms of their wild existence no longer outweighed the bitter winters and rugged conditions that took more and more of a toll on their aging bones and muscles with each passing year, the three of them had decided it was time for a change.

Texas had beckoned, along with thoughts of starting up a horse ranch, something Firestick had some limited experience with from his younger days. They found what they were looking for in the grassy valley that surrounded Buffalo Peak. At a spot just west of the town, they built a sturdy ranch house and began putting together a herd.

It got off to a good start and promised to be everything they'd hoped for — except for an awareness of the frequent outbursts of violence in the nearby town, and the lack of any established law and order to try and keep it under control. Seeing the good citizens of Buffalo Peak — the ones who were trying to make it a decent place that would grow and amount to something — getting whipsawed by an unrestrained handful who didn't give a damn about decency stuck hard in the craws of the former mountain men. To the point where, on more than one occasion, they finally stepped in and put a stop to the antics of some of the hell-raisers.

Out of that came an offer from the town council to put on badges and serve as full-time marshal and deputies. They could still run their horse ranch, so long as they arranged for one or more of them to be in town a reasonable share of the time in order to settle any problems that arose. If the offer came as a surprise, then their agreement to give it a try came as an even bigger one.

Nearly three years had passed since then. The ranch was doing well, the town was growing, and things in general were working out okay. This was still the Western frontier, though, so flare-ups of gunplay and other kinds of trouble still cropped up from time to time. But when it did, the three former mountain men proved quite capable of handling it.

Entering the front office area of the jail, Firestick was met by the aroma of fresh-brewed coffee. He was also welcomed by a pair of friendly faces and the wet snout of a dog nudging his leg, wanting to be petted. The faces belonged to his deputy Moosejaw and Sam Duvall, a widower and former New York City constable who'd come out West for his health and who served as a part-time jailer for times when there were owlhoots being kept in the lockup overnight. The wet snout was provided by Shield, Sam's dog who accompanied him wherever he went. Beartooth, Firestick's other deputy and close friend, was busy out at the ranch that morning and wouldn't be in town until later.

"Any luck findin' Arthur?" Moosejaw asked, pouring a cup of coffee from a dented old pot taken off the stove in the middle of the room and holding it out to the marshal.

Taking the cup and then balancing it in one hand while he reached down to give Shield a good scratching behind the ears, Firestick said, "None. Nobody's seen him around this morning. Or, if they have, they ain't sayin' so."

"Yeah, that's pretty much the same thing I ran into when I asked around," reported Moosejaw. He was the youngest of the three former mountain men by a handful of months. He was also the largest, standing nearly six-six, a little thick through the gut but thicker by far through the shoulders. He had a broad, fleshy face, blunt nose, and a wide mouth quick to display a grin. But when provoked, his friendly giant persona could turn into just about the last thing you'd want to see, especially if you were unfortunate enough to be the cause of the provocation.

"When is Clint Harvey due in to pick up his boys?" Sam wanted to know. The tuberculosis that had driven him West had indeed been diminished by the drier, warmer conditions, but it still left him a rather frail-looking individual suffering occasional coughing fits. He remained tough spirited and outspoken, however, and was a well-regarded member of the community.

"I expect him any time," Firestick answered, straightening up from petting Shield and walking around to take a seat behind his desk.

"If you ask me," said Sam, "I don't really think you're going to have any trouble from Arthur."

"Why do you say that?"

"Because I bend my elbow fairly regularly at the Lone Star Palace," explained Sam, "and I've gotten to know Arthur pretty good. Sure, I can understand how he's wanting some payback from Retlock for clubbing him alongside the head with a sawed-off and making him look bad that night. Chalk it up to professional pride. But everybody seems to be forgetting one thing."

"And that is?" Firestick prompted him.

"That same pride, in my opinion, wouldn't allow Arthur to take his anger out on a one-armed man — which is essentially what you made Orval, at least for the time being, when you blasted the hell out of his gun hand."

Firestick puckered his chin thoughtfully. "You may have a point. Gotta admit I never looked at it that way. All I know is that the talk I've heard goin' around has it how Arthur has been blowin' about the way he's gonna thrash Orval just as soon as he can get his hands on him."

"Bah. You know how unreliable talk that gets spread like that can be. It's more likely Arthur made a simple comment, in anger, about how he'd like to get his hands on Orval at some point to square things, and it got blown out of proportion. That's a far cry from him planning something right away while Orval's laid up with only one wing." Sam spread his hands. "But, like I said, that's just my opinion."

From where he'd wandered over to gaze out the front window, Moosejaw said, "Looks like we'll get the chance to test your opinion pretty soon. Clint Harvey and a couple of his men are comin' down the street now, headed this way."

CHAPTER 5

Firestick rose up from the seat he'd just gotten comfortable in. "Good enough. I'd just as soon get this over with so Harvey can take his men back to the ranch and keep 'em there for a while. If Arthur is on the prod, that'll give him time to cool down."

"Also give Orval a chance to get his hand back in shape in case a confrontation between the two of them has to take place somewhere down the road," Sam pointed out.

"Let's take it one step at a time," said Firestick. "Sam, you might as well go get those three out of their cell. Moosejaw, how about you step outside and keep an eye peeled in case Arthur *does* decide to show up and try to cause trouble?"

Both men moved as instructed. Moosejaw left the door open on his way out and a moment later Clint Harvey strode through.

The men who'd ridden up with him stayed outside.

"Mornin', Mr. Harvey," Firestick said.

"What's so good about it?" Harvey groused in return. He was a short, squat man, built along the lines of a tree stump, with shaggy eyebrows, a dour expression, and slightly overlong arms that ended in surprisingly delicate-looking hands.

"Didn't say it was a *good* mornin'. Just stated it, friendly-like, as a time of day," Firestick replied.

Harvey scowled. "Yeah. Well, I guess there's no arguing that much."

There came a faint clanging of steel on steel from the other side of the thick door that led back to the cell block.

"I take it you're getting ready to release my men?" Harvey asked.

Firestick nodded. "That's right. There's only the matter of coverin' the cost of damages caused by them and they'll be all yours."

"I need to square that with the saloon owner?"

"I've got his bill right here. I can give you a receipt and then see to it he gets the money. Tell the truth, I'd just as soon you got your men — leastways those three — on out of town without any saloon stops."

Harvey grunted. "I suppose that's under-standable." He dug a wallet out of his vest pocket. "If you show me that bill, I'll take care of it."

Firestick took a sheet of paper from his desk — Earl Sterling's estimate for the dam-age done to his saloon — and handed it to the rancher. The amount hadn't seemed unreasonable to the marshal and apparently not to Harvey, either, since he didn't hesi-tate to withdraw enough to cover it. Fire-stick took the money, scrawled "paid" and his initials at the bottom of the paper, and handed it back to Harvey.

As he folded the receipt and slipped it in his pocket along with the wallet, the rancher said, "And there's no fines or anything to add to that?"

Firestick shook his head. "Not this time. Works in their favor that those three ain't made a habit of causin' trouble in the past. Long as they steer clear for a while, let things calm down, and then — should go without sayin' — don't repeat any foolish behavior in the future, we can call it even."

"Sounds fair enough," Harvey allowed. Then, as if just remembering, he added, "I understand one of my men was wounded?"

"That's right. I had to shoot Orval Ret-lock in his gun hand."

"How bad?"

"Frank Moorehouse fixed it best he could. Won't ever be good as new again but, given some time, Frank figures Orval should get back sixty, maybe seventy percent use."

"But Moorehouse is no real doctor."

"True. But he's all we got. If Orval was to travel to Presidio or somewhere and visit one with full bona fides, maybe that doc could do some better fixin' and give him a better outlook." Firestick hesitated. "Ain't my decision and I'd never tell the kid to his face, but I think it'd be a waste of time. I think he's gonna have to face losin' partial use of his hand."

"Still, you can see where it would be a mighty hard thing for a strapping young fella like him to accept."

"Coulda been worse. I coulda shot and killed him and been well within my rights to do so," Firestick pointed out bluntly.

Before the subject could be discussed further, the door leading back to the cell block opened and three men came through it — Tom Willis and Sully Hutchins walking ahead of jailer Sam Duvall. The two just-released prisoners looked subdued and embarrassed as they cast furtive glances toward Clint Harvey.

"We're might sorry about this, boss,"

mumbled Willis.

"And mighty grateful you came to fetch us out," added Sully.

"I back the men who ride for me . . . within reason," said Harvey. "Where's Retlock?"

Willis and Sully suddenly looked even more ill at ease. It was Sam who answered, saying, "He won't come out."

"What? What do you mean he won't come out?" Harvey demanded.

Sam shrugged indifferently. "Just what I said . . . He's refusing to leave the cell. Says a one-armed man ain't no good to you or himself or anybody else. Says he might as well just stay behind bars and rot."

Harvey scowled. "That's ridiculous. He still has *some* use of his hand, doesn't he?"

"That's what we been tryin' to tell him, boss," said Sully. "Right now, yeah, it's all swole up and powerful sore. But when the bandages come off and he's able to start workin' it some, the doc says he'll still be able to do quite a bit of stuff with it."

"But he ain't wantin' to hear any of that," Willis added glumly. "He keeps sayin' a man without his right hand ain't no man at all, he's worthless."

"Maybe he'd listen to you, boss," suggested Sully. "Maybe you can talk enough sense into him to get him to at least try."

When Harvey looked his way, Firestick said, "Go ahead. Give it a try. He can't stay in there at the town's expense forever."

They trudged back into the cell block. Sam led the way. Harvey, Willis, and Sully followed, with Firestick bringing up the rear.

Orval sat on the edge of a cot in one of the two cells. Its door was wide open. He sat with his head hung down, elbows resting on knees. His right hand was heavily bandaged.

Harvey stepped into the cell. "Orval? What's this nonsense about you not wanting to come out of there?"

Orval slowly raised his head. "What's the use, boss? I come out, I ain't gonna be no good to nobody." He held up his damaged hand. "This thing is gonna keep me locked away from what I can do for the rest of my life. Might as well just leave all of me locked away."

"That's awful shortsighted, seems to me," Harvey told him. "Every indication is that you'll still be able to use that hand to a certain degree. More than half, the doc says. Sure, I know it's bound to be frustrating and awkward and it's a hell of a lot easier for somebody else to say, but if you try hard and stick with it there'll be plenty you can do. A strong, healthy fella like you — maybe even more than expected. But you'll never know if you quit and don't even give it a try."

Orval's gaze drifted past the rancher and locked on Firestick standing outside the cell. His bottom lip curled. "Damn you, Marshal. Why didn't you just go ahead and put that bullet in the back of my head and spare me all of this?"

"Come on, boy. You surely don't mean that," Harvey said.

Orval turned his glare on him. "Don't I? How the hell do you know what I mean?"

Some color crept up Harvey's neck and over his cheeks. He looked like he was teetering between sympathy and anger. "It's hard to believe anyone would put the same value on their life as their hand. That's all I was trying to say."

Orval's eyes continued to bore into him. "You're big on throwin' that word 'try' around. You sayin' *you'll* give me a try? You'll still hire me on, even as a cripple?"

"I came here to bail you out, didn't I? Yes, I have every intention of you returning to work at the High Point. You'll need more time to heal, I understand, and even after that there's bound to be some limitations on what you'll be able to do. But I'll still expect a full day's work out of you and have every reason to expect I'll get it."

"Come on, Orval. You can't get much fairer than that," urged Sully.

"Get on out of there and join us back at the ranch," Willis said.

Orval's gaze swept over all of them, lingering hotly on Firestick for an extra beat. Then, heaving a great sigh, he pushed himself up off the cot. "What the hell. Reckon I got nothing to lose," he muttered to no one in particular.

They shuffled back out into the office area. For a moment, as they edged around one end of the marshal's desk, everyone was bunched closely together. In that instant, using his size and strength to full advantage and moving with speed born of desperation, Orval lashed out with his right elbow and sent everyone around him staggering a step backward. At the same time, his left hand streaked down and snatched Firestick's Colt out of its holster. Sweeping the gun in a short arc, his off hand holding it rather awkwardly but still effective enough at such short range, he leveled it on the marshal's stomach and yelled, "Now you pay, you cripple-makin' son of a bitch!"

A gun roared shatteringly within the confines of the room.

But it wasn't Firestick's Colt. It came from the Schofield .45 fisted by Moosejaw, who was coming back in from outside and was just in time to spot the tormented Orval's attempt at revenge. The heavy slug hurled by the Schofield smashed into the side of Orval's neck, exiting in a spray of gore and slamming the big man hard against the back wall of the office. He sank slowly to the floor, leaving a scarlet streak as he slid down. Though he never got off a shot, Firestick's Colt stayed in the grip of his lifeless hand.

CHAPTER 6

"We're makin' better time than we figured. I'm expectin' now we oughta make it in by tomorrow afternoon or so. Sound about right to you?"

"Yeah, I'd say so. Long as we don't get hit with no more hard rain."

Charlie gazed out under the front edge of the cave within which they sat, sweeping his gaze across the star-sprinkled sky, and said, "No sign of anything brewin' up there as far as I can see."

"True enough. Long as it stays that way," Josh allowed. "But you remember what ol' Ma said back there at Jepperd's Ford — how she reckoned the spring rains weren't done yet and more would be showin' up before long."

"Yeah, and I also remember pretty damn well how Ma had a kind of sour outlook on just about everything," Charlie said, his own expression taking on a touch of sourness at the memory. "Plus, we've come quite a spell from where she's familiar with the weather patterns. Ain't to say it *ain't* gonna rain no more, neither — not here nor there, either one. All I'm claimin' is that it don't look like nothing is due around here anywhere soon."

"Okay, okay. I can go along with that. I can see the same clear, starry sky as you, can't I?" Josh frowned. "But the dang rain ain't hardly the biggest thing on my mind. Whether it holds off or don't, we're still gonna be makin' it to Buffalo Peak before long. What we're gonna do when we get there? That's the part I been ponderin' on more than anything."

"What's to ponder? We're gonna find ourselves a couple right nice gals, get hitched, and settle down. That's what we decided months ago, ain't it?"

"Yeah, that part ain't changed," Josh agreed as he fed a couple of fresh sticks into the crackling campfire that separated the two of them. "But how we go about reachin' it, that's the thing."

"On account of those ideas Pierce Torrence tried to sell us on, you mean?"

"Well, yeah. He made some awful interestin' points. I won't say he sold me completely, but he sure set me to thinkin'.

If he hadn't, I wouldn't still be chewin' it over in my head all this time later. You sayin' he didn't make no impression on you at all?"

Charlie reached out and snagged a final piece of bacon that lay in the frying pan. "No, I can't claim that. Like you, I been grindin' on it a fair amount myself." He held up the bacon. "You want half of this?"

"No. Go ahead, kill it."

Charlie bit off some of the bacon. As he chewed, he said, "At first I thought Torrence was pokin' some fun at our expense. You know, takin' us for a couple rubes, stringin' us on to see how gullible we were. But, the more he talked, danged if what he was sayin' didn't start to make more sense."

"Yeah. Yeah, that's the same as it was for me," Josh said, his head bobbing. "And then, when that Leticia gal — and, oh my, wasn't she an eyeful and a half ? — started to chime in with Torrence, she made it sound all the more like something worth considerin'."

"Swore that's the way all women, down deep, want a man — a real man — to act. Grab 'em, haul 'em off somewhere to show 'em some hard lovin' while convincin' 'em you're the *hombre* who'll always be able to take care of 'em, and then claim 'em for your lawfully wedded."

Charlie popped the last of the bacon in his mouth, licking the grease off his fingertips as he chewed and continued to talk. "Ain't no denyin' that sounds a whole lot quicker than attendin' ice cream socials and square dances and whatnot, tryin' to cull some filly out of the herd while at the same time there's other stallions all around pawin' at the ground, tryin' to get her attention, too."

Josh's head was bobbing some more. "That's right. And then, if you finally *do* find a filly who takes an interest in your scent, next you got to meet her ma and pa and go through that whole sashay of convincin' 'em you'll be a good provider who truly has deep feelings for their daughter and you ain't just some rascal lookin' to crowd her into a horse stall somewhere for a tumble in the straw . . . Whew! It's like a body has to climb over one hill after another before you ever get to the one that has gettin' married finally waitin' at the top."

"Sorta makes you see why fellas like Romo are so committed to stayin' single, don't it?"

"Maybe. But that ain't us." Josh frowned. "Say, you ain't crawfishin' on me, are you? We made up our minds that we've reached the time for settlin' down and gettin' married. Right?"

"Yeah, that's right. Take it easy, I ain't nohow crawfishin'." Charlie finished chewing and swallowed down the last of the bacon.

Using a sawed-off section of tree trunk for a stool, Pierce Torrence sat alone on the front porch of Ma Speckler's nameless saloon. The evening still carried the warmth of the day, though cooling quickly. The only sign of any kind of cloud in the sky was the thin curl of smoke rising up from Torrence's cigarette.

As he took a hard drag, the quirly's tip glowing bright red in the shadows cast under the narrow porch overhang, the screen door opened behind his shoulder and Leticia Beauregard emerged from inside. She had a knit shawl wrapped around her shoulders.

"I wondered where you'd gotten to," she said.

"Just sitting out here thinking. Kinda enjoying looking up at the sky and not seeing rain pouring out of it for a change."

Leticia held out her hand and he passed her his cigarette. She took a long drag, handed it back as she exhaled a plume out into the darkness. "Jesus, we've got to go somewhere where you can get some decent smoking tobacco," she said.

"Ma says it's the best she carries."

"Maybe so. But that doesn't make it good. Lord, you could crumble up crusty old buffalo chips and roll something better than that."

"You speaking from experience?"

"Some things you just know." Leticia stuck out her tongue and made a face. "I'm glad I only take a few puffs a day. And until we get some place where you can buy something better, I think I'll hold off having even that much."

"You might be in for a considerable wait. I haven't made up my mind yet where we're headed next."

Leticia picked up an empty wooden bucket, turned it over, and sat down on it. She leaned forward to rest her elbows on her knees, and the low-cut front of her blouse sagged open, nearly baring her ample breasts.

Torrence grinned with one side of his mouth. "If Romo should happen to wander out here, you'd better sit up straighter. If he saw you like that, he'd be apt to walk off the edge of the porch and break his fool neck."

"If he was going to injure himself from being distracted by ogling me," Leticia said offhandedly, "he would have done it a long time ago. I swear, he's got eyes that can look sideways, like a horse, even when he's facing forward. And, believe me, he *never* stops looking."

Torrence emitted a low chuckle. "Yeah, when he's not on the job, he's got pretty much a one-track mind. When it's time, though, he's all business and I know I can count on him."

Leticia regarded him for a moment, then said, "So when is it going to be time?"

"What do you mean?"

"When is it going to be time for business? For a job?"

"I just got done telling you, I haven't made up my mind yet."

"But you're closer than you pretend. I can always tell. That's what you're doing out here now — running things through your mind, considering, maybe even planning a little . . . I'm just curious what you might be leaning toward."

Torrence met her gaze. "Maybe you're too curious. You've heard how that worked out for a certain cat."

"I'm no cat. I'm a woman."

Torrence took a final drag on his cigarette, flipped away the butt. Then he chuckled again. "Very well, my curious kitten. It may amuse you to know that I'm thinking about a little place called Buffalo Peak."

Leticia arched a brow. "Buffalo Peak? Isn't that . . . ?"

"Yes. It's where those two drifters who passed through here the other night are headed. As a matter of fact, their babbling is what got me to thinking about it as a possible spot for us to pay a visit."

"Is that a proposal? We're not going there to get married, are we?"

"I was thinking of something more along the lines of eloping with all the money they have in their bank."

She smiled. "For that, I would be honored to serve as a bridesmaid."

Torrence stood up and began to pace. "Everything those simpletons said about the place — except for the nonsense about getting married — sounded quite accurate. I was telling the truth when I told them I'd heard of the area before. The quiet little town in the valley below the Vieja Mountains, well isolated from any other town close by, surrounded by a growing number of cattle ranches and farms. You add all that up and what else do you get? A plump little bank somewhere smack in the middle, that's what. There's got to be, in order to handle the money for the merchants and ranchers and the like. It may not be the richest haul we could go after, but it's like a ripe, juicy peach on a low-hanging branch . . . it's too damn good to pass up."

"What kind of law do they have protecting it?"

"That's another thing that makes it attractive. Actually, overhearing somebody talk about the law in Buffalo Peak is what first piqued my interest. They put badges on a couple mossy old mountain men who also run a string of horses outside of town. Part-timers. Fresh from trapping beavers or skunks or whatever. And now they split their time between wrangling hayburners and keeping the peace. Does that sound too fearsome for us to dare go up against?"

"What it sounds like is more and more inviting all the time," said Leticia, eagerness evident in her voice.

"Yes, it does, doesn't it?" Torrence nodded as if in response to his own question. "In fact, hearing myself say those things out loud pretty much made up my mind."

"What about those two drifters, though? If we're going to be heading that way soon, is there any chance of them queering our play in case we run into them when we get there?"

Torrence shrugged. "I don't see how. In

the first place, we're not going to be lol-lygagging around for very long once we arrive. You know our style — smash and grab, in and out quick. If we *should* happen to run into Charlie and Josh, we could merely say that hearing them carry on about Buffalo Peak made it sound so inviting we decided to pay a visit for ourselves. Simple as that."

"That works." Leticia gave an abrupt little laugh. "Besides, if they follow your advice about picking out their future brides, then they should have already been there and gone by the time we show up — gone with the lucky women of their choice slung over their shoulders."

"We should only be so lucky."

"Why do you say that?"

"Isn't it obvious? If Charlie and Josh took my advice seriously — along with some very sincere-sounding input from you, I might add — and they really *did* proceed to haul off a couple fair maidens the way we suggested, can you imagine the turmoil such a thing would put the town in? That's why I said it would be lucky for us. It would be a distraction that would make plucking the bank even easier."

Leticia's brow furrowed. "But it's not possible for somebody — especially *two* somebodies — to be gullible enough to truly swallow that line of bunk you fed them . . . is it?"

"When I started out," Torrence said, his expression sobering as he replayed the scene in his mind, "I certainly never thought so. I could see right off they were a pretty dull-minded pair, so I set out to have a little fun. You know, stringing them along a little. But thinking back, the more we carried on the more they seemed to be gulping it down. Damn, now I'm not so sure! I think they may have actually believed us."

"Jesus," Leticia murmured. "I hate the thought of them maybe dragging off a couple innocent girls all on account of . . ."

"Never mind that! Charlie and Josh aren't the kind to hurt anybody, even if they did go through with . . ." Torrence let his words trail off. Then, abruptly, he smacked his right fist into his left palm. "But if they end up doing something we can take advantage of, then by God we're not going to pass it up. Come on, I think it's time to go inside and let Romo and Black Hills know we'll be riding out in the morning."

CHAPTER 7

"It troubles me to see you like this," Kate Mallory was saying. "You've had to shoot and kill men in the line of duty before. And before that, up in the mountains, you killed to survive. Animals, Indians, other trappers looking to rob you of your pelts . . . I don't mean to imply you ever took it lightly or that killing was easy for you. But always in the past, when it was necessary, you were able to come to grips with it for that reason. Because it was necessary. I realize it's easier to say from my position — the outside looking in — but I'm not sure I understand why this is so different, especially since you're not even the one who pulled the trigger on Orval Retlock."

As he sat listening to these words, Firestick hung his head morosely over the glass of bourbon Kate had poured for him. The two of them were in Kate's private office at the Mallory House, the hotel Kate had taken over following the death of her parents. It was late. The building around them and the street outside were quiet. An oil lamp affixed to the wall had its wick set low, casting Kate's smoldering dark beauty in a soft glow.

After settling in the area, starting up the horse ranch with his partners, and taking on the job of town marshal, Firestick had thought his move down out of the mountains was working out about as good as it could get — until he met Kate. Not only met her and felt a stirring for female companionship like he'd thought he was long past, but in time discovered she harbored similar feelings toward him.

Their relationship of well over a year now remained rather private, not exactly a secret to many people around town but also not something they overtly displayed. As two people who'd gone a long time without a romantic interest in their lives, they were willing to take a little longer and let things develop at a comfortable pace.

Rolling the glass of bourbon slowly back and forth between his palms, Firestick replied to Kate's comments, "I think maybe that's the part that's botherin' me the most, the fact that I left it to Moosejaw to pull the final trigger on Orval, yet I was the one who killed him. By shootin' him in the hand to begin with, just cripplin' him, I killed his spirit just as sure as if I'd put that first bullet in his brain. He even said as much himself. I let him live with that crippled spirit until somebody else had to come along and finish the job for me."

"But he was trying to kill you. Moosejaw had no choice but to do what he did."

"No, Moosejaw didn't. But I did. The first time I tangled with Orval in the Lone Star Palace, I shouldn't have wounded him the way I did."

Kate looked confused, on the brink of incredulity. "Are you saying it would have been better to kill him on the spot?"

"The way he looked at it, it would have been. For some men, takin' away their right hand is like takin' away everything they are, a part of 'em they can't stand to be without. You've seen fellas who came back from the war missin' a limb, an arm or a leg, maybe both. Lord knows how many of 'em might better have been killed outright in battle, the way they saw it. Some adapt, some never do. They either end up blowin' their brains out or turn into useless puddles of misery. Lookin' back, I figure Orval's time in that cell gave him too much time to think and he panicked over seein' himself maybe goin' that route."

"So what happened to him was unfortunate. Maybe even tragic. But there's still no call for you to heap so much of it on yourself."

Firestick threw back his bourbon and then brought the emptied glass back down heavily on the desktop that separated them. "Damn it, Kate, you don't even shoot an animal out in the wild and leave it to run off just wounded. You either do the job right to begin with or you follow up and finish it quick and clean. You don't leave the poor dumb beast to suffer."

"But you weren't out to kill Retlock in the first place," Kate pointed out. "You were there to tame down the trouble that he was a big part of causing. You tried to give him a break by disarming him before somebody *did* get killed."

"I could have just clubbed him across the back of the head like I ended up doing anyway," Firestick argued, "or maybe put my bullet in the meaty part of his arm instead of bustin' his hand all to hell."

"Yes. And since he was armed with two guns from what you yourself told me — one of them being a sawed-off shotgun — he could have found a way to cut loose and harmed a whole lot of people, one of them possibly Beartooth or maybe even you, if you would have wasted time sorting through all your options instead of taking fast and effective action."

"Orval Retlock, if he was still around, might have something to say about that 'effective' part."

Kate had picked up the bourbon bottle to pour some more. She stopped abruptly with the bottle raised partway. "Alright, that's about enough. This second-guessing, self-pitying person sitting across from me is not the man I know and fell in love with. I'm proud it was me you chose to open up to, and I wish I had more to say that might be helpful. But I don't . . . except I wish that other fella would come back around now."

Firestick regarded her for several seconds, his expression hardening some, his mouth tightening. Then, slowly, his features relaxed. He managed a lopsided smile.

"Tell you what," he said. "You finish pourin' some more of that bourbon instead of just wavin' the bottle around, I think that other fella might be ready to have himself a slug."

Kate poured. "But before you drink that, maybe I do have one more thing to add," she said.

Firestick wrapped his hand around the

glass but didn't raise it.

"I think a part of what's bothering you about Retlock is a . . . I want to say fear, though that's not a word very applicable to anything about you . . . a fear that if anything ever happened that left you physically impaired the way he saw himself, you might have the same kind of outlook toward it as he did."

Firestick's response was very calm, almost matter-of-fact. "I think you're right. If I lost my right hand, or an arm or a leg, I believe it'd really knock me low. I don't know if I could handle it."

"I think you could. You're the strongest man I know. And I don't mean just physically, but mentally and spiritually, too."

"That's for others to say, not me." Firestick shrugged. "But as far as endin' up in the kind of sorry condition we're talkin' about, it ain't something I fear. If it came to that, if I was strugglin' with it hard, my way out is already set."

"What do you mean? I don't see you as the suicidal type."

"Wouldn't have to be. Beartooth or Moosejaw would take care of it for me, same as I would for either of them if the situation was reversed. It's a kind of pact we made with one another many moons ago."

Kate's eyebrows lifted. "Well. I guess I can't top that."

Firestick took a pull of his bourbon. "It's not a contest, Kate. What you mean to me . . . us bein' able to talk like this . . . Well, men are kinda funny. Even after all the years me and Beartooth and Moosejaw have stuck together, I don't think I ever could've had this particular conversation with either of them."

Kate reached across the desk and put her hand on his. She smiled. "I'm glad to hear you say that. I never want to come between you three — not that anybody ever could — but at the same time I'm glad to know I hold a special place with you."

"Don't ever doubt that, gal."

Kate withdrew her hand and sat back in her chair. The corners of her mouth curved up in a different way, her smile turning impish. "On second thought, when I said I couldn't top that old pact of yours, maybe I was selling myself short. A couple things occur to me that I bet could at least make a pretty darn good run for the money. It's been a while since you've been up to my apartment, in case I'm not speaking plain enough."

On the nights when Firestick was the one who made the late rounds in town, he invariably finished up with a stop at the Mallory House to spend some time with Kate. Usually she would be waiting for him in her office where they would visit and share a couple of drinks, like tonight. When the mood moved them, they would sometimes retire to Kate's apartment at the rear of the hotel where they would pass the time a bit more intimately.

So when Kate extended her invitation tonight, there was certainly no hesitation to the response.

Rising and coming around the end of her desk, she said coyly, "Since it *has* been a while, you remember the way okay, don't you?"

"With my eyes closed," Firestick assured her as he, too, stood up. "And having you in the lead, I can always feel my way."

"That's what I'm counting on," said Kate, brushing by him and letting one hand trail lightly across his cheek.

CHAPTER 8

"There now, sir," announced Eb Squires as he removed the protective striped cloth that had been draped over the front of the man in his barber's chair. "All trimmed and shaved from the neck up and ready for the freshly drawn, steaming hot bath waiting for you in the back room."

The man in the chair sat up straight and leaned forward a bit, though without making a move to rise right away. First he took the time to carefully study his reflection in the wall mirror, lifting his chin and then turning his head slowly to either side.

"I hope everything looks satisfactory, Mr. Shaw," said Eb. "I didn't apply any hair tonic or bay rum, since you'll be bathing right away. But there are bottles of each back there for you to use when you get out of the tub, along with some body talc and a brush and comb. Oh, and a mirror, too, of course."

Rupert Shaw uncoiled from the chair and smiled. He was a moderately tall, trim, classically handsome man in his middle thirties. He had pale brown hair and equally pale brows above clear green eyes. When he aimed his smile at the barber, he displayed even, white teeth. A small mole just above the left corner of his mouth appeared to be the only flaw in his features.

"Very adequate, my good fellow. Very satisfactory indeed," he told Eb. He then turned to a third man also present in the barbershop, an individual who had been seated, waiting patiently, but who'd come to his feet as soon as Shaw did. "Pay Mr. Squires, Oberon. Be sure to give him a generous tip."

"I appreciate that," Eb was quick to say. "It's really not necessary, but I do appreciate it."

"Nonsense. Good service, especially provided on short notice, deserves proper recompense."

The man Shaw had addressed as "Oberon" — one Oberon Hadley in full — counted out some crisp bills from a thick wallet and handed them to Eb. In sharp contrast to Shaw, Hadley towered four inches over six feet tall, was massive through his trunk and shoulders, and had a rough-hewn, gloriously battered face that no one had likely ever referred to as handsome and certainly not in the past dozen of his near-forty years after it began to accumulate the marks of many a conflict. He was dressed in a well-cut suit of top-quality material, much as Shaw, but on Hadley the outfit looked about as ill suited as boots on a buffalo.

To Eb's eyes, however, the wad of bills the big man held out made him look just fine.

Gesturing toward a curtained doorway at the back of the room, Shaw said, "I gather my bath is through there?"

"That's right," Eb replied. "My boy Harley is back there, too, heating some more water in case you want it. If you need anything else, let him know. If he doesn't respond quick enough, raise a holler to me and I'll see that he hops to it."

"I laid out your fresh clothes back there as well, Captain," said Hadley, addressing Shaw. "I'll be after gettin' me own trim and shave from Mr. Squires here, then I'll be back to check on you."

"Sounds like I'm being cared for almost to the point of being pampered." Shaw smiled again. "Not that I'm complaining, mind you."

At that moment, the front door of the shop burst open rather recklessly and a large man sauntered in. He was of a height and girth equivalent to Hadley, clad in rumpled, dusty range clothes, and sporting a chinful of bristly black whiskers. Milling behind him, part of them still out on the boardwalk that ran in front of Squires's barbershop and extended to other businesses lining the east side of Sierra Blanca's main street, were three more men of a similar stamp, though not as large. The dust from their clothing and wide-brimmed hats lifted in a gust of wind off the street and swirled into the shop.

"Hey, close the damn door," Eb barked irritably from where he was placing the money he'd just been paid into a cash register. Then, turning, when he saw who the new arrival was, his chin sagged noticeably and his face turned a shade whiter.

Black Whiskers peeled back his lips to form a sneer. "What's your bitch, Squires? How the hell do you expect customers to get in if they don't use the damn door?"

Eb's head bobbed agreeably. "Of course, Ollie. That only makes good sense. I . . . I was reacting to the dust, that's all. Customers expect a barbershop to be clean and free of dust."

"That's what brooms are for, ain't it?" Ollie Tamrack countered. "*Hombres* like me and my boys come in here to get whisker-

84

scraped and scrubbed down, then it falls to you to clean up afterwards. That's the way it goes. Besides, it gives that half-wit boy of yours something to do. What else would he be good for?"

Behind Tamrack, the other cowboys smirked and chuckled.

Eb frowned. "Come on, Ollie. I've asked you not to talk like that when you come around. Harley hears and he's got feelings, too, you know."

"Does he? If he ain't got all his marbles, how do you know he's got any feelings?"

"He's my son." Eb's mouth compressed into a thin, straight line. "I've seen him hurt enough times. Believe me, he has feelings."

"If you say so." Tamrack waved a hand dismissively. "All I care about is that he's got a tub of hot water ready for me. I came here for my usual Thursday shave and bath and I'm already runnin' late, so I ain't in no mood for any lollygaggin'. The gals over at Miss Hollie's get pure disappointed if I keep 'em waitin' too long!"

This last part he delivered with some added volume and he turned his head a bit as he said it, making sure the men behind him got the full benefit. They responded with raucous whoops and some laughter. "Those gals' disappointment would be the only thing that's pure over at Miss Hollie's!" somebody said, and then there was more laughter.

But Eb wasn't laughing. He suddenly looked very sober and troubled.

After clearing his throat, the barber said, "I'm afraid there's, uh, going to be a problem with that, Ollie."

"What do you mean a problem?" Tamrack wanted to know.

"With the bath . . . there's not going to be one available for a while."

"What the hell are you talkin' about? It's a bath — soap and water. The crick run dry or something?"

Eb swallowed, the Adam's apple in his neck bulging. "No, there's plenty of water. It's all heated and ready, in fact. But . . . but these other gentlemen are ahead of you."

Tamrack, his face growing flushed to a shade of near purple, raked his eyes over Shaw and Hadley who had been standing quietly by, looking on with expressions of interest and a hint of mild amusement.

"*These* duded-up varmints?" Tamrack snarled. "These are the 'gentlemen' who are standin' in the way of me and my boys gettin' what we came here for?"

"They're visitors from England, passing

through on the El Paso to Presidio stage run," Eb tried to explain. "The coach broke down on the trail, barely made it into town. It won't be repaired and ready to roll again until sometime tomorrow. So these fellas are stranded overnight and they —"

"I don't give a damn about any of that!" Tamrack cut him off. "All I care about is that I'm bein' put out by these nancy-boy lookin' sons of bitches and I don't like it one bit. Damn you, Eb, you know me and my boys come into town every Thursday for a few drinks and to have a romp at Miss Hollie's. We give you our business every time, regular as can be, to get spruced up for visitin' the gals."

"Yes, you do, Ollie," Eb agreed. "And I appreciate it. But you don't *always* make it in and never at a set time. You said yourself that you're running late today, so how —"

"Stubborn, stupid goddamn cows don't exactly have pocket watches, Squires."

"I can't help that," Eb replied, growing indignant and starting to show some spine in the face of Tamrack's bullying tone. "Just like I can't be expected to wait around all day and keep a tubful of hot water ready for if and when you might decide to show up."

Tamrack took a step forward. "You're soundin' kinda mouthy, you little pipsqueak.

87

Who the hell do you think you're talkin' to that way?"

"Perhaps," said Rupert Shaw, speaking softly yet with force from where he stood near the curtained doorway, "you'd like to hear my response to that question. Although, on second thought, I think you're going to get it whether you wish to or not."

CHAPTER 9

Tamrack stopped short, his mouth gaping open in disbelief. Under sharply furrowed brows, his eyes cut to Shaw.

"Please," Eb blurted nervously. "I don't want no trouble in here."

"Too damn bad what you don't want and too damn late for there to be no trouble," Tamrack growled, shifting his weight and starting to take a step toward Shaw.

But before he covered any ground, his way was blocked by Hadley. "I think ye'd best be standin' where you are and havin' a listen to the captain."

"I heard all I want and more out of that fancy-pants," Tamrack responded. "He made the mistake of meddlin' in my business and now he's gonna pay." Behind him, the other three cowboys crowded in closer through the door.

"The mistake will be yours if ye take another step," warned Hadley.

"I guarantee if you don't get out of my way you'll be makin' a bigger one."

Then, without waiting to see if his words had any effect, Tamrack suddenly cocked his shoulders and swung his club of a right fist in a looping roundhouse aimed at Hadley's jaw. Even quicker, the big Englishman thrust up his left forearm and blocked the blow. Sweeping Tamrack's arm away and down, Hadley backed up a step, bent his knees and upper body slightly, then lunged forward. Putting the full weight of his body mass into it, he slammed hard into Tamrack's middle and drove him backward.

A great gust of air exploded out of the cowboy as he flopped forward over one of Hadley's thick shoulders. Once he had his man going in reverse, the Englishman grabbed him securely by his leather belt, jerked upward, and lifted his feet off the floor. Now carrying Tamrack folded over one shoulder like a sack of grain, Hadley continued to rush forward, ramming into the knot of cowboys filling the doorway.

As the staggering, stumbling, off-balance cowboys virtually exploded out onto the boardwalk and into the street, Hadley lumbered out through the doorway himself, still holding Tamrack in his grip. On the lip of the boardwalk, he stopped short and unloaded his burden, dropping Tamrack's feet to the ground and giving him a shove that sent him stumbling drunkenly into the midst of his still-reeling men.

Inside the barbershop, a stunned Eb Squires stood looking out the door with his mouth formed into a perfect "O." "Good God!" he exclaimed. "I never saw anything like that in my life."

"Keep watching," advised Shaw calmly as he moved past him, heading toward the front door. "It's likely not over with." Pausing, he said over his shoulder, "Do you have a law officer in this town?"

"Uh, yeah. Sure."

"Probably be a good idea to send for him. How about a doctor?"

"Uh-huh. We got a doc, too."

"Send for him as well. In fact, it might be best to send for the doctor first."

In response, Eb made as if to go out the front door. But thinking better of that, he instead turned and hurried out the back way through the curtain.

Shaw continued leisurely out the front and stepped onto the boardwalk next to Hadley. The latter had stripped off his suit jacket by this point and stood slowly rolling up his shirtsleeves as he addressed the cowboys he'd scattered but who were now beginning to regroup. Though it was clearly visible to the men in the street, he seemed unmindful of the short-barreled, pearl-handled revolver that rode in a smooth leather shoulder holster formerly hidden by his jacket.

"If ye lads have had enough rough-housin'," he said, "it might be a good idea for ye to reconsider listenin' to what the captain has to say."

Beside him, Shaw took note that all the cowboys wore guns holstered on their hips. In anticipation of this, as he exited the barbershop he had slipped a large bore, over-under derringer from his vest pocket and now held it at waist level, aimed in the general direction of the men in the street.

"As far as any continuation of this matter," he added to what Hadley had already said, "let me advise you that, in case any of you are considering reaching for the weapons at your disposal, my large friend here is every bit as capable with his own revolver as he is with his fists. Furthermore, as you can see, I am quite prepared to provide some assistance."

"How about you take that pea shooter and shove it up your rear end before one of us does it for you," snarled one of the cowboys backing Tamrack.

"Stow that kind of talk, Nelson," said a

disheveled-looking Tamrack, still sucking hard to regain some of the wind that had gotten knocked out of him. "He's already got the drop on us, you fool."

"That's only a two-shooter he's holdin'. Even if he can hit anything with it, he can't get us all," argued Nelson.

"Very observant. Which barrel would you prefer to be emptied on you?" Shaw asked mildly.

By now, several citizens and tradesmen who'd been going about their business on Sierra Blanca's main street had halted what they were doing in order to more closely observe the scene that was playing out in front of the barbershop.

"No need for that, no need for shootin' irons at all," said Tamrack, absently rubbing his bruised ribs. "But that don't mean this is over. Not by a bucketful. No man puts his hands on me and dumps me on my ass without me gettin' a piece of him in return." He jabbed a forefinger in the direction of Hadley. "That means *you,* big fella. I say we go ahead with this but keep it between just you and me. You havin' any?"

Hadley smiled. "It's mighty kind of ye to extend that invitation before I had me shave and bath, lad. I'd've been most annoyed to have gotten all cleaned up and *then* had to scuff about with ye. So, to show my gratitude, I promise to try and keep from hurtin' ye too bad."

"Don't do me any favors and for damn sure don't expect the same kind of promise in return. I aim to break you in two!" With that proclamation, Tamrack stripped off his gunbelt and handed it to Nelson, adding to him and the other cowboys, "This is strictly between him and me, you understand? The rest of you stay out of it."

Acting in kind, Hadley pulled the revolver from his shoulder rig and held it out to Shaw, saying, "This won't take long, Captain. We'll have ye in that tub before the water gets too cold."

He stepped off the boardwalk then, and the two big men met out in the dusty street. Tamrack led it off, not waiting and quickly demonstrating that he had learned very little from their encounter inside by immediately throwing another whistling roundhouse right. Once again, Hadley blocked it. Only this time he followed up by landing a sharp right hook to Tamrack's ribs and then a slashing left cross to the jaw.

Tamrack staggered back but stayed on his feet. His expression looked stunned, though, as much from surprise as from the power behind the rapidly landed punches.

The men closed again, colliding like two warring bulls, trading a series of in-close punches. Tamrack threw his fists like heavy clubs, pounding blindly, on instinct, while Hadley's return blows came quicker and with greater accuracy, landing jarringly each time.

They separated and circled one another warily. Tamrack was breathing hard, beginning to drip sweat. A thick stream of blood poured from one nostril. A sheen of sweat shown on Hadley's face, but there were no other marks and his breathing seemed only slightly elevated.

Along the street, on either side, more people were gathering to watch.

Tamrack made another rush, this time leading with his left. The move came quickly enough that Hadley was unable to block it. Instead, he twisted his body away and took only a glancing blow to the side of his head. It still had some sting to it, but the overall result turned out to be more costly for Tamrack. Not landing the punch as solidly as intended threw him momentarily off balance and exposed to a quick retaliation from Hadley. The big Englishman swung a smashing backhand with his left fist, followed almost instantly, as his body twisted around, by a hammering right.

Tamrack was knocked staggering, his legs wobbly, streams of blood gushing from both nostrils now as well as from his mouth.

Hadley went after him, throwing jabs to his face and hooks to his body. Tamrack was driven back, managing to block a few of the blows but taking the brunt of most of them while unable to throw anything of his own in return. Then, with a surge of desperate strength, Tamrack planted his feet and halted himself. Dropping his head and shoulders, he ducked a pair of punches and rammed forward into Hadley's middle. Now, suddenly, it was Hadley being backed up with Tamrack relentlessly driving into him.

They reached a hitch rail just off to one side of the front of the barbershop. The small of Hadley's back slammed hard against the rail, and he was forced to bend backward over it by a flurry of blows from Tamrack, hammering down on his chest and face. An excited ripple went through the cowboys in the middle of the street.

Wanting to finish it, no matter what it took, Tamrack leaned close over his opponent and slammed upward with his knee, aiming for Hadley's groin. But the big Englishman twisted his body at the last second, and the knee pounded into his hip instead. As part of the same movement, Hadley jerked his right arm free, pulling it momentarily across his chest, then he slammed back with the elbow, driving it hard into Tamrack's chin.

The big cowboy staggered to one side. Hadley finished twisting free and suddenly he had Tamrack in his grip and was forcing him facedown over the hitch rail, raining double-fisted sledge-like blows onto the back of his neck. Tamrack's body sagged and started to go limp. Hadley brought it to an end by jerking his own knee upward to Tamrack's face where it hung down on the back side of the hitch rail. The big cowboy recoiled from the blow, straightening up but then immediately falling over backward and landing flat on his back in the dusty street. It was clear to all watching that he wasn't going to be getting up under his own power anytime soon.

The three cowboys bunched in the middle of the street stood poised, uncertain, finding it hard to believe what they'd just witnessed and not quite sure what to do next.

A spare, leathery-faced man, wearing a walrus mustache and a marshal's star on his chest, stepped out of the crowd and spoke in a deep, calm, authoritative voice.

"Just stand easy, boys," he advised. His hand rested casually on the butt of the Colt riding in a holster on his right hip. Holding it there, his seen-it-all-before pale eyes swept slowly over the whole scene. They paused for just an extra beat on Shaw and Hadley. "*Everybody* can take it easy. You had your show. It was a fair fight — and a pretty good one from what I saw — but now it's over. So you can break it up and go on about your business . . . Go ahead. Like I said, the show's over."

As the crowd began to disperse, a second man came out of it. He was a plump middle-ager with a pair of round spectacles perched on the end of his nose, carrying a well-worn doctor's bag.

"If you're looking for a patient, doc, I'd say you've got a pretty good candidate right there," said the marshal, jerking his chin toward Tamrack.

The doctor walked over, adjusting his spectacles for a closer look. "Well now. What have we here . . . Ollie Tamrack?"

"What's left of him."

The doctor looked around. "Who do we have to thank . . . er, I mean, who's responsible for this?"

"That would be me, sar," spoke up Hadley from where he stood, once more on the boardwalk, using a handkerchief handed to him by Shaw to wipe the sweat from his face and dab at the trickle of blood leaking out one corner of his mouth.

"What of your injuries?"

"Nothing an overdue barbering and a hot bath won't take care of," Hadley told him. "Best see to that lad there. He wouldn't go down easy. I had to be a mite rougher on him than I intended."

"Yeah, doc. Quit wastin' time and take care of Ollie, damn it. He looks like he might be hurt bad," said one of the cowboys in the street.

The doctor smiled. "Oh, I'll take care of him alright. I'll savor every minute, every stitch, and hopefully a cracked bone or two. After all the times I've been called upon to treat the victims Ollie has beaten down and stomped, I've been looking forward to the day when I could treat him for a taste of the same."

CHAPTER 10

"So you can see the fix I might end up in if I allow myself to get caught in the middle."

Firestick shrugged. "Then the simplest answer, it seems to me, is to avoid the risk of gettin' caught in the middle by steerin' clear of the whole thing. Just tell Frenchy you're not interested."

"But I *am* interested. That's the problem. I'd be a fool not to be. Think of the added business she could bring to my place."

"Yeah. And the added trouble when the whole works blows up . . . which it's pretty much guaranteed to do, sooner or later."

Dan Coswick — commonly referred to as "Irish Dan" even though he'd never been any closer to Ireland than Galveston Bay — sat slumped in a straight-backed wooden chair hitched up in front of the marshal's desk. He was a man in his late forties, craggily handsome, with eyes that always seemed to have a hint of sadness about them, and a lantern jaw set with a wide, expressive mouth. His thick, curly hair, once fiery red in color and the source of his nickname, was nowadays shot with enough gray to dilute the redness considerably. And the expressive mouth was presently turned down at the corners in a frown of consternation.

"You really figure it's that much of a guarantee?" Coswick said, questioning Firestick's assessment. "I mean, there's at least a chance it might work out, don't you think?"

"Always a chance, I reckon," conceded Firestick. "But I think there's a bigger one that Frenchy will end up goin' back to Sterling by the time it's all said and done. Then where will that leave you?"

"Depends," Coswick said stubbornly. "I could be out the expense I go to build her a proper stage. But if she sticks with me for even just a few weeks, the increase in business would probably be enough to cover that. Hell, with the big spring festival coming up in just a couple days and all the cowboys who'll be flocking to town for that, I might break even in one big night if I was able to advertise having Frenchy performing at my place then."

"So you break even, money-wise, and in

the meantime grow an ulcer wonderin' if and when Sterling might retaliate somehow."

Coswick scowled. "If he came at me like a man, face on, I'd have no worry. But he strikes me more like a duded-up sneak. A back shooter, if he wanted to get even bad enough."

"If he shoots you, I'll arrest him."

"A fat lot of good that would do me by then!" Coswick blustered. "Are you taking me serious about this or not?"

Firestick spread his hands. "Dan, I'm takin' you as serious as I can. There ain't much I can do based on what *might* happen. If you came here for my opinion, I already gave it. Steer clear of the whole thing. You'll only end up holding the short end of the stick."

Coswick sank back in his chair, looking dejected. "Ah, dang it, I guess I already know that's most likely how it would go. I guess I came here hoping you'd tell me a different way of looking at it. I'm not an overly greedy sort. You know that. I do a decent level of business at the Silver Spur, plenty to meet my needs. But I just can't shake the thought of how much better it could be if I had Frenchy Fontaine doing her song and dance numbers at my place.

And, truth to tell, the old he-goat in me can't help thinking how nice it would be to just plain have Frenchy around, close-like."

Firestick cocked an eyebrow. "Now you're really reachin' for trouble."

"I know, I know. I get a dose of the fool in me from time to time."

Firestick leaned forward and rested his elbows on the desktop. "The trouble between Frenchy and Sterling that caused her to move out on him, any idea what caused it?"

Coswick wagged his head. "Frenchy never said. All she told me when she came around was that she'd left Sterling, needed a job, and wanted to know if I was interested in taking her on as an entertainer at my place."

"Okay, that's what Frenchy said. But you don't spend all the time you do shovin' drinks across the bar at the Silver Spur without hearin' the story behind most everything that goes on in this valley. So what are you pickin' up that way?"

"The talk I hear," Coswick said, squirming a little in his chair, "is that the big blowup came over that new dove Sterling hired a short time back."

"The one they call Cleo, by any chance?"

"Yeah, that's the one. Apparently Frenchy thinks there's something going on between

103

Cleo and Sterling. So Frenchy gave Sterling a choice — 'either she goes, or I do.' I don't know what Sterling's response was, but I guess it's clear enough it didn't suit Frenchy. So she left."

"The strawberry blonde strikes again," muttered Firestick, leaning back in his chair.

"How's that?"

"Never mind. I was just thinkin' out loud."

"Okay. How about, while you're thinking, you consider one more thing for me?"

"Like what?"

"Well," Coswick said, his expression growing very earnest, "since Frenchy is staying at the Mallory House after moving out of her apartment at the Lone Star Palace, it occurs to me how much better women are about opening up and discussing things with other women than they are when it comes to —"

"No," Firestick said bluntly. "I can see where you're headed and the answer is no."

"You haven't even heard me out."

"I don't have to. I heard enough. You want me to talk to Kate to see if Frenchy has shared anything with her about what her feelings are and how things stand between her and Sterling. That'd put me in the middle and Kate, too. No."

"Aw, come on, Firestick. It'd help me a

lot if I —"

"No. End of conversation."

The statement was helped along when the front door opened and two well-dressed men walked in. One was tall, trim, and quite handsome; the other towered over him, was massive through the torso and shoulders, and had a face that nature hadn't been particularly kind to in the first place, before being further mistreated, it appeared, by being pounded upon numerous times since then.

"My apologies for the unannounced intrusion, gentlemen," said the handsome one. "If we're not interrupting anything crucial, I am in hopes we might have a few words with the marshal."

Firestick stood up. "I'm Marshal McQueen. It so happens our business here was just finishin' up" — this with a meaningful glance toward Coswick — "so sure, I've got some time to spare."

Advancing with outstretched hand, the newcomer said, "Excellent. I am Rupert Shaw, formerly a captain in the Queen's British India Army, 92nd Highlanders Infantry. My companion is Oberon Hadley, formerly a sergeant with same. We just arrived on the stagecoach from El Paso after an unexpected layover in Sierra Blanca."

Firestick reached across his desk and shook hands with each man. "This," he said after taking his hand back and using it to gesture in the direction of Coswick, "is Dan Coswick, one of our town's leadin' businessmen."

Coswick stood up and additional handshakes were exchanged. "I run a saloon called the Silver Spur," he said. "If you gentlemen are going to be spending any length of time in Buffalo Peak and are given to strong drink on occasion, I hope you stop by my place. You'll find fair prices and a fair measure poured every time."

Hadley made no comment but at the words "given to strong drink on occasion" his otherwise stony expression displayed a brief but unmistakable flash of heightened interest.

Shaw nodded and said with a thin smile, "We may very well be staying in the area for an extended period of time, and I assure you we've been known to indulge in strong drink on occasion. So we will remember your kind invitation and try to make it a point to stop by your . . . I'm sorry, what was the name of your establishment again?"

"The Silver Spur. You can't miss it, it's right down the street."

"Okay, Dan," Firestick said, showing some

impatience. "I expect these gents came here with something more in mind than hearin' you go into an advertisin' spiel. And if I ain't mistaken, you were on your way out to take care of some important business elsewhere."

Coswick grinned as he started for the door. "In other words — skedaddle. Right?"

"Couldn't've said it better myself."

Halfway out the door, Coswick couldn't resist tossing over his shoulder, "Don't forget, fellas — the Silver Spur. Hope to see you there."

Once the saloon owner had departed, Firestick motioned to the chair he'd recently vacated. "You gents are welcome to have a seat, take a load off," he said. "There's another chair over by the wall you can pull up."

"That won't be necessary, Marshal. Our intent is to take up only a minimal amount of your time," explained Shaw. "Mainly, we wanted to introduce ourselves and advise you of our presence in your town. Beyond that, I will tell you we have come all this way looking for a young lady. My former fiancée, to be perfectly candid. I have information that, as recently as four months ago, she was living on one of the ranches in the valley. I have every reason to hope and believe she is still there and that you can help me locate her. Her name is Victoria Kingsley."

CHAPTER 11

Firestick had withstood physical blows that left him feeling less stunned than he was in that moment.

"Victoria Kingsley . . . my former fiancée . . ."

As the impact of those words shivered through him, his mind raced. Yes, he was familiar with Victoria Kingsley. Very familiar. What he wasn't very familiar with, he realized, though not for the first time, was her past. But this was the West; such things weren't that uncommon. Out here there was no shortage of folks who chose not to reveal much about their pasts, and it was an accepted thing. The West was a place for new beginnings, for fresh starts, and what had gone before didn't matter so much as how people conducted themselves in the here and now.

And Victoria was someone who conducted herself just fine. She was a good person and a close friend. The fact she'd never spoken of a "former fiancé" back in her native England indicated to Firestick that it was something she likely wanted to forget. Yet here he was now, come all this way looking for her.

It crossed Firestick's mind to be deceptive, not reveal his relationship to Victoria, give himself a chance to first advise her about Shaw showing up and see how she wanted to play it. But the marshal wasn't much of a hand for lying, and in this case it was bound to only make things more awkward when the truth came out. Everybody in town knew that Victoria worked at the Double M as cook and housekeeper for the former mountain men and their *vaqueros*. All Shaw had to do was mention her name practically anywhere and he'd find that out. So trying to dodge the fact now was pointless.

All of these thoughts passed through Firestick's mind in a flash. He aimed not to let anything show on his face but wasn't sure how well he succeeded.

Something prompted Shaw to ask, "Are you acquainted with Miss Kingsley, Marshal?"

Firestick gave a measured nod. "Matter of fact I am. Know her well. That ranch she lives on, as a matter of fact, belongs to me

— well, me and a couple pals of mine who are also deputies for the town. It's a small horse outfit we operate on the side. Miss Victoria is our cook and housekeeper."

Shaw's brows pinched together. "You mean Victoria functions as a servant girl?"

His tone and words did a pretty good job of putting Firestick's own brows in a furl. "Well, 'servant' ain't exactly a word we use much in these parts. Miss Victoria has a job, does it well, and we pay her an agreed upon wage. That's the way it works."

"You'll have to pardon my reaction, Marshal," Shaw replied, still looking like he had a bad taste in his mouth. "But Victoria comes from a very well-to-do Welsh family. The thought of her traveling all this way to perform . . . well, menial tasks, I don't know how else to put it, is . . . er, rather unsettling."

"Reckon you got a right to your opinion," Firestick said, his teeth on edge. "Though I'm pretty sure Miss Victoria don't look at it that way."

"And you profess to know her well enough to make that presumption?"

"I said it, didn't I?"

Shaw scowled and tugged fussily at the lapels of his expensive jacket. "Very well. There's no sense wasting time on a difference of perceptions. If you will provide us directions to this ranch of yours and advise where we might rent some horses, my companion and I will leave you to your other duties, Marshal."

Firestick wagged his head. "Not quite so fast. We got a funny habit around here of bein' a mite protective of our womenfolk. That includes not settin' 'em up for some smooth-talkin' stranger who comes along and claims to be an old friend or even fiancé."

"Are you questioning my credentials, sir?"

"Not necessarily. I got no call to think you're other than who you say you are. But that don't matter. In fact, what you told me about yourself is part of what makes me a little curious and inclined to be cautious."

"I've never been a fan of riddles, Marshal. If you have a point to make, please get to it."

"Okay. You say you're Miss Victoria's former fiancé. For starters, that makes it plain the romance and planned weddin' got called off for some reason. Why, I don't know or especially care. But what I do know is that she's been in the states for three or four years now, right here in Buffalo Peak for over half that time, yet she's never spoke of you and you haven't come lookin' for her until now. Can't help but make me wonder whether or not she *wants* to see you."

"I assure you she would not turn me away," Shaw said. Muscles at the hinges of his jaw bulged visibly, and a flush of anger was creeping up over his cheeks.

"If that's the case, then there's no problem. But I think it's only reasonable, after all this time, to give her a bit of advance notice before you go bargin' in on her and sort of wallop her alongside the head with your appearance."

Shaw's nostrils flared and he appeared ready to respond angrily. Beside him, Hadley looked on, his expression anxious and a bit uncertain.

In a low, calm voice, he addressed Shaw, saying, "The marshal makes a valid point, Captain. A fair shock 'twould be to Miss Kingsley if ye showed up unannounced so. There's no doubt she'll welcome you with open arms, but think about how much more welcoming she'll be if she's had some time to primp and prepare. Ye know how women are about such things."

Slowly, the high color drained from Shaw's face. His eyes remained fixed on Firestick, but the glare in them also cooled.

"Alright," he said rather abruptly. "The two of you have made me see the error of my ways. Of course Victoria deserves some prior advisement of me being here — so as not to 'wallop her alongside the head' with it." He paused to show a somewhat sheepish grin. "I guess my own eagerness to see her, after planning and looking forward to it increasingly over these past weeks, caused me to fail giving proper consideration for her reaction. But that only curbs my eagerness temporarily. How long do you need to get word to Victoria, Marshal?"

"I normally return to the ranch for supper," Firestick replied. "But, since we're already well on into afternoon, I reckon I could go a mite earlier. The question then becomes how long Miss Victoria will need. She may want to send word back and invite you to supper — for which you'd be more than welcome as far as me and my pards are concerned — or she'd maybe rather wait until tomorrow. However she calls it, I'll get word to you as soon as I know."

"Needless to say, I will be waiting anxiously."

"I take it you're stayin' at the Mallory House Hotel?"

"Indeed. We'll be sure to wait right there until we hear from you." Shaw paused, a sterner expression returning to his face. "One more thing, Marshal. In case, after all this time, Victoria has any initial reluctance at the prospect of seeing me again . . . tell her I'm not prepared to take no for an answer."

CHAPTER 12

On most days, business along Trail Street, except for the saloons, tapered off by late afternoon. That was the case again today as far as the normal course of trade and shopping. But different kinds of activity — associated with getting ready for the spring festival scheduled to be held on Sunday, day after tomorrow — was very much in evidence. Last-minute preparations by volunteers were in full swing all up and down the street.

Among other things, as he walked from the jail building, Firestick saw a colorfully lettered banner being strung high across the full width of the street between two tall, specially erected poles. It read: 10TH ANNUAL SPRING FESTIVAL — BUFFALO PEAK, TEXAS. The folks accomplishing the task seemed cheerful and excited, as did other groups who could be seen hanging up bunting and decorating shop windows.

Normally, Firestick would have shared in the upbeat mood. He'd always enjoyed the festival in the past and was looking forward to it again this year. Or he had been, anyway, until the back-to-back visits from Dan Coswick and the two Englishmen weighted his thoughts with other concerns. What he needed now, to help balance those concerns, was somebody to talk to about them before he rode out to the Double M.

He found what he was looking for in the large, grassy area out behind the town's First Baptist church. Kate Mallory was there. Along with her, helping to set up tables for the big picnic that would be the centerpiece of the festival, were Moosejaw and his lady friend Daisy Rawling. Elsewhere across the area, others were putting up decorations and making preparations for the Sunday night square dance.

Kate looked up and smiled at the sight of Firestick approaching. She had her hair pulled back with a patterned headscarf tied over it. Her cheeks were mildly flushed, and in the soft gold tint of the afternoon sun she looked so good that Firestick wanted to stop and just stare at her, drink in her loveliness. But that wasn't feasible under the circumstances, so the best he could do was keep his eyes trained on her as he drew near.

"This is a nice surprise," she greeted. "Did you come to lend a hand?"

"No, afraid not," Firestick said, not waiting to get right to it. "In fact, I have to pull one of your number away. Moosejaw, I need you to put this business aside and take over looking after the town for me. I've got to ride out to the ranch."

Moosejaw had no trouble discerning the soberness in his tone and reading the same on his face. "What's goin' on?" he asked.

"We've got a situation," Firestick told him.

Moosejaw frowned. "Hope you can make it clearer than that."

Firestick glanced around. There was no one else in their immediate vicinity. If he had his 'druthers, he would have preferred to discuss this with Kate and Moosejaw only. Daisy, who was a great gal and totally devoted to Moosejaw, also happened to be quite outspoken and unfortunately often lacking in discretion. But seeing no way to exclude her, at least not politely, he proceeded to have the talk he'd come for.

Quickly, Firestick related how he'd been paid a visit by Shaw and Hadley, what their stated purpose was, then ended by repeating the bombshell statement from Shaw about being Victoria Kingsley's former fiancé. Upon divulging the latter, he found himself facing three stunned, open-mouthed expressions.

"Good heavens," Kate finally said, the first to find her voice. "What a shocking piece of news that is."

"Is it?" asked Firestick, regarding her closely.

She frowned. "What kind of question is that? Of course it is. Who could think otherwise?"

Firestick puffed out his cheeks and exhaled a quick gust of air. "I was hopin' maybe . . . well, seein's how you and Victoria have gotten kinda chummy over the past year or so . . . I thought she might possibly have mentioned something to you about havin' been engaged back in England. Hell, for that matter, has she ever talked much at all about her past?"

"No, she never has. Not really," Kate said. "Oh, she's told me some general things about England, about living over there, about some of the different customs and the different terms they have for certain things . . . I never gave it a lot of thought before, but Victoria seldom opens up much about anything of a personal nature."

"Except about her cousin Estelle — the girl who traveled to America with her and who encouraged Victoria to come in the first place," spoke up Daisy. "She mentioned her a couple times when the three of us were talking, remember?"

"Yes, that's right," said Kate, nodding. "She does speak occasionally about Estelle."

"She always says I remind her of Estelle," said Daisy. "Not in appearance or anything, she says, but because Estelle was kinda feisty and didn't take no guff off nobody."

Daisy beamed a bit at what she clearly took as a compliment. She was short, even for a gal, and particularly in contrast to the towering Moosejaw. But what she lacked in height she made up for in sass and an abundance of womanly curves, to the point of appearing on the plump side at first glance. But closer examination revealed the "plumpness" contained a layer of surprising muscle that came from being the town blacksmith, a position she took over after her late husband passed away. Her femininity, despite the ample curves, was often masked by her work attire of a man's shirt and either trousers or bib overalls, but none of that hid a pretty face highlighted by luminous brown eyes and a brilliant smile, all capped by a profusion of yellow curls cut functionally short. The smile was far more frequently on display since she and Moosejaw had begun seeing each other and, though she still favored trousers and boots over skirts or dresses, there was no mistaking a certain glow about her that only came from a young woman in the full bloom of a romance.

"Unfortunately," said Kate, "Estelle's feistiness wasn't enough to make her immune to getting ill. Very ill. When she eventually died, it was a sad and difficult time for Victoria, the meek one, who suddenly had to fend strictly for herself."

"I never knew any of that," said Moosejaw somberly. "And I sure never heard nothing about no fiancé from back across the sea."

"According to Shaw," Firestick said, "Victoria comes from a very well-off family. When I told him she was our cook and housekeeper out at the ranch, he seemed surprised and a little put off that she was, in his words, a 'servant girl.' "

Daisy wrinkled up her nose. "He sounds to me like a stuck-up English dandy. I don't like him already."

"I got a hunch that wouldn't be a hard conclusion for a lot of people to reach," allowed Firestick. "But there's one in particular I'm worried about."

"Beartooth," said Moosejaw.

Firestick nodded. "Exactly. He don't take much to snooty behavior from anybody in

the first place. And if it came from somebody showin' up to lay some kind of claim
on Miss Victoria to boot . . ."

Moosejaw grunted. "Won't be pretty. And
it's apt to turn that way real quick-like."

"Out of jealousy, you're saying?" asked
Kate.

"Reckon that's the closest word for it,"
Moosejaw replied.

"But Beartooth has never expressed any
feelings like that about Victoria — never
tried to lay his own 'claim,' as you put it, on
her."

"Come on, Kate," said Firestick. "We all
know those two have been dancin' around
their feelin's toward each other for over a
year now. Anybody can see it."

"Every time I try to bring it up, try to
nudge 'em together, you all tell me to mind
my own business," Daisy reminded the others.

"That's water under the bridge for right
now," Firestick said. "What matters now is
how I let Victoria know about this Shaw
character and then — providin' she's willin'
to see him — how I keep Beartooth from
wantin' to tear him apart, especially if he
starts spoutin' off with some high and
mighty remarks."

Moosejaw wagged his head. "I can pretty

much guarantee you ain't gonna keep Beartooth from *wantin'* to tear this gent apart. I figure the best we can hope for is that the two of us will be able to hold him back."

"If he feels that strong about Victoria, then he should have spoke up at some point during all the time he's had before now," Daisy said.

"Maybe so. But that's water under the bridge, too, like Firestick already said," Moosejaw responded irritably. "Re-hashin' that part now don't gain us nothing."

"I think we also need to remember that Victoria deserves some consideration," said Kate. "If she wants to see this old suitor, then she certainly has the right, no matter what Beartooth thinks. On the other hand, since she fled to America after their engagement ended and has never spoken of it or attempted to stay in touch — well, I'd take that as the behavior of someone who no longer seems interested in the man or whatever their relationship was."

"I wondered about that, too," Firestick conceded. "But at the same time, she must have kept in contact with somebody back there. Shaw came here knowin' she was somewhere in this valley."

"Didn't you know? She exchanged letters once in a while with another cousin in

London," Kate said. "Not very often, just enough to keep track of her parents. Again, she was never very specific. But reading between the lines, I got the impression her folks were against her coming to America so she avoided direct contact with them and used the cousin as a sort of go-between."

"Yeah. I remember takin' letters from her to post in town a time or two," said Moosejaw.

"Guess I got left in the dark about that." Firestick shrugged. "Not that it was — or is — any of my business. But at least it explains how Shaw knew where to find her. The cousin in London must have let something slip."

"It still doesn't answer whether or not Victoria wants to see Shaw, though," said Kate.

Firestick sighed. "No, it don't. Comes right back around to only one way to find out. I've got to go out to the ranch and let her know he's here. See what she wants to do about it."

"And if she *doesn't* want to see him?"

"I'll worry about that if and when the time comes." Firestick twisted his mouth ruefully. "But Shaw's already made it clear he didn't come all this way to be turned down."

CHAPTER 13

From behind the bar at the Silver Spur Saloon, Art Farrelly pushed a pair of tall, frothy beers in front of the two cowpokes who'd just bellied up on the other side. "There ya be, fellas. Coldest, crispest beer served south of Denver," he proclaimed.

Josh Stallworth shelled out some coins for payment, then wrapped his fist around the handle of one of the mugs and tipped it up for a long, thirsty pull. Beside him, Charlie Gannon did the same.

They lowered their half-drained mugs together. Emitting a satisfied belch, Charlie said, "I can't prove your claim about coldness, mister, and I doubt you can, either — but I've got to admit this here's some mighty prime stuff. It surely does hit the spot."

"And then some," added Josh.

Farrelly grinned. "We don't get no complaints. And, purely for the sake of seein' to it the quality stays high you understand, I sample it regular-like myself, just to make sure."

All three had a good chuckle over that.

Fishing out some more coins, Josh said, "I don't know how long it's been since you've done any samplin', but how about havin' a round on us so's you don't fall behind?"

"How can I refuse a generous offer like that?" Farrelly grabbed a mug and filled it for himself. Hoisting it high, he said, "Here's to good old days and better new ones."

At the far end of the room, a wide space had been cleared and three men were busy beginning to fashion a platform of sorts from the assortment of fresh-cut lumber that had been brought in and stacked close by.

Above the din of hammering and sawing, Josh said, "Looks like you're in the midst of betterin' your new days by sprucin' the place up some."

"Aye. That's the decision of the boss," said Farrelly. "They're building a stage for Frenchy to start performing on."

"Frenchy?" echoed Charlie.

"Frenchy Fontaine," said Farrelly. He frowned. "If you fellas don't know who she is, you must be new to these parts."

"Just got into town a handful of minutes ago."

"Well then, that explains it. Frenchy Fontaine, you see, is a song and dance gal. A real Frenchy she is, and a real beauty to boot. Voice like an angel and a set of legs like . . . well, er, like an angel, too, I guess. And, boy, she don't mind kickin' 'em high and showing 'em off."

"You sound like you've seen her perform plenty of times already," said Charlie.

"Every chance I could." Farrelly glanced rather furtively to either side. "Bein's how she used to do her show down the street at the Lone Star Palace, see, I used to have to sneak in for a peek once in a while. I had to be careful the boss didn't catch wind I was doin' business at the competition. But it was worth the risk, I'll tell ya. And now, lo and behold, Frenchy's gonna start doing her act right here at the Silver Spur. Her opening night will be Sunday. Far as I'm concerned, that'll be the high point of this year's spring festival."

Josh and Charlie drank some more of their beers.

"Yeah, as we rode in we saw signs all over about this festival shindig. Looks like it's a pretty big thing around here, eh?" said Josh.

"Oh, you bet. Big church service in the

morning, belly-bustin' picnic on the church grounds at noon, rodeo in the afternoon, foot-stompin' square dance that night. And, of course, the usual spillover from all that coming around regular-like to do some whistle-wettin' right here. With Frenchy makin' her, whatyacall, debut, we're expecting that spillover to be the biggest ever."

Josh flashed a wide grin. "Sounds like a heck of a good time. Reckon we couldn't've hardly picked a better time to show up."

"You fellas figure on stickin' around hereabouts?"

"Could be. If we find what we're lookin' for," said Charlie.

"Well, if you're lookin' for ranch work, you're right — you couldn't hardly have timed it better," Farrelly said. "Every wrangler, ramrod, and ranch owner in the territory will be in town over the weekend. If you're wantin' to sign on to an outfit, you should have plenty of opportunities."

"That's good to know," Charlie allowed. "But in the meantime, for the night or so, we're gonna need a place to bunk. Something hopefully with a roof over our heads for a change. We saw a hotel when we was ridin' in, but that's likely a bit rich for our blood. Anything in town for a couple drifters pinchin' their pennies a mite tighter?"

"Matter of fact there is," Farrelly answered. "Go see Hans Greeble at the general store. He's got a big loft up over his storeroom where he rents out spots for fellas passin' through, like you boys, to spread their bedrolls and be warm and dry. Bathin' and laundry arrangements can be made, too, all for real reasonable prices."

"Sounds like what we need. Thanks for the tip."

"Don't mention it. Be sure to stop in again. And don't forget Frenchy's big debut on Sunday night."

Earl Sterling sat behind the desk in his office at the rear of the Lone Star Palace. He was groomed and dressed to his usual precision, but he nevertheless looked haggard, worn down. His expression was grim, his eyes bleary and bloodshot.

Arthur, his brawny head bartender and bouncer stood before the desk, looking uncomfortable as he shifted his weight from one foot to the other.

"Are you sure of your information?" Sterling said. His gaze was not focused directly on Arthur but rather fixed balefully at a spot somewhere over his left shoulder.

"Not much doubt, boss. There's carpenters over at the Spur now, building a stage for her to perform on," replied Arthur.

Sterling's mouth stretched tighter, the corners turning down even more. "Two back-stabbing snakes," he muttered. "An ungrateful bitch and a conniving bastard who couldn't beat me in straight-up competition on his best day. So now Coswick jumps at the chance to take advantage when he thinks I'm already rocked back on my heels."

Arthur worked his lower jaw faintly, like he was ready to say something, but then held off.

"To hell with both of them," Sterling declared. "Frenchy was wore out as an attraction around here anyway. The cut she took for the added business she supposedly brought in was way out of line with what she actually drew. Good riddance. Let Coswick find that out for himself. He'll dump her quick enough when he does — he won't put up with her like I did. Let her try to come crawling back to me then and see where I tell her to go."

"Frenchy was with you a long time, boss," Arthur said.

"So what?" Sterling finally shifted his eyes to the big bartender. "A long time can be too long, and that's the point it reached with us. I started seeing the first signs of it when she tried to talk me out of bringing in some doves like I wanted. Jealousy, that's all it was. That's the way a woman gets when you let them hang around for too long. They think they got some kind of claim on you, how you should think and what you should do." Sterling jabbed a thumb into his chest. "Well, not this *hombre.* The only person who makes rules for me is *me.*"

Arthur nodded. "Whatever you say, boss. But I was wonderin', er, what about Frenchy's things?"

"What do you mean 'things'? What about them?"

"Well, the way she went out in such a big hurry she left a lot of her things behind. You know, some clothes and personal odds and ends. Said as she was going out the door that she'd be sending somebody around to pick them up, but nobody's showed up yet."

"Then she'd better get it taken care of pretty quick or I'll throw the damn stuff out in the street. If she's gone, she's gone all the way."

"Uh-huh. I understand that. I just didn't know if you'd, er, already sent Miss Cleo to start doing that."

"If I sent Cleo to start doing what?" Sterling demanded, clearly getting exasperated.

"Throwing out Frenchy's stuff. I met her coming down the stairs when I was headed this way and that's where she said she was going — back to Frenchy's apartment to clear it out. She said she didn't want any of that slut's trash cluttering up the place — her words — for when she got ready to move in herself."

Sterling shot to his feet. "I never agreed to that!"

His movement was so sudden and his voice so harsh it caused Arthur to take a step backward. "I didn't know, boss. That's why I was wondering."

"See how women sink their clutches in you and try to maneuver you, Arthur?" Sterling threw his arms wide. "A damn little trollop — how bold can you be? I let her turn my head for a few seconds, feed her a line or two about thinking she's something special, and . . ."

Sterling stopped abruptly, his face flushing with a mixture of anger and embarrassment for saying more than he'd meant to. "Never mind. I'll go straighten out Cleo. You get word to Frenchy, go yourself if you have to, and tell her she's got twenty-four hours to clear out the rest of her stuff. Tell her to send somebody. Not, for God's sake, to come herself. I don't want to see her around here again and I sure as hell don't want her and Cleo to run into each other. All I'd need would be for an eye-gouging catfight to break out between those two on top of everything else!"

CHAPTER 14

When Firestick got to the Double M, he found Victoria and Beartooth both outside by the horse corral. They were watching Jesus Marquez, one of the ranch's *vaqueros,* breaking a steel-dust mare he had galloping in circles within the enclosure. The mare seemed to be behaving and responding fairly well as Firestick rode up. But judging by the way the animal was breathing hard, the sweat and dirt streaking Jesus's face, and the thick haze of dust still hanging in the air, it was evident that not very long ago a heck of a battle between bronc and rider had taken place.

As Firestick reined up close to where Beartooth and Victoria were leaning against the corral fence, Beartooth turned and squinted up at him. "You just missed a good show. Likely better than most of the bronc bustin' anybody'll see at the festival rodeo on Sunday. That little mare had a double-barreled load of fight in her. 'Bout gave Jesus more than he could handle."

"He stuck with it, though," said Victoria, also turning. "I don't know how, but he did. It's nothing short of amazing to me the way he's able to stay on those raw, wild horses when they leap and twist so violently in their attempts to buck him off."

Victoria was an attractive, full-bodied woman a few years short of thirty. She had thick, richly textured chestnut hair, a finely sculpted face, and striking blue eyes that left a lasting impression on everyone who met her.

Looking down at her now, standing there in her simple yet flattering dress and half-length apron with the breeze slightly stirring her hair, Firestick tried to picture her — knowing what he'd recently learned of her background — in an elegant gown in a posh upper-crust setting. It was an easy picture to make, even though Firestick's experience with posh settings was pretty limited. Still, the point was that Victoria — like Kate, for that matter — had the grace and beauty to blend against any backdrop and only make it the better.

Firestick was drawn from his appraisal by Miguel Santros, Jesus's uncle and the ranch's second full-time *vaquero,* responding to Victoria's comments about bronc riding. From where he also stood leaning against the corral fence, he said, "Experiencing how much better it is to stay *on* the horse, instead of getting thrown *off,* is a great skill developer." A wry smile spread across his weather-seamed face. "Although, speaking from experience, I can say that even remaining on a bucking bronc is not the most comfortable way to spend one's time."

As he added the last, Miguel absently placed the palms of his hands to the small of his back and ran them down over his flat rear end. As Jesus's mentor and one of the best men around when it came to gentling and training horses, the old *vaquero* certainly knew whereof he spoke.

"I can only imagine, though, even that is painful," said Victoria with a rueful smile of her own. "I ache for days after merely *watching* a bronc being ridden down."

Overhearing this from inside the corral, Jesus steered the mare over closer and said, "Not that I want to cause you any pain, Miss Victoria, but I hope you're going to come to the rodeo on Sunday and see me ride there. I plan on placing pretty good in some of the events and bringing home a few ribbons."

Now Victoria's smile changed to one of dazzling fondness that she beamed at the young rider. "I'm sure you will, Jesus. And of course I'll be there watching and cheering you on."

Jesus responded with a faint blush and a grin so wide it nearly split his face in two.

"And if I don't get back to the kitchen," Victoria added, "I may have plenty of time to watch because I could be at risk of losing my job. Since the marshal is home early that means Moosejaw isn't likely to be far behind, and I still have some finishing touches to put on the supper I'm planning to serve."

As she started toward the main house, Firestick stopped her, saying, "No need to hurry off, Miss Victoria. Moosejaw won't be along any time soon and I came early because I have something I need to talk to you about . . . you and Beartooth both."

Victoria paused, looking puzzled.

Recognizing the seriousness in his old friend's tone and expression, Beartooth's brows pinched closer together. "What's goin' on?" he wanted to know.

Heaving a weary sigh, not looking forward to this but at the same time wanting to get it over with, Firestick swung down from his saddle. Looking on, Miguel also saw the seriousness in Firestick's manner and understood that what he'd come to talk about was meant only for those he'd named. Signaling Jesus with a faint jerk of his head, the two *vaqueros* drifted away.

"Mainly," Firestick started out, "this has to do with Miss Victoria. But I figure you got a stake in hearin' it, too, Beartooth."

Victoria's expression was impassive, waiting patiently for Firestick to continue. But patience wasn't exactly Beartooth's strong suit. "We already got that part. You made it clear you wanted to talk to the both of us," he said. "So what's the big mystery? Get to it."

Firestick's gaze settled on Victoria. "A couple strangers showed up in Buffalo Peak a little while ago. Got off the stage from El Paso. Came all the way from England. One of 'em is a gent named Shaw. He's askin' around for you, Miss Victoria. Unless everything he told me is a pack of lies, I expect you've got some kind of idea why."

Strangely, Victoria's reaction was very calm. In fact, it amounted to no reaction at all. At least not outwardly. Except for her eyes cutting away from Firestick and shifting to gaze out over the prairie, vaguely in the direction of town, her expression barely changed.

Beartooth, on the other hand, looked confused and increasingly frustrated in the silence that followed Firestick's statement. After his eyes had cut back and forth several times between Firestick and Victoria, he said, "Well, *I* got no blasted idea why. Who is this Shaw character, anyway? And what's his interest in Victoria?"

Firestick didn't say anything. Left it up to Victoria to answer.

After several beats, still gazing away, she began speaking with very little inflection in her voice. "Rupert Shaw comes from a wealthy family in Sheffield. His father is prominent in the steel industry there. Only a few months separate Rupert and I in age. From the time we were twelve, our parents began encouraging — some would say *pushing* — each of us toward eventual marriage to one another. Rupert had no objections, nor did I . . . in the beginning.

"Just before we turned twenty, we became engaged. But our wedding was postponed to give Rupert a chance to serve in the military. His father thought it would be an asset for him, would look good on his résumé, give him added stature for his future in the business world. It was while he was away, allegedly serving our country in some godforsaken corner of the world, that

I realized I didn't love him. Never really had. I was . . . relieved to have him away and did not look forward to his return. Oh, I don't mean I wished him harm or anything dreadful like that. I just didn't want to face a future as Mrs. Rupert Shaw.

"The only person I could share my feelings with, the only one I could trust to understand, was my cousin Estelle. She was getting ready to embark on her lifelong dream of coming to America and specifically to the West. She encouraged me to come with her and suddenly I — the meek, obedient, always sensible girl who never did anything impulsive or daring — wanted that more than anything. I informed my shocked and dismayed parents, wrote a long letter to Rupert, being as kind and trying to explain my feelings as best I could, and then . . . to America I came."

Not until she'd finished speaking did Victoria turn her gaze back to Firestick and Beartooth. Then, with a somewhat wistful smile, she added, "And now, it appears, my past has caught up with me."

"Only if you want it to," Firestick was quick to say. "There was no sense in me tryin' to shade Shaw. He came here knowin' you were somewhere in this valley. Since everybody in town knows your name and that you live and work out here at the Double M, he was bound to find that out. So I leveled with him, but said I'd have to talk to you first before directin' him to you. If you tell me now that you don't want to see him or have anything to do with him, then that's the way it'll be. We'll make sure he stays away from you."

"Damn betcha we will," said Beartooth emphatically.

For the first time, Victoria looked a bit distressed, indecisive. She raised the fingertips of one hand to her temple, saying, "This is so sudden and unexpected. He came all this way . . . I don't quite know what to . . ."

As her words trailed off, Beartooth, looking equal parts anxious and anguished, said, "You don't still . . . I mean . . . do you *want* to see him?"

Victoria looked away again, not giving an answer right away.

In the silence that suddenly hung heavy over the three of them, Firestick looked up and spotted two riders in the distance, coming from the direction of town. Both sat their saddles well — one tall and erect, the other taller still and much thicker through the torso and shoulders. Peering more closely, it only took a second for the marshal to recognize who they were.

Through clenched teeth, he said, "It appears, Miss Victoria, that your former fiancé ain't very strong on holdin' to agreements he makes."

CHAPTER 15

The two riders came galloping into the Double M compound and reined up in front of the corral. At the sight of Victoria, Rupert Shaw's eyes shone with delight. Murmuring her name, he wasted no time starting to climb down out of his saddle.

"Hold it right there, mister!" Firestick stepped in front of Victoria as he issued the sharp command.

Shaw froze in a partially dismounted position. "What is the meaning?" he demanded. "I came thousands of miles to —"

"I don't give a damn how far you came," Firestick cut him off. "That was your choice, nobody else's. What I care about is that you dogged me out here when we agreed you would wait back in town until I had a chance to talk to Victoria. To advise her you'd showed up here, and find out if she was interested in seein' you."

"Of course she's interested in seeing me,"

Shaw insisted. "We go back to childhood together, for heaven's sake."

"I ain't heard her say so yet — because you didn't give us the chance to finish discussin' you. And none of that changes the fact of you breakin' our agreement for you to hold off until I got word back to you. You were gonna wait at the hotel, remember?"

"Please!" Shaw's tone was disdainful. "Any so-called agreement between us was hardly a binding matter. That may have been your impression, but not mine. I wasn't about to waste time waiting in a stuffy hotel room, knowing I was so close to what I'd come so far for. Oberon and I rented horses from the livery, and when we saw you ride out of town, we followed. It's as simple as that."

"Then here's something else that should be real simple for you," Firestick grated. "You got five minutes to get the hell off my property. And since our land stretches for a good distance in every direction, you'd best get a move on."

"You can't be serious," Shaw said indignantly, still poised with one leg partly raised to dismount.

"Try me. And keep in mind, the clock is already runnin'."

During this exchange, Hadley's right hand shifted subtly above his saddle horn and undid the single button holding the front of his suit jacket closed.

But Beartooth didn't miss the move. Taking a long step to one side in order to distance himself from Victoria, he let his right hand drop close to the Colt riding on his hip and said, "And you there, big boy — if that paw of yours makes one more twitch toward the weapon I suspect is inside that coat, I'll blow you so far out of the saddle you'll think you're on your way back to England."

Shaw's mouth fell agape. He craned his neck to try and make eye contact with Victoria, still blocked by Firestick's bulk. "Good God, Victoria! Have you no sway over these ruffians? Is this the kind of life you lead by choice — or are they holding you hostage?"

Placing a restraining hand on Firestick's shoulder, Victoria stepped around him. "Enough!" she declared. "Enough of this anger and ugly talk. I'll have no one hurt on my account."

"Nobody's gonna get hurt if they have the sense to back off," Beartooth told her. "You don't have to talk to these men if you don't want to."

Victoria gave him an uncertain glance. "That's just it. I *do* want to talk to them. Or, rather, I feel I need to. I owe Rupert that much. I have for a long time."

Beartooth's shoulders sagged visibly. He held Victoria's eyes for a long moment. Then, in a low voice, he said, "Okay . . . if that's the way you want it."

"Thank God!" exclaimed Shaw with a sigh of relief. "At least someone is showing a measure of good sense."

Victoria spun on him with fire in her eyes. "There's certainly none coming from you, Rupert Shaw! These men you brand 'ruffians'? They are among the finest gentlemen I've ever known. It is you who are being rude and impudent, as usual. Giving me pause, I must say, as to whether or not I *should* listen to anything you have to say."

"Forgive me if I spoke too hastily or harshly," responded Shaw. "Surely you can see how I might be feeling a bit desperate here. But I assure one and all that the last thing I'm looking for is to cause trouble or make enemies."

Victoria continued to scowl at him for several seconds. Gradually the heat cooled in her eyes. Glancing first at Firestick and then Beartooth, she said, "I appreciate both of you wanting to protect me, but there's really nothing here that represents any kind of threat. If you don't object, for reasons I've already explained, I'd like to have some time with Rupert."

"Of course we don't object," said Firestick. "It's always been your decision."

"Long as you're comfortable with it," Beartooth told her.

Firestick motioned toward the house. "Go on over to the front porch where you'll have some shade and some privacy. We'll stay back here, out of the way."

Victoria smiled fleetingly. "I shan't take too long. I know you'll be wanting your supper."

"Take as much time as you need."

Shaw at last finished dismounting and walked beside Victoria as she took Firestick's suggestion and led the way to the shaded front porch. Hadley remained in his saddle until they reached the hitch rail in front of the house. Before leaving the corral area, he made a point of letting his gaze linger meaningfully on Beartooth.

The two former mountain men stood looking after the trio. Until Firestick turned away and said, "Come on, us standin' here gawpin' ain't hardly givin' her the privacy I promised."

"I didn't make no promises," Beartooth

muttered, even though he turned away, too. "I ain't likin' this whole thing worth a damn."

"Can't say I do, either," allowed Firestick as they began walking slowly along the corral fence. "But what can we do? Victoria's a woman growed and as long as she's in no danger and it's what she wants, we can't force our will on her. She's not our prisoner here."

"But she belongs here, dammit. Not with that duded-up slicker," Beartooth insisted.

"She's not *with* him. She's just talkin' to him for a few minutes."

"But that's the whole idea, leastways from the way he's lookin' at it. He didn't go to all the trouble of comin' clear across an ocean and most of the country just to *talk* to Victoria. He wants her back."

"Yeah, I suppose he does. But he never wanted her to leave him in the first place, remember, yet she did. I think it's safe to say Victoria has a mind of her own. If she was interested in goin' back to him, don't you reckon she would have made a move in that direction by now?"

"Maybe she did. Maybe she sent for him."

"Now you're talkin' loco. She had no idea he was comin'."

"How can you be so sure? You don't know

any more about her — *really* know — than I do. Maybe not as much. She's never opened up about her past to anybody. She sure as hell never mentioned comin' from wealth and bein' engaged to that Shaw jackass."

"That kinda falls under the heading of bein' her own business, don't it? Her past was and is a private matter, if she wants it to be. After all, she's only an employee around here."

Beartooth stopped short. "Now wait a minute. That's a helluva thing to say. And you know it ain't true. You know good and well she's more than that. She's . . . well, the truth of it . . . what I'm tryin' to say is . . ."

"What you're mumblin' and stumblin' about is that you're in love with her," Firestick said.

Beartooth's eyes widened. He swallowed. "Yeah. Yeah, I am. How'd you know?"

"Because I got a pair of eyeballs and half a brain, that's how. Me, Moosejaw, Kate . . . we've all seen it. And you know Daisy has been ridin' the two of you every chance she gets."

"Yeah, but that's just Daisy . . . Do you think Victoria knows? I mean, *really* knows?"

"Have you ever told her?"

149

"You know I haven't."

"Then how is she supposed to *really* know?"

"The rest of you saw it."

"Most gals have a kinda funny notion about things like that. They want to hear the words, want the fella to do something to *show* his intentions. Ain't too many of 'em around like Daisy."

Firestick added that last part with a wry grin, aiming to lighten the moment a bit, recalling how Daisy had basically thrown a headlock on Moosejaw and *told* him he was in love with her — which, fortunately, turned out to be the case.

Beartooth dug the toe of one boot in the ground and managed a weak smile. "Might be better if more of 'em were."

"So what are you gonna do now — about these feelin's of yours toward Victoria, I mean?" Firestick prodded.

Beartooth's smile faded and he looked up, his expression turning uncertain. "What *can* I do? What should I do? I've never been in this kind of fix before."

"You *fight* for her, that's what you do, you damn lunkhead," Firestick said, his tone turning somewhat frustrated. "And by that I don't mean go back there and knock the hell out of Shaw. Or his pet ape, either, in case I ain't bein' clear. I mean you fight by not wastin' no more time lettin' Victoria know how you feel. See what her feelin's are for you. Unless I'm wrong, I think you'll find she's got a heap of unspoken fondness just like you been carryin' around."

Beartooth's eyes bored into him. "But what if you *are* wrong?"

"Then, if you're convinced you love her and want her bad enough, you fight that much harder."

Beartooth set his jaw firmly, absorbing Firestick's words. His expression conveyed his gratitude for the encouragement and support but he seemed unsure how to reply.

Inside the corral, Miguel had approached without notice. Into the silence between the two former mountain men, he said, "*Señors* . . . Another rider comes from the east. Riding very hard."

Firestick and Beartooth looked around, quickly swinging their attention to the east and the approaching rider. The man was indeed riding hard, coming fast. As he drew closer, they recognized him as Gabe Hooper, a young man who worked for Pete Roeback at the town livery.

Hooper came galloping into the compound and checked down his horse sharply. Billows of dust swirled around him.

"Whoa there, young Gabe," said Firestick. "What lit a fire under you?"

"Miss Kate sent me," Hooper said, breathing hard. "She said to tell you to come right quick. Four hardcases showed up in town a little while ago. Four mean-lookin' cusses if I ever saw any. Got trouble written all over 'em. Deputy Moosejaw is keepin' an eye on 'em, but Miss Kate is worried something bad is gonna bust loose and says you oughta come in case he needs a hand."

CHAPTER 16

Travel back and forth between the Double M and town, when there was no reason to hurry, normally took close to an hour. Reacting to the message carried by Gabe Hooper, Firestick dug his heels hard into his horse and cut that time in half. Since his mount was already saddled and ready, he lit out immediately, telling Beartooth to saddle up and follow as quick as he could. Hooper was advised to rest his animal before heading back.

With the sun hovering just above the western horizon and sinking fast, the lengthening shadows of late afternoon filled the draws and the eastern slopes of the low hills as Firestick pounded along. He was coming in at a slight angle from the northwest. Ordinarily he would swing onto the west end of Trail Street where the jail building lay near the outskirts.

On this occasion, though, he didn't want

his sudden appearance to trigger anything if tensions were already running high in town. So instead he sharpened his angle of approach and came in behind the Mallory House Hotel. Tying his horse out back near the privy, he went in through the rear and up an interior hallway to the front lobby. He was in luck, finding Kate there, watching anxiously out the front window. Frenchy Fontaine was with her, her beautiful face looking pinched and strained by deep concern.

Kate turned at the clump of Firestick's boot heels entering the lobby. "Elwood! I'm so glad you got here." She was the only one around town who called him by his given name.

"I take it things are still hangin' fire?"

"So far. I don't know for how much longer."

Out through the window, the street looked quiet, void of any activity. Word had apparently spread that there was trouble in the air.

"So what's goin' on exactly?" Firestick asked. "Gabe said something about four hardcases showin' up lookin' for trouble."

"That about sums it up."

"Where's Moosejaw?"

"Down the street a ways, in front of

154

Daisy's blacksmith shop where he can keep an eye on things."

"And where are the hardcases?"

"Across the street, in the Silver Spur. The only place they've been since they hit town."

"So what's so troublesome about 'em? They threatenin' somebody or something?"

"In a manner of speaking," said Kate. "They came looking for somebody — that newest girl Earl Sterling hired over at the Lone Star Palace."

"The one called Cleo?"

"That would be the one," Kate said.

"The dirty little *putain*!" hissed Frenchy. "I tried to warn Earl against bringing in those kind of girls. I told him it would lead to nothing but trouble, but he wouldn't listen. In the beginning, I have to admit, it wasn't too bad. Then *she* showed up — conniving, backstabbing, manipulating Cleo. In no time at all she had all the other girls hating her and everybody but a pathetically smitten Earl seeing what she truly was. It was disgusting to watch — not to mention personally humiliating."

Firestick frowned. "I can appreciate all that, and I'm sorry for you, Frenchy. But what does it have to do with —"

Kate cut him off, explaining, "Frenchy was in the Silver Spur when those hardcases came in. She was there to check out the stage that Coswick is building for her because she's going to start performing there, in case you haven't heard. Anyway, as soon as those rowdies showed up they started asking for Cleo. They were sent by a man named Kilbourn, they claim, who had an exclusive contract with Cleo back in El Paso. According to them, she broke it and ran out on him. They're here either to take Cleo back or collect an undisclosed amount of money she supposedly owes this Kilbourn."

"So why are they at the Spur when Cleo is at the Palace?"

Kate shrugged. "I guess they came to town not knowing exactly which saloon they'd find her in. They picked the wrong one to start with but then decided they liked it there and would stick with it."

"I slipped out the back as soon as I could, but not before I heard someone tell them where Cleo could actually be found," said Frenchy. "Once they knew that, they sent Art Farrelly, the Spur bartender, over to the Palace with their demands. Either Cleo or the money."

"Let me guess. Cleo don't want to go with 'em and either don't have or refuses to pay the money. And Sterling is backing her."

"That's where it stands," said Kate. "The men from Kilbourn have given until six o'clock for their demands to be met one way or the other. If not, they're going to the Palace to take what they came for."

Firestick glanced at the clock on the wall behind the registration desk. It was ten minutes of six.

"Has Moosejaw confronted the hardcases in any way?"

Kate shook her head. "No. So far it's only words. I think he's waiting to see if they actually try something."

Firestick nodded as if in approval.

At that moment, Thomas Rivers, Kate's right-hand man around the hotel, came into the lobby from the adjoining dining room. Marilu, his plump, round-faced wife, who was head cook and overseer of housekeeping, was right behind him. In his hands, Thomas was gripping the Greener shotgun he normally kept behind the bar in the hotel's small barroom. Thomas was a big man, big enough so that the Greener looked almost like a toy wrapped in his thick fingers. The expression on his coffee-colored face was intense.

"You be needin' some backup with that bunch across the way, Marshal, I'm standin' here ready," he announced.

157

"My man ain't no shirker when there's trouble needs facin'," said Marilu proudly.

"Everybody knows that," Firestick replied, addressing them both. "And there's nobody I'd rather have sidin' me than Big Thomas. But grateful as I am for the offer, this is a job that's best for me and my deputies to handle. Moosejaw is right down the street and Beartooth is comin' in hard on my heels."

"That's still only three to their four," Thomas pointed out.

Firestick grinned. "I can't help it the odds are stacked so bad against 'em. Besides, the hot air those loud mouths are blowin' is likely to cool down and dry up once they see three determined star-packers standin' in their way."

"I don't know about that," Frenchy said. "They looked to me like a very rough bunch."

"It's still a job for me and my deputies to handle," said Firestick firmly. He tossed another glance at the clock. "Now, I need to slip down to the blacksmith shop in order to let Moosejaw know I'm here. Beartooth will be showin' up any minute. Thomas, the best way you can help is to stay right here with that shotgun in case the trouble shows any sign of spillin' out of the street and comin' this way."

"It does, I'll make sure it gets stopped real short," Thomas said.

Beartooth came pounding up just as Firestick exited the rear of the hotel. "I saw your horse and came over here instead of the jail," he said. "What's goin' on?"

Firestick gave him a quick rundown, ending with, "I'm on my way now to let Moosejaw know we're here. He's keeping an eye on things from Daisy's blacksmith shop, ready to step out if and when those jaspers make their move. How about you go down to the alley that runs beside Moorehouse's barbershop and take up a position there. After I tell Moosejaw we're here, I'll settle in somewhere between you two. Then, when Kilbourn's men come out of the Spur, we'll step out and show we're ready for 'em."

Beartooth nodded. "Sounds good. If they stay in a bunch, we'll have a three-way line of fire on 'em. They'll have to be mighty nervy — or stupid — to try anything in the face of that."

Firestick grunted. "Trouble is, they just might be. I naturally want to avoid a shootout if we can, but if they don't give us a choice, then at least the street looks clear of citizens."

"You make the call. But if you open the ball," Beartooth said, yanking his Winchester from the saddle scabbard of his horse, "I'll be ready."

A handful of minutes later, Firestick reached Daisy's blacksmith shop and again came in through the rear. He found Moosejaw and Daisy at the front of the barn-like structure, past the forge area, standing to one side of an open sliding door and peering out at the street. He announced himself from a safe distance back.

Once Moosejaw's face had snapped around, a smile quickly curved his mouth. "Can't say I'm sorry to see you," he said. "I didn't know if you were comin' back to town or not."

Firestick grinned, too. "Kate sent word you had a spot of trouble shapin' up here. Didn't want you to hog all the fun for yourself."

"He wouldn't've been on his own," Daisy said, holding up the long-barreled shotgun she was gripping in her fists. "I was ready to back his play."

Firestick rolled his eyes. "Jesus Christ, is everybody in this town shotgun happy?"

"What do you mean?"

"Never mind. Just stand at ease with that thing, okay? Me and Beartooth are here now

160

to back Moosejaw. Let us handle it; it's what we get paid for."

"Beartooth's here, too?" Moosejaw asked.

"He's down the street, in the alley by Moorehouse's," Firestick explained. "Now that you know we're here, my idea is for me to take up a position in between you two. When those hardcases come out of the Spur, we'll show ourselves and let 'em know we mean business if they don't call it off and hightail out of town. If they're hell-bent on tryin' us, we'll have no choice but to show 'em what a purely bad idea that is."

"I like it," Moosejaw was quick to say. "You'll be in the center, so you take the lead on lettin' 'em know how things stand. Me and Beartooth will be ready to jump in when needed."

"Done. It's gotta be six by now, so I'd better hurry up and find me a spot."

CHAPTER 17

Cutting once again behind the buildings that lined this side of Trail Street, Firestick worked his way through a gap between a bakery and a boot repair shop too narrow to be called an alley. There was a large rain barrel taking up most of the opening at the street end, providing good cover for him to settle in back of. This placed him almost directly across from the front door of the Silver Spur Saloon on the opposite side of the empty street. The sinking sun was casting long shadows from some of the building peaks out into the dusty, deeply rutted strip that separated them.

Firestick barely had time to drop into a half-crouch behind the barrel before the Spur's batwings slapped open and four men emerged. They were indeed a hard-looking lot — scruffy, unshaven, narrow-eyed, loaded down with guns and shell belts bristling with heavy caliber cartridges.

Striding half a step ahead of the others was a tall, rangy specimen wearing a cream-colored hat. Crowded in behind him were two galoots of average height, one decked out in a tobacco-colored bowler, the other wearing a flat-crowned Stetson. Both carried rifles. Bringing up the rear was a potbellied Mexican sporting a brace of pistols worn for the cross draw.

Exiting the saloon, the four turned immediately to their left — Firestick's right — and started in the direction of the Lone Star Palace on the same side of the street.

That was all Firestick needed to see. He straightened up, edged around the barrel, and stepped out onto the boardwalk on his side.

"Hold it right there, gents," he said in a level voice, loud enough to carry across the street. In his peripheral vision, he saw Moosejaw ease out onto the edge of the street in front of the blacksmith shop. Down to his left, Beartooth also moved into view.

The four men stopped. The leader locked eyes with Firestick, his expression showing nothing. Slowly, his gaze dropped to the badge on Firestick's chest. Then, just as slowly, he looked first one way, then the other to take note of the two deputies. Behind him, the other three appeared poised, wary. The knuckles of the two rifle-men whitened as they gripped their weapons tighter. The Mexican shifted his body so that he was facing Firestick and both of his holstered pistols were clear of the man closest to him.

"You got some kind of business with us, Marshal?" asked the leader.

"Believe I do," said Firestick. "More to the point, your intentions are my business."

"Not sure I follow you. We're just four long riders passin' through your town. We had ourselves a few drinks at this here saloon, and now we're on our way down to the other one where we understand they got sportin' women. Before we ride on, we reckoned we might have ourselves a mattress dance or two . . . providin' the gals ain't so homely they change our minds, that is. And seein's how you *allow* sportin' gals in your town to begin with, such intentions can't hardly be against the law, can they?"

"Wouldn't be . . . if you was tellin' the truth."

The leader's mouth pulled tight. "You callin' me a liar?"

"You're tellin' me a whole different story than you been spoutin' to everybody else since you hit town. What would you call it?"

The width of the dusty street separating

the two men filled with tension.

At length, the leader said, "She ain't nothing but a dirty little whore, Marshal. And a sneakin', cheatin' one at that. She ain't worth puttin' yourself to no trouble over."

"Strange advice comin' from you," said Firestick, "seein's how you and your boys have already gone to a lot of trouble over her — ridin' all this way from El Paso the way you have."

The leader shrugged. "Times are hard. It's a payin' job for us to bring her back."

"Me and my men have payin' jobs, too. Part of what's expected for that pay is to protect our citizens from bein' drug away against their will."

"Are you kiddin' me? A citizen? I repeat, she ain't nothing but a whore," the leader sneered. "She broke a contract and cost the fella who hired us a serious amount of money. She needs to be held accountable for that."

"You got a copy of the contract?"

"What!"

"You heard me. The contract she's supposed to have broke — you bring a copy of it?"

"Hell no, we didn't bring no contract! We look to you like paper-shufflin' lawyers or some such?"

Firestick's eyes turned flinty. "What you look like to me," he said, "are four *hombres* who rode a long way for nothing. If you're smart, you'd best ride back out of town and forget what you came here for."

The tension in the air grew heavier.

"That ain't gonna happen," the leader said in a flat tone. "We ain't the kind to take on a job and not see it through to the end."

"You're real close to the end," Firestick told him. "You can get the rest of the way there by turnin' around like I gave you the chance . . . or you can find it right here."

Firestick tensed as he said the words, about ninety-nine percent sure the hard-cases weren't going to ride away. The only thing that surprised him was the fact it wasn't the leader who made the next move — it was the potbellied Mexican with the twin Colts.

He drew both six-guns and was mighty quick about it, extending them at arm's length and triggering both simultaneously. Luckily for Firestick, his aim wasn't nearly as impressive as his flashy draw. Bullets ripped the air past the marshal's shoulder and thumped into the rain barrel.

Firestick went into a diving roll to his right, clawing for his own gun as he did so. He ended up on one knee behind an awning post in front of the boot repair shop. A long wooden sign in the shape of a boot was nailed to the post, providing some narrow yet welcome cover. From behind this, the marshal began returning fire.

By then, everybody was blazing away. Sizzling lead and rolling clouds of powder smoke filled the street.

Down the street, in front of Moorehouse's barbershop, Beartooth was levering and firing his Winchester in rapid succession, taking aim at the Mexican who'd opened up on Firestick. Two of his bullets found their target, spinning the man partway around and slamming him back against the front of the Silver Spur. A Colt flew from the Mexican's left hand. He turned his body again, staggering, sliding along the front of the building, trying to lunge to safety through the batwings. He was waving his right hand wildly, continuing to trigger random shots. More bullets from Beartooth chewed the outer wall behind the Mexican's head. Just when it looked like the Mexican might make it through the door still on his feet, Firestick planted a .44 slug just above his left ear, blowing off his *sombrero* and part of his skull. The Mexican finally made it through the batwings — as a carcass that hit and skidded loosely on the sawdust-sprinkled floor.

In front of the blacksmith shop, crouched behind a high-walled wheelbarrow, Moose-jaw traded shots with the two hardcase rifle-men. The one in the derby was peppering his position heavily, levering and shooting back in the same rapid-fire manner as Bear-tooth was down the street. The other rifle-man, the one in the Stetson, had taken a couple methodical shots but seemed far more interested in trying to squirm low and find some cover behind a watering trough in front of the boardwalk. He didn't get low enough before a .45 caliber slug from Moosejaw's Schofield drilled into his throat, just below the Adam's apple, and flipped him onto his back. A spout of blood from his destroyed throat arced up and splattered against the side of the trough he'd been try-ing to get behind.

Seeing his pard go down so enraged the derby-hatted *hombre* that he tried to take advantage of Moosejaw's momentary lapse in follow-up fire — while he was reloading — by rushing out into the street and aiming an even more intense volley at the wheel-barrow. It was as if the damn fool forgot there were still two more lawmen engaged in the fight. Firestick reminded him by shooting him in the thigh and knocking him to the dirt.

Before the marshal could finish the rifleman he'd spilled in the middle of the street, the leader of the hardcases, who'd been surprisingly slow in drawing his pistol and joining the fray, diverted Firestick's attention by sending a pair of bullets hammering into the boot sign he was still behind. The sign rattled and spit slivers, but was thick enough to prevent the slugs from chewing through.

Leaning down lower, reaching under the heel of the wooden boot, Firestick triggered a return shot at the hardcase leader. His bullet scored truer, slamming dead center into the tall man's chest. The leader's head jerked back and he went up on his toes. In the same instant, a Winchester round from down the street, courtesy of Beartooth, whistled in and hit less than an inch from where Firestick's shot had struck. The leader flung out his arms and was driven backward through the Spur's plate glass window.

Out in the street, the remaining wounded rifleman had made it up on his good knee. He'd lost the derby hat but was still clutching his Winchester. He was lifting it again as Moosejaw, his Schofield now reloaded, rose up behind the wheelbarrow and drew an unwavering bead on the man. The big deputy tried to give him a chance, saying, "Drop it. You don't have a prayer." But the rifleman wasn't having any. He continued deliberately raising his weapon until it reached a point where Moosejaw had no choice. He squeezed the trigger and put a bullet in the middle of the stubborn fool's forehead.

Everything went suddenly and totally silent. For over half a minute, there was no sound or movement. Even the three lawmen stood motionless.

Then, all at once, like a picture coming to life, men began pouring out of the saloons and other folks began appearing in shop doorways and windows. Beartooth came slowly walking up the street, reloading his Winchester as he strode along. Firestick, too, took time to reload his .44 before stepping out into the street and moving toward the fallen men. Moosejaw was wrapped in a big embrace from Daisy before he gently disengaged himself and also moved toward where the bodies were sprawled.

Only when he heard one of the onlookers say, "Look, the deputy's wounded" did Firestick realize Beartooth had been hit. There was a tear in his shirtsleeve, high up near his left shoulder, and some fresh blood was trailing down to the crook of his arm.

"It's nothing," Beartooth was quick to scoff. "Just a bullet burn, barely broke the skin. That crazy Mexican throwing those wild shots before he went down almost got lucky when he threw one my way."

"Too close for comfort," muttered Firestick. His gaze swept again over the sprawled bodies. Through gritted teeth he added, "They weren't much, but by damn, they stood their ground and made a fight of it tryin' to finish the job they took on. You can't deny 'em that."

His gaze lifted and happened to fall on Earl Sterling, who'd pushed his way to the front edge of the crowd. He was ashen faced and somewhat disheveled looking. His eyes went from Firestick to the men on the ground, then back to Firestick again. "My God, Marshal, I . . . I don't know how to thank you."

"Don't thank me. Don't say a damn word to me," Firestick growled.

Sterling's eyes widened. He looked bewildered.

"Four men dead and one of my deputies wounded," Firestick went on, his voice grating. "Once again on account of that . . . that troublemakin' blonde you hired, Sterling. And we both know this ain't the first blood spilled over her. She's poison, but you're the only one who can't see it. She's makin' a blasted fool out of you!"

"Take it easy, Firestick," Beartooth said.

Sterling looked like he wanted to say something but dared not.

Firestick wasn't done. "Well, you can let her make a fool out of you if you want. But I've had it. One more piece of trouble related to her — and I mean if she as much as sneezes and gives somebody a cold — I'm runnin' her pretty little ass out of town. And if you don't like it, you can make dust with her!"

"Alright, that's enough," Beartooth said, this time putting a hand on Firestick's shoulder and turning him away from Sterling.

"That's enough for everybody," said Moosejaw, joining in also to try and calm things down. "All of you clear out now. Get home to supper, go on about your business . . . If you want to do something useful, somebody send for the undertaker."

CHAPTER 18

Saturday morning dawned bright and clear and in no time at all Buffalo Peak was bustling with activity in preparation for the upcoming big event. Outlying families were already arriving in wagons or on horseback, prepared to sleep over with friends in town or, in some cases, to camp on the outskirts — whatever it took to be certain not to miss a minute of the festival.

Through this busy throng, Charlie Gannon and Josh Stallworth strolled slowly along, taking in the sights and making plans for what they'd come here to do. The previous evening, when the trouble broke out, they'd been up in the loft over the general store playing red dog with a couple other drifters who were spreading their bedrolls up there. By the time they got down to the street, everything was over and the deputies were shooing everybody back to their own businesses. Not wanting to draw attention to themselves and not having a particularly strong interest in somebody else's bad luck anyway, they'd retreated back to the loft.

This morning, they'd taken breakfast in a little café where the portions were generous and the prices reasonable. The talk around them had been a mix of embellishments about the shoot-out and equally excited chatter about the festival. Again aiming not to draw attention to themselves, Charlie and Josh merely listened and took their time over their meals.

Now, all but invisible in the scurry of people coming and going up and down the length of Trail Street, they were just killing time and refining their plans.

"Seems to me," Charlie was saying, "if we're gonna go ahead and do this thing, then makin' our move right in the middle of these big doin's that have got everybody so excited might work in our favor."

"How so?" Josh wanted to know.

"Well, reason it out. There's gonna be gobs of people around, all payin' attention to what their own little groups are doin' and at the same time folks switchin' back and forth between groups and different activities. So, once we've picked out the gals we want to take for wives, we just wait for the right time when they're on the move —

separated from whatever group they've been with, on their way to somewhere else, see — and then *snap!* we close in. We take 'em to where we'll have our horses and everything waitin', and we can be miles out of town before anybody even figures out they're missin'."

Josh looked puzzled. "But why won't they be missed right away?"

"Because of the crowd size and everybody driftin' back and forth and movin' around. Don't you see?" Charlie spread his hands for emphasis. "If a gal ain't in one place, everybody there will think she's off visitin' with some other friends or whatever. If she ain't with the other friends, they'll think she's with the first bunch. It could be a couple hours before they figure out she ain't with nobody. Nobody but us, that is. You startin' to get the picture?"

Josh nodded. "Yeah. Yeah, I am now. It ain't like we'd be snatchin' a gal who went out in the backyard to hang up clothes and then in a few minutes somebody in the house would be wonderin' what's takin' her so long."

"There you go. Now you got it."

They'd reached the east end of town where a corral and holding pens had been set up for the rodeo. Cowboys and animals

175

from several of the surrounding ranches in the valley had already begun showing up. The air was filled with the yips and whistles of the wranglers, combined with the tattoo of horses' hooves and the bawling of some of the bulls brought in for riding competition.

"Maybe we oughta enter some of these rodeo events and see if we could make some extra money," mused Josh. "Bet we could show these Texas punchers a thing or two."

"I expect we could," Charlie allowed. "But we ain't got time. If things go right, I hope we'll be ridin' hard *away* from here tomorrow while some of these boys are gettin' their guts jarred loose tryin' to stay on the back of an ornery critter only too happy to do exactly that. Besides, we're okay on money as long as we dole it out careful-like. The cash we got from that Oklahoma rancher gave us more money than we ever had at one time, didn't it? We need to use it to get square with our new wives, then we can start figurin' what we'll do to get by in the future."

They turned away from the rodeo pens and headed back toward town.

Josh grinned. "Boy, don't that sound good? Money in our pockets . . . Wives soon to be had . . . Plannin' for the future . . . I gotta say, Charlie, it wasn't that long ago those kind of things seemed a million miles away to me. Hell, I figured I'd be pushin' around cattle until I was too old and creaky to climb up in the saddle. And then, after that . . . well, I don't know."

"Well, now you *do* know, Josh," Charlie told him. "We got us a plan. We're gonna by-God stick to it and I got me a feelin' it's gonna work out just fine."

"I have to admit, Oberon," Rupert Shaw was saying, "that I am utterly and increasingly baffled."

"By what, Captain?" Hadley asked around a bite of thick bacon.

"By everything currently surrounding us." To emphasize, Shaw made a broad circular motion with one hand. "By this . . . this *American West* that everyone seems to find so fascinating. Ever since William Cody — or so-called Buffalo Bill — toured the continent with his boisterous crowd and their equally boisterous presentation of alleged showmanship, it's as if practically the whole world has become enthralled with the 'Wild West.' Everything past the Mississippi River is held up as some sort of Promised Land where adventure and romance and great hopes for the future wait around every corner to any daring to seek it.

"Rubbish, says I. More like behind every rock or cactus or impassible mountain range lurks yet another expanse of hardship and primitive conditions. Not to mention danger in the form of everything from that which slithers across the ground to beasts that howl in the night to hostile natives plotting revenge against everyone with pale skin."

The two men were having a late breakfast in the dining room of the Mallory House Hotel. Most other guests had eaten and departed by now and so, in this interval before the lunch crowd started to gather, they had complete privacy. They were seated before the wide front window with a bustling Trail Street in evidence on the other side of the glass.

With a forkful of scrambled eggs and more bacon raised partway to his mouth, Hadley paused and said, "Ye have to admit, sar, that we witnessed some splendid scenery from the train."

"If I want scenery," replied Shaw, "I can go to an art gallery or take a ride through the English countryside. A ride, I might add, that would be supremely more comfortable than any of those lurching, soot-spewing trains we traveled on. Not to mention the abysmal, bone-jarring stagecoaches!"

Hadley scrunched his face a bit at the mention of the latter. "True enough on that, Captain," he agreed before going ahead and pushing his fork into his mouth. As he chewed, he added, "But maybe it's good for body and soul to once in a while take a break from too much comfort. After all, sar, we endured far worse conditions when we was servin' the Queen in hell-hot Afghanistan where we drove Ayub Khan and his bloody heathens back through Baba Wali Pass."

"I'm afraid that's a more thoughtful outlook than mine, old friend," Shaw said with a wry smile. "Having fulfilled my obligation to the Queen and her military, I'm more than happy to be done with rugged conditions and mean to enjoy a life of comfort and wealth to the fullest — apart from this current undertaking, which I question my pursuit of more each day."

Marilu, the cook and hostess for the dining room, appeared at that point. With a big smile on her face, she said, "Are you gentlemen findin' everything satisfactory?"

"Indeed, my dear lady," Shaw assured her. "Everything was most delicious."

"Very much so," agreed Hadley as he scraped his plate clean.

"Can I get you anything else? More tea

maybe? A roll with some fresh-made apple butter to go with it?"

"Not me. I'm too full already," said Shaw. Then, casting a sidelong glance over to Hadley, he added, "My large friend here, however, seldom reaches that condition. Something more for you, Oberon?"

Hadley cocked a bushy eyebrow. "Too tempting ye are, lass. That apple butter sounds too good to pass up. I'll have some, with a splash more of tea if ye please."

Marilu beamed. "Always pleased to see a man with a big appetite. Be right back with more."

"I'll make one concession," Shaw said after she'd departed, "by admitting that most of the food we've been served has been decent. And, Lord knows, plentiful."

Hadley grinned. "See, Captain. Not everything about this trip has been bleak."

"But let's not get carried away." Shaw scowled. "I said the food was decent — but not *better* than the fare back home. And apple butter is hardly enough of an exotic rarity to have traveled all this way for."

Hadley's forehead puckered. He looked like he wanted to say something to lighten his companion's mood but couldn't come up with anything.

Seeming to sense this, Shaw heaved a sigh

and said, "I'm sorry, Oberon, for being in such poor humor. Let's face it, the thing that has me baffled and bothered beyond all else is Victoria. Finding her living in these conditions and showing not the slightest interest — certainly no eagerness — to return to England is nothing like what I expected. Naturally I'd hoped that my arrival here might rekindle some spark of the feelings she once had for me. At the very least, even if she continued to profess no love for me, I believed that, having had her adventure in this new world and especially with Estelle no longer present to egg her on, she would be ready to come back home.

"Once there, admittedly, I planned on doing everything I could to get her back on a path to the altar. Maybe it's wounded pride due to the way she broke both our engagement and my heart, but I've never really gotten over her. I've always felt that if I could see her again, spend some time with her, I'd have a chance at winning her back."

"And ye still do, Captain," insisted Hadley. "It's not your way to give up so easy."

Shaw gave a halfhearted shake of his head. "No, I'm not giving up. Not yet. But I have to confess I'm feeling rather discouraged. You saw her out there yesterday. How she acted, how she looked."

"Aye. She's lost none of her beauty, that's for sure."

"It was more than that. Yes, she's lovely as ever. But beyond that she looked happy, content . . . Damn it, she looked *at home* in that rustic setting."

Marilu returned bearing a tray set with a small pot of fresh tea, two rolls, and a small cup of apple butter. Sensing the men were in deep conversation, she placed the tray on the table and promptly retreated, saying only, "Just holler if you need anything more."

Once their hostess was gone, Shaw said, "That's what bewilders me so. Back in England, either as my wife or simply under the circumstances under which she grew up, Victoria could be living a life of leisure and comparative luxury. She could have servants waiting on her instead of functioning as little more than a scullery maid for those three ruffians out at that ranch."

Shaw paused, frowning, then quickly amended his statement. "My apologies if that sounded disrespectful. I know you come from a working-class background, Oberon, and your mother was a maid. I have full regard for people who do honest work at all levels of society. My point was merely meant to express my confusion as to why anyone — namely Victoria — would willingly regress *down* to a lower, harder station."

"Understood, sar," Hadley said, though somewhat tightly.

"And those men she works for," Shaw went on, lifting his eyebrows. "Three former mountain men — a more primitive lot you could scarcely find anywhere short of the Indian tribes who used to roam these prairies or perhaps aborigines on some remote island. Their names alone — Firestick, Beartooth, Moosejaw — sound like characters used to frighten children in some crude fairy tale."

Generously applying a spoonful of apple butter to one of the rolls Marilu had brought him, Hadley said, "Judging from the talk this morning about how those three faced down a pack of toughs out in the street last night, I think they're a wee bit more real than anything out of a fairy tale."

"That's another thing — gunfights in the middle of the street! Participated in by the very men Victoria has surrounded herself with!" Shaw rolled his eyes in exasperation. "What kind of environment is that to want to be part of, I ask you? Does that sound like the behavior of civilized human beings?"

"I hardly think it's an everyday occurrence," Hadley suggested. "And from all reports, the four scoundrels who got shot down were a hard lot who were bent on making trouble even after they were given every chance to walk away."

"It's still a highly undesirable state of affairs," Shaw insisted. "It only strengthens my resolve to do everything in my power to encourage Victoria away from here."

"Are ye not meeting with her again today?"

"Yes. She's coming into town for some duties associated to this festival thing they're having tomorrow. She's agreed to make time to join me for tea and a further chat."

Hadley grinned. "Polish up that golden tongue I've heard ye use a time or three in the past, Captain. If ye don't mind me saying, that is. As long as she's willing to talk, ye still have a chance to sway her to your way of thinking."

Shaw smiled, too, albeit a bit wistfully. "That's certainly my intent, Oberon. Like I said, I'm not ready to give up . . . not yet."

CHAPTER 19

Over breakfast at the Double M Ranch that Saturday morning, moods had been mixed.

Firestick was still brooding about the previous evening's events, particularly how the troublesome dove Cleo had once again figured into them. He'd never been moved to run anyone out of town before, and despite what he'd told Sterling, he wasn't anxious to start now. He didn't even know if he had the legal authority to carry out the threat.

Moosejaw seemed fairly relaxed and comfortable as far as how things had turned out with the hardcases. He saw it simply as something that had to be done. He was more troubled by Firestick's gloominess and the anguish he knew Beartooth was going through due to Victoria's former fiancé showing up.

As for Beartooth, he was doing his best to hide that anguish, but to his old comrades who'd spent too much time with him not to see the signs, it was clear the matter was grinding on him.

Victoria had been waiting up when the three got back from town last night, and her attention had turned immediately to Beartooth's wounded shoulder. Even though Frank Moorehouse, the town barber who doubled as the closest thing Buffalo Peak had to a doctor based on his war experience as a medical aide, had already treated the shoulder and declared it nothing serious, Victoria insisted on re-examining and re-bandaging it. Her focus on the wound and the time she took tending to it served to distract from any detailed discussion of either the shooting or how things had gone with her and Rupert Shaw. As far as the latter, she said only that nothing had been resolved and that she would be seeing and talking with him again, this time in town.

So this morning, that unresolved issue was the thing that still hung in the air heavier than anything else. Both Firestick and Moosejaw recognized the need for Beartooth and Victoria to have some time alone. For that reason, both of them ate their breakfast rather hurriedly and then professed the need to get into town right away to tend to matters of vague urgency and importance.

As soon as they were out of the house and on their way to the barn to get saddled up, Victoria once again turned her attention to Beartooth's shoulder.

"I noticed you were moving that arm rather stiffly all through breakfast," she said.

"Yeah, reckon I was," Beartooth allowed. "But that's kinda to be expected, don't you think? Bound to loosen up, though, after I use it durin' the course of the day."

"Probably. But it still bears having another look at. Did the bandage bleed through during the night?"

"Not that I could see."

"Well, unbutton your shirt so I can check it out."

As Beartooth began undoing his shirt, Victoria rose up from her place at the table and walked around to stand behind him. More than ever before, Beartooth became instantly and keenly aware of the closeness of her. Of the scent and the woman heat that emanated from her. Of the soft pressure of her breast touching his bared shoulder as she leaned closer to examine the wound. He swallowed, the lump in his throat feeling as big as the plate on the table before him.

"No, it hasn't bled through. That's a good

sign," Victoria murmured. "And there's no redness around the area that might indicate infection. That's also good."

"So you might as well just leave the bandage in place, eh?"

"Perhaps. But, since I'm going into town later anyway, I can always pick up some more inexpensive sheeting for fresh bandages. I think it's safest to go ahead and change this one and take the opportunity to add some more of that ointment Mr. Moorehouse gave you."

Beartooth made a face. "That stuff stings worse than the doggone bullet did when it split my skin in the first place."

"Oh, don't be such a baby," Victoria said, smiling faintly. "I'm going to take this off and then let the wound air out for a bit while I go get the ointment and scissors and some clean material for a new bandage."

She began carefully untying the knot that held the bandage in place. As she worked at this, Beartooth slowly turned his head and regarded her beautifully concentrating face from only inches away. Once she had the knot undone, sensing his close scrutiny, her own eyes lifted and met his.

"Victoria . . ." Beartooth said in a low, husky voice.

"What is it? Why are you looking at me

like that?"

Maybe he was imagining it, but Beartooth thought he heard a trace of huskiness in her voice, as well. He swallowed again. "Don't you know? Don't you have any idea what's goin' on inside my head right now? God, this would be a whole lot easier if you did."

"What would be easier? Me re-doing your bandage?"

"No. That's not what I'm talking about at all."

"I . . . I'm sorry. But you're not making a great deal of sense."

Beartooth's mouth pulled tight with frustration as he fought to find the words. "I know I'm not. It's just that . . . there's so much I've been holdin' back from sayin' for so long . . ."

Reaching up, he wrapped each of her wrists in his hands and gently tugged her around in front of him. Then he stood up, still holding her wrists, and pressed her trembling hands tight to his chest. "You know me well enough to know I ain't much of one for speeches. And I got no way with flowery words like probably roll off the silver tongue of that Rupert character. But havin' him show up here and bringin' with him the possibility you might be goin' away . . . Well, that made me realize something.

Something that's been buildin' stronger and stronger inside me for a long time now but I've been too much of a lunkhead to say or do anything about it." Beartooth paused, his expression twisting anxiously as he continued to gaze down at Victoria. "Lord-amighty, gal, do you *still* have no idea what I'm tryin' to say?"

Victoria had her head tipped back, looking up to meet his gaze. The hint of a smile touched her lips. "Are you telling me you don't want me to go away with Rupert?"

"That's exactly what I'm tellin' you! I don't want you to go away with anybody."

"Why?"

"Why?" Beartooth echoed. "Well, ain't it plain? I . . . I want you here. You belong here. You need to stay."

"I *need* to stay? That's your only reason for not wanting me to go?"

"No! There's lots of reasons. I want you to stay because . . . well, because . . . Aw, can't you tell? Ain't it written all over my face . . . ? I want you to stay because I'm in love with you, doggone it!"

Slowly, still gazing up at him but now wearing a dazzling smile, Victoria withdrew her hands from his grip. Then, equally slowly, her palms glided up over his chest and cupped around the back of his neck.

Just before she tugged his head down so that their lips could meet, she murmured, "It's about bloody time you got around to letting a girl know how you feel!"

CHAPTER 20

In town, Firestick and Moosejaw split up. Firestick got off at the jail, turning his horse over to Moosejaw for stabling, along with the big deputy's own animal, at Roeback's livery until they were needed again at some later point in the day. Moosejaw stated his intention to take a turn around town to see how things were shaping up for tomorrow's big festival day before re-joining Firestick at the jail.

In the meantime, the marshal had to write up a report of last night's shoot-out to present to the town council this morning. Immediately following the incident, a couple of the members had cornered him on the street and requested that he do so. They'd scheduled a nine-o'clock meeting in a conference room at the bank to review the matter with him and the rest of the council.

Not surprisingly, given his background, the paperwork aspect of marshaling was

Firestick's least favorite part of the job. But it came with wearing the badge, so he'd not only learned to accept it but had actually gotten pretty good at documenting things to the satisfaction of the council. Since they gave him plenty of leeway and stayed out of his hair for the most part, he reckoned the least he could do was shove some paperwork in front of them from time to time if it helped keep things that way.

The other thing Firestick meant to take care of this morning was get a telegram off to the sheriff in El Paso. Firestick had never met the man personally, but they'd exchanged wires a time or two in the past and the sheriff — his name was Broward — had always seemed competent and accommodating.

On this occasion, Firestick wanted to advise Broward about the four hardcases sent by a man called Kilbourn — all allegedly from his town. Only a limited amount of identification had been found on the four victims, yielding merely the names Jepson and Grover for two of them. Firestick hoped this would mean something to the sheriff — enough that he could see to it a message was delivered and made clear: Don't send any more men or they'll meet the same fate.

At the moment, these thoughts were

relegated to the back of Firestick's mind as he worked on his report for the council. Having started a small fire in the office stove to heat up the pot of leftover coffee sitting on top of it, the marshal took a break from his scribbling and got up to go over and see if the coffee was hot yet. Finding that it was, he had just snared a cup and poured himself some when the front door opened and someone came in.

The identity of his visitor was enough of a surprise to nearly make him spill some of the coffee he'd just poured.

Cleo, the soiled dove from the Lone Star Palace Saloon, pressed the door closed behind her and stood there with alternating traces of determination and uncertainty playing across her pretty face.

After a moment of somewhat awkward silence, she said, "You know who I am, don't you?"

"I do," said Firestick.

The girl's mouth tightened. "And I know that you don't like me."

Firestick considered this statement a moment before answering. "Not necessarily accurate to say I don't like *you,* miss. What I don't like is the trouble that flares up around you."

"And that's all my fault? I've never been

the one to club somebody or start waving a gun around and acting like a jackass."

"No. You've never been a clubber or a gun waver," the marshal admitted. "Nor have you ever had your skull split open or taken a bullet. But others have, and you tend to be in the middle whenever that happens."

"And because of that you're going to run me out of town. What about the men who've been *directly* involved in those outbreaks of trouble?"

"Some of them are dead," Firestick pointed out. "You might say they've left town permanent-like."

Cleo's shoulders slumped and a new emotion played across her face, a touch of sadness. "And you think I've ever *wanted* that — that I get some kind of thrill from having men fight over me and end up beating and sometimes killing each other?"

Either she was a hell of a good actress — which, of course, gals in her line of work were expected to be, at least to some extent — or she was genuinely bothered by the kinds of incidents under discussion. In any event, Firestick suddenly felt a lessening of the hostile feelings he'd built up toward her. It struck him that he'd never given her the slightest benefit of a doubt or even bothered to get her side of any of the disturbances. In that way, he realized, he was guilty of treating her as contemptuously as the men who regularly passed her around and used her with little or no feelings toward her humanity.

Plus, he had to admit to being impressed by the guts it took for her to show up here this morning and air her side of things. Maybe he was getting gullible in his old age, but damned if he didn't feel inclined toward giving her a fair hearing.

"Reckon your side of it ain't exactly been no picnic, either," he said, taking the hard edge off the tone he'd been using up to now. "Why don't you take a seat and maybe we can come up with a better plan than me havin' to run you out of town. There's enough coffee in the pot for another cup if you'd like some — though it's heated over from yesterday so I've got to warn you it's mighty stout."

Cleo shook her head. "No thanks."

She moved forward and sat down in the chair hitched up in front of the marshal's desk. Firestick settled into his chair on the other side.

"Those men who got shot last night," Cleo said, "do you know their names?"

"Only two of 'em. Jepson and Grover."

Cleo's mouth tightened. "I figured they'd

be part of it."

"The other two had no identification on them. One wore a derby hat, the other was a feisty, potbellied little Mexican packin' twin Colts in cross-draw holsters."

"Bob Miller and Diego Olmos," Cleo said glumly. "They all work . . . or worked, I guess I should say . . . for Josiah Kilbourn."

"Kilbourn. That's the name they used. Said he hired 'em to bring you back on account of you broke a contract with him and took off owin' him money."

"That's a lie!" Cleo's eyes blazed. "I only took what was owed me, and I never had no kind of contract with Kilbourn. One person can't lay claim to another. In case everybody forgot, we fought a war not too long ago that freed slaves."

"Whatever his reasons, Kilbourn seems to want you back awful bad. Bad enough to pay four men to come after you."

"They're on his payroll. It wouldn't have cost him any extra to send them to try and fetch me back. The only reason he wants me is because I made him a lot of money. Trouble was, the things he wanted me to start doing in order to earn it . . . well, I refused. When he threatened me, you're damn right I took off."

Once again Cleo's eyes blazed angrily.

Then, abruptly, they shifted, took on a vaguely sad, faraway look that she aimed down at the floor. "Look, Marshal, I know what I am. I make no bones about it. I'm a whore. I could make excuses, tell you a sad story about my bad breaks. But what would be the point? I'm what I am and where I'm at because I'm a girl who does what she has to in order to get by." She lifted her gaze and fixed it on him flat and steady. "But there's a limit, even for whores. At least there is for this one. And I won't go beyond that for Kilbourn or anybody else."

Without knowing what Kilbourn had demanded of this girl — without *wanting* to know, beyond what he couldn't keep from imagining — Firestick felt a strong surge of loathing for the so-called man. "What's the lowdown on this Kilbourn varmint?" he said. "How much power does he have in and around El Paso?"

"A pretty fair amount among the lowlifes and criminals."

"What about Broward, the sheriff there-abouts? He do anything to try and stand in Kilbourn's way, or is he paid to step aside?"

"Far as I know, Broward's on the up and up. But he can only do so much. Kilbourn is a slippery snake who knows how to slither in and out of the swamp he operates in without sticking his neck out too far."

Firestick nodded. "That's good to hear. About Broward, I mean. I've had a few long-distance dealin's with him in the past and that was my take on him — that he was honest. I'm fixin' to get a wire off to him this mornin' and fill him in on what happened to Kilbourn's boys when they came around here. I expect him to bend Kilbourn's ear with the news. Any luck, that should be enough to make Kilbourn back off from tryin' anything more where you're concerned."

Cleo's eyes brightened. "That would be a relief. And I guess I owe you an overdue thanks for last night, too. I'm sorry one of your deputies got hurt and four men had to die, but I'm certainly grateful you stopped them from getting to me. Lord knows, Earl wouldn't have put up much resistance and Arthur couldn't have stopped them alone."

Firestick shrugged. "It's what me and my deputies get paid for, miss. We wouldn't be worth much if we let a pack of scruffy jackals swagger in here and ride off with one of our citizens."

"Not even a whore?" Cleo said.

"That's your word, not mine," Firestick told her. "It's not for me to judge you or look down on what you do. My only problem is with the trouble that's cropped up around you practically since you hit town."

"So that still stands then, doesn't it? The Kilbourn problem may be solved but there's still the rest of it."

"There is if it keeps up."

Cleo looked dismayed. "But what am I supposed to do? How do I control the actions of customers who show up and decide to act wild and foolish? It's my job to be appealing to men. Not to sound vain, but I happen to be a little younger and maybe a little prettier than some of the other girls. No matter how nice I try to be to them, they hate me out of plain jealousy. Earl Sterling's girlfriend, Frenchy, is a classic example."

"Stealin' another woman's man ain't exactly a way to get in good graces with other gals," Firestick pointed out.

"No woman can steal another woman's man if he's truly satisfied with what he's got in the first place," Cleo insisted. "And it's not like I went out of my way to lure Earl — he came to me all on his own. He's my boss and, especially considering the way I make my living, how could I turn him down? That makes just another example of what I'm trying to say. Men want to be with me and they get impatient, make trouble.

Short of getting out of the business — which I see no opportunity to do — I don't know a way to control the feelings and actions of others."

Firestick wagged his head. "I'm afraid I can't help you there. I don't usually get called in until the trouble's already busted loose. But you're right, controllin' it shouldn't fall strictly to you, either. I'll talk to Sterling about keepin' a tighter lid on the customers who come around. As for his own actions, it's up to him to sort them out. He was with Frenchy for a long time. In fairness to you and her both, I'd say he better make up his mind how he really feels."

"So how does that leave things between you and me?" Cleo sighed. "Are you running me out of town or not?"

"I never said that was a certainty," Firestick told her. "What I said was that it might have to come to that if things didn't straighten out."

Cleo eyed him warily.

"Look," he added. "It took guts for you to come here this morning and lay things on the line like you've done. I give you credit for that. How about we leave it that I won't go out of my way to crowd you as long as Sterling starts doin' a better job of gettin' things tamed down at the Palace? See where that takes us."

Cleo stood up. "I can live with that. It's better than packing my bag and moving on yet again. Thanks for your time."

CHAPTER 21

The front door had scarcely closed behind Cleo before it clicked open again. So fast, in fact, that Firestick looked up from the report he'd returned his attention to expecting it would be the dove coming back in about something she'd forgotten.

He was correct in that it was an attractive female coming through the doorway. But that was as far as it went. It wasn't Cleo. It was Kate Mallory.

Pressing the door closed behind her, she leaned back against it and then just stood there regarding him with one eyebrow prettily arched.

Firestick stood up behind his desk. "Kate. This is a surprise."

"Yes. I can see where it would be." Her tone dripped with sarcasm.

Obviously she must have seen Cleo exiting. Must have practically bumped into her. And now she was in a mood to tease Firestick about it . . . at least he was pretty sure she was teasing. She couldn't *seriously* think Cleo's presence here indicated anything improper. Could she?

"Come on in, have a seat," the marshal urged her. "I haven't had time to make a pot of fresh coffee yet. But I can get one goin' if you'd like some."

"No, that's alright," Kate answered coolly. "I wouldn't want you to overdo it, having already been so busy this early in the day."

Firestick folded his arms across his chest and cocked an eyebrow of his own. "Alright, go ahead and have your fun. But you know it wasn't what you're pretendin' to think it was."

"All I know is what I saw with my own two eyes," Kate said. "There are only so many conclusions one can draw from that."

"Yeah. Well, the only *right* conclusion is that she was here strictly on business."

"Oh, I don't doubt that. Then the question becomes . . . her kind of business, or yours?"

"Okay. That's about enough." Firestick scowled. "As you likely know by now, I've got a report to write for the council meeting at nine. So I don't have time to fool around."

Kate being a member of the town council,

Firestick figured she'd gotten notice of the meeting.

"Does that mean the 'no fooling around' rule also applied while Little Miss Cleo was here?" she prodded.

Firestick scowled some more, said nothing.

At last Kate put away the act and came forward, smiling. "Lucky for you, I'm not the jealous type. I must admit, though, I was a little surprised by the sight of your visitor who just left."

"So was I," Firestick admitted, relieved to see her smile. "I was even more surprised to find out she ain't quite the schemin', troublemakin' little hussy I had her pegged to be."

"Oh? Does that mean you won't be in such a big hurry when it comes to, and I quote, 'runnin' her pretty little ass out of town'?" Kate had been in the street last night and had obviously overheard the marshal's words to Earl Sterling.

Firestick twisted his mouth ruefully. "Ain't necessarily out of the question, not altogether. But, for the time bein', let's say it don't seem quite as urgent as it did when I said those things."

Kate came around the end of the desk and placed her hands on his chest. "I'm glad to see you've cooled down some. You were coiled awfully tight last night. That's why, when I saw Moosejaw up the street and he told me you were in town, I wanted to come and find out how you were."

Firestick put his arms around her and laced his fingers behind the small of her back. "Like you said, I've cooled down some. I'm okay now — better still, with you around."

"After our talk the other day, following the shooting of Orval Retlock and the way it troubled you . . . well, with the shooting of those four men last night and especially knowing I was the one who encouraged you to go confront them, I wasn't sure . . ."

Firestick spread his mouth in a reassuring smile. "You worry too much. Those skunks from last night ain't worth it. They got what they deserved. Hell, they were the type practically born for it. In their case, it was just a matter of time. With Orval, it was different. If things hadn't taken the bad turn like they did, he could've got his bullyin' ways straightened out and had a future, maybe made something of himself. That's the shame of it, what made it different with him. But it's past now. I guess it went the way it was written. I got it squared in my head . . . I'm okay. You don't have to worry."

Kate pressed hard against him for a long moment, feeling good in his arms. "That's good to hear," she said. Then she leaned back a bit and looked up at him. "So now allow me to move on to another worry. How do things stand with Beartooth and Victoria? How did her talk with the Englishman go?"

"Far as I know, nothing's settled," Firestick replied. "When we got back to the ranch last night and she saw Beartooth had been wounded, that was what got all of her attention."

"At least she didn't give any indication that Shaw had swept her off her feet and she was ready to go back with him. That's a good sign, wouldn't you say?"

"Reckon you could take it that way. She'll be talkin' with Shaw again today, when she comes into town later. In the meantime, me and Moosejaw left Beartooth behind at the ranch this morning so he could have his chance to talk with her."

"Do you think he's ready to actually let her know how he feels about her?"

"I believe so. It's built up in him something fierce now that the thought of maybe losin' her to this Englishman has hit him." Firestick made a face. "If he *don't* get around to levelin' with Victoria about his feelin's now, then he deserves to have her stole away."

Kate pulled gently out of his embrace. "All we can do is hope it works out for both of them. Now you'd better get back to your report and I've got plenty else to tend to myself. But before I go, I'll get a fresh pot of coffee cooking for you."

"Oh . . . my . . . lord."

Josh Stallworth stopped short in his ascent up the stairs leading to the sleeping loft over Greeble's General Store. He halted so abruptly that Charlie Gannon, coming up behind him, bumped his shoulder against Josh's rump.

"What the hell you doin', stoppin' like that?" Charlie demanded.

"I'm pausin' to drink in the vision of an angel," Josh replied in an odd, almost dreamy tone.

The two men were three-quarters of the way toward the top of an outside stairway that extended up the back side of the building. The area behind the store included a sort of meandering lane, not really an alley, that wound behind several of the businesses on this side of Trail Street. What Josh was referring to — and where his gaze was locked — was the sight of Cleo walking along this lane on her way from the jail to the Lone Star Palace Saloon.

Charlie obviously saw her, too. "Okay, I'll give you that she's a vision. Mighty pretty gal," he allowed. "But I ain't sure about the angel part and I don't see how you can be, either."

"I don't need to know nothing more than what I can see. To me, she's an angel and that's all there is to it," Josh said firmly. "What's more — she's gonna be the one, Charlie."

"The one what?"

"The one I'm gonna take for my bride. Ever since we got here — just like you been doin' — I been walkin' around studyin' the different gals we see. There's been a lot of pretty ones and some of 'em I sorta thought in my head would probably be okay for me. But one glance just now and all that went out the window." Josh heaved a big sigh. "Ain't no sense lookin' no more. Not for me."

"Then good for you," said Charlie. "Now all you got to do is figure out how you're gonna know where she'll be tomorrow in the middle of all the hoopla so's you can grab her when we're ready to light out."

"Don't worry. Now that I got her picked out, I ain't about to fail at bein' able to find her again when it counts." Josh's eyes had never left Cleo as she moved farther away down the lane. Now, briefly, he cut a glance down at Charlie a couple steps below him. His expression turning somewhat concerned, he said, "But what about you, Charlie? You're gonna want to be gettin' a gal picked out for yourself pretty quick, too, ain't you?"

"Don't worry. I got plenty of time," Charlie said. "I ain't necessarily lookin' to pick one out in advance. I figure with the picnic and all the other activities goin' on, there'll be plenty to choose from and I won't have no trouble spottin' a good one when the time is at hand."

"Well, if that's the way you want to do it, then I guess that'll work out okay." Josh's gaze had returned to Cleo, who by now had proceeded several buildings down the lane, all the while oblivious to the men watching and discussing her. As Josh continued to watch, she turned and went in the back entrance of the Lone Star Palace Saloon.

"Whoa now," said Charlie, who was also watching. "Did you see that?"

Josh answered, "Yeah, she went in that building down the way. She was bound to be headed somewhere."

"You know what that building is, don't

you? That's the saloon that's been pointed out to us as havin' workin' gals available."

"Yeah. So?"

Charlie gave him a look. "Your 'angel' is goin' in there, Josh. Ain't you worried she might be . . . well, one of the doves?"

"Those kind of gals ain't hardly ever out and about this early in the day, Charlie. More likely she's a cleanin' lady or maybe a barmaid showin' up for work."

"Yeah, I don't dispute she must be showin' up for work. But she didn't look much like no cleanin' lady I ever saw. Don't it bother you there's at least the chance she might, you know, be there for that other kind of work?"

Josh continued to stare at the back door of the building his angel had disappeared through. He looked thoughtful, not responding right away. Then, abruptly, he said, "No. That don't matter to me. If that's the way it is, then it's something I'll be savin' her from. She's still my angel, and I still aim to make her my wife."

On the crest of a low hill off to the northwest, four riders sat their horses and gazed in the direction of Buffalo Peak less than a mile in the distance.

When Pierce Torrence finally lowered the

binoculars he'd been holding to his eyes for the past minute, Leticia Beauregard, mounted to his left, said, "Something sure kept you looking. What did you see that was so interesting?"

"Lots of activity going on down there," Torrence replied.

Leticia frowned. "Hell, I can tell that much even without the glasses. A town of any size on a Saturday morning — you'd expect there to be a lot of activity."

"Of course. But I mean a level of activity that's unusually high, even for a Saturday morning."

"Enough of it, looks to me," said Black Hills Buckner, on the other side of Torrence, "that it's even spillin' *out* of the town. Ain't that some tents and campsites I see scattered around the edges?"

"Yes, it is," Torrence confirmed.

"And there's more pourin' in," added Romo Perlison from where he was reined up next to Black Hills. He pointed. "There's a wagon loaded with what looks like a whole family rollin' up over yonder. And a ways to the west of them there's some riders comin'."

"Only thing I can think of that brings folks flocking from all around that way," said Leticia, "is a public hanging. Must be somebody pretty important."

"You're on the right track, my dear," Torrence told her. "But it's not a hanging."

"What is it then?"

"Just an old-fashioned community celebration. A festival of some kind. There's a banner stretched high across the middle of the street identifying what exactly it is they're celebrating, but the angle from here is wrong for me to be able to read all of it. I can only make out that it ends in 'Festival.' "

"Well, that don't make no never mind to me," said Romo. "One festival is as good as another. Let's spur these hayburners on down there and join in the fun."

"Not so fast," Torrence was quick to counter.

Romo's face stretched with a pained expression. "Aw, come on, Pierce. Not even for a little while? When the good Lord plops something like this down in front of you, it's like an omen. A *good* omen! It'd be a shame, almost a sin, not to take advantage of it."

"The only thing we're here to take advantage of is the money in the bank that's somewhere down there," Torrence reminded him.

"And all this activity and people in town means lots of business for the stores and saloons and that means lots of money that will end up in that bank," added Leticia. "There's the *real* good omen in this!"

"So where's the harm in havin' a little fun first — eatin' some spicy food, maybe swingin' our hips to a dance or two if they got a band playin' — and *then* hittin' the bank?" Romo pleaded. "Didn't you ever hear of sometimes combinin' business with a little bit of pleasure?"

"Shut up, Romo," growled Black Hills.

Romo glared at the big man. But he kept quiet while doing it.

"The thing we've got to remember," said Torrence, "is that we've managed to get our descriptions plastered on a fair number of wanted posters over the past year or so. The four of us, especially with Leticia being a woman and Black Hills being as sizable as he is, make a fairly distinct group. So even while we haven't pulled any jobs in this area before, that doesn't mean our descriptions haven't circulated this far. What it does mean is that the days of all of us riding into a town and giving the place a good looking over before we do what we came for are gone. We need to be smarter than that."

The gang leader paused to let his words sink in, his gaze raking the faces of all about him before he continued, "Arriving here to find this festival going on — whatever it's about — is what's known as a two-edged sword. The edge that works in our favor, as Leticia recognized, is that it means an extra influx of money into the town, into the bank we aim to hit. The edge that works against us is all the extra sets of eyes and guns that are on hand while the merriment is taking place. In other words, the much greater chance of being spotted and recognized, and that many more men available to give chase after we commit our robbery."

"So what's the answer?" Leticia said. "How do we take advantage of one, yet guard against the other?"

Torrence smiled tolerantly. "Patience. As is often the case, that's the short, simple, wisest answer. By my reckoning, today is Saturday. That means tomorrow is Sunday, when the bank will be closed. Since we didn't come equipped with dynamite to stage an after-hours robbery, that leaves the choice of either attempting to carry out some slapdash plan today or waiting until Monday when the bank re-opens — at which time it will be at its plumpest with deposits from festival business."

Romo made a face. "Jeez. You mean we rode hard all this way just to hold off another couple days before we do anything?"

"What we came all this way for was to rob a bank," Torrence bit off from between clenched teeth. "Circumstances now dictate the way to do that with the best chance for success, and the least risk, is to wait until Monday. Now, unless you think you've got a better idea for how to get it done and are ready to take over running this outfit — that's the way it is."

Romo quickly withered under the flinty gaze that accompanied Torrence's words. "Sure, Pierce. Whatever you say. I was just . . . I didn't mean . . ."

"Shut up, Romo," Black Hills growled.

CHAPTER 22

The meeting with the town council went well, although it dragged out quite a bit longer than anyone came prepared for. All five council members had busy schedules to keep, especially with the upcoming festival activities.

They passed around Firestick's report on last night's shoot-out and each scanned it dutifully, though they all seemed quite familiar with the details in advance. Kate's relationship with the marshal was no secret to anyone on the council, yet there was no questioning the merit of her complimentary words, and the rest of the council — to Firestick's discomfort and embarrassment — readily added to the praise.

Then they got into a general discussion about ongoing trouble related to the Lone Star Palace's soiled doves, as well as possible retaliation from cohorts of the four men who'd been cut down. Firestick managed to ease concerns about the latter by reporting on the telegram he'd sent to the El Paso sheriff and how he believed it would effectively stop any further trouble from that source.

As far as trouble stemming from the Lone Star Palace doves, he informed the council of his plans to impress on Earl Sterling the necessity for keeping tighter control over future outbreaks of trouble in his saloon.

Unless, he tossed out for consideration, they wanted to reconsider outlawing prostitution within the city limits. This turned into a hot potato that ended up taking considerable time. Much as some were uncomfortable with the whole moral issue, it came down to a practical consensus that — given the growth of surrounding cattle ranches and thereby the increasing number of restless young cowboys showing up in town to spend their money and "have a good time" — the availability of willing doves to help these roosters let off some steam was arguably better than what they might pursue as an alternative.

So, when all was said and done, Firestick was left to proceed with the steps he'd outlined and once again continue handling matters as best he saw fit.

Quitting the bank building where the meeting had been held, Firestick paused on the boardwalk out front to talk more with Kate. It was nearly noon now and the day was bright and warm under a cloudless sky, only a faint hint of breeze. With sunshine pouring over her and even with the bustle and dust of traffic moving up and down Trail Street in the background, Kate looked nothing short of stunning. Her pale skin took on a golden hue in the sunlight, and her glossy black hair shone in marked contrast.

"Didn't you ever hear it's not polite to stare?" she teased, tilting her head back to return Firestick's adoring gaze.

"Hang what's polite and what ain't," he replied gruffly. "Anybody looks as fine as you *deserves* to be stared at. It ought to be illegal not to. And, since I'm the law hereabouts . . ."

"So you want other men looking at me the way you are now?"

"I couldn't hardly blame 'em . . . long as I didn't catch 'em at it."

Kate gave a little laugh. "You lay down some rather peculiar laws, Mr. Marshal."

"Maybe so. I'm also mighty good at

enforcin' 'em. Reason I know is, that bunch of folks in there" — he jabbed a thumb over his shoulder, indicating the bank — "just got done tellin' me I was. Thanks to some promptin' from you, that is."

"They all know what a good job you do for our town. I just thought I'd take the chance to remind them."

Firestick frowned. "Well, I wish you wouldn't. It was kinda embarrassin'."

Kate placed a hand on his chest and smiled impishly. "Would you rather I tell them about other things you're particularly skillful at?"

"Probably best hold off on that, too. Leastways not in front of the whole council. Especially not Trugood, the bank president — I expect it might give him a heart attack. Just talkin' about those soiled doves a while ago got him so het up he broke out in a hard sweat and blushed red as a boiled tomato." Firestick arched a brow. "If I didn't know better, I might think he's got a particular weakness when it comes to those doves."

Kate's eyes widened. "Really?"

Firestick grinned slyly. "Let's just say he seems to know his way up and down the back stairs of the Lone Star Palace real good. Now, since the bank holds a note on the Palace, maybe he's just doing a thorough job of keepin' an eye on his business interests."

"That's scandalous," Kate said with mock severity. "It's almost as bad as a certain hotel proprietress I've heard tell of who carries on illicitly with a scalawag of a law officer."

"Tsk, tsk. What's the world comin' to?"

Kate glanced around as if suddenly aware of their surroundings. "I don't know, but us standing here in public talking about such things is probably worthy of a scandal all on its own. Will you be coming by the hotel for lunch in a little while?"

"Is that an invite?"

"I believe Marilu has roast pork on the menu."

"Now *that's* an invite if I ever heard one. I'll be there."

CHAPTER 23

Beartooth and Victoria rode into town together. In her time at the Double M, Victoria had become quite an accomplished horsewoman, finding free time to take long rides several afternoons a week. To facilitate this, she had fashioned a number of split-skirt riding outfits for herself. Additionally, the men of the ranch had presented her with a horse of her own, a steel-dust gelding who was spirited yet wholly responsive and devoted to Victoria. And on her last birthday, the men had arranged through Hans Greeble at his store in town to order her a pair of fine, tooled leather riding boots all the way from Dallas.

Today she was decked out in those boots, her finest riding outfit, and a cream-colored Stetson perched atop her thick mane of chestnut hair. Before they'd left the ranch, she had said to Beartooth, "When Rupert sees me riding up astride a horse dressed in this outfit, I may not have to break it to him that I definitely won't be returning to England with him. He may be so shocked by this display he no longer will want anything to do with me."

Beartooth frowned. "What's so shockin' about it? The way you're dressed looks mighty fine to me."

"That's just it. To you here in America or at least out here in the West, I may appear perfectly presentable. But in the society Rupert comes from, a woman in a split skirt and boots riding *astride* a horse would be unthinkable."

"How the heck *else* is there to ride a horse?"

"Why, side-saddle, of course, for a woman of proper breeding. Even Lady Godiva, when she took her notorious ride wearing nothing but her long tresses, had the decency to sit her horse side-saddle."

Beartooth's eyebrows lifted. "And *that* would be considered less shocking than a proper ridin' skirt?"

"Well, perhaps not *less* shocking." Victoria laughed. "Let's just call it shocking in a different way."

Beartooth grunted. "Wouldn't shock me to find out that fancy-pants Rupert does his ridin' sidesaddle."

When they reached the edge of town, Victoria reined up, saying, "You've probably got things you need to do, so we may as well separate here. I'll go ahead and meet with Rupert for tea and the further discussion I agreed to. Later, I'll be helping with festival preparations on the church lawn. Will you come around?"

"Try to keep me away."

"And then at some point we need to go down to where they'll be holding the rodeo. Jesus and Miguel will be there, and they'll be expecting us to stop by."

"We won't let 'em down," Beartooth said. Then, after a long pause during which he regarded Victoria closely, he added, "You sure you don't want me around when you talk to Rupert?"

Victoria shook her head. "It isn't necessary. Really. It's not like he's going to harm me or anything. We'll talk . . . everything will be fine."

"Will you tell him about us? I mean, as far as explainin' your reasons for choosin' to stay here?"

Victoria considered for a moment. "I may, I may not. I'll see how the conversation goes. If I don't mention us, please believe it would have nothing to do with any reluctance on my part to announce far and wide the feelings we've discovered for each other. But, at the same time, I expect I *will* have some reluctance for wounding Rupert any deeper than necessary. You understand, don't you?"

"Sure," said Beartooth. "It's your decision. You handle it however you think best."

When Beartooth got to the jail, he found Firestick and Moosejaw already present in the office. It was rare when all three were in town and at the jail at the same time. More often than not, one of them was back at the ranch or involved in something that kept them scattered except for the breakfast and supper get-togethers at the Double M.

As soon as Beartooth walked through the front door, his longtime pals pinned him with questioning looks. And before any words were spoken, the wide grin that spread across his face gave them their answer.

"It's all settled, fellas," he said, busting with the need to crow about it. "Victoria's gonna stay right here and not go back to England. What's more, me and her talked it over and . . . well, it turns out she's got the same feelin's for me as I do her!"

Grins almost as wide as Beartooth's spread across the faces of Firestick and

Moosejaw.

"I knew it. I knew it all the time," said Moosejaw.

"Didn't I tell you?" said Firestick. "The first step was gettin' around to lettin' her know how *you* felt."

Beartooth held up his hands, palms out. "Much as I hate to admit when you're right, you sure had it pegged. And I'm doggone happy I listened to you for once."

"Just don't go makin' a habit of it. I wouldn't know how to act."

"You might have to get used to it," Moosejaw said. "Now that he's got a steady gal in his life, his days of bein' stubborn and not listenin' to anybody are all but over anyway."

"We'll have to see about that," Beartooth countered. "But then, if anybody'd know about gettin' his marchin' orders from the gal in his life, I reckon it would be you."

They all had a good-natured laugh over that.

"Here now," Firestick said abruptly. "I think this is an occasion that calls for a little more than well wishes and friendly warnin's about bein' steered by the women we know damn well we're lucky to have latched on to." From a bottom drawer in the desk, he produced a long-necked bottle of red-eye. Holding it up, he announced, "I think a drink or three might be in order."

"Seein' how you're the marshal and we're just lowly deputies, I don't hardly see how we can argue the point," said Beartooth.

Moosejaw fetched three tin cups from behind the stove and Firestick splashed a generous amount into each. When the former mountain men all had a cup in hand, Firestick raised his in a toast. "All kiddin' aside, old friend," he said to Beartooth, "I hope you and Victoria make each other as happy as you deserve."

"I second that," added Moosejaw.

The three cups were tipped up and hearty gulps drained.

Hiking a leg and taking a seat on the end of his desk, Firestick said, "Kinda hard to believe, ain't it? Only a handful of years back, we drifted down out of the mountains, leavin' pretty much the only way of life we'd ever known, and came here lookin' for a place to settle, wonderin' if we'd ever really fit in anywhere. Now look at us. Our ranch is doin' decent, the town has not only accepted us but looks to us for its protection, and we've each found gals that it appears we're ready to settle down with. I'd say we fared pretty well, wouldn't you?"

"Hard to argue, considerin' how survivin' the winter and havin' some pelts to sell come spring was about the best we had to look forward to before," agreed Beartooth.

"That, and hangin' on to our scalps," said Moosejaw.

Firestick smiled ruefully. "Yeah. The owl-hoots we have to deal with from time to time since we pinned on these badges might be lookin' to kill us, but at least they ain't out to take our top knots."

They had another good laugh over that.

The echoes of that laughter were still hanging in the air when the front door suddenly flew open and Arthur, the bouncer/bartender from the Lone Star Palace Saloon, burst in. He was out of breath and sweating and his words came in rapid gasps. "Marshal . . . you gotta come quick . . . It's the boss . . . he's been drinking all night and all morning . . . He's gone wild drunk . . . I can't stop him . . . he's out to kill Irish Dan Coswick!"

Firestick sprang to his feet. Beartooth and Moosejaw quickly set aside their cups.

"Where is he?" Firestick wanted to know.

"He's out in the street in front of the Silver Spur. He's callin' Coswick out, threatening to shoot him on sight!"

"Shit!" Firestick spat. He motioned toward the gun rack on the back wall and said to Moosejaw, "Grab one of those street sweepers and bring it along — Arthur, you stay here out of the way!"

CHAPTER 24

The three lawmen boiled out of the jail building and headed down the street at a trot. Instinctively, they fanned out. Beartooth and Moosejaw went to either side, moving close along the front edge of the boardwalks. Firestick proceeded down the middle.

They hadn't gone far before a shot rang out from up ahead. Then another.

Unlike last night, the street wasn't empty. Far from it. Mid-day on a Saturday before the spring festival had people flocked in from far and wide. The boardwalks were crowded with shoppers going from business to business. The street itself was congested with wagons and horsemen on the move.

When the shots sounded, however, the scene changed quickly. At first there was a slight pause, as folks were confused by exactly what to think. Then somebody shouted "Gunfight!" and it was instantly repeated by a dozen lips. Men cussed, women gave frightened squeals and shooed their children ahead of them toward safety. Those on the boardwalks clamored frantically to get inside the various shops. The teamsters and riders out in the street scattered almost as frantically, either turning their rigs or horses around and putting distance between themselves and the gunfire or, in a couple cases, abandoning their wagons where they stood and also ducking into the closest doorway.

By the time Firestick and his deputies neared the Silver Spur, almost the exact same area out front where last night's shooting had taken place, the street and boardwalks had cleared. But windows and doorways were crowded with gawking faces.

Earl Sterling stood in the middle of the street, facing the already bullet-riddled Silver Spur with its front window still boarded over from last night's damage. He held a long-barreled pistol in each hand and was weaving unsteadily on his feet. The man known for his nearly impeccable grooming was nowhere to be seen. Sterling's hair was an unruly mess, he was unshaven . . . he was minus his ever-present tie and suit coat. His vest was only partially buttoned — crookedly at that — and part of his shirttail was hanging out.

As the lawmen got closer, they slowed their approach.

If Sterling noticed them, he paid no attention. Suddenly rearing back his head, and staggering a half step backward as a result, he shouted loudly, "Coswick, you backstabbing, woman-stealing, gutless yellow dog bastard! Step out here and face me like a man! Don't make me come in there and drag you out!"

As if to put an exclamation point on his challenge, Sterling raised the gun in his right hand and fired a round at the boarded-over window. The bullet slammed into the wood with a loud smack.

Firestick came to a halt about fifteen yards short of Sterling. He extended his arms to either side, signaling Moosejaw and Beartooth to also stop.

Sterling shouted again, "Damn you, Coswick! I know you can hear me in there!"

"Of course he can hear you," Firestick said in a voice strong enough to be heard but not so loud as to give Sterling too much of a start. He went on, adding, "The whole town can hear you, and you're makin' a jackass of yourself."

Sterling turned jerkily, unsteadily. He glared at Firestick through bleary eyes. "You don't need to concern yourself with this, McQueen. You only care about my whores not causing trouble, remember? This is going to be a fair fight between Coswick and me . . . *if* the yellow bastard has got the stones to step out and face me."

Firestick shook his head. "I can't let that stand, Sterling, and you know it. You're disruptin' the whole town on the busiest day of the year and endangerin' innocent folks all up and down the street. Now put those guns down and back away before somebody gets hurt."

"The only one who's going to get hurt is that gutless, woman-stealing Irishman!"

"He didn't steal your woman," Firestick grated. "You chased her away and all he did was give her some place to go."

"How the hell do you know what happened between Frenchy and me?"

"The whole town knows. Like I said, you just keep makin' a bigger jackass out of yourself. You got nobody to blame for your troubles but yourself."

"Shut up! You don't know what you're talking about!" Sterling hurled the words so violently that he lurched off balance and staggered, barely able to keep himself from falling.

"What I do know," said Firestick, bringing

233

his hand to rest on the grips of the Colt holstered on his hip, "is that if you keep wavin' those guns around and actin' wild, you'll force me to end your troubles permanent-like."

From where they stood off to either side and slightly back from Firestick, Beartooth and Moosejaw were poised and ready, too. Moosejaw held the shotgun at his waist, its barrel at a forty-five-degree angle, ready to snap level. Beartooth's fingertips danced lightly on the grips of his own holstered Colt.

"You know me, you know my meaning," Firestick said, his voice sandpapery. "Don't force it, Sterling."

Sterling stood with his feet planted, body weaving. His bleary eyes moved jerkily from one deputy to the other and then back to Firestick again.

"No! Stop it! Stop this, Earl, before it's too late!"

The wailing voice, female, cut across the tension-filled street like a knife.

For only a fraction of a second, Firestick took his eyes off Sterling and cast a quick glance over toward the Mallory House where Frenchy Fontaine emerged from the front door. She took several quick steps out into the street and then slowed uncertainly as she drew nearer to Sterling. The latter turned his head and body — lurching, unsteady still — to face her.

"Dammit, Frenchy, stay clear of him," Firestick growled.

But instead of causing her to back away, his warning only propelled her the rest of the way forward. She ran to Sterling's side and threw her arms around him, either purposely or inadvertently pinning his own arms to his sides. The sudden move nearly toppled Sterling in his drunken state, and it was only thanks to Frenchy that the two of them remained upright.

"For God's sake, Earl, quit this insanity before you get killed," she urged him. "Please! Drop the guns and end this."

Gazing down at her face only inches from his, Sterling's expression crumpled and he looked ready to weep. "I only did it for you, Frenchy," he said, his voice thick. "I don't want to lose you. I had to stop Coswick from taking you away from me."

And then, in a delayed reaction to her request, both of his hands opened and the pistols he'd been holding thumped to the ground.

Firestick rushed forward. Beartooth and Moosejaw converged from either side. When he got close enough, Moosejaw kicked away one of Sterling's dropped guns. Firestick leaned over and scooped up the other one.

Still gazing down at Frenchy's face, Sterling seemed oblivious to any of this. "Please say you ain't gonna leave me," he half-sobbed. "Please give me another chance."

Before Frenchy could answer, Beartooth placed one hand on her shoulder and one on her forearm. He gently but firmly pulled her away from Sterling, saying, "Let us handle this now."

When Frenchy started to back away, Sterling suddenly lunged at Beartooth, striking down his arm. Then, shouting "Leave us alone!" he swung his fist in an awkward, looping right cross aimed at Beartooth's face.

The deputy easily leaned away so that the intended blow missed.

Thrown off balance by the wild swing, Sterling staggered and might have fallen if Moosejaw, letting go of his shotgun, hadn't stepped up behind him and grabbed him before he could do so. Seizing Sterling's arms in two powerful grips just above the elbows, Moosejaw jerked him upright, pulling his elbows close together behind his back and lifting him up on his toes. "Take it easy, buster. Time for you to calm down."

"Don't hurt him!" Frenchy pleaded.

"That's kinda up to him, ma'am," Moose-jaw told her in a surprisingly calm voice.

"Stop fighting him, Earl! It's no use."

Firestick stepped forward, shoving the confiscated pistol into his belt, and pressed between Sterling and Frenchy. "You've helped enough. It's time for you to stand out of the way now," he said to the distraught woman. Then, turning to Sterling, he said, "And it's time for you to listen to her. You're damned lucky this didn't turn out worse for you or somebody else."

Sterling, still half-suspended and helpless in Moosejaw's grip, abruptly dropped his chin onto his chest and began to sob openly. "I'm so sorry. I couldn't stand the thought of losing Frenchy."

Firestick caught Moosejaw's eye and gave a jerk of his chin. "Get him out of the street. Take him to the jail where he can sleep it off."

"What are you going to do to him?" Frenchy wanted to know.

Firestick sighed somewhat irritably. "You heard what I said. Nothing more than that for right now. I'll decide more after he sobers up and we've had a chance to talk to him."

Sensing the marshal's annoyance, Kate came out of the hotel and put an arm around Frenchy, saying, "Come inside, honey. You've done enough. Come in and try to relax."

All up and down the street, others were emerging from the shops and doorways where they'd ducked for cover. At first they were subdued and quiet but then, gradually, they became more animated and the buzz of conversation grew in volume among them.

Dan Coswick came out of the Silver Spur and strode over to the marshal. "I told you," he said excitedly. "I told you just the other day that Sterling was bound to make trouble."

"Yeah, you told me," Firestick replied. "And then you went ahead and hired Frenchy to work at your place anyway."

Coswick scowled. "You're blaming me for this?"

"The only one I'm blamin' direct is the fool who came here makin' threats. Knowin' it likely would lead to trouble, you *could* have held off and gave him and Frenchy some room to see how permanent the rift between 'em was. That's all I'm sayin'." Firestick held up his hands, palms out. "But you and me yammerin' at each other now ain't gonna change what's done. The only thing left for you to do is decide if you're gonna press charges against Sterling for shootin' up your place. You can let me know on that. For the time bein', though, you'd best get back inside and handle your customers — this is the kind of thing that'll get their thirsts worked up yappin' about it."

Still scowling, Coswick turned away and stomped back into his saloon.

As Kate was taking Frenchy back inside the hotel, Victoria squeezed through a knot of people crowding the doorway and hurried out to where Beartooth was standing. "Look at your arm," she said. "When he tried to strike you, he opened up your wound."

Beartooth looked down at the spot just below his left shoulder where fresh blood had leaked through his bandage and the material of his shirt. "I'll be danged," he said. "He sure couldn't throw a punch worth beans, but he must have done that when he shoved my arm away."

Chapter 25

"No matter how it happened, we need to get it fixed again," said Victoria firmly. "We can either go find Frank Moorehouse or you can come inside the hotel with me and I'll see if Kate has something I can use to re-bandage it."

Beartooth grinned at her. "You or Frank Moorehouse? Now let me think real hard on which one I'm gonna choose."

Suddenly Rupert Shaw, who had followed Victoria out from the dining room where they'd been having tea, was standing beside them. "I beg your pardon, Victoria," he said, "but you and I have an interrupted discussion to finish. Don't you think that matter would be best left to the attention of a physician?"

"I assure you I'm perfectly capable of dressing this wound, Rupert. I've done so twice already," Victoria informed him. "Besides, our town has no full-time doctor or physician."

Shaw arched a brow. "Why doesn't that surprise me? Yet another appalling condition of this bucolic hinterland you seem to find so appealing."

"Mister," Beartooth said, his teeth on edge, "if I knew for sure what all those forty-dollar words meant, I'm thinkin' they might piss me off."

"I'll thank you to refrain from using vulgarities in front of the lady," Shaw said stiffly.

"If you don't back off real sudden-like," Beartooth replied, "you damn sure won't be thankin' me for what I do next."

Firestick turned from where he still stood close by. "Beartooth," he cautioned in a low voice.

"Don't worry, I ain't gonna hurt him. He just needs to horn out of what don't concern him," Beartooth said. As he was speaking, Hadley loomed up behind Shaw, causing the deputy to add, "And that goes for his pet ape, too."

"Stop this!" Victoria said sharply. "We all just finished witnessing one display of foolishness; no one wants to see another."

"It seems to me," said Shaw, "that displays of foolishness are very common around here. Perhaps daily, judging by the two I'm aware of in only the short time I've had the displeasure of being here. All the more reason for me to implore you to get away from this dreadful place. If you will return with me to the dining room so we can finish our discussion, my dear Victoria, it may not be too late to convince you that —"

"It's no use, Rupert," Victoria cut him off. "I'm not going back to England. Not with you, not ever. My home is here now and here is where I intend to stay."

As she said these words, Victoria — either subconsciously or perhaps purposely — pressed herself closer to Beartooth. Viewing this, Rupert's expression changed. Turned hard and cold.

"Now I see," he said, his voice barely above a harsh whisper. "It is more than this wretched land that holds you here. What's more, your deception in not immediately revealing this speaks volumes for your own awareness of how sad and ridiculous such an attraction on your part truly is."

"Was I you, I'd be careful with your words. You've been warned once," advised Firestick in the same low voice he'd used to caution Beartooth.

But Shaw ignored him. His eyes were locked on Beartooth, pinning him with a hateful glare. "And you . . . Despite knowing full well the comforts and fine life that await Victoria back where she belongs, you encourage her to forgo all of that? For what? For you? For a gun-toting, bloodstained ruffian who can never hope to give her a fraction of what she deserves? Do you know how selfish and loathsome that makes you?"

"My choices are my own, Rupert!" Victoria insisted. "This is America. That's the way things are done here."

His eyes narrowed, his chin thrust out stubbornly, Shaw said, "I have no further words for you, Victoria. Not at this time. Your overly romanticized foolhardiness has clouded your mind. I have to forgive you for that. But this cad. This seducer of the innocent — for him there can be no forgiveness. For the honor of your family's good name, I must hold him to account!"

Meeting Shaw's eyes with his own flinty gaze, Beartooth said, "You gonna stand there flingin' words the rest of the day, or you gonna do something to try and back 'em up?"

"I will be only too happy to back them up . . . on a field of honor. Providing, of course, you have the backbone to face me in such a manner."

"Rupert, that's absurd!" protested Victoria.

"What the hell's he talkin' about?" Beartooth wanted to know.

"Unless I'm mistakin'," said Firestick, "you just got challenged to a duel."

"Precisely," confirmed Shaw. "I naturally would not expect you to comply in an impaired physical condition. I therefore suggest two days from now. That will allow time for you to heal and for the festival that is so important to your community to be over with. We will select a remote spot — not the middle of a dusty street, much as that seems to be favored around here — where there will be no risk of inadvertently injuring any onlookers. The choice of weapons, either sabers or firearms, is yours to make."

"Hell, I'll fight you any way you want. Guns, knives, clubs, it don't make no never mind to me," said Beartooth, rolling his shoulders, getting worked up. "And we don't need to wait no two days or even two seconds. I'm fit to go right now."

Shaw snorted disdainfully. "Such a barbaric response does not surprise me. That nevertheless isn't how it's conducted by proper and honorable gentlemen — even if only one of us qualifies as such."

By this point, a growing number of people who had just emerged after taking measures to stay clear of the previous shooting were now drawing in closer, watching and listening to this new conflict that obviously was brewing.

"That's about enough with the highfalutin words and all the rest," spoke up Firestick, addressing Shaw. "You seem to be forgettin' one thing: I'm the law around here and I ain't gonna stand by and allow some duel to take place, any more than I allowed the attempted shoot-out that just got over with to play out."

Shaw smiled thinly. "On the streets of your town, Marshal, you have every right to hold that line. But unless I am mistaken, your jurisdiction ends at the town limits. You'll recall I clearly stipulated this matter between your deputy and I take place *not* on any street but rather at a remote location. That being the case, I don't believe you have any legal standing to interfere. Unless, of course, Mr. Beartooth needs you to bend the rules in order for him to avoid facing me as I have challenged."

The marshal started to respond but Beartooth cut him short. "Save your breath, Firestick. This insultin' blowhard called down the thunder, I aim to see he gets what he's askin' for. And not you or anybody else had better try to stand in my way."

Shaw's smile widened, showing lots of

teeth. "Most excellent. I shall say good day for now. I and my second, Mr. Hadley, will scout the surrounding countryside and select a suitable spot for our meeting. We will advise same when you send word on the time and weapons of your choice."

Shaw turned and started back into the hotel. He paused for just a moment to make eye contact with Victoria. But then, without either of them speaking, he turned the rest of the way and proceeded on inside.

CHAPTER 26

Once again the town bounced back quickly from the interruption of gunplay and violence. With the festival only a day away and the fact that this time no one had even been shot, let alone killed, the incident became a subject for wagging tongues but without really affecting any important plans already under way.

This was true for most citizens as well as visitors who'd flocked in from miles around to enjoy the celebration. For a handful of folks more directly involved, however, it was a different matter.

Earl Sterling, obviously, had jeopardized the operation of his successful saloon on one of the busiest nights of the year. He had put into question his standing in the community and the continuation of the business going forward. However, even though Sterling was passed out in a jail cell and too drunk to know it, at least a short-term salvation for the Lone Star Palace presented itself in the form of Frenchy and Arthur joining forces to keep the place running for the time being. An embittered Dan Coswick appeared to be left with his much ballyhooed new entertainer no longer available to make her debut at the Spur.

There was also no lack of tension between Firestick, Beartooth, and Victoria over Beartooth's insistence on accepting Rupert Shaw's challenge to a duel. While Firestick could understand, on a personal level, how Beartooth couldn't back away from something like that, in his role as marshal he could hardly show support for it, no matter where the event took place.

For Victoria it was as simple as her statement to Beartooth: "I didn't admit my love for you only to have it put to the test mere hours later by you agreeing to risk your life in such a preposterous undertaking!"

The weight of the pending duel hung over them the whole day.

"It's not something I make a habit of doing," Pete Roeback said as he leaned on a pitchfork in one of the horse stalls of his livery, "but as long as I've got the space available and you're willing to pay a little extra to use it, I guess we can work out a deal. After all, you've been pretty good customers, boarding your horses here and then buying that new animal from me and all."

"We appreciate it, Mr. Roeback," Charlie Gannon assured him. "It'll allow us to stick around for at least part of the shindig tomorrow — the big picnic and maybe a smidgen of the rodeo — without skippin' all of it or losin' another whole day before we light out."

"I can understand not wanting to miss the festival, being as how you've been here in town for a couple days now and have got caught up in all the hoopla over it," Roeback said. "Folks *do* have a mighty good time, I'll tell you that. Ain't sure why you don't just hang around an extra day, but I reckon that's your business."

"It's temptin' to do that, don't think it ain't," said Josh Stallworth. "You've got such a nice, pleasant town here. But our brother is shorthanded on his ranch up in Kansas and we promised to go give him a hand. We already feel guilty for tarryin' here in Buffalo Peak for as long as we have, not to mention plannin' on stretchin' it into tomorrow. We can't wait another whole day."

"That's right. The longer we stay here, the better we like it and find it harder to leave," added Charlie. "And the pretty ladies you have in this town — whooee! We stick around much longer, I'm apt to fall in love and want to settle down forever."

Roeback chuckled. "Yeah, we do have some mighty fine-looking gals hereabouts. Even an old married rooster like me can't help noticing that. As far as being a nice, peaceful town, though — not saying it ain't, mind you — I'm kinda surprised you'd come away with that impression given the shooting ruckuses we've had in the short time you've been here."

"Everything is relative, Mr. Roeback," Charlie told him. "We've been in some mighty rough towns and know how to spot 'em pretty good. Yeah, there's been some excitement in the last couple days, but it's easy to see that ain't the regular way of things around here."

Roeback nodded. "Well, it's good to hear you can see that. So you go ahead and buy your supplies and bring 'em on back here when you've got everything you need. I'll be around. You can put 'em in the store-room, then, where they'll be handy for you to grab and load up your pack animal when you're ready to head out tomorrow."

"We're much obliged, Mr. Roeback," Josh said earnestly. "When we get back, we'll settle up our bill for use of that storeroom plus one more night for our horses and all."

Charlie and Josh quit the livery barn and ambled out into the afternoon bustle on Trail Street. The day had grown hot and the lack of any breeze left a fine layer of dust in the air, stirred up by the comings and goings of so many people.

"Well, we got that taken care of," Charlie said as they walked along. "Now all we got to do is stock up on supplies, get 'em stashed for quick grabbin' when we need 'em, and sit tight for one more night. Then, tomorrow is the day we make our big move."

"Boy, I can hardly wait." Josh smiled dreamily. "To think that by this time tomorrow I'll have Miss Cleo hugged up tight against me in my saddle. Makes me 'bout ready to bust from havin' to wait that long."

Charlie frowned. "How do you know her name is Cleo?"

"I asked around about the strawberry blonde from the Lone Star Palace. Wasn't hard to find out. I figure Cleo must be short for Cleopatra, that famous queen from way back in history. That's how I'm gonna treat her, too, once she comes around to takin' a shine to me — like a queen."

"Do you think that was a good idea, drawin' attention to yourself by askin' about her that way?"

Josh shrugged. "Don't see the harm. In the first place, nobody knows me. In the second place, a gal as pretty as Miss Cleo is bound to have plenty of men askin' after her. Besides, when the women we pick go missin' and everybody starts thinkin' on it and askin' around, they're likely gonna remember us anyway. But they still ain't gonna know who we are or where we went, so none of it will matter much."

"I suppose. Us bein' strangers and all, we'll come to mind for sure. Still kinda wish you hadn't done that askin' around, though."

"Okay. While we're wishin' then, maybe I wish you hadn't told that livery fella back there about findin' the gals in town pretty enough to take one of 'em for a wife. Ain't that drawin' the same kind of attention?"

Charlie scowled. "Shit. I never thought . . . Gotta admit you make a proper point, though. I say the thing for us to do from here on out is to make sure neither one of us speaks careless anymore. We're close to accomplishin' what we set out to do; we don't want to make problems now at the last minute."

"Amen to that," Josh said. "I don't think neither of us has done anything too drastic.

But you're right about bein' extra careful all the same. We concentrate on gettin' our supplies — makin' sure to be real thorough so's we'll impress our gals by thinkin' of everything that'll keep 'em comfortable and well fed — then we lay low for the rest of today and tonight and be ready to give it our all tomorrow."

"You got it, pard. That's the ticket, sure enough."

The sun was setting, casting deepening shadows between slanted fingers of rock and into the numerous arroyos that twisted through the foothills of the Vieja Mountains. A lone horseman, coming from the direction of town, rode into the mouth of one of these arroyos. He checked down the speed of his animal as the ground within the narrowing passageway ascended steadily and grew rockier. The horse's hooves began to clack loudly, faintly echoing.

After a couple hundred yards, the arroyo suddenly flared wider and opened onto a flat, oval-shaped area with stands of scrub brush and a handful of scrawny trees along the outer edge. Opposite these, the inner edge of the oval reached under an outward sloping rock wall that eventually rose up and blended into the higher peaks.

Under the rock overhang, Black Hills Buckner and Romo Perlison squatted beside a low-burning campfire. Leticia Beauregard was on her feet, moving toward the center of the oval to greet Pierce Torrence as he came riding in.

Swinging down from his saddle, Torrence growled, "It's sure good to see how you were keeping a sharp lookout while I was gone."

"Relax," said Black Hills, rising to his full towering height and moving forward from the fire. "I had you spotted out on the flats twenty minutes ago. Wasn't nothing else movin' anywhere in sight, just like there ain't been all afternoon."

"And anybody comin' up that arroyo, the way sound echoes in those rocks," added Romo, "will announce themselves like a marching band beatin' a drum."

"All the same, it's better to know if somebody is coming before it gets to the point of being able to hear them."

"We know the coast is clear for the time being," said Leticia, reaching up to loosen the bulging canvas bag tied behind Torrence's saddle. "So the only sound I'm worried about hearing is that of us chowing down on some decent food you better have brought back with you — something besides the jerky and beans we've been getting by on for too damn long."

Torrence grinned. "A person can go a long way on jerky and beans."

"Uh-huh," said Leticia. "And you can go just as far with a little variety in your belly, too."

She pulled the bag down, slung it over her shoulder, and started toward the fire.

"I'll see to your horse, boss," said Romo. "You go ahead and take a load off, then you can fill us in on the layout of that town while Letty is whippin' up supper from whatever grub you brung back."

A surprisingly short time later they were all seated around the fire balancing plates piled high with pan biscuits, stewed tomatoes, and slabs of crisp bacon. A fresh pot of coffee bubbled on the edge of the coals, and some canned peaches awaited to be served for dessert. The last sliver of the sun had dropped behind the western horizon, leaving a pinkish-gold glow low in the sky, and the air was rapidly starting to cool.

"As we could tell by the number of riders and wagons we saw dribblin' in all day," Torrence said, "the town is packed. The big event is what they call their Spring Festival. Tenth annual. Even though you can bet the whole place will be jumping tonight, the main day for the official activities — a church picnic, rodeo, evening square dance, and whatever else — will all take place tomorrow."

"Oh, man," groaned Romo even as he shoveled in a mouthful of food, "don't I wish I could join in on some of that celebratin'."

"Wish all you want," Torrence told him. "While all that's going on, we sit tight right here. But then, along about mid-day on Monday, when the visitors to town have thinned out and those who are left are still hungover and wore out and the money that's been raked in over the weekend has been deposited in the bank — that's when we do our celebrating."

"How does the bank look?" Leticia asked.

Torrence smiled confidently. "Easy pickings. A cracker box. I went in and changed a torn twenty-dollar bill for some coins, got a chance to look it over real good. I'll sketch out a drawing and we'll have time to go over it tomorrow."

"Speakin' of tomorrow," said Black Hills, "I still got some more explorin' I want to do in this rock pile, but I already got a couple pretty good routes for us to use on our getaway. Be confusin' as hell to anybody tryin' to follow us and damned hard to track over this broken ground."

"That's your department, big man. I leave our escape route to you," Torrence told him. "I'm thinking, however, that we may want to give ourselves an added edge by taking a hostage."

"A hostage?" echoed Leticia.

"That's right. We've used them before."

"Yes. But I've never liked it." Leticia frowned. "I don't like how we treat the hostages when we're done with them."

Torrence regarded her as if finding her reaction genuinely curious. "You surprise me, my dear. After all this time, I thought you were as hard on the inside as anybody I ever worked with — harder even, than many."

"I've never flinched from doing whatever has to be done. And never will," Leticia responded. "I'm just questioning the necessity, that's all. If the bank is a cracker box and the town law is only a couple long-in-the-tooth former mountain men, I guess I just don't understand the need for an added edge like a hostage."

"You raise a fair question," said Torrence. "But here, as the quaint old saying goes, is the fly in the buttermilk: The picture painted to me of this town's law enforcement turns out to be quite inaccurate. Learning this was one of the benefits of me going into town and giving things a good looking over.

"In the first place, there are three appointed lawmen to deal with, not just two. A marshal and a pair of deputies. And, yes, they are all former mountain men, long-standing friends, and they have a small horse ranch just outside of town that they run in addition to their peace-keeping duties. It's true they've got a few years on them also. But observing them personally made it evident they're still strong and robust and very far from doddering under the weight of their years. And when there's trouble in the town, they've proven themselves time and again — as recently as last night and again this afternoon, just a few hours before I rode in — to be very efficient at handling it. The incident last night involved four gun toughs with whom the marshal and his deputies shot it out and left dead in the middle of the street."

Torrence paused to let his words sink in while his gaze drifted over the three faces turned to him. Then he said, "So, based on this, I trust you'll see why I think giving ourselves an extra edge may be in order. In addition to a quicker and more efficient response than I'd anticipated once we've hit the bank, I feel it's also worth considering that the marshal and his deputies *are* former mountain men and therefore likely have some strong tracking skills. Taking nothing away from Black Hills' skill at obscuring our trail, that still has to be weighed as a factor when it comes to them pursuing us."

Nobody spoke right away. Until Leticia, her mouth twisting wryly, said, "Okay. You've made your sale. A hostage it is."

Torrence smiled. "I thought you'd see it my way."

"One more thing," said Leticia. "What about those two marriage-minded oafs from back at Ma Speckler's? Any sign of them while you were in town?"

"Nary a one," replied Torrence. "Either they've come and gone or were lost somewhere in the crowd. Either way suited me just fine. It wasn't like I *wanted* to run into them."

CHAPTER 27

The big day finally arrived.

Everything kicked off with an early morning pancake feed down by the rodeo arena. Then church services would be held by popular Pastor Bart at the First Baptist Church. Children's games, a market for selling or trading homemade food and other goods displayed by wives and craftsmen from around the area, and the dreaded but inevitable speechifying by local dignitaries were slotted to be held over the next couple hours. The belly-busting mid-day picnic, what many considered the high point of the day, came next. Rodeo events followed that. And capping it all off would be an evening of dancing and musical entertainment.

The folks from the Double M rolled out at the crack of dawn, skipping breakfast at the ranch and aiming to be present for the pancake feed. Miguel and Jesus were already in town; like many other wranglers from surrounding ranches, they had camped overnight on the rodeo grounds to be with the horses they would be using for the riding and roping events they'd be participating in.

Firestick, Moosejaw, Beartooth, and Victoria rode in on their own individual mounts. In addition to its lovely rider, Victoria's horse also carried a large carpetbag containing a carefully folded dress and other accessories into which she'd change at Kate's place, trading her riding clothes for the sake of being more fashionably attired during the course of the day.

The festival events awaiting all of them served to provide a welcome diversion from the stress that still existed over the looming duel. After returning to the ranch last evening and enduring a very tense supper punctuated by bursts of argument on that subject, Firestick had finally demanded a truce from any further discussion until after the festival. They all had obligations as far as the celebration, he pointed out, and their personal feelings shouldn't get in the way of meeting those. So, while the unmistakable cold shoulder now and then and a measure of overall awkwardness couldn't be suppressed completely, they had proceeded on that basis. Only Moosejaw, who was more or less on the periphery of the conflicting emotions, made any attempt at genuine good cheer, but his efforts fell mostly flat.

Once in town, the four of them promptly split up. Firestick stopped at the jail, where the services of Sam Duvall and Shield had been enlisted once again to spend the night keeping watch over Earl Sterling. Moosejaw went to the blacksmith shop to pick up Daisy so they could attend the pancake feed together. Beartooth stayed with Victoria — the two of them maintaining a determined silence — as far as the Mallory House, where Victoria took her carpetbag and went inside to use Kate's apartment for changing. Beartooth went on down to the rodeo area to check on Miguel and Jesus and then partake of some of the pancakes.

When Firestick entered the office, he was met by the welcome aroma of fresh-brewed coffee. Sam Duvall stood beside the stove, pouring himself a cup of the steaming mud. Shield lay on the floor nearby, his ears perking up at the marshal's entrance but otherwise remaining still.

"Just in time," said Sam, looking around. "Got a brand-new batch here."

"I know. I can tell by the smell," Firestick replied. "Nothing smells as good as fresh coffee in the morning. And I can't think of too many who brew it better than yours, Sam."

The old constable smiled. "I take that to mean you'd be interested in a cup?"

"You bet. We lit out so early from the ranch this mornin' we didn't take time for breakfast or even some mud."

"To start out and ride this far with no coffee in you — the very thought makes me shudder."

"Dang near inhuman, ain't it?"

Firestick held out an empty cup while Sam tipped the pot once more and filled it. After blowing a couple cooling gusts into the cup and taking a careful sip of its contents, Firestick tipped his head toward the door to the lockup. "How'd our guest behave last night?"

"Nary a peep out of him. From the times I looked in, I don't think he hardly moved a muscle. But then, just a little while ago, I heard him groaning. I figure his peaceful night is about to be offset by a mighty miserable morning when he gets fully woke up to his hangover."

Firestick grunted. "And the damn fool will have earned every bit of it."

"So what are you going to do with him?"

"I ain't rightly sure," Firestick admitted. "As you well know, we're kinda short on havin' an official set of town rules and regulations. I'm sure nobody would argue if I fined him or kept him jailed some amount of time for disturbin' the peace or reckless behavior with a firearm or some such. But I don't know how much difference that would really make. Hell, it might be more trouble than it'd be worth."

"It would keep me busier than I truly want to be if I had to spend too many nights in a row coming here to look after him, I can tell you that," said Sam. "But if that's what you decide, I won't let you down."

"I appreciate that, Sam. That's why I said keepin' him jailed might be more trouble than it's worth. Some kind of heavy fine is probably more in order." Firestick drank some of his coffee. "Reckon a big part of it'll come down to how much of a stink Dan Coswick wants to make. He's the one Sterling was makin' threats against and whose building took a couple bullets."

"I got a hunch that after Dan cools down you'll find him more reasonable than you might think," Sam said. "But you're right, he's the one who's in a position to demand some charges against Sterling if he wants to push it."

"I expect he'll be around before too long, then I'll find out. In the meantime, you've been stuck here all night and those pancakes must be callin' to you. You and Shield both, since I know you'll be flippin' him a few of those flapjacks, too. So go ahead and take off . . . go enjoy the festival. Check in with me later, in case I decide to keep Sterling behind bars another night or on the chance some other idiot does something worth gettin' locked up for."

"But what about you? Since you went without breakfast at the ranch, those pancakes must be calling to you, as well."

"Don't worry about me. I'll grab me some sooner or later. Beartooth or Moosejaw will be back to spell me after they've had their fill — if there's any left for anybody, that is, after Moosejaw cuts a swath through 'em. But as long as I got some of this in me now" — Firestick held up his cup of coffee — "I'll get by. So go ahead before Moosejaw lays waste like a herd of locusts."

Chapter 28

Oberon Hadley didn't like the way things were shaping up. Didn't like it one bit.

He'd viewed the opportunity to travel to America with Captain Shaw as a grand adventure, the opportunity of a lifetime. And from his own perspective, it had been all of that and more. He'd liked this big, raw, sprawling, boisterous country right from the start. He'd even liked the crowded, smoky eastern cities. There was a kind of energy and swagger about the people and the way things got done that appealed to him.

Then, as he and the captain had traveled farther and farther west, the vastness of the land and all its rugged beauty had awed him even more — not to mention the people, who were so leathery tough and resilient yet at the same time friendly and often curiously gentle.

That was the America Hadley saw and

came to believe he was getting an accurate and fond sense of. At the same time, unfortunately, Captain Shaw had a very different reaction. He disliked the absence of formalities, the outspokenness and impertinence of what he saw as the common folks. He hated the lack of certain luxuries, had no appreciation for how Westerners overcame and adapted to harsh conditions. His displeasure over these conditions was regularly voiced, and his annoyance was often displayed in rude behavior toward those around him.

That Shaw was openly elitist came as no revelation to Hadley. Signs of that had been evident when they'd served together in the Queen's Army. But within military structure and the chain of command, the captain had enjoyed enough power to satisfy his sense of superiority while at the same time not allowing him to be too overbearing with his subordinates. What was more, he had very early on formed a liking for — and dependency on — one Sergeant Hadley. This had won Hadley over, allowing him to overlook some of the captain's high-handed ways and at times even be able to intervene and blunt some of his more obnoxious intentions. And then, when it counted the most, in the heat of the battle for Baba Wali Pass during the Anglo-Afghan War, Captain Shaw's disbursement of the troops under his command had proven a key piece of strategy that helped carry the day.

The captain's actions in that battle had been enough to offset any reservations Hadley might otherwise have had when, after the Afghan conflict was over and they'd both been discharged from the army, Shaw offered him a job as his personal aide. The former sergeant accepted. The position held far better promise than any of the other job prospects available to him, and in the two years since he'd seldom had any regrets.

But now that had changed.

Hadley very much regretted his current situation. The captain's behavior — his refusal to accept the latest rejection from Victoria and his insistence on carrying through with this duel against the deputy known as Beartooth — was nothing short of bizarre and wrong. And it trapped Hadley right in the middle.

The way the former sergeant saw it, if the duel took place there was small chance of yielding a positive result for anybody. If the captain shot Beartooth, he might very well face legal repercussions since he was the one who initiated everything. If Beartooth shot the captain — which Hadley feared was more likely, given the deputy's skill with a handgun — then Shaw stood to end up wounded or possibly dead.

What would then be expected of Hadley? Should he seek revenge, or merely see to it the captain's remains got returned home? As far as that went, once news of the incident spread might there be an international furor that in some way tried to hold Beartooth accountable or perhaps dictated what Hadley's role should be?

In the hours since the captain had made his challenge and set the whole thing in motion, Hadley had tried more than once to get him to reconsider. But he was never allowed to even finish any of the reasoning he attempted to present.

Shaw seemed almost maniacally determined to go through with the duel. Yesterday afternoon, after he'd issued his challenge, he had purchased a .45-caliber Colt revolver from a local dealer. Then he'd insisted he and Hadley ride out and search the countryside for a suitable spot to hold the contest. Now, first thing this morning, they were returning to conduct some target practice.

For the time being, Hadley had given up trying to dissuade the captain from what he was so hell-bent on doing. But that didn't mean he was ready to give up entirely. The whole notion was foolish and wrong. One way or another, Hadley knew he had to find a way to stop it from happening.

In a large stall near the rear of Roeback Livery's main barn, Charlie Gannon and Josh Stallworth were nearly finished lashing their supply bundles onto the backs of the packhorse they purchased the day before from Pete Roeback. In the same stall, already saddled and ready, were the pair's regular mounts. Except for the occasional scrape of a hoof from one of the horses elsewhere in the barn, the place was silent. Roeback and his hired help were all gone to the pancake feed.

"I understand how we got to have everything ready so's we can ride out quick once we've selected our brides," Josh was saying. "But I can't help wonderin' if it's a good idea to get our horses and supplies loaded up like this and then just leave 'em for a spell."

"What else are we gonna do with 'em?" Charlie wanted to know. "Lead 'em around with us everywhere we go until we're ready to light out?"

"No. I understand we can't do that. It's just . . . well, what if somebody takes a notion to mess with our stuff, steal some of it or something, while there's nobody

270

around?"

Charlie chuckled. "You mean some dishonest rascals like us?"

"A damn thief is what I mean. No other word for it." Josh took the wadded-up end of a section of rope he'd just knotted to secure one of the bulging bundles on his side of the horse and tossed it over for Charlie to use on his side. Then, frowning deeply, he said, "But I don't like hearin' you call us dishonest, Charlie. That ain't what we're doin', is it? I mean, yeah, at first we're sorta snatchin' the gals by surprise and a little against their will. But our intentions ain't bad. Not evil bad, like we're kidnappin' 'em for money or something. Soon as we get 'em convinced what we're about, that we full intend to do right by 'em — marry 'em proper and provide for 'em and all — well, then that'll square things. Won't it? The gals will be able to tell anybody who might have started out after us that everything turned out okay. Ain't that the way you see it?"

Grunting a little as he tugged on the rope Josh had tossed over, pulling it tight, Charlie said, "Yeah, the way you laid it out sounds good to me. No, we ain't rightfully dishonest fellas. If we was, we would've found a helluva lot easier way to build up this nest egg we're workin' with now than bustin' our humps at wranglin' work for all the years we did. But you're also right in sayin' that the way we plan to start out with these gals is gonna look wrong at first and put us on the dodge for a while in the beginnin'. That's all I meant by that 'dishonest fellas like us' remark."

"Okay. Good. I'm glad we're lookin' at things the same way."

"As far as anybody messin' with our stuff on account of how we're gonna be leavin' it here for a while," Charlie added, "I don't think there's hardly no worry about that happenin'. There's some risk, I suppose, but we're gonna have to live with it. Most folks around are basically honest and, especially today, they're way more interested in the big town festival than anything else."

"Yeah, I guess that's all there is for it." Josh looked thoughtful for a minute and then abruptly broke into a grin. "The thing on everybody's mind right now is the big pancake feed down by the rodeo arena. And I gotta say, my mind is strayin' in that direction, too. So let's finish up here and head in that direction ourselves. While we're chowin' down and minglin', maybe you'll get your sights set on the gal you aim to take for your bride . . ."

CHAPTER 29

As Firestick had predicted, it didn't take Dan Coswick long to come around wanting to talk about the charges he might be interested in filing against Earl Sterling. What the marshal hadn't predicted was that Coswick didn't come alone.

Firestick had just stepped back into the office after going to check on a moaning and wretchedly hungover Sterling, when the front door opened and Coswick came in accompanied by Frenchy Fontaine, Cleo, and Big Arthur.

"If I didn't know better," Firestick said, his eyebrows lifting, "I might think I was seein' things on account of inhalin' too many secondhand alcohol fumes from my visit back there to the lockup just now."

"I can understand how you believe you may be hallucinating," said Frenchy, her lush mouth twisting wryly. "But trust me, you are not. The four of us — quite to our own surprise yet in our individual self-interests — have reached an agreement on some things we feel you will be interested to hear."

"Oh, you got me interested, alright," Firestick assured her. "Why don't you pull some chairs over closer, have a seat, and tell me about these agreements."

"We're okay standing," said Cleo. "This won't take that long."

"What are your further intentions to punish Earl for his behavior yesterday?" asked Frenchy.

Firestick folded his arms. "To tell you the truth, I ain't rightly made up my mind yet. A lot of it is gonna depend on what charges Dan here is lookin' to make."

"None," Coswick said bluntly. "There wasn't no harm done to my place except for a couple bullet holes in the boards that had been put up due to the damage from before. As far as the threats and the rest . . . I'm willin' to chalk that up to the booze. I've done plenty of dumb things my own self when I had too much red-eye in me. And, let's face it" — he cast a sheepish glance in Frenchy's direction — "I was awful fast to horn in on the situation between Sterling and Frenchy, trying to turn it to my benefit. I ain't saying I deserved to get shot over it, but a pop on the nose from Sterling wouldn't have been out of line."

"He's being unnecessarily gallant," Frenchy was quick to say. "Everyone knows it was I who went to him about a job at his place. Because of that and because Dan went to the trouble and expense of building a stage for me, I have agreed to perform at the Silver Spur on alternating weekends through the summer."

"What's Sterling gonna say about that?" Firestick wanted to know.

"If he knows what's good for him, he'd better go along with it," Cleo said. "Otherwise he'll lose Frenchy completely again — and for good this time. He'll lose her both as his entertainer and his lover. And he won't have little ol' me to fall back on as a replacement, either."

"And what do you get out of this?" Firestick said.

"Cleo and I reached a truce," Frenchy answered. "I no longer blame her for Earl's stupidity. He was using both of us. Nor do I begrudge her and the other girls continuing to work at the Palace. Frankly, it is good for business and, since I am going to insist on a percent of the business if I stay with Earl, then I have to take that into consideration."

"And don't forget me," Arthur spoke up.

"Yes. Arthur deserves a cut, too. We've both been with Earl for a long time. Last night and today are not the first times we've bailed him out when he got himself in a fix. It's past time for him to do right by us."

"Sounds reasonable to me," Firestick said.

"And," interjected Cleo, "to get back to your question about what I get out of all this — first of all, to keep my job. Providing Earl has the sense to go along and the Palace keeps running, that is. If so, then Frenchy and Arthur are gonna put me in charge of the rest of the girls to make sure we quit sniping amongst ourselves and do our part to keep rowdy customers in line so a certain ornery lug of a lawman don't keep comin' around trying to put the run on us."

Firestick grinned. "Sounds like a pretty ambitious undertakin'. But one I like the sound of all the same."

"So where does that leave your decision on what to do about Sterling?" asked Coswick. "How long are you going to keep him locked up?"

Firestick regarded the quartet before him for a long minute before he said, "Tell you what. In the spirit of this bein' festival weekend and considerin' the way you four have ironed things out, I'm willin' to go easy on him. Let's make it time served and a fifty-dollar fine for disturbin' the peace. How does that sound?"

He got looks of satisfaction and relief for an answer.

"But, right at the moment, your boy is still pretty deep in the miseries of bein' hungover," Firestick told them. "I'd advise lettin' him sweat it out a while longer before you hit him with all those conditions you've cooked up. Come back with the fifty dollars in two or three hours, and he'll be all yours."

Frenchy smiled and gave a nod of her head. "I'll be here."

"And I'll be with her," Arthur added, "in case the boss needs some help mindin' his manners and recognizing the good deal he's being offered."

After the contingent from the local saloons had left, Firestick found himself feeling pretty good. If only he could figure out some way to get around the duel that still loomed between Beartooth and Rupert Shaw, he could allow himself to feel a whole lot better.

As he was reflecting on this, the door opened and something more to make him feel good came through it. Kate.

While Firestick stood smiling at the sight of her, she moved toward him saying, "I saw your other visitors leaving — including once again the little dove Cleo. I must say, that seems to be turning into a habit I could find annoying if I thought about it very hard."

"Take it easy. You saw that she was part of a group, didn't you?"

"Yes, and that was something of a surprise in itself. Especially seeing her walking shoulder to shoulder with Frenchy and Frenchy not reaching over to try and claw her eyes out."

"They've called a truce," Firestick informed her. "In fact, the whole bunch of them came here in sort of an alliance. One that includes Earl Sterling, too, although he don't know it yet."

"Okay. You've succeeded in getting me past my annoyance and making me intrigued," said Kate. "So tell me the rest of it. What's going on?"

Firestick gestured toward the chair in front of his desk. "Have a seat and I'll fill you in. But first, what is that you got with you that I can't help but notice smells so good?"

In her hands Kate was holding a small squarish package wrapped in a cloth dinner napkin. "You mean this?" she said coyly, lifting it slightly. "Well, it started out being a couple of fried egg sandwiches that Marilu made up for me to bring over to you after Victoria told us you'd ridden in without breakfast and might not make it to the pancake feed before everything was gone. But then, when I saw Cleo twitching her tail out of here again, it helped remind me that you have a prisoner in the back who needs feeding, too. I've been debating with myself whether he should get both sandwiches or maybe only one."

"Let me solve that question for you. Sterling is too hungover and sick to keep even a bite of anything down. So you can put those sandwiches right here," Firestick said, tapping a finger on his desk, "and I'll see to it they get took care of."

"I just hope I'm not contributing to the starvation of a poor prisoner." She placed the wrapped sandwiches on the marshal's desk, then took a seat in front of it as Firestick moved around and sank into his own chair. "Now tell me about this alliance that Frenchy and Coswick and the rest worked out."

While he ate, Firestick gave her a quick rundown on what he'd heard from his four previous visitors. When he'd finished, Kate leaned back in her chair and said, "I wondered what happened to Frenchy — why she never came back to the hotel last night.

I heard that she and Arthur joined together to keep the Palace running after you locked Sterling up. I just never realized she threw her negotiating net wide enough to get the others to cooperate with her."

"However it came to be," Firestick said with a shrug, "what they put together don't sound like a bad deal to me. Providin' Sterling goes along with it, that is. Which I think he probably will because he's got too much to lose if he don't. Coswick comes out of it with a sort of win because he gets Frenchy entertainin' part of the time at his place, and Sterling makes out okay, too, because he keeps her all the rest of the time. And Arthur and Cleo got a stake in keepin' the Palace runnin' and makin' sure it operates more peaceful-like. If it all hangs together, then it actually works out tidier than I had any reason to expect at the start of the day."

"I agree. *If.*" Kate studied him. All of her coyness was gone now, her expression very serious. "But there's something apart from all of that that still has you troubled, isn't there?"

"Shouldn't be hard to figure out," Firestick said as he lifted his second sandwich to take a bite.

"The duel between Beartooth and Rupert Shaw?"

Firestick nodded, chewing.

"Victoria's beside herself over the same thing. It's all she talked about when she stopped by my place a little while ago to change her outfit."

"Was Beartooth with her?"

"No. I think he accompanied her as far as the hotel, then went on to the pancake breakfast by himself. When I left to come here, Victoria was headed that way, too, with Marilu and Big Thomas."

"If Victoria's so worked up about it," Firestick said, "then it seems to me she'd be better off talkin' directly to Beartooth."

"I get the impression they're hardly speaking at all. She says he refuses to listen."

Firestick sighed. "Yeah, that's true enough. The damn stubborn mule. What about Shaw? He's the one who started it. Did she try talkin' to him?"

"Not this morning. He's nowhere around where she *could* have tried to talk to him. He and that big Hadley left the hotel practically at first light. I think they went out of town somewhere to practice shooting. In case you didn't know, Shaw bought himself a gun yesterday — a big, fancy Colt .45."

Firestick swore under his breath. "That's

just great."

"He's obviously taking this whole duel thing dead serious," said Kate, her brows pinching together.

"Yeah, and that's exactly how he's gonna end up — dead," Firestick said bitterly. "He can buy all the fancy guns he can get his hands on and he can practice from here to the second coming, but it won't do him any good. If he goes up against Beartooth, Beartooth will kill him. It's that simple."

Kate eyed Firestick closely. She gnawed her lower lip for a moment, then said, "Maybe you could talk to Beartooth. Get him to —"

"I tried that yesterday when it was first bustin' loose," Firestick cut her off. "How far did I get?"

"But now that he's had a chance to cool down some, maybe —"

Firestick cut her off again. "No. Nothing I can say will change his mind."

"How do you know if you don't even try?"

"Because I know Beartooth."

"But you're the marshal. You're expected to try and stop this kind of thing. Let alone the fact that Beartooth wears a badge himself, doesn't he realize — or care — the spot he's putting you in?"

"You heard Shaw. If they take it outside of

town, I have no legal jurisdiction over what they do."

Kate's dark eyes flashed. "That's a feeble excuse if I ever heard one! I know you. If you really wanted to, that's not something that would stop you from . . ."

Her words trailed off. The heat went out of her eyes but she kept them locked on Firestick. In a quieter voice, she said, "I think I'm beginning to understand. You won't try to stop Beartooth because you refuse to ask him to act differently."

Firestick didn't reply. He looked away from her gaze and concentrated instead on the empty napkin on his desk.

"In his place," Kate continued, "you would do exactly the same. You can't ask him to do something you wouldn't do yourself."

Now Firestick lifted his eyes and met hers. "There are some things a man can't step around, Kate. Not and stay a man. Shaw threw this in his face, called him out in front of the whole town. I appreciate why Beartooth can't back away from that. And you're right — I'm damned if I'll ask him to."

Chapter 30

Charlie and Josh had eaten their fill of pancakes and were drifting away from the crowd still gathered near the rodeo arena where the breakfast feed was beginning to taper down some. Not all of the tables that had been set up were filled to capacity like they had been earlier, even though most of the diners still remained in the area, milling and visiting. A handful of industrious men had begun taking the tables that were now empty and moving them up the street to the grassy area behind the church where the noon picnic would be held.

Not wanting to get asked to join a work detail that might detain them when they were ready to make their move, Josh and Charlie put distance between themselves and any such risk. As they meandered up Trail Street, once past the churchyard where more preparations were taking place, the street around them turned basically empty of other people.

"We ain't gonna have much luck findin' you a woman up this way, Charlie," Josh pointed. "Pickin's are about as slim as a ghost town, what with everybody back the other way either by the church or still at the pancake feed."

"You think I can't see that?" Charlie said irritably.

"Speakin' of seein' — did you spot any likely bride candidates in the crowd back there?" Josh asked. "You're gonna have to lock your sights on one sooner or later."

"You want to tell me something else I already know?" grumbled Charlie. "Yeah, I saw plenty of gals back there who would have suited me just fine. But the circumstances wasn't hardly right for slingin' one of 'em over my shoulder and walkin' off. I need to catch one out on the edge of the pack where I can grab her and slip away without nobody noticin'. We'll have to go back and mingle some more when everybody starts driftin' up to the church. That grassy area out back where there's some trees around the edges looks like it'll give me a better chance than the way it was with all that open space around the rodeo arena."

"I reckon," Josh allowed.

"In the meantime, as long as we're up this

285

way, we might as well duck in and check on our horses. Make sure everything's okay."

"Yeah, that'd be a good idea," agreed Josh. "You know, speakin' of ideas, here's another one you might want to consider."

"What's that?"

"Well, I made sure to look real careful but I didn't see no sign of Miss Cleo back there at the pancake feed."

"Did you really expect to? Come on, Josh — an upstairs saloon girl like her? You think the goody-goods of the community would allow gals like that to mingle right in the thick of their precious festival? There's only one place for their kind, and they know it as well as anybody."

Josh's face reddened with anger. "Yeah. Bunch of stinkin' town phonies. Most all the men back there would trade their fat cow wives for a beauty like Cleo in a heart-beat. But they have to act all goody-good, like you said, in order to pretend otherwise and treat the girls like dirt as part of their act."

They were entering Roeback's Livery by this point and Josh peevishly smacked the edge of his fist against a corral post as he walked past. "But that's gettin' away from the idea I was tryin' to get to," he continued. "The thing is, see, not havin' Miss Cleo down there amongst all the others is a good thing for me. After you've picked out your gal and we're ready to light out, I know right where Cleo will be and I can snatch her away pretty easy."

"Yeah, we already went over that," said Charlie. "So where does this big new idea come in?"

"Don't you see?" Josh spread his hands. "There's three or four other upstairs girls at the Palace, ain't there? Since you ain't picked out nobody else yet and the ones you've spotted are turnin' out to be sort of tricky to get to, well, how about considerin' one of those other Palace gals?"

They'd reached the rear stall where their horses were. One look made it quickly evident neither the animals nor their supplies had been trifled with.

Charlie pinned Josh with a direct gaze. "Look, pal, I don't want to hurt your feelin's and I'll never speak bad of anybody you take for your wife. But a girl like that — an upstairs gal — that ain't what I'm lookin' for, okay? Maybe it ain't fair, considerin' how I've been willin' to lay with plenty of 'em, as you dang well know. But to take one for my bride . . . well, I'd never be able to get past thinkin' about all the other men. Now that ain't sayin' nothing against you, if

287

you're able to. Plus, your Miss Cleo is rightfully a real cutie. But I've had a look at those other gals from the Palace and . . . well, there ain't nothing there to help me change my mind, if you get what I mean."

Josh's shoulders sagged. "Okay, if that's how you feel. I sure can't argue against those other gals not bein' able to hold a candle to my Cleo. It was just a notion I had, probably 'cause I'm anxious to get on our way."

"I know you are. I am, too." Charlie clapped Josh on the shoulder. "Just bear with me, pard. I promise to make up my mind and cull me a bride out of the pack before too much longer."

They wandered back down the length of the livery barn. As they emerged out the front, they saw Kate Mallory coming down the empty street on her way from the jail to the rodeo arena.

Charlie took one look at this dark-haired beauty, glanced over at Josh standing beside him, then swung his eyes back to Kate again.

A moment later Charlie stepped forward. "Excuse me, ma'am."

CHAPTER 31

Firestick had just finished brewing a fresh pot of coffee and pouring himself a cup when the front door opened behind him. He turned, expecting it to be either Beartooth or Moosejaw coming to spell him. Instead, he was surprised to see it was Sam Duvall returning, his dog Shield at his side.

"Hey fellas," Firestick greeted. "Get your fill of pancakes already?"

"Matter of fact we did," Sam answered. "I seem to recall heaping my plate full several times. Too damn many times, to tell the truth — now I feel so stuffed I can hardly walk."

"Well, you made it this far," Firestick pointed out. "What about my two deputies? They still crammin' their faces? I expected one of them to be comin' back around by now."

"They would have. Leastways Moosejaw would have," Sam said. "He was on his way, in fact, when he got interrupted. That's why he asked me to come fetch you instead."

"Fetch me for what? Where is he?"

"He's waiting for you at the Mallory House."

"What happened? What's wrong?"

"Calm down . . . it's nothing real serious. But it involves those English fellows. So I'd just as soon they explain it to you when you get there."

Firestick held out the cup of coffee he'd just poured. "Here. Even though you claim to be full of pancakes, I've never seen you when you didn't have room for a cup of coffee. This is fresh brewed but you're still gettin' a bad trade for the pot you left me earlier — I flat don't make it as good as you."

"I'll manage," Sam said, taking the cup as the marshal started for the door. "But what about our guest in the lockup?"

Over his shoulder before going out the door, Firestick said, "He's startin' to come around. I poured a couple cups of your brew down him and I think he thinks he's gonna live on account of feelin' too sick to die. In case Frenchy and Arthur from the Palace show up before I get back, they can claim him as long as they pay the fifty-dollar fine. I'll fill you in on the rest when

I get back."

As he approached the Mallory House, Firestick could see that things were pretty well wrapped up at the pancake feed and a strung-out mass of folks were slowly threading their way from there up to the church where Pastor Bart was scheduled to start his service before long.

Entering the hotel, the marshal found a small knot of people gathered in the lobby. Moosejaw was there. Daisy was at his side, looking quite fetching with her golden hair pinned up and wearing a yellow-trimmed summer dress in considerable contrast to her customary attire of boots, overalls, and a man's work shirt. Also present were Victoria, Oberon Hadley, and Rupert Shaw. The latter was occupying one of two plush armchairs positioned by the front window. The others stood looking on as Frank Moorehouse, his medical bag at his side, leaned attentively over Shaw.

"What's goin' on?" Firestick asked, stepping up beside Moosejaw.

The big deputy tilted his head toward the man in the chair. "Shaw got throwed by his horse. Seems to be banged up pretty bad. Frank is examinin' him to see just how bad."

"Where'd it happen?" Firestick said.

Before Moosejaw could respond, Shaw spoke from where he was sprawled back in the easy chair. "I'm perfectly capable of speaking for myself, Marshal. It wasn't my voice box that got damaged."

Firestick looked over at him. "Alright, mister. Go ahead then."

"The accident happened out by that tall rock formation to the east. A 'butte' or some such nonsensical term, I believe you call it? The one the town is allegedly named after." Shaw was referring to the towering rock upthrust called Buffalo Hump Butte that lay a few miles east of town and was, indeed, the feature from which the town took its revised name of Buffalo Peak. He went on, "At any rate, it was there that Oberon and I rode out to early this morning to do some target shooting. When we were ready to return, that stupid idiot of a horse I'd rented from the livery unexpectedly reared up and dislodged me from my saddle."

"Was he startled by a gunshot?"

"The shooting was all over by that point. The miserable beast acted up for no reason whatsoever! Had there been any cause or justification, I would have been prepared. I am, after all," declared Shaw, "an excellent horseman."

"Even the best rider can be caught off guard by a spooked animal," Firestick said.

"Be that as it may, that particular wretched beast should never have the opportunity to surprise another rider. He should be put down immediately!" Shaw's nostrils flared. "In fact, the first chance I get I am going to insist that the livery operator do so."

"Comes to that, Pete Roeback might not be real cooperative," Firestick warned. "He thinks mighty highly of his horses. I'm surprised he'd rent you one that had any skittishness in him."

Shaw pulled his head back indignantly. "Are you suggesting I was somehow at fault?"

"Never suggested nothing of the kind," Firestick said. "It's just that Roeback is one of the best horse gentlers and tamers around. Him and my man, Miguel. But by the same token, there are some horses who all of a sudden decide to show a contrary streak and surprise even the best."

"Well, whatever the cause," said Moorehouse, straightening up, "the result is that the fall appears to have left Mr. Shaw with either a fractured or severely sprained right forearm and wrist. Probably some badly bruised ribs, too, judging by the pain he exhibited when we lowered him into the chair. In any event, the best I can do is to bind his middle to ease any sharp breaths that will aggravate the ribs until they've had a chance to mend. Same for the arm and wrist — bind it and splint it, fashion a sling to limit movement until the damage heals. I can supply some pills, too, but a stiff shot of bourbon every now and then will provide the same effect."

"Aye. Now there's the kind of injury to have, eh, Captain? One that calls for a frequent nip of the spirits," said Hadley, clearly trying to lighten the mood of the moment.

Shaw made no response except to give him a baleful look.

"So there's no way of tellin' how bad the break to his arm is?" asked Firestick.

"I can't say for sure there even is a fracture," said Moorehouse. "There isn't much swelling, so I think it's safe to say it's not a severe one. But fracture or bad sprain, either one, is going to be pretty painful for a while."

"In the event you'd like some confirmation to your diagnosis, it hurts like bloody hell right at the moment," said Shaw.

"I have some material for wrapping and fashioning a sling over at my shop," Moorehouse said. "Unless Kate has some things here we could use."

Firestick looked around. "Where is Kate anyway?"

"We thought she was with you," said Victoria. "The last I saw her, she was going to bring you some sandwiches at the jail as I was leaving here with Marilu and her husband to attend the pancake breakfast."

"Yes, she did bring me sandwiches. But then she left to go join up with the rest of you. That was quite a while ago," Firestick said, not bothering to mention that Kate had been in a bit of a huff when she parted from him.

Moosejaw wagged his head. "I never did see her show up down where they were servin' breakfast."

"Where's Beartooth? Is she with him?"

"When we headed up here after Hadley came around to say Shaw was hurt," Moosejaw said, "I saw Beartooth go over toward the rodeo pens where Miguel and Jesus were. No surprise he didn't give much of a hang about Shaw's trouble. But anyway, Kate wasn't with him — nor over by Jesus or Miguel, neither."

Firestick frowned.

"She must have gone to the church to help with something there," Daisy suggested.

"Much as I appreciate your concern for

the lovely Miss Mallory," Shaw spoke up, "I think it's safe to presume she *will* make a reappearance. In the meantime, is it too much to ask that someone provide the, er, doctor with the materials he requires to finish administering to my injuries?"

"My shop isn't that far away," said Moorehouse. "I'll go get what I need, be back in a few minutes. Until then, keep that arm propped up and stay still."

As Moorehouse went out the door, Firestick looked at Moosejaw. "You know your way to Kate's bar," he said, referring to the hotel's small barroom that was adjacent to the lobby area. "You mind goin' and bringin' back a bottle of good bourbon? Grab some empty glasses, too, while you're at it. It might only be the middle of the morning, but I got a hunch there might be a couple of us" — here he shot a sidelong glance at Hadley — "willin' to join Shaw in a slug. Strictly in the spirit of medicinal purposes, of course."

Moosejaw went to do as requested. Daisy trailed after him.

As they were leaving, Shaw tipped his head back against the chair, closed his eyes, and expelled a long, ragged breath. Suddenly his eyes re-opened wide and his head lifted again. He cut his gaze back and forth between Firestick and Victoria. "Just in case anyone is wondering," he announced, "this in no way absolves that ruffian Beartooth from answering my challenge to a duel tomorrow."

"That's preposterous!" exclaimed Victoria. "Just as you acknowledged Beartooth was in no condition to fight with the far lesser injury of his re-opened shoulder wound, you certainly are in no shape to face him with a broken arm. He wouldn't agree to go against you with such a disadvantage anyway."

"He has no choice, unless he is the dishonorable coward I've suspected him of being all along," said Shaw. "You see, it will not be me in my current damaged condition he will be facing. It will be me in the form of my second — Oberon."

"Now wait a damn minute," growled Firestick. "This whole duel thing was your crazy idea to begin with. Now you're tryin' to say you expect it to go on without you even bein' part of it?"

"In a manner of speaking, yes, that is indeed what I am saying. Much to my personal disappointment, I must add," Shaw stated. "Nevertheless, once the challenge has been made and the date of the engagement set, it cannot be postponed or re-assigned indefinitely due either to whim or inconvenience to one of the principals. That is the whole purpose for naming seconds. You heard the diagnosis of what passes for a doctor in this godforsaken corner of creation you call a town. There is no way for him to say for certain how long my healing may take. And I certainly do not intend to linger here for an uncertain amount of time. Hence, the matter will be settled with Oberon acting in my stead, and afterward we will take our leave on the next available stagecoach."

Victoria swung her attention to Hadley. "And you are willing to go along with this? To put yourself in a position where you may kill — or be killed — over a matter you have absolutely no personal investment in?"

"But I do have a personal investment, ma'am," said Hadley, a curious mix of sadness and somberness gripping the battered mask that was his face. "I gave my word when I agreed to be the captain's second. There's no way I can fail to honor that."

"The only question, my dear," said Shaw, "is whether or not concepts like honor, commitment, and bravery mean anything to someone like this uncouth lout who's managed to addle you with foolish notions of romance."

"Mister," said Firestick, his voice turned

gravelly, "that's twice in just a handful of minutes you've used your highfalutin lingo to speak poorly of my friend. He ain't here to defend himself, but I am. You might want to keep that in mind. Because if you don't, you're apt to piss me off. Comes to that, you might also want to keep in mind that my way ain't to mess around with no fancy la-de-da rules or field of honor bullshit. I'll come at you sudden and full bore, and the only thing that sprained arm of yours will mean to me is something I might decide to rip off and beat in your smug face with."

Shaw's mouth dropped open and he turned a full shade paler than he already was. Behind him, Hadley's body went rigid and his eyes became cautious, measuring.

Before either of them could say or do anything more, the lobby door opened and Frank Moorehouse came back in. With him came Frenchy Fontaine and a dark-haired, nervous-looking young woman.

Chapter 32

"Firestick," said Moorehouse hurriedly, somewhat breathlessly. "I think you need to hear this right away."

Suddenly the tension in the room shifted to Moorehouse's tone and anxious expression.

"What is it?" Firestick wanted to know.

At that, Frenchy stepped forward. Motioning toward the young woman who'd entered with her, she said, "Marshal, this is Janice, one of the upstairs girls at the Palace. Janice, tell the marshal what you saw."

The girl seemed hesitant, finding it hard to get started at first. But once she did, the words started coming quicker and easier. "It was an hour or so ago. Maybe a little longer. I . . . I heard a noise outside my room, out in the hallway. I was only half-awake but I got up to see. When I looked out, there was nobody there. But I was awake by then and I needed to, uh, do some personal business. Only the chamber pot was full, so I took it down the back stairs and out to dump it. And that's when I saw them."

"Saw who?" Firestick prodded.

"The men riding away on horses. Two of them. They were leading a third horse loaded with bundles of stuff. Cleo was riding with one of the men and another woman was riding with the second man."

The muscles in Firestick's gut started to tighten. "Did you recognize the men? Or the other woman?"

Janice shook her head. "I don't remember ever seeing either of the men before. They were turned mostly away, riding off, so I didn't have a real good look. But nothing looked familiar about them. The other woman I was pretty sure I'd seen around town before. But us girls from the Palace don't get out too much so I wasn't positive. Not at first. But the more I thought about it, the more something felt kinda wrong with the whole thing."

"Do you think the women were bein' takin' against their will?"

"I can't say for sure. In both cases, the gals were sitting in front so the men had to have their arms kind of around them in order to work the reins. That could've meant they were holding them in place or, like I said, just steering the horses."

"Did the women appear to be strugglin' or fightin' back against the men?"

"Not from what I could tell. That's why I didn't say anything right away. If you know Cleo, well, she can be kind of wild spirited and independent sometimes." Janice paused, casting a sidelong glance at Frenchy and nibbling at her lower lip before bringing her eyes back to Firestick. "I thought at first she might be riding off somewhere to do a, you know, kind of a private session with those men. But I kept thinking about that other woman and how she didn't really fit. That's when I finally remembered where I'd seen her before and who she was. Or at least who I'd been told she was. The lady who runs and owns this here hotel."

The tightening in Firestick's stomach suddenly jerked into a knot, so quick and hard it was like a punch to the gut.

Victoria gasped audibly and Moosejaw uttered a curse, not quite under his breath.

"When Janice finally got worried enough to go to Frenchy with what she'd seen," Moorehouse said, "Frenchy immediately took her to the jail to find you. I ran into them when I was returning from my shop and brought them here."

Firestick heard the words, but they were blurred by the great rushing roar in his ears and the blood pounding in his veins. His beloved Kate! Abducted? He could think of no other reason that would explain her riding out of town in the company of two strange men without taking time to notify him. But why? Taken by who? And how did Cleo fit in? Had she also been abducted or was she part of some twisted plot?

Standing there, half-stunned, Firestick had no answers. He only knew he needed to set things in motion for the sake of finding some — and fast!

With so many folks on hand for the festival, Pastor Bart was holding his service on the lawn out back of the church proper. Practically everyone currently in town was in attendance.

The only people who weren't consisted mostly of the handful scrambling under the direction of Firestick. Moosejaw, Daisy, Victoria, and Moorehouse scattered to search and make sure there was no sign of Kate anywhere in town. Beartooth and Miguel were also alerted and joined the search. Young Jesus was dispatched to take care of a very particular matter for the marshal.

While the others were looking, Firestick

asked Frenchy and Janice to show him the area behind the Lone Star Palace where Janice had seen the horsemen and the women. He studied the tracks they'd left and committed to memory everything about them that might help him spot them again in the future.

"From the looks of these," he said to Janice, "they appear to have headed off to the south. Did you happen to watch them long enough to see if they continued that way after they got clear of the other buildings and houses?"

Janice shook her head. "No. I'm sorry, I didn't. I saw them, noticed the things I've told you, then went about my business emptying the chamber pot and went back upstairs." Frowning, the girl's eyes went from Firestick to Frenchy and then back again. "Am I in trouble for not saying something sooner?"

"Of course not," said Firestick. "I'm just glad you spoke up when you did."

"What do you think it means, Marshal? Where do you think those men are going with Cleo and Miss Kate?" asked Frenchy.

"Damned if I know," Firestick muttered. He stood gazing off to the south, his forehead puckered with concern, not saying anything for several seconds. "If they continue south, it ain't all that far before they'll be in Mexico."

"What does that gain them? What's in Mexico?"

"What it gains 'em — they might think — is that nobody from this side of the border will follow 'em across because no lawman or posse has legal jurisdiction down there."

Frenchy looked into his eyes and said, "But that won't stop you, will it?"

"Not one damn bit," Firestick grated.

The searchers began re-converging at that point. Their grim expressions, even before any words were spoken, gave Firestick all the answer he really needed. He'd held out little hope that Janice's identification of Kate was a mistake, but it had been necessary to get confirmation all the same.

"Kate is nowhere to be found. Not anywhere in town," Beartooth summed up. He and Victoria had returned together and they stood side-by-side now. It crossed Firestick's mind that there was nothing like tragedy or a sudden twist of trouble to make people get past the petty differences in their lives.

"Nobody's seen her since she went to take you those sandwiches," Moosejaw added glumly.

"Somebody saw her," Firestick said

through clenched teeth. "Walkin' alone after she left the jail — and that's when they took her."

"So what do you make of it? Kidnapping?" Frank Moorehouse asked.

"That'd only make sense if whoever took those gals was lookin' to gain money with a ransom demand." Firestick wagged his head, the movement barely perceptible. "Kate's hotel is worth some money, but the only one able to free it up for any kind of payoff is Kate herself. If that's what those two varmints were after, seems to me they would have just stuck a gun in her face and robbed her. And expectin' ransom for the girl Cleo . . . well, that's even a worse fit."

"Hate to speak poorly of somebody who ain't here to defend herself," said Moosejaw, "but you think there's any chance Cleo might be part of it? Might be in cahoots somehow with the two riders?"

Frenchy and Janice gave him angry looks, but the towering deputy ignored them, keeping his eyes on Firestick.

"If she was, which I find doubtful," said the marshal, "it would go right back to what would be the point? You got to figure the whole thing is for some kind of gain. If Cleo was part of it, then that would seem to narrow it down to money — and that leads to what I said before about the best one in a position to pay money for Kate is Kate herself."

"So if Cleo ain't part of it," said Beartooth, "what else does that leave?"

Firestick motioned toward the tracks on the ground of the lane they were standing on the edge of. Then he raised his arm, pointing southward. "Sign leads off that way. To the south. Means they're likely headed for Mexico. It could be they're figurin' on stayin' down there or it could be they're makin' a run that way for only a little while, to throw us off because they reckon we won't chase 'em across the border."

Moosejaw's eyes took on a flintiness. "If they reckon that, my reckonin' is that they're plumb wrong."

Firestick nodded. "Goes without sayin'. But here's the thing. Gettin' back to the reason for takin' those gals, I see it as boilin' down to one of two purposes. Either those two riders took 'em for themselves . . . or they took 'em to sell somewhere down in Mexico."

Victoria gasped and clutched Beartooth's arm. Frenchy winced. Janice's hardened features simply stayed blank.

"You don't have to go very far down that way to find *banditos* or slavers who'll pay a pretty penny for white women," Firestick went on. "If I was a bettin' man, unpleasant as it is to think on, that's how I'd lay my money."

"Bastards!" hissed Daisy, pressing close against Moosejaw.

"So why are we standin' here jawin' about it? Let's saddle up and get the hell after 'em," exclaimed Beartooth.

Firestick raised a hand, palm out. "Hold on. You gotta know I want to do that worse than anybody. But they've already got a two- or three-hour head start. Another hour or so ain't gonna make that much difference. What's more important is to take some time to make the smartest plan and best preparations. *Then* we go after 'em!"

"What plans and preparations? What have you got in mind?"

Firestick raked his eyes over everyone gathered around him. They came to rest on Frenchy and Janice. "Can't tell you gals how obliged I am for comin' forward like you done. If Janice hadn't seen what she did and been willin' to speak up about it, this whole thing would be even more puzzlin' than it is. But you can take your leave now and go on about your own affairs. The rest of us will be headin' over to the jail and hashin' out the best way to proceed from here. Oh, and Miss Frenchy? You can gather up Arthur and come fetch Sterling as soon as you're ready. Forget about the fine. We'll call it even."

Chapter 33

Josh and Charlie set a steady, moderately brisk pace for their ride away from Buffalo Peak. With the packhorse heavily laden and their mounts carrying double, even though the women were relatively light, they didn't want to risk wearing out their horses this early on the first day. The sun was already at its peak, blazing white hot in a cloudless sky, meaning the next few hours would grow hotter still.

Charlie figured they'd covered fifteen miles, maybe closer to twenty, when he spotted a stand of scraggly trees along the base of a low, rocky ridge just ahead. He reckoned this looked like a good spot to take a break and signaled to Josh. They slowed their horses and turned them in where the trees threw patches of dappled shade. Each man swung down from his saddle and then reached up to ease down the woman who'd been riding with him.

Both women had their hands tied in front of them with rough twine and were gagged by bandannas jerked tight across their mouths and knotted behind their heads. When Kate's feet touched the ground, she staggered and weaved a little. Charlie quickly grabbed her by the shoulders and steadied her. As soon as Cleo touched down, on the other hand, she seemed quite steady — enough so that she immediately hauled off and kicked Josh in the shins and then followed up with an attempt to drive her knee into his groin.

Josh's high-topped leather boot absorbed most of the impact from the kick. And he'd been in enough barroom brawls to have learned how to turn his hip against an attempted groin shot. So the most devastating effect of Cleo's aggression was that she was jarred off balance and ended up falling onto her rump.

Josh lunged forward and leaned over her, clucking with concern. "You got to take it easy or you'll hurt yourself," he cautioned. "Are you okay?"

Cleo's eyes blazed up at him and her throat strained as she loosed what would have been a tirade of angry words if the gag in her mouth hadn't made them unintelligible.

Looking on, still with his hands on Kate's shoulders, Charlie chuckled. "It's a good thing she's gagged, Josh, elsewise I think you would have just got another workin' over from her sassy mouth."

"Well, what do you expect?" said Josh, scowling. "We ain't took no chance to talk to 'em yet, to explain what this is all about. They're probably scared half to death, thinkin' the worst. You would be, too, in their position right about now. My Miss Cleo just showed she's got spirit and is a fighter, that's all. Ain't a doggone thing wrong with that."

"Then there ain't no time like the present to start pitchin' our case," replied Charlie. "We can tell 'em what's goin' on while the horses are coolin' down before we water 'em. This'll be our chance to water the gals, too, and start showin' we mean 'em no harm, only comfort and good things. I got to warn everybody right now, though, that if that spitfire of yours — or mine, either, for that matter — takes a notion to try a kick at my stones, I'll flatten her and it won't be because she fell off balance that she hits the ground. I don't cotton to beatin' women in general, but something like that is crossin' the line to where a clobberin' would be called for."

"That's fair enough, I reckon," allowed Josh. "But just steer clear of my spitfire and you won't have no worry. Won't be long, though — once these gals understand what we're about — where there won't be no need for that kind of stuff to enter into it at all."

Charlie nodded. "And if we're gonna get to that part, we might as well start in. Like I said, I'm sure they'd welcome a drink and maybe some grub. So, since we're well out of range for raisin' a holler to do 'em any good, we can go ahead and get rid of their gags." As he said this, Charlie began untying Kate's bandanna. Glancing over at Josh, he grinned crookedly and added, "Though I'll wager that one of yours is gonna spit out a good, loud earful all the same."

A moment later, as soon as the stifling cloth was removed from her mouth, Cleo made Charlie's prediction come true by unleashing a string of angry curses and threats.

"You lowdown, grubby-pawed bastards! I don't know what the hell you think you're doing, but I'll see your balls cut off and stuffed in my pocket before this is over!"

"Whooee! Such language!" Charlie exclaimed. "Can't you at least try to tame it down some on account of there bein' a lady present?" He tugged the gag out of Kate's mouth and then turned her around to face him. Smiling, he said to her, "You *are* a lady, ain't you, darlin'? I could tell right off, from just one look."

Kate's gaze met his, her eyes and expression icy. "My mama taught me that a lady is as a lady does," she said with the same chill in her voice. "But if she knew what I was thinking right about now, I doubt she would find it very ladylike even by that broad interpretation."

Charlie's smile stayed in place. "Sounds to me like that was just a classier way of sayin' you agree with Little Miss Foulmouth."

Kate gave no reply, just continued to regard him with her icy stare.

"Well, under the circumstances," Charlie said with a sigh, "I reckon I can't blame you too much. But you'll come around. It's just a matter of time before both of you gals — providin' you got good sense — will get it through your heads that me and Josh mean you no harm, only good. Good for you and good for us, too."

"It'll be a cold day in hell before I look at the likes of either of you and see anything good!" sneered Cleo.

"Aw, come on now. Don't be like that.

Some things you just need to give a chance," said Josh. He lifted the canteen from his saddle and held it out to her. "Here. You got to be thirsty after that hard ride. Take yourself a long, cool drink and try to calm down some."

Cleo glared first at him and then at the canteen. For a minute it looked like she was going to refuse the drink, maybe even knock the canteen away. But then the fact she *was* hot and thirsty won out. She took the canteen in her two still-bound hands and lifted it to her lips.

Charlie produced his own canteen and held it out to Kate, saying, "Even your hot-tempered friend sees the sense in cooperatin' at least a little. Here. Have your own self a drink."

After the women had slaked their thirst, Charlie and Josh took their own turns with the canteens. Then they instructed Kate and Cleo to go sit down in a grassy spot by the trunk of one of the trees while they tended to the horses — watering them out of their hats before hobbling them where they could munch at some of the sparse grass that was available.

Turning back to where the women sat, Josh said, "You gals want anything to eat? We got jerky, some biscuits, airtights of peaches and different things."

"This will be a short stop and we won't be makin' another until we halt for night camp across the border. So if you want anything in your bellies besides some more drinks of water between now and then," Charlie advised, "you'd better speak up."

"What we want," said Cleo, "is to know what this is all about."

"Where are you taking us — and why?" added Kate.

Following an exchange of glances between him and Josh, Charlie ambled over and squatted near the women. Josh came and stood beside him.

"Okay. The long and the short of it," said Charlie, "is this: We've taken you gals to be our brides."

Kate and Cleo couldn't have looked more dumbfounded if he'd sprouted a bushy tail and yipped like a coyote.

"Now we know this ain't the way such things are generally done," Charlie went on. "But me and Josh also know we ain't very polished on, whatyacall, social graces. And we ain't spring chickens no more, and we don't fool ourselves that we're overly handsome. So it shouldn't be hard to see that the chance for meetin' and courtin' gals to become our wives in the regular way has, well, sorta passed us by. But we ain't ready to just leave it at that. We're hard workers, basically honest, and we could be good providers for a wife and family. That's what we want to show you — that we can be decent, dedicated, good husbands. Once we win you over, why, we figure nature will then just take its course."

"That's the most insane thing I've ever heard," said Kate in a strained, partially hushed whisper.

Josh shook his head. "No, not rightly so. That's the way it was done long, long ago. A fella would pick his mate, show her he meant business and could take care of her, and that was that. All the fol-der-al about courtin' and goin' to dances and meetin' the family and the rest of that kind of stuff came along later on. Me and Charlie are meanin' to go back to the old ways, skip over all the clutter, and get right to what matters."

"And that don't mean we're right away lookin' to violate you or some such, neither," Charlie was quick to add. "Like I said, that's where we're willin' to let nature take its course. Once you see how we treat you and provide for you, you'll come around in time."

"You fools," said Cleo. "Don't you know

what kind of girl I am? You can have your way with me — play house with me, if that's what you want to call it — any night of the week and twice on Saturday for just a handful of dollar bills. You don't have to hogtie me and drag me out into the desert just to —"

"Stop that!" Josh cut her off. "That life is over for you. I don't want to hear you speak of it no more. When you become my wife, you're gonna be startin' from scratch. Startin' decent. Nothing that came before is gonna matter."

Cleo regarded him and for a moment, her sassy boldness slipping. It left her looking bewildered and a little frightened. "You *are* insane."

"Do insane people plan as careful and thorough as we have?" said Charlie, scowling. He swung his arm, motioning toward the horses. "See that pack animal over there? See all those bundles piled on his back? Those are supplies. There are things in those bundles — utensils, clothes, foofaraws — that any wife in the territory would give her eye teeth to have at her disposal. The place where we're takin' you, you'll get to wear those things and use those things, and you'll start to get the idea that bein' the wives of Charlie Gannon and Josh Stallworth ain't such a bad notion at all."

"Where is it you're taking us?" Kate asked.

Charlie smiled smugly. "After we make a little dodge down into Mexico for the sake of throwin' off any busybodies who might come after us, we'll angle back up to the northwest and re-cross into good ol' Texas again. Me and Josh got in mind a spot we passed through once durin' our driftin' days. Little place where they struck silver a few years back. But then the vein ran out and the town that sprung up and thrived for a while emptied out. Just some old buildings left now. But there's a few sturdy ones amongst 'em. Places just right for turnin' into temporary homes where we can take the time to get to know one another with nobody else around to bother us."

"Place has a right pretty name, too," said Josh. He smiled at Cleo. "Real promisin' name for us to start a bright, promisin' future together. It's called Bright Rock."

CHAPTER 34

"Bright Rock," Keefer Fleming muttered sourly. He lifted the bottle of tequila he held loosely in one hand and took a long, gurgling slug. Lowering it, he passed the back of his free hand across his mouth. His squinted eyes made another hundred-eighty-degree scan of his surroundings, and the expression on his face conveyed the same sourness as his tone. "Bright Rock," he repeated. "Boy, whoever came up with that name sure as hell saw things different than the way they look to me. What I'm seein' now is about as bright as a sun-baked old buffalo chip layin' out on the prairie somewhere."

To one side of Fleming, leaning against a porch post of the building that at one time had been a hotel, Vic Mason let his own gaze drift down the length of the sand-filled, tumbleweed-strewn street lined on either side by dusty, sagging, empty structures.

"Yeah, the old place is definitely lacking signs of life or luster these days," he agreed. "But if it was anything like most boom towns at their peak, I bet it was something to see back when."

"Maybe," Fleming grunted. "But it'd take a helluva strong imagination to picture it any different now."

Fleming was a tall, rangy thirty-year-old with bushy, wheat-colored sideburns, blunt nose, and a somewhat weak chin. His eyes were a shade too close together beneath brows so pale and sparse they were almost invisible, making the eyes stand out in an oddly stark way. He carried himself with an insolent slouch matched by a mouth whose lower lip seemed perpetually curled with an insolence of its own.

In contrast, Mason was a rigidly erect individual, broad shouldered and solidly built though a dozen or more years older than Fleming. He was an even six feet tall, but his bearing and strong physique made him seem larger. He had curly black hair, a hooked beak for a nose, and seen-it-all-before dark eyes that often carried a bemused glint but could turn in an instant to flash with dangerous fury.

Both men wore fully packed shell belts around their waists and shiny revolvers on their hips, riding low and loose in well-oiled holsters.

"Well, however you choose to look at it," Mason declared as his gaze made another sweep down the empty, abandoned street, "you might as well learn to like the view. Because it's all we're gonna be seein' for the next two or three days."

"There's a dismal thought," groaned Fleming. "You really figure it'll be that long before those gun-hungry greasers show up?"

"Most likely," said Mason. "We made considerably better time than I expected for gettin' here — even with Hawkins packin' a bullet in him. That puts us a couple days ahead of schedule. On top of that, there was always a window of a couple days for Estarde to meet us here. Him fightin' his revolution and all, he don't exactly run on a precise schedule."

"Long as he don't lag too far behind in his schedule and the damn revolution gets over without him."

"That would be unfortunate." Mason shrugged. "But if it came to that, really only a minor inconvenience. The way they brew up fresh revolutions down in Mexico, it's only a few weeks between 'em. That means cases of guns are always in demand. For the uprising that's currently takin' place, or the next one due around the corner."

Fleming grunted again. "Talk about your cockeyed optimism."

"Maybe optimism. Maybe just realism." Mason pushed away from the porch post and stood up straight. "Either way, it's better than standing around pissin' and moanin' about it, the way you seem to favor. What's so bad if we got to cool our heels here for a couple, three days? We're finally shed of the army patrol that was blisterin' our heels up in Arizona, we've got shelter and shade here, and we've got plenty of supplies to see us through. The hard part is done. Sittin' and bidin' our time for a bit don't seem like such a hardship for the money we'll be wrappin' our hands around when we fork over those firearms."

"Okay, okay," said Fleming, making a placating gesture. "No need to get so hot under the collar, Vic."

Any further exchange between the two was interrupted by the hollow clump of boot heels coming from inside the empty building at their backs. A moment later, a third man emerged from the old hotel. He was a stocky specimen somewhere between the ages of Fleming and Mason. He possessed sad eyes set deep in a weather-beaten face, and a wide mouth with thick lips. At the moment he wore neither a gunbelt nor a jacket or vest. He was carrying his hat in his hands. His face was beaded with sweat, more was dripping from his uncombed mass of hair, and his shirt was soaked.

Both Mason and Fleming turned to face him.

Fleming said, "Jesus Christ, Lefty, you look like you been put through the wringer."

"You think it's hot out here, try it inside. It's like an oven, not even a breath of air moving," replied Lefty Gramlich, the sweat-drenched man.

"How's Hawkins holdin' up?" Mason wanted to know. "You able to get him halfway comfortable?"

Lefty's face clenched with anguish. "A little comfortable, I guess. For the time being. But . . . he's getting worse, Vic. He's a tough old buzzard, I don't have to tell you that. The long ride down from Arizona was awful rough on him with that bullet in his leg. I thought we was keeping the wound dressed and cleaned pretty good. But when I changed his bandage just now, I saw it. Gangrene's setting in."

"Are you sure?"

"Gangrene rot has a stink you don't ever forget once you've experienced it," said Lefty woodenly. He'd been a medical aide during the war and had seen many horrors attached to the carnage and wounds of battle.

"Now that we're settled in one spot," said Fleming, "what about getting that bullet dug out?"

Lefty shook his head. "I ain't good enough. That's the main reason I never tried on the trail. It's too deep, smashed and splintered into fragments on his big thigh bone. Something like that would require the hand of a skilled surgeon under better conditions. Besides, even if the fragments were dug out now, it's too late to stop the infection."

"And there's no chance he can survive the infection?" Mason's words were half statement, half question.

"None," Lefty responded bluntly.

Mason gave it several seconds, then said, "What about takin' the leg? What chance would that give him?"

Lefty averted his gaze and dug the toe of his boot into the warped, weathered boards of the porch deck. When he lifted his eyes again, he said, "Not much better. Under these conditions, maybe ten or fifteen percent more than doing nothing."

"Jesus," said Fleming, licking his lips. "How much suffering will the poor devil do? We're packing plenty of tequila and whiskey. Enough to keep his pain pretty well dulled, right?"

"In the beginning," Lefty allowed. "Toward the end . . . there ain't enough whiskey in Texas."

Mason had been silently staring off at nothing in particular ever since getting his answer on Hawkins's chance for survival. Continuing to stare off, he said now, "I've rode with Clem Hawkins for a lot of years. During the war and since. Longer than any of the rest of you boys been with us. Never once knowed him to play me false or let me down. Leastways not until he took that bullet up in Arizona." He turned slowly to face the other two. "For all those reasons and more, I can't let my old friend check out the way you just described, Lefty. Do you understand what I'm sayin'?"

Both Lefty and Fleming averted their eyes, unable to meet his stony gaze.

"Where's young Beaudine?" Mason asked.

"Down at the far end of town, keeping watch like you sent him to do," answered Fleming.

Mason's gaze cut in that direction for a moment, then came back. "Clem sorta took Beaudine under his wing when the kid first joined up with us. Beaudine has looked real fondly on Clem ever since."

"Like an uncle, almost a second father," Lefty agreed.

"I think the kid would have trouble understandin' the thing I figure needs doin'. Be hard enough on him to come back and find out Clem passed sudden-like in his sleep. But he could handle that much, eventually. He don't need to ever know more."

The silence from Lefty and Fleming amounted to mute agreement.

Abruptly, Fleming said, "Maybe you'd better let me take care of it, Vic. You don't have to —"

"No," Mason cut him off. "He's my old runnin' pard. It should fall to me." He extended his hand toward Lefty. "Lend me your knife. Won't do for the kid to hear a gunshot. Stay out here and make sure he don't come back unexpected-like."

Lefty silently took the knife from his belt sheath and handed it over. Mason took it and started into the hotel. Half a step through the doorway, he paused and looked back over his shoulder. "I appreciate your offer from a minute ago, Fleming, I want you to know that. But you'd better also know that when I come back out and for as long as we have to wait here, I don't want to listen to no more bellyachin' from you about how rough you think you got it."

CHAPTER 35

By the time Jesus Marquez got back to Buffalo Peak and rejoined those gathered at the jail, a plan for going after the women and their abductors had been decided on. It wasn't a plan everybody was happy with, but Firestick was adamant about holding to it and there was no budging him.

What it boiled down to was that only the marshal and Moosejaw would give chase. Two men could travel faster and be less detectable than a whole posse when they got ready to close in on their quarry, Firestick explained. He included himself in the pair of pursuers for obvious reasons, Kate being one of the abductees, and he chose Moosejaw to accompany him because the towering deputy was the best tracker in the territory, superior even to his former mountain men buddies.

Beartooth would stay behind to uphold the law in Buffalo Peak. Also, though it wasn't spoken out loud, there was a matter of the personal issues he had hanging fire.

A handful of quick, quiet inquiries, done as discreetly as possible to avoid disrupting the festival, provided possible identities for the abductors as two recently arrived drifters going by the names of Josh and Charlie. Hans Greeble reported selling them a large stock of supplies from his general store, and Pete Roeback confirmed that they'd bought a packhorse from him to haul said supplies.

This didn't prove anything solid, but if it *was* the same two men who'd ridden off with Kate and Cleo — which seemed more likely than not — then it implied two things that gave Firestick a small measure of relief: One, they were provisioned well enough so that the women wouldn't be deprived of food or basic needs; and two, since the provisions were so plentiful, it seemed to indicate the abductors might be planning to keep the women with them for a time rather than being in a hurry to sell them off.

Armed with this information and their basic plan, Firestick and Moosejaw needed only to provision themselves before riding out. This was promptly seen to with aid once again from Greeble and Roeback. The latter furnished two sturdy horses for each man . . . Greeble gathered up a couple sacks of trail supplies for them to take along.

The final item was the thing Jesus had ridden back to the ranch to fetch especially for Firestick — his finely crafted Hawken rifle. The gun he had carried for so many years up in the mountains and the very weapon — accurate at legendary distances and delivering a .50-caliber slug with deadly force — that had figured prominently in him coming to be called "Firestick." With luck and the right circumstances, a chance might present itself for Firestick to drop one of the men from far enough away so that he'd go down before he ever heard the shot that killed him. And then the second man would quickly follow.

At any rate, just having the Hawken along, lashed securely behind his saddle and primed to deliver hellfire retribution, made Firestick feel better.

Once Firestick and Moosejaw had ridden away, Jesus and Miguel left to go check on their horses and make final preparations for the rodeo. Seeing how forlorn Daisy looked following the departure of her man, Frank Moorehouse tried to help ease her mind by coaxing her to accompany him to the picnic, which was under way by then. And since Frenchy and Arthur had shown up to take

Earl Sterling off Sam's hands, they invited him to join them.

This left Beartooth and Victoria alone together for the first time since their rift over the pending duel had resulted in them barely speaking to one another except for the time they'd spent looking for Kate.

Refusing to revert to that kind of behavior, especially under the circumstances, Beartooth turned to Victoria as soon as the door closed behind Daisy and the others. He walked over to stand before her and took her hands in his.

"With all the trouble and uncertainty swirlin' around," he said, "this seems like a mighty poor time for us to sulk and steer clear of each other over a damn fool like Shaw. If we let something like that change the way we feel, then those feelin's must not be very strong after all."

"But they are!" Victoria insisted, her words coming in a rush. "It's my feelings for you that made me so upset and angry at the thought of you being forced into that insane duel. Not angry *at* you — but desperate with fear over the thought of you getting hurt or killed."

Beartooth's mouth twisted disdainfully. "The day I can't shade a struttin' peacock like Rupert Shaw —"

"But anything can happen when two men aim and fire pistols at each other," said Victoria, cutting him short. "And you musn't take Rupert so lightly. He was, after all, a captain in the Queen's Army and is widely regarded a crack shot. What's more, I remember hearing stories when I was a girl growing up back in England about how duels could sometimes turn out in very unexpected ways."

"This ain't England," Beartooth reminded her.

Suddenly recalling the conversation she and Firestick had had with Shaw following his accident and realizing Beartooth hadn't yet heard about what happened, Victoria said, "Besides, there's been a change. It's no longer Rupert you'll be facing on the so-called field of honor. It's now scheduled to be Oberon Hadley."

"What are you talkin' about?" Beartooth scowled. "I can't say I've ever liked the looks of that big ox. But my beef is with Shaw, not him."

Victoria quickly explained to him about Shaw's injury from the horse fall and how, fulfilling his role as a second, Hadley was prepared to take Shaw's place in the scheduled duel.

"That's the craziest thing I ever heard of!"

Beartooth exploded. "Two men declare they're mad enough to fight each other but then, at the last minute, one of 'em skips aside and motions for some other fella to step in to do his fightin' for him? We got a name for that kind of thing where I come from, and it's chickensh—"

"Rupert can't very well handle a gun with his arm broken. You understand that, don't you? And knowing you, you'd take no satisfaction in beating a man who's crippled."

"So we wait until he's healed. Ain't like I'm in a particular hurry to kill him. I'm only in this at all because Shaw called me out. That don't mean I'm willin' to take the life of some other poor fool and let Shaw dance away safe and clear."

Victoria's brows pinched together anxiously. "But what if there was a way to see this through without anyone getting hurt or killed?"

"Me just walk away from it, you mean? Come on, Victoria, you can't ask me to do that. It just ain't in me to —"

Once again Victoria cut him short, saying, "No. There is a way that's perfectly within the practices and rules of dueling and considered acceptably honorable by most." She gave a little shake of her head. "It

334

surprises me how much I remember about dueling lore. It was a passion that my uncle Edward loved talking about — not that he ever participated, mind you — and for a time I was enthralled by his tales. It's all been rushing back through my mind, last night and this morning, ever since Rupert forced all of us to consider the wretched practice.

"At any rate, there is a term called 'deloping.' I remember giggling when I first heard it because I thought it sounded like a couple getting halfway through an elopement but then stopping and turning back and not going through with it after all. In the dueling world, of course, it's nothing like that. Although I guess you could say it's a means of calling something off — the bloodshed that might otherwise result."

Beartooth gently squeezed her hands, which he was still holding. "If there's a point to this, gal, I sorta wish you'd get to it. So far you're not makin' a whole lotta sense."

"What deloping amounts to," Victoria said, "is an act whereby both principals in a duel purposely shoot to miss their opponent. The mere exchange of gunfire is seen as a satisfactory response to the challenge originally issued, and the two principals may then walk away considering the matter resolved."

Beartooth was speechless. Victoria gazed up at him, waiting for a response. Finally he gave her one. "With all due respect, darlin', to your country and your uncle Edward and anybody who ever bravely stood and faced a bullet in a true duel . . . this delopin' thing is an even more idiotic notion than somebody like Hadley steppin' in as a second. Hell, why don't the two fellas involved just face each other and holler 'Bang! Bang!'? It'd make about as much sense."

"I'm not making a case for the sense in it," Victoria told him. "The whole concept of dueling falls pretty short in that regard. I'm merely offering an acceptable way to handle Rupert's stupid challenge without you or Hadley, either one, risking your lives over it. If Rupert himself were still involved, I wouldn't even bother bringing this up. I doubt he'd ever consider it an option in the first place, and even if he did, I would not trust him to shoot clear."

Beartooth let go of her hands and turned away. He rocked his head back and groaned. "How do I get myself into fixes like this?"

Victoria looked on quietly, feeling his frustration, not knowing what to say next.

Abruptly, Beartooth turned back to her. "But listen to me feel sorry for myself. Miss

Kate and that other gal are ones with real problems — in the hands of those two varmints who made off with 'em for who knows what reason. And my two best friends are ridin' straight into the teeth of possible danger to try and get 'em back. What I've got on my plate here don't hold a candle to that."

"But it's still nothing to take lightly," Victoria said. "And having concern over it hardly amounts to feeling sorry for yourself."

Beartooth moved close to her again. "Maybe not. But it's concern for another day — tomorrow. What I got to take care of today, what Firestick left me in charge to do, is look after this town. Word is bound to start spreadin', if it ain't on everybody's tongues already, about those stolen women. I got to keep a lid on that, not let panic set in, try to keep the festival from fallin' apart or let a bunch of rambunctious fools decide to form a vigilante group and join in on the chase. *That's* where my attention has to be for right now." He put his hands on her shoulders. "All I need to know is that you'll be behind me in whatever I do."

Victoria slipped her arms around his waist. "No. I won't be behind you. I'll be right at your side."

CHAPTER 36

The storm rolled in out of the southwest. It came fast, as the day wore into late afternoon. Thickening black clouds rapidly swallowed the clear sky and blazing sun.

Firestick and Moosejaw had found the spot where their quarry had stopped to rest in the shade of some scraggly trees running along the base of a low, rocky ridge. Footprints of two women mingled in with those of two men confirmed they were following the right trail. Signs that the women had been allowed to walk around and even sit in the shade for a time seemed to indicate they weren't being treated too shabbily, at least so far.

The pursuers took the opportunity to switch their saddles to fresher mounts and pause for a short break themselves, cooling and watering the horses and giving them a breather. The storm clouds were visible along the southwestern horizon by then, climbing higher and darker.

"Damn, I don't like the looks of that," Firestick muttered, eyeing the threatening line of darkness as he lowered his canteen.

"Me neither," said Moosejaw, gazing in the same direction. "The trail so far has been easy to follow. I figure we've closed the gap between us by an hour or more. If that storm delivers a hard rain, though, it'll mess up their tracks and change things in a hurry."

"Damn," Firestick said again. "And not a chance in hell to catch up with 'em before it hits, is there?"

"I don't see how. We'd have to ride these horses half to death, and even then . . ." Moosejaw let his words trail off.

Firestick's mouth pulled into a tight, straight line. "All the same, we gotta keep pushin' on. Maybe that storm will blow itself out before it reaches us."

It wasn't to be. Not even close. When the storm hit, it slammed with full fury. The churning, wind-whipped clouds were ripped open by pitchforks of brilliant lightning that released bursts of ground-shaking thunder. Rain slanted down hard and cold and drenching. Except for the blinding lightning, the erasure of the sun by gray-black clouds turned the fading brightness of afternoon into the gloom of dusk.

Firestick and Moosejaw had time to shrug into their rain slickers as they saw the gray wall of water bearing down on them. Otherwise they were caught out in the open and had no choice but to bend their heads against it and keep urging their horses forward. At length, they came to a shallow gully with sloped walls and a sudden bend where a ragged, north-facing cliff had long ago broken away in such a manner that it created a concave, cigar-shaped area into which they were able to tuck themselves and their horses. It wasn't ideal, but it blunted most of the direct rain and was high enough up on the slope that they'd be above any sudden rush of water in case a flash flood came swirling down the gully. The men squatted there on their haunches, cocooned inside their slickers, while the horses stood with lowered heads, bunched resolutely together as deep as they could get in the scooped-out area.

By the time the fiercest part of the storm began to subside, the sun had long since set and full night was upon them. Almost as quickly as the storm had built, once it passed the clouds began to break apart and here and there faint glimmers of starlight could be seen peeking through.

The former mountain men mounted up and once again went on the move, looking for a better spot than the muddy gully to make night camp. It took nearly an hour before they came to a small stand of trees. These were thick enough that the ground directly at their base yielded enough dry twigs to fuel a fire. In short order, the men had some coffee cooking and the horses, after each receiving a handful of grain, were hobbled with access to a few patches of graze.

"So far," said Moosejaw, the flicker of the campfire flames dancing on his broad face as he got ready to raise a cup of freshly brewed coffee to his mouth, "they've been traveling in a fairly straight line. Always due south. In the morning we'll reach the Rio Grande, which I expect they already made it across before they got caught by the storm. Finding their trail again is gonna be a mite tricky."

Firestick didn't respond right away, thoughtfully chewing a bite of beef jerky that he'd softened with a swallow from his own coffee cup. "How far you figure they were ahead of us when the storm caught 'em?"

After taking some time of his own before answering, Moosejaw said, "I'd say between an hour and a half and two hours."

"Okay then," Firestick said slowly, his gaze focused on the fire but seeing something far beyond the flames. "If we calculate how fast they were travelin' up to the time the storm hit 'em, and reckon that backward to where the storm hit us . . . we ought to be able to come up with a reasonable idea of how far they got before they had to stop. That make sense?"

"As a rough guess, yeah," Moosejaw allowed. "Keep in mind where the storm hit 'em and where they stopped might be two different places. We had to forge on for a fair distance after we got caught in it, remember?"

"But we kept pushin' hard even though we saw the storm comin'," Firestick pointed out. "Since we've seen indications those two skunks are treatin' the women fairly decent as they go along, I got a hunch they might have took shelter *ahead* of the rain."

Moosejaw shrugged. "Okay. You could go with that. But you'd still have to call it some rough calculatin' because there'd be no way of knowin' *how far* ahead of the storm they might have stopped."

"I'm still willin' to go with it, even as a rough calculation," Firestick said. "Here's what I'm gettin' at. When we start out again in the mornin', there ain't much sense tryin' to pick up their trail right away because we know it's gonna be washed out by the storm. So I say we head due south once more, ridin' hard, gamblin' they didn't suddenly veer off a different way. No sense wastin' time tryin' to cut sign, not at first, until we've gone as far as we calculate they made it before they ran into the storm. *There* is where we fan out and start lookin' to cut fresh sign — either where they camped or after they started out again. The ground will be soft after the rain and from that point their tracks oughta stand out even plainer."

"Once we find 'em, yeah."

"That's why we look sharpest for a likely shelter spot. You've seen how few of those there are on this flat ol' prairie. If our calculatin' takes us close to as far as they got, there ain't gonna be that many decent spots to choose from. The right one will tell us where they camped the night."

Some of Moosejaw's skepticism appeared to lift. "Goin' about it that way would give us our quickest chance to pick up their trail again," he conceded.

"Damn betcha," Firestick declared.

CHAPTER 37

On the other side of the border, the land had quickly turned more rugged, with barren, choppy ridges cut by twisting arroyos and tall upthrusts of ragged, sun-blasted rock. It was a harsh land, but one thing it offered was a number of cave-like cuts into the jagged, sawtooth-topped upthrusts, which held the promise of shelter from the storm boiling in out of the southwest.

Josh and Charlie weighed the approaching storm against these ragged openings and knew they had to make a quick choice of one suited for protecting the women, horses, and themselves. Hard, chilly gusts of wind thrown ahead of the storm were already stinging their faces with bits of sand and gravel by the time they spotted a cavernous half-dome that appeared a good fit for their needs. In short order they were huddled within, and when the lashing rain came it never touched them.

"This is a prime example of what you can count on from me and Josh when it comes to protectin' and providin' for you," said Charlie, addressing Kate and Cleo as he held out cups of steaming coffee to them. "No matter the situation that might come along, we've got the savvy to make the best of it."

Even though they glared while doing it, the women took the coffee, its warmth welcome against the chilly gusts the storm brought. The women still had their wrists tied in front and in addition each had a leg iron clamped around one ankle and then attached to a spike driven securely into the rocky ground. The chain gave them a movement range of three or four feet, and the shackles were cushioned against their skin by wraps of soft leather. Each had a thick, dry blanket draped over her shoulders.

From where he was forking strips of bacon into a sizzling skillet resting on the coals of a campfire, Josh looked over his shoulder and said, "We even thought to pack a bundle of kindling and sticks to feed a fire in case we got caught unexpected this way. Like Charlie said, we're men of savvy and experience who've learned to take care of ourselves and will always be sure to do the same for our wives."

"I guess you didn't take the time to notice," said Cleo through clenched teeth, "but both of us happened to be doing pretty good jobs of taking care of our own selves before you came along to drag us to hell and gone out here in the middle of nowhere. And it surely didn't include being chained up in a sandy, gritty ol' cave with a thunderstorm ripping all around us."

Josh smiled tolerantly and said, "But it also didn't include a husband to share the burden of tough times and then the good ones to follow and the workin' together to see 'em keep gettin' better."

"Don't you remember who you're talking to?" sneered Cleo. "I had me a husband every night of the week. Hell, I had several of 'em most nights. I had 'em lined up outside my door, waitin' their turn to —"

"Stop it!" Josh shouted. "I told you I don't want to hear that kind of talk. You're better than that, and that life's behind you now. You don't have to think about it no more, and you never need to speak of it. You'll see. You'll become my wife and never have to worry about bein' a . . . a . . ."

"Whore!" Cleo hurled the word. "That's what I was and there ain't no two ways about it. Whore! My own mother said that's what I was and all I was ever gonna amount to."

Josh took a step toward her. "Then she was wrong! She was wrong and in order for a mother to ever say something like that to her own daughter, she must have been —"

"A whore, too?" Cleo smiled bitterly. "Yeah, she was. Dear ol' Mom."

Josh stood frozen, poised in a half crouch. His expression was anguished and he gripped the bacon fork in one hand almost as if he wanted to thrust it at Cleo. Abruptly, his shoulders sagged and he turned away, turned back to his skillet. In a low, barely audible voice, he muttered, "You're better than that."

Watching him, for the briefest moment Cleo's expression softened and something — Sympathy? Regret? — passed across her face. Then it was gone. She looked away and glared down into her coffee cup.

Except for the roar and howl of the storm, everything was quiet for several minutes. The understandable tension and awkwardness that had gripped the four ever since riding out of Buffalo Peak was increased following the exchange that just took place. By the time coffee cups had been refilled and plates of bacon and beans were being passed out, however, it settled back some.

But there was still little or no conversation, and Josh and Cleo studiously avoided looking at one another.

Partway through emptying her plate, Kate spoke up. "I can't help wondering how you picked out the two of us for your wives," she said. "I gather you had some awareness of Cleo's situation. But how much did you know about me?"

She swept her eyes over both of the abductors but lingered mostly on Charlie since he was the one "claiming" her for his own.

"I knew all I needed to know about you, darlin', from just one look," Charlie promptly replied. "The fact you was walkin' all by yourself, passin' right there in front of my eyes, was like a sign. An omen. It all came together that you was the woman meant to be my bride."

"What if I'm already married?"

"I don't see no ring on your finger. Married women never part from wearin' their weddin' ring."

It crossed Kate's mind to lie, to try and convince him that she *was* married and there was some logical explanation for not wearing her ring. But she couldn't think of a good reason. Furthermore, she somehow sensed Charlie would instinctively know she wasn't telling the truth and she feared it might anger him. Anger him to the point of worsening her treatment as well as Cleo's. She didn't want that for the simple reason stricter treatment would surely lessen the chance for some kind of opening she could possibly turn into an escape. The way it was now, the captives were being given certain amounts of leeway and she hoped this might eventually yield some advantage. Kate didn't want to risk losing that sliver of hope.

"While it's true I may not be married to a man," she said now, turning a bit coy, "there are certain things in some people's lives to which they are so committed that it's practically like a marriage. It's rather common among professional men — bankers, lawyers, storeowners, and such — to hear them say 'I'm married to my job' or 'married to my work.' Haven't you ever heard that?"

Charlie scowled. "No, I never did. And I'm glad of it. Sounds pretty stupid to me."

"Be that as it may," Kate continued, "I fall into that category. You see, I own and operate the hotel back in Buffalo Peak. The Mallory House. I'm married to it, in a manner of speaking. I don't know if you heard any talk about it while you were in town, but it is quite successful."

"You mean that fancy joint right on the main drag?"

"Exactly."

Charlie snorted. "All it took was one look for me and Josh to see that place was too rich for our blood. I guess that'd be some folks' idea of success."

"And you say that whole shebang belongs to you? You run it all on your own?" said Josh, also taking an interest.

"Naturally I have a staff of employees who help me," Kate answered. "But the deed is free and clear and strictly in my name. I inherited it after both of my parents were struck down in an influenza epidemic."

Charlie smiled slyly. "Hey, you hear that, Josh? I'm not only gonna have me a real pretty wife, I'm gonna have me a rich one, too. If, of course, Miss Katie here ain't lyin' her pretty little head off."

Kate felt a flush of anger burn her cheeks. She fought to control it but couldn't keep it completely out of her tone. "Why would I lie about something you could so easily disprove? All you have to do is ask anybody in Buffalo Peak. You'd have verification in a matter of seconds."

"Oh, now there's a grand idea," Charlie scoffed. "Sure, we turn around and ride back into a town where we just stole a couple pretty women, tap some good citizen on the shoulder, and say, 'Excuse me, but could you tell me if one of the women I stole owns and runs the fancy hotel there across the street?' And then what? By the time Mr. Good Citizen is done spittin' out his answer, I got a whole passel of law dogs snarlin' at me from behind the muzzles of their rifles and shotguns. How doggone dumb do you think I am, darlin'?"

"If you're dumb enough to think you can snatch a pair of women who are complete strangers to you and then ride off and be able to convince them you're their dream husbands because you're clever enough to find a dry cave in a thunderstorm," Kate replied in an angry rush, "then the measure of your dumbness is beyond comprehension!"

Charlie threw back his head and crowed with delight. "Whooee! Looky here, Josh — you ain't the only one who grabbed hisself a spitfire. I got me one with a whole lot of sass in her, too!"

Kate's anger flared hotter than ever. "You want sass, you cackling moron? You're calling down more of it than you can begin to imagine. I tried to give you an easy way out, was working my way toward offering you money — a ransom, if you will — to end this insanity and let us go. But now you've laughed that off. So let me tell you the rest of what you didn't bother to find out about me.

"Back in Buffalo Peak, it so happens, I am a very special friend to the marshal there. You can take that however you want. But how you *should* take it, if you had any sense, is to know that he will be coming after me. He will be relentless in his pursuit, and when he catches up it will be the sorriest day of your pathetic lives!"

Charlie smirked throughout this tirade. When Kate paused to catch her breath, he said, almost lazily, "Well now. That was quite a spiel, darlin'. And you might have even given me cause to worry a little bit if not for a couple of things. Number one, I figure you're probably lyin' through your pretty little teeth again — which is really a bad habit, and one we're gonna have to work on as time goes by. Number two, even if you're tellin' the truth about that marshal bein' sweet on you and comin' to fetch you back, I'll remind you that we have crossed the border into Mexico. Which means no law dog from Texas or anywhere else up north has one lick of say down here. What's more — supposin' he was bold enough to come chargin' across the border anyway — after this frog-strangler of a rain finishes gushin' down he won't have a chance in hell of pickin' up any sign to try and follow. He'll be plumb out of luck, and as far as holdin' out hope for him to come ridin' to your rescue, so will you."

"You go ahead and believe that," said Kate, her tone now turned to ice. "You sleep real comfortable tonight thinkin' you've got it all figured out. And I'll do the same. Because I have complete confidence in Marshal Firestick McQueen. No border and no amount of rain will be enough to stop him. He's coming to get me and God have mercy on anything or anybody who tries to stand in his way."

CHAPTER 38

The storm that cut a swath along both sides of the border did not reach as far north as Buffalo Peak. The evening sky clouded over during the final handful of rodeo events and stayed that way during the street dance that was the final activity of the daylong festival, but nothing more than a few distant lightning flashes came of it.

The mood of the festival stayed high throughout, even in the wake of the abduction. Word of the incident spread all during the mid-day picnic, and there were a few occasions when fear and panic, surging abruptly though thankfully in small pockets, threatened to take hold. But Beartooth was right there, steadily threading his way in and out of the tables, always with Victoria in hand and always somehow managing to be near one of these pockets of distress whenever it was building. He quickly soothed the concern, pointing out that Firestick and

Moosejaw were on the job, pursuing the abductors with fierce intent to catch up and rescue the women.

"Who would you bet on?" Beartooth would invariably say, flashing a reassuring grin. "Two lowdown, women-stealing skunks . . . or two all-around double-tough *hombres* who also happen to be the best trackers in the territory?" In no time he would have the frowns and worried expressions erased and replaced by agreeably bobbing heads and even a few confident smiles.

"I never would have guessed," Victoria said, squeezing Beartooth's hand while aiming a bright smile at him, "what a skilled diplomat and manipulator of public sentiment you are."

Beartooth arched a brow. "I ain't exactly sure what all those fancy words mean, but could it be there was a compliment somewhere in the mix?"

"Indeed there was. And I know that the marshal," Victoria added, "would be just as impressed as I am by how you were able to put those people at ease and make them believe everything is going to be okay."

"Yeah," said Beartooth, his expression turning somber. "I only hope I wasn't feedin' 'em all just a line."

Victoria appeared taken aback. "What do

you mean? You have faith in Firestick and Moosejaw, don't you?"

"Ain't nobody better at doin' what they set out to do." Beartooth scowled. "But out there in the wild, things got a way of suddenly turnin' against a body. Even the best. Me and those two rascals have made it through more than a few of those bad turns and managed to always come out with our hides intact. But those times it was the three of us workin' together. Now, split up the way we are, it ain't the same. You can see how it's bound to gnaw at a body some, can't you?"

"I suppose," Victoria said. "But what is it that's gnawing at you? Worry about them? Or feeling guilty that you're not out there with them?"

"Don't rightly know if I see the difference," replied Beartooth. "Either way, it leaves a fella feelin' a mite uncomfortable."

"Maybe," said Victoria, "you need to listen to your own words. Who would you bet on?"

"Hell. That's easy. Firestick and Moosejaw. All the way."

They'd been slowly making their way from the picnic area to the rodeo arena, talking as they walked along.

Victoria stopped walking. Beartooth, still holding her hand, stopped, too. He looked down at her impossibly blue eyes gazing up at him. "And I," she said, "will always bet on you . . . and us . . . all the way."

Suddenly unmindful of the people all around them, Beartooth was moved to kiss this beauty before him. He was leaning in to do so when a voice at his shoulder suddenly spoke and interrupted the moment.

"Excuse me, Beartooth. But I just ran across something kinda curious that I think you might be interested in."

Beartooth turned to lock eyes with Pete Roeback. Reading the eager, earnest expression on the liveryman's face, it was clear he had no clue what his poor timing had broken up. Nevertheless finding it hard to keep the exasperation out of his voice, Beartooth said, "This better be good, Pete."

Playing to the hilt his disdain for all things American, Rupert Shaw refused to attend any of the festival activities. After being tended to by Frank Moorehouse, he retreated to his hotel room and remained there, sulking, nursing his injuries, and impatiently waiting for tomorrow's duel to be over with so he could then, in his own words, "Get the bloody hell out of this godforsaken rubbish bin of a town."

Oberon Hadley, on the other hand, continued to be fascinated by the raw energy and spirit of this place called America. Once he'd seen to it that Shaw was settled in his room and a noon meal had been delivered from the dining room, he decided to venture out and see what the festival had to offer. He was mindful of the fact that his association with Shaw, who'd managed to make himself unpopular in the eyes of many, might cause his own presence to be less than welcome as he mingled amidst the throng, but Hadley was hardly a man who shied away from the mere possibility of a confrontation.

During his service in the Queen's Army, he'd set foot in many a corner of the globe where the British colors were cursed and sometimes even spat upon. Yet it had never prevented him from trodding among the locals in his free time and visiting more than a few grog shops that he left in shambles when some of the other patrons took exception to him sampling the establishment's fare in their presence. He never went looking for trouble — and that certainly was true today, especially with the pending duel already on his plate — but he'd be damned if he would walk wide of anywhere just because a scuffle *might* ensue.

To the big Englishman's delight and mild

surprise, when he ventured out at the height of the mid-day picnic, he encountered no rancor in anyone's treatment of him. Oh, there were a few sidelong glances and perhaps an unkind word or two murmured under someone's breath that he could have challenged. But the overall merriment of these kind, honest, hardworking people was far too appealing for him to give any serious thought toward participating in any disruption. Plus he was simply having too good a time himself to want to ruin it by being thin-skinned. What he concentrated on instead was quaffing considerable quantities of homemade beer, sampling a wide variety of food, listening to and exchanging a few ribald jokes, and even flirting a bit with a couple of young ladies who were somewhat on the plump side, just the way he liked them.

As the picnic wound down, Hadley was swept up in the flow of folks who began migrating toward the rodeo arena. *Here* was the feature of the scheduled festival events he'd been looking forward to the most. While Captain Shaw seldom passed up the opportunity to disparage Buffalo Bill's Wild West after viewing it once during its tour through England, Hadley had made a point of seeing the show twice and both times was wildly impressed and exhilarated by the performances — particularly the riding and roping and horsemanship of the "cowboys." The chance to see more of the same here today, in a more intimate setting and this time demonstrated by those who actually lived the life and did the work every day, had him feeling almost as excited as a little kid.

The calf roping was finished and the bulldogging had barely begun, however, when Hadley's eager viewing was drawn away in a most unexpected manner. It came in the form of Victoria Kingsley, who had threaded her way through the cheering crowd to find him and now tugged on his sleeve to get his attention.

When Victoria first started to speak, Hadley couldn't hear her over the din. He had to stop her and then motion for her to start over after he'd leaned down closer in order to make out what she was trying to tell him.

"Please come with me. There's something you need to see."

Much as Hadley hated to leave the rodeo, there was no missing the sincerity and sense of urgency in the girl's tone. Refusing her request did not seem like an option.

Ten minutes later, they had extracted themselves from the rodeo crowd and Victoria had led the way up Trail Street to Roe-back's livery. By this point, Hadley's internal alarms were starting to jangle, telling him to beware of a possible trap, while at the same time the sentimental part of him resisted believing that Victoria — the former fiancée to his captain, even though now estranged — would be part of anything intended to do him harm.

But when they'd gone only a short way into the livery barn and Hadley spotted Beartooth waiting just ahead, he slowed his steps and came to a halt. In deference to the day's heat, Hadley had gone out minus his jacket. He did wear a vest, though, and concealed under it was the shoulder holster and short-barreled revolver he seldom was without. At the sight of Beartooth he had instinctively shrugged his shoulders in a practiced move that shifted the vest slightly forward on his frame, loosening the way it hung over his chest for the purpose of providing easier access to the revolver in case he needed it quickly.

When Hadley stopped Victoria stopped, too, though only after she'd gone a couple steps ahead of him. Looking back, she said, "What I want to show you is in the horse stall where the deputy is standing."

Reading and understanding Hadley's

reluctance, Beartooth said to him, "Take it easy, big fella. Ambushin' ain't my style. If it was, you'd already be dead."

"Our purpose in asking you here," Victoria added, "is aimed toward preventing bloodshed, not causing it."

Hadley considered for a minute, then proceeded toward Beartooth again. "Someone had better start clarifying what this is all about and doing so quickly," he said, "or I will be turning and leaving."

"That will be your prerogative," Victoria said. "But after you've seen our purpose in bringing you here, I am in hopes you won't be in such a hurry to go."

When they reached Beartooth, Hadley saw that inside the stall he was standing in front of was a sleek bay mare. Also in the stall, standing beside the horse, was another man Hadley recognized as Pete Roeback, owner and proprietor of the livery who had rented horses to the Englishmen on more than one occasion.

Roeback nodded. "I trust you remember me."

"I do," said Hadley tersely. "And I remember that horse by ye, too. That's the devilish beast what threw Captain Shaw earlier today and nearly broke him in two."

"That's what we want to talk to you

about," said Beartooth.

Hadley frowned. "What more is there to say? The animal is improperly trained, not to be trusted. I'd go so far as to suggest she might be ready for a bullet to the brain in order to make sure no future rider is thrown or trampled even worse."

"I take exception to that," Roeback was quick to say. "I've had that mare for over three years. Trained her myself. I've ridden her countless times and have even had women and children on her back with never a hint of trouble. Captain Shaw rode her himself on two prior occasions without incident."

"Horses can change, suddenly develop a mean streak," Hadley said.

Roeback shook his head. "No, they don't. Not the horses I train and care for. That's what bothered me so much about Marge here supposedly spookin' so bad without reason. The sight or sound of a rattler — maybe. But even then I ain't so sure she'd spook as wild as you and Shaw described."

Hadley's eyes narrowed. "Ye wouldn't be suggesting me or the captain are lying, would ye?"

"All I'm suggesting is that there had to be a reason for Marge to rear and bolt that way. And I think I found it."

"What with the abduction of those women and the festival kickin' off and everything right on the heels of you and Shaw gettin' back to town," Beartooth explained, "Pete here didn't get a chance to give Marge a good lookin' over until just a little while ago. What he found caused him to fetch me. Victoria also came along. After we'd had our look, she suggested gettin' you in on it, too. She also suggested you'd cooperate easier if she went for you alone."

"A pretty lass is hard to say no to," Hadley allowed. "But now that I'm here, I still don't know why."

Lifting a lantern off a nail on one of the stall posts, Roeback held it up over the mare's right flank and said, "Step over here and take a look. You'll get your answer."

Hadley entered the stall and leaned to peer closer at what Roeback was indicating. What he saw was a small, deep puncture mark in the sleek hide right about where the edge of a saddle blanket would be.

The big Englishman straightened up, saying, "So what is it?"

"You tell me and we'll both know," said Roeback, an edge to his tone. "Which is to say, I can see it's clearly a puncture wound but I can't be certain what made it. What I *can* be pretty certain of, though, is that whatever it was — if jabbed suddenly and unexpectedly into Marge's flank — would be enough to cause her to act the way you and Captain Shaw described."

"Yes, I suppose it would. But I still don't see . . ." Hadley's voice trailed off and suddenly his face clouded with suspicion and anger. "Wait a minute. Are ye implying that me or the captain abused your horse in some way?"

"Not you . . . but maybe Shaw," said Beartooth.

"What in bloody hell for, man?"

"To make the mare rear up exactly the way she did. Resultin' in him bein' dumped from his saddle."

"Are ye daft?" Hadley's expression was twisted with half anger and half befuddlement. "Why would any man purposely cause a horse to throw him and risk injuries such as the captain suffered — or worse?"

Nobody said anything for several seconds. Beartooth and Victoria exchanged glances. And then, in a low, measured voice, Beartooth said, "Maybe a man facin' an upcomin' event that carried an even bigger risk . . . and was countin' on a few bruises and a fracture or two as a way to get out of goin' through with it."

It took a second for Beartooth's full meaning to sink in. But the instant it did, Hadley spat an enraged curse and surged out of the stall toward him. Fast as the big man was, however, he wasn't faster than Beartooth's draw. Hadley only managed one long, lunging step before he was brought up short by finding himself staring down the muzzle of Beartooth's .45-caliber Colt, raised and pointed square at the bridge of his nose.

"Settle down, mister!" Beartooth said through gritted teeth. "You and me have already got a date to trade bullets — tomorrow. I wouldn't be in a hurry to rush it none."

Hadley was literally trembling with anger, his huge fists hanging at his sides, clenched so tight the knuckles pressed bone white against the skin. "Ye are a blackguard and a coward," he seethed. "Impugning a fine and noble man's honor when he is not present to defend it himself and too stove in to do so even if he was!"

"That 'stove in' part is the whole point of this," said Beartooth. "Don't you find it mighty convenient how a mare with a history of bein' nothing but gentle would suddenly and for no reason act the way Marge did?"

"But there *was* a reason," Roeback insisted. "I showed it to all of you."

"That small puncture proves nothing," Hadley told him. "Ye said yourself ye didn't check that horse for several hours. She could have got that wound any number of ways — maybe something as simple as brushing up against a nail sticking out of the wood somewhere in her stall."

"Yeah," Roeback snarled, "and maybe from some sneaky bastard poking the sharp end of a nail or the tip of a penknife into her rump on purpose!"

"As soon as I get done with this deputy tomorrow —" Hadley started to say.

But Victoria cut him short. "Stop it! Stop it, all of you!" Her eyes locked on Hadley. "You can blame me for causing these suspicions against Rupert. It stems from an incident I'd all but forgotten about and then remembered only after I saw the puncture wound in that horse. The incident I'm talking about happened when Rupert was in the army, serving in Afghanistan during a battle for some obscure mountain pass."

"Baba Wali Pass." Hadley bit off the words like they were a bitter taste in his mouth. "There was nothing obscure about it to those of us who fought there. It was in that battle that Captain Shaw showed his gallantry and skill of command and played a major role in winning the day."

"Yes, he received many medals and was lauded as quite the hero. My cousin Estelle received letters from back home telling all about it. She read them to me and I was proud and happy for Rupert," said Victoria. "But the letters also mentioned there was some sort of cloud over the incident, and for a time Rupert's role in the battle and whether or not he was deserving of his medals came into question due to allegations from some of the men in his command."

"Slackers and liars!" Hadley exclaimed. "Men who'd earlier been ridden hard by the captain for their poor performance of duties and went looking to get even in the lowest, pettiest of ways by calling into question his bravery." He glared even more fiercely at Beartooth as he said the last.

"The allegations against Rupert's actions that day had to do once again with a horse, did they not?" pressed Victoria. "A horse that was mysteriously shot out from under him just as his troops began their charge."

"It was the height of a battle! Bullets were flying everywhere, cutting down men and horses alike," Hadley said. "What is so mysterious or suspicious about Captain Shaw's mount taking a ball?"

Victoria replied, "The timing, among other things, I would say. It happened, as I recall from what was contained in the letters, right as the charge was set in motion. As a result, Rupert was spared the thickest, bloodiest part of the fighting that followed. In fact, his detractors accused him of shooting his horse himself, for that very reason."

"Black lies!" Hadley boomed. "I was there, I saw firsthand what happened. True, the captain went down and was unable to participate in the full charge without a mount. But it was his strategy and leadership, the timing of his order to strike an enemy flank that was weakened and wavering for only a precious few moments, that played a key part in taking that bloody pass. Had the captain hesitated and not acted as decisively as he did — whether he was at the spearhead of the charge or not — the overall success of the day would have suffered greatly."

There was no questioning the passion or conviction in Hadley's words. At least not when he began the statement. And yet, as he wound down, there seemed to be a faint lessening, a weariness, in the punch of his delivery. And the glare he kept fixed on Beartooth also appeared to lose some of its white-hot intensity.

Nobody said anything for several moments.

And then, slowly, Beartooth lowered his Colt. "As you said, you were there," he declared. "Nobody can question your personal bravery or your perception of what happened. All the same, I think you're mistaken in your high opinion of Shaw. I'm of the opinion he's a lowdown skunk and a conniver who manipulates others to do his dirty work for him. Meanin', with all due respect, I think he has in the past — and is once again now — playin' you for a sucker. Understand I got no particular hard feelin's toward you. But make no mistake . . . You stand in front of me tomorrow with a pistol in your hand, I won't hesitate to kill you."

CHAPTER 39

As is often the case following a hard night-time storm, the following morning dawned bright and clear.

Josh and Charlie rose with the first light, rousted and fed the women, then took care of the horses before loading up the pack animal once more. They were on their way before the bottom edge of the sun had fully cleared the horizon.

"We'll be spendin' part of the day still down here in Mexico, ridin' over some rocky ground that won't leave a trail anybody short of an Apache could follow," Charlie told the women as they were finishing up their breakfast. "Then, in the afternoon, we'll cut north again — northwest, to be exact. Come night, we'll be back in Texas. That'll be our last night on the trail. After that, we'll be in Bright Rock where we'll be stayin' for a spell and makin' our homes together."

"The old, abandoned town might not look like much at first," Josh added. "But we plan on fixin' up a couple of the buildings right nice. Like Charlie said, we're gonna turn 'em into homes where you gals will come to know and appreciate us."

"I already have a home. You dragged me away from it," Kate said bitterly.

"There's a difference between a place to live and a home with a husband and family," Charlie said. "I aim to show you what that difference is."

A surprisingly quiet Cleo just listened and gazed over the rim of her coffee cup with an odd, faraway look in her eyes.

North of the border, Firestick and Moosejaw also broke camp with the sun and were on their way south a short time later. They took time only to tend the horses and to make a small, quick fire over which they boiled some coffee. Otherwise they settled for beef jerky that they ate once in their saddles and on the move.

They didn't speak more than twenty words during all of this. There was no need. They each knew what to do, and the grim expressions on their faces said all that needed saying.

■ ■ ■ ■

In the foothills of the Vieja Mountains north of Buffalo Peak, Pierce Torrence and his group also rose early. They went about their morning rituals unhurriedly, taking time for a substantial breakfast before tending to their horses and then packing their gear and striking camp.

"I want to ride into town a little earlier than I first indicated," Torrence had announced during breakfast. "Closer to, say, ten than noon. That will still give the businesses time to have deposited the money they took in over the weekend. The bank will be nice and plump for the picking, and the town in general should still be a bit groggy in the aftermath of their big festival.

"We follow our standard routine. Letty goes in first. Black Hills and I follow, and we all make our withdrawal from behind drawn guns. Romo stays outside guarding the horses and watching the street. That will include deciding on a decent-looking horse from the nearest hitch rail that we can use to carry the hostage we'll be taking with us."

"Who'll pick the hostage?" Leticia asked.

"Me," said Torrence. "I'll grab the best

choice from whoever happens to be in the bank when we're ready to haul out." He paused, let his gaze rake meaningfully over the others. "You all know I normally don't advocate gunplay unless it's absolutely necessary. But this time I'm saying to play it a little different. Anything you see wearing a badge — fill it full of lead. The law dogs in this burg are former mountain men, remember, so likely better than average at tracking. Understood?"

"Fillin' a law dog full of lead," echoed Romo, smiling broadly. "You don't have to tell me twice, boss."

Beartooth had decided to spend the night at the jail. In the absence of Firestick and Moosejaw, he meant to remain in town as much as possible.

The way things stood now, the duel was still scheduled to take place at two o'clock this afternoon out near Buffalo Hump Butte. Beartooth wanted to believe that the discussion with Oberon Hadley the previous evening might have accomplished something, might have given the devoted aide some serious reluctance about going through with his part. But at the same time, he had a sinking feeling it hadn't been enough.

Victoria, who'd returned to the ranch last night with Miguel and Jesus, was due back in town sometime this morning. She planned to make a final appeal to Hadley by suggesting the idea of the deloping option. Though Beartooth had scoffed at the ridiculous-sounding practice, he secretly hoped that maybe — just maybe — it might provide a last-minute alternative to him having to kill Hadley. Much as the deputy disliked Shaw, he had no hard feelings against the man he was slated to face in his place. In fact, he found that he'd formed a grudging respect for the big, ugly, stubbornly loyal jackass . . .

In his room at the Mallory House, Rupert Shaw rose earlier than was his custom. In spite of his aches from the previous day's horse fall, his spirits were high and he felt very energized. At his room's washbasin, he even hummed a bit as he went through his morning ablutions. Any observer with knowledge of the man's alleged injuries — particularly the cracked ribs and fractured arm — who witnessed the way he moved and leaned over the basin with no strain and the dexterity with which he handled a hairbrush in his right hand, would surely have found these acts at least surprising, if not highly suspicious. Only when he was finished at the washstand and had dressed, bending freely at the waist and using both hands to pull on his socks and trousers, did he carefully re-wrap the splint to his forearm and then hang it in a sling suspended from around his neck.

That accomplished, he walked over to the door that accessed the room adjoining his and knocked loudly. After a minute, the door opened and a tousle-haired Oberon Hadley poked his head into the opening.

"Sorry if I woke you, chum," Shaw greeted him. "But it's time to get on with what has the makings of a most memorable day. I'm not sure what accommodations are available in this establishment, what with the proprietress abducted and all, but I trust breakfast can still be arranged. If so, I wish to have something sent up to my room and I ask that you join me."

Hadley blinked puffy eyes and back-handed a yawn. "As ye wish, sar. As soon as I get . . . Hold on here — you're all dressed already. Ye should have woke me sooner so I could have assisted, what with your bad arm and all. How did ye manage?"

"Quite tediously and awkwardly. I'm sure you would have found it amusing to watch." Shaw smiled. "But I can't bother you with every little thing. I managed, and well enough. Though I will need some help getting my boots on."

"To be sure, Captain."

"But that can wait. First, let's get some breakfast in us. After that, I need to make a trip to the bank and arrange for some traveling cash. While I'm out, I'll also purchase our stagecoach tickets for the first transport out of this loathsome place once you've acted in my stead and taken care of that wretched deputy. I doubt even that will be enough to jolt my beloved Victoria out of her foolish romantic daze, but at least I will have saved her from the clutches of that backwoods ruffian."

Hadley's scarred forehead puckered with deep seams. "About that, Captain . . ."

"Yes? What is it?"

But the big man couldn't meet Shaw's penetrating gaze. First he dragged his huge paw of a hand down over his face. Then he shoved it back the other way and ran it through his close-cropped hair. Sighing, turning back into his own room, he said, "Never mind, sar. I'll get that breakfast ordered."

CHAPTER 40

Four riders reached the outskirts of Buffalo Peak a handful of minutes past ten. Gazing down the length of Trail Street that stretched before them, they saw only a moderate amount of activity. At the far end, the last of the wranglers who'd participated in the previous day's rodeo were gathering up their gear and their horses and getting ready to head back to the ranches they'd ridden in from. Behind the Baptist church, a few people, mostly women, were beginning to clear away chairs and tables left over from the picnic.

While Torrence, Black Hills, and Romo lagged behind, Leticia rode on ahead down the street. Clad in a long, tan-colored duster and a slouch hat, she drew no particular interest from the scattered few moving around on the boardwalks to either side.

In front of the bank, she reined up and dismounted. Once she had tied her horse to the hitch rail, she shed her duster to reveal that underneath she was wearing a well-fitted pale yellow dress with a scooped front that displayed a rather daring amount of cleavage. Quickly folding the duster and shoving it under one of the thongs that held the bedroll in place behind her saddle, Leticia next removed her slouch hat and shook loose her mane of dark hair. Hanging the hat on the saddle horn, she turned to step up on the boardwalk and march into the bank with a smile on her lips and her prominent breasts thrust proudly out ahead of her. Inside, the attention she had failed to garner out on the street was instantly replaced by the total focus of every man in the bank.

When Torrence and Black Hills entered only a couple of minutes behind her, not a single head turned to look at the new arrivals — until their guns suddenly flashed into view, aimed at the startled faces of the tellers behind their screens of flimsy, wide-spaced bars. Torrence announced in a loud voice, "This is a holdup! Everybody do exactly as you're told and nobody has to get hurt. You'll all live to tell your grandkids about it!"

"And that includes you, sweetheart," Leticia cooed to Ezra Ballard, the plump, elderly bank guard, as she swept a nickel-plated revolver from the folds of her skirt and shoved its muzzle under his nose. "Drop that shotgun — slow and careful — then get over there with the others."

Using his left hand and gripping it near the end of its twin barrels, Ezra lifted the shotgun resting in his lap, leaned over, and laid it gently on the floor beside the stool where he was sitting. Then he stood up and shuffled obediently the way Leticia was urging him. Even in that tense moment, he still couldn't keep his rheumy old eyes from drifting to her breasts.

After Torrence had locked the front door and pulled the window shades, he helped Leticia herd all of the tellers and customers, along with Ezra, to one end of the bank's lobby. While they were doing this, Black Hills kicked open the waist-high swinging gate that led to the area behind the tellers' counter. When bank president Jason Trugood came barging out of his office, he was immediately met by Black Hills's long-barreled Colt jammed in his face.

"Welcome to the party," growled Black Hills. "You're just in time to help me fill up a bag with all that money you've got cluttering up the joint."

"You'll never get away with this!" Trugood

blustered.

"Reckon you must see things different than I do," Black Hills countered. "Because it looks to me like we already are!"

In the lobby, all those now gathered there were being ordered to lie facedown on the floor. Mostly there was stunned silence among them as they obeyed. One of the tellers, a frail young woman, sniffled quietly. One of the customers, however, a well-dressed dandy with one arm in a sling, attempted a show of protesting loudly.

"This is an outrage!" he sputtered. "You can't make people grovel on the floor like animals. Where is the law enforcement to prevent such treatment?"

"You'd better hope they don't show up, Fancy-pants," Torrence told him. "Because if they do, bullets are sure to start flying and then a lot of innocent folks might end up on the floor permanent-like. Which is going to happen to you for sure if you don't shut up and do as you're told!"

Huffing indignantly, the man in the sling lowered himself to the floor.

"Alright. Keep them there and keep them quiet," Torrence said to Leticia. "I'm going to help gather up the money."

As he hurried behind the tellers' counter, Torrence couldn't keep from smiling smugly. It was all going well, according to plan. In a matter of minutes, they'd be riding clear with a haul of easy money.

What he couldn't know was that, outside, the potential for trouble was taking shape. That shape was the towering form of Oberon Hadley coming across the street from the Mallory House, seemingly headed for the bank.

From where he stood leaning casually against an awning post just off center of the bank's front door, Romo tracked the approach of the big man. He was in place for the purpose of handling just this kind of unexpected problem. He'd done so in the past and was prepared to do so once again, though he found himself wishing the size of what he was going to have to deal with wasn't quite so damn big.

By the time Hadley stepped up on the boardwalk, there was no doubt that the bank was his destination. As he started to reach for the door handle, Romo flipped the butt of the cigarette he'd been smoking out into the street and said, "It's locked. They're closed for a little while."

Hadley looked over at him even as his hand closed on the doorknob. "What's that ye say?"

"The bank," Romo said. "It's closed. The

door is locked."

Hadley confirmed this by trying the knob and finding it wouldn't budge. "What the bloody hell? They *were* open earlier. I saw people going in and out."

"True enough," Romo agreed in an easy, relaxed manner. "I was on my way in myself. That's when some clerk-lookin' fella stuck his head out and said he was lockin' the door. But only for a short time, he said — some kind of emergency staff meetin'. Whatever that means."

Hadley frowned. "In the middle of the morning? With customers inside? That's bloody odd, wouldn't ye say?"

Romo grinned sheepishly. "I'm afraid I wouldn't know, to tell the truth. Afraid I ain't never had much truck with banks. Never had enough money to need one."

"No matter, they wouldn't lock up and hold a staff meeting with customers inside," insisted Hadley, his frown deepening. "I have a friend in there and I know for a fact he hasn't come back out yet."

Romo stood a little straighter, easing his weight off the post. He was beginning to feel edgy about this *hombre* and the fact he was being stubborn when it came to accepting the simple explanation for why the bank was closed. "You sure about that friend of yours?" he said, keeping his tone light, just being curious. "They wouldn't let me in, so I don't think they *are* allowin' customers to remain inside while they're havin' their powwow. Maybe your friend came out and you just didn't notice."

Hadley regarded him for a minute. Romo had trouble reading his expression. He thought he might have seen brief ticks of annoyance and maybe suspicion. Enough of the latter, in fact, to cause him to shift his gun hand ever so slightly closer to the revolver on his hip.

But then, abruptly, the big Englishman grinned. "That must be it. Me friend must have finished his business sooner than I expected," he said affably. "I'll be havin' to look elsewhere for him, then. Good luck with your wait, chap. Hope it's not too much longer."

With that, he turned and ambled away. Not back across the street, but on down the boardwalk toward a string of stores and shops.

Romo breathed a sigh of relief and leaned back against his post again, though still a bit unsettled. Damn, they were taking their time in the bank. What the hell was keeping them?

Twenty yards down the boardwalk, Hadley stepped into the recessed doorway of a hat shop. He pressed his back against the door, having no intention of opening it and entering the shop. He stood very still, his mind churning, replaying the exchange he'd just had with the man in front of the bank. *Something was wrong.* He might be a stranger to America and its ways, but locking the door to your business during prime hours to allegedly hold an emergency meeting with your staff while customers were also still inside — and Captain Shaw *was* still inside, Hadley was certain of that — just didn't seem logical.

Hadley pictured the way all the shades were drawn over the bank windows, long before the day's heat had built to an uncomfortable level or before the afternoon sun would be slanting directly down on them. And how the man out front was positioned . . . a lookout perhaps? Then there were the four horses tied close and ready at the hitch rail . . . ready to be ridden away hard in a getaway?

The former sergeant thought about the rousing "dime novels" he'd read to pass the time during the trip across the country. He knew, of course, they were wildly embellished accounts of daring, imaginative exploits. But, at the same time, he'd also read enough newspaper articles detailing events of a similar nature — gunfights, raids, stagecoach and train holdups — to know there was a real-life core to those gaudy embellishments.

With sudden conviction, Hadley knew that a bank robbery was in progress . . . and Captain Shaw was in the middle of it! Acting with the speed of that thought, Hadley's hand darted inside his coat and under his vest and reappeared gripping his short-barreled .38 revolver.

Although not a man to act on impulse, neither was Oberon Hadley a man to stand by and fail to get involved when warranted. But what was prudent in this situation? What action should he take if there were four armed robbers with who knew how many innocent customers and bank employees at their mercy if shooting broke out?

He replayed in his mind's eye the street scene he'd taken in upon first exiting the hotel. Hardly anyone out and about and none who looked like strong candidates to stand against violent criminals. Farther back up the street, nearly to the end, the adobe jail building had stood silent and deserted looking. Where in the hell was that deputy? Whatever other feelings Hadley might have about the man he seemed destined to face in a duel later this day, he marked him as strong and competent, the kind of man you'd want to stand shoulder to shoulder with in case of a confrontation.

Suddenly, all of Hadley's contemplation was shoved aside by a shout coming from the direction of the bank, followed immediately by the tramp of feet on the boardwalk and the rapid-fire voice of a man barking orders.

Hadley leaned out of the recessed doorway to see what was going on. He did so too eagerly, without taking adequate precaution — and it damn near earned him a bullet to the skull.

Standing wide legged in front of the bank, with his gun drawn, Romo Perlison was ready for the big man to pop back into view. He'd had a hunch the English ox hadn't been satisfied with the story he'd been fed and might be lurking to cause trouble. When he saw him lean out of the doorway with a gun in his fist, that gave him his proof and he didn't hesitate to trigger two rounds meant to splatter the troublemaker's brains.

Hadley's reflexes — amazingly quick,

especially for a man his size — along with Romo's hurried aim, combined to keep him alive. One bullet sizzled through the air exactly where his head was a fraction of a second earlier; the other splattered against the doorway's wood frame a half inch too high even if he hadn't ducked.

Hadley threw himself back into the recess, slamming hard against the door. He immediately dropped into a low crouch in case more bullets came. They did. Two more pounded in at an angle, hitting at the same height as before. Chewing wood, rattling window glass.

"Stop wasting bullets unless you've got a sure target!" somebody shouted.

Then other shouts began to ring out from other places up and down the street.

"Bank robbery!"

"They're hitting the bank!"

"The bank's being robbed!"

Risking that the first shout to not waste bullets had come from one of the robbers and that it wasn't just a ruse, Hadley poked his head out at knee height for another quick peek around the edge of the doorway. His first glimpse, before Romo's slugs drove him back, had been startlingly brief yet enough to brand certain images into his senses — images he fervently hoped were mistaken. Unfortunately, what he saw now, with this second look, was confirmation they were not.

In the midst of the bodies emerging hurriedly from the bank and scrambling to the waiting horses, there was one that did not belong, was most definitely not part of the robber gang . . . Rupert Shaw! He was being roughly jerked and shoved by a tall, lean man with a pencil mustache. The same man — clearly the leader of the gang — barked more commands. In his free hand he held a long-barreled revolver, and he frequently waved its muzzle so it pointed at the captain's head.

Hadley didn't need to see any more to know with gut-wrenching certainty that he was looking at his captain being grabbed for a hostage. Any shred of doubt was erased a moment later when the man with the pencil mustache hollered loud and clear, "We got us a hostage here. Any of you fools try to stop us, I guarantee Fancy Dan will be the first to die!

"You sonsabitches stand clear and let us ride out of here. A posse comes boiling out too sudden or too close, the first thing they're going to catch up with is Fancy Dan's corpse. They give us some breathing room, on the other hand, we'll let him go unharmed after a day or so. Make sure your law dogs understand that loud and clear."

By the time Pencil Mustache was done talking, his gang — including, shockingly, a curvy, attractive woman in a yellow dress whom Hadley at first took for another hostage until he saw her waving around a gun with the rest of them — was mounted. The captain, his arms tied painfully behind his back with the cloth from his sling, was thrust onto a fifth horse being led by the leader.

"If you ever want to see Fancy Dan alive again, remember everything I said!" Pencil Mustache shouted as a final warning.

Seconds later, the group had wheeled their horses and were thundering away in a cloud of dust. As they passed the jail building, they peppered it with a random volley of shots, blasting away chunks of adobe and riddling the thick wooden door.

As the gang rode off, Hadley stepped out of the hat shop doorway. Along with a handful of others along the street, he watched the robbers disappear in a dust haze. That was all anybody could do. The big Englishman was squeezing his pistol so hard it had cut into the ball of his thumb. Yet he hadn't dared to raise and fire it for fear of risking the captain's life.

CHAPTER 41

Beartooth came running down the middle of Trail Street, .45 in hand, from the direction of the rodeo arena. But he was too late, had been too far away to arrive in time to do any good.

After making an early pass through the whole town shortly after the stores and shops had opened for the day's business, Beartooth had returned to where yesterday's rodeo had been held because he'd sensed trouble possibly brewing when he was there the first time. A handful of wranglers from different brands had closed down the saloons the previous night and then had used what meager slice of night was left to catch a couple hours' sleep in their bedrolls before rising to get headed back to their respective ranches. Trouble was, a number of them had woke up hungover and belligerent, and some jibes about who'd done well and who'd made poor showings in yesterday's events ended up being traded. Beartooth was on hand to keep things from getting out of hand when tempers flared. But a little while later, when he looked back and saw that not all of the wranglers had departed yet, he returned to make sure things weren't heating up all over again. That's what he'd been involved in when he'd heard shots fired from far up the street, and his attention was drawn only in time to see the robbers pouring out of the bank and making their getaway.

By the time Beartooth reached the area in front of the bank, the street was filled with excitedly jabbering citizens. Some shouted questions, others clamored to tell what they had seen and heard. Unfortunately, all of this was happening at once and as a result the deputy was getting bombarded with noise that was impossible to make much sense of.

Suddenly a pair of shots split the air and everybody went silent, many of them ducking away in alarm.

Oberon Hadley stepped forward. People in his way scattered aside. Lowering the pistol he had raised above his head to fire the shots, he said, "For the love of sanity, ye bunch of nattering nits! Give the man some breathing room and let him hear one person at a time."

From the boardwalk in front of the bank, a harried looking Jason Trugood wailed, "My bank has been robbed — cleaned out! A posse needs to go after the scoundrels!"

"That's right," a voice in the crowd agreed. "We need to get saddled up and ride out pronto. What are we waiting for?"

"What about the hostage?" argued Mabel Grant, who ran the bakery across the street. "We all heard what would happen to him if a posse gave chase too soon."

"What's this about a hostage?" Beartooth wanted to know. "Who was taken and what was said about what would happen to him?"

Once again everyone started clamoring in unison.

This time Beartooth cut them off himself, shouting, "Quiet down, dammit, or I'm never gonna get the straight of this!" He swung his gaze to Hadley. "What about it, big fella? Did you see what happened?"

"Enough," Hadley answered curtly. He gave a quick, concise rundown of everything he had seen and heard, including rough descriptions of the robbers and the fact the hostage they'd taken was none other than Rupert Shaw. When he was done, he said, "Does that sound like the work of any gang who's operated before in your area?"

Beartooth shook his head. "Can't say it does, no. Especially not the part about a woman. That's a new wrinkle for sure, leastways not one I ever heard tell of."

"What difference does it make who they are and whether or not anybody ever heard of them?" Trugood demanded. "They're bank-robbing scum, that's all you need to know! And you should be taking out after them, not just stand here talking!"

Beartooth backed him up with a flinty look. "You'd best take it easy, Trugood. I'll decide what I need to know, along with what action I'll take and when." He gestured to the employees flocked around the bank president. "Get him back inside and try to settle him down. Get a shot of bourbon in him. Where's Ezra Ballard?"

The old bank guard edged forward. He wore a tormented expression. "I'm right here, Beartooth," he said meekly.

"What happened inside, Ezra?" the deputy asked. "Give it to me straight and quick."

"It all went so fast," Ezra answered. "They came in like nothing special. The woman first, the two men a couple minutes after her. Then all of a sudden they whipped out their guns. The woman, too. She had hers jammed in my face before I . . . there was nothing I could do to stop them."

"What made them settle on Shaw as their hostage?"

"I'm not sure. The Englishman . . . was that his name — Shaw . . . ? He put up a fuss when they made everybody lay on the floor. I guess that made the leader of the gang mad. Once they'd gathered up the money, they yanked Shaw back to his feet and ripped his sling off, used it to tie his wrists behind his back. They drug him out that way."

Beartooth cast a sidelong glance over at Hadley. "Your captain seems to have a winnin' way with folks wherever he goes," he said wryly.

"Aye," Hadley said tersely. "But he's still my captain. That means I have to do something to try and save him. What about you?"

"Nobody robs a bank in my town and rides away free, if that's what you're askin'," Beartooth told him. "But what do you make of the threats against the hostage's life?"

"If they were issued by honorable men," Hadley replied, "it might mean something. Since that was hardly the case, I believe — and I suspect you do, too — they'll only keep him alive as long as he might be useful. The likelihood of them turning him loose unharmed, no matter how long pursuit is delayed, is less than zero. The only chance for the captain to make it out of this still breathing is if we go take him away from them."

"You'd go along with attemptin' that?"

"Try and stop me."

Beartooth eyed him for a long count. "No, I don't believe I'd care to. But tell me . . . A few hours out on the trail are you and me gonna have to stop and fight that stupid duel?"

Hadley shook his head. "The duel is off. Permanently. You have my word on it."

"What if we save Shaw's hide and he says different — still insists on goin' through with it?"

"In that event," Hadley said with a cocked eyebrow, "I will personally stuff him in a steamer trunk and not let him out until we're on the ocean halfway back to England."

Beartooth set his jaw and tipped his head in a quick nod. "That's good enough for me. Let's start puttin' together a posse."

CHAPTER 42

The drastic transition to the harsh, broken land they found once they'd crossed the border made the attempt by Firestick and Moosejaw to pick up the trail of their quarry even more difficult than they'd anticipated. Wearing grim, determined expressions, they doggedly set about scouring for fresh sign.

With the sun climbing higher and hotter overhead, they pursued the plan Firestick had laid out of riding to a point that was as far as they estimated the abductors and the women could have reached. Then the former mountain men began fanning out in wide sweeps, looking for either a trail or a campsite where those they were after had spent the night.

Unlike the gently rolling prairie up north, the terrain here was so chopped by arroyos and ridges and stands of rock that might offer suitable shelter, the necessity to explore each one was frustratingly time consuming.

At first, there were numerous ground depressions holding pools of water from last night's rain that kept the horses well slaked through this tedious process. As the day wore into afternoon, however, either the relentlessly beating sun or the thirsty land had dried up all of these — all but a few stubborn, secluded tanks lurking in deeply worn pockets hiding in the perpetual shade of the tallest rocks.

Upon reaching one such spot, Firestick signaled a halt. The horses were weary. The pounding sun and the precarious, punishing slopes had combined to take a toll on them. Nor were the men, no matter how rugged and determined, left unscathed.

After cooling the horses and then watering and securing them with feedbags hitched over their snouts, Firestick and Moosejaw laid up at the base of a rock column where the wind had sand-scoured a smooth-edged cutout, like an open mouth, within which lay a welcome slice of shade.

"Hard to believe, ain't it?" Moosejaw mused as he gazed up at the rocks looming over them after lowering his canteen once he'd taken a long gulp of the cool tank water with which he'd just filled it, "that some year this little sand cut will wear deep enough to topple that whole mighty wall."

Firestick lay on his back beside him, hat tipped forward over his eyes. "Long as it don't come tumblin' down until we're gone from here," he mumbled, "I can't say as I particularly care. I just don't want to have to move sudden-like any time soon."

"I hear that," Moosejaw agreed. "I think all the quick is tuckered out of me right at the moment."

Firestick thumbed back his hat. "Jesus. How long have we been badge-toters in Buffalo Peak? Goin' on about three years now, right? Have we softened up so much from town livin' in that short amount of time? Used to be we could hike and climb the high mountain trails for days on end without hardly drawin' a quickened breath. Now look at us. We been on horseback most all day and here we sit puffin' like we was the ones carryin' saddles on our backs."

"That blazin' sun don't help any," Moosejaw pointed out. "Back in the mountains, we was used to trees and shade and cooler air. And much as we might hate to admit it, we was a site younger then, too."

Firestick shoved himself up on one elbow. Scowling, he said, "That only matters if we let it. We catch our breath here for a minute or two longer and then, when we start out again, our second wind will kick in. We can't let up."

"Never said nothing about lettin' up. Just wishin' for maybe a cool breeze and a fresh whiff of youth if there was any floatin' around, that's all."

"While you're at it, wish for some fresh tracks to follow. That'd give us all the boost we need," Firestick declared. "We might not be as spry as we used to be, but we can still follow sign with the best of 'em. We just need a few scratches on the ground to get us started again, dammit."

Moosejaw eyed his friend of many years. He could sense the anxiety and worry in him, deeper than he'd ever seen before even though they'd been in plenty of tight spots together in the past. But a woman one of them was in love with had never been part of it before. That was the difference, and Moosejaw had no trouble appreciating it. All he had to do was picture Daisy as one of the abducted gals they were after.

"Don't worry, pard," he said now, making his tone as reassuring as he could. "Their sign is out there. It's just a matter of time before we cut it."

"I know," Firestick said. "I just keep thinkin' how that time is draggin' by for us . . . and I can't help but wonder how it must be for Kate."

"She knows you'll be comin' for her," Moosejaw told him. "No matter how tough she has it, that will keep her goin'."

It was well into the afternoon before they at last found the cavernous half dome where the abductors and the women had camped the previous night. They would have weathered the storm in relative comfort here. What was more, there were again signs — discarded empty tins that had once held canned peaches and stewed tomatoes, ground markings indicating bedrolls separating those of the women from the men, a latrine dug in a private spot, and so forth — that indicated the women had been fed well and treated decently.

What was most intriguing of all, however, were some scratchings they came across that had nothing to do with a trail leading away. On a patch of sand near the latrine — possibly scratched there at the last minute before the group rode away — were these words: *BRIGHT ROCK NW.*

"What do you make of it?" asked Moosejaw after bringing it to the attention of Firestick. "I took a long gander around and I don't see no bright rock or shiny rock or nothing that seems to fit — not to the northwest or no other direction, neither."

"Bright rock NW," said Firestick, reading the words out loud. "I got to believe it was put there as a message to us, either by Kate or that Cleo gal. But I'm blamed if I can cipher what it's meant to tell us."

The two men walked out from the cavern and together took another look around, to the northwest and every other direction. But they saw nothing that seemed to fit the words.

"The tracks away from here lead off to the northwest. That's one thing," said Moosejaw.

Firestick frowned. "Yeah, but we'd've seen that much regardless. Those words were meant to tell us something more." He paused, then said the words again, as if repeating them would somehow help them make sense. "Bright rock . . . Bright rock NW."

"They were fresh-scratched in that patch of sand, so it ain't like they were left by somebody else using that cavern some earlier time," Moosejaw mulled, thinking out loud.

Abruptly, Firestick lifted his chin. "Wait a minute. Hold on. I recall hearin' some old-timers back in town talkin' a few times. There was some town off to the west of

Buffalo Peak, quite a few years back. They hit silver in the hills nearby and a community sprung up fast, a boomtown. But then the silver died out and so did the community. It's abandoned now, a ghost town. But wasn't the name something like Bright Rock?"

Moosejaw's eyes went wide. "No, it wasn't 'something like' Bright Rock — that's exactly what it was! I've heard stories about it, too. Yeah! And west of Buffalo Peak would be roughly northwest from where we're standin'."

The two men locked eyes for several beats, a silent excitement building between them.

Finally, Moosejaw said, "That must be it. Right? The abductors let on they were headed for Bright Rock and one of the gals left it as a clue for us."

"Seems that way," Firestick said.

Now Moosejaw frowned. "But why ride clear the hell down here into Mexico only to turn around and go back up there?"

"I had a hunch all along that cuttin' for the border might only be a ruse, remember? A way to discourage a posse or any lawmen from crossin' to where they didn't have no legal standin', leavin' the owlhoots to turn north again later on. So that don't surprise me so much. The only question, as far as

403

I'm concerned, is whether or not those words in the sand are legitimate."

"What do you mean?"

"What if," Firestick elaborated, "it was one of the abductors who scratched those words there? To make us think exactly what we're thinkin' and send us off on a wild-goose chase while they continued in a whole different direction?"

"What about the tracks leadin' that way? To the northwest, I mean?"

"How long are we gonna strain our eyes and slow ourselves down tryin' to follow tracks over this rough ground if we think we already know where they're gonna lead us?"

Another tense silence hung between them until, in a plainly exasperated tone, Moose-jaw said, "Damn it, there are times when you can think something to death. Sooner or later, you got to go with your gut and *act.* You taught me that more than anybody."

"So what are you sayin'?"

Moosejaw shook his head. "Ain't for me to say, old friend. Kate's your woman. You got to make the call."

Firestick glared at him for a moment and then slowly turned his head and looked off to the northwest. When his face turned back, a corner of his mouth lifted wryly. "My gut says Bright Rock."

Moosejaw's mouth spread in a full grin. "That's what I was hopin' to hear. Let's get mounted and get a move on."

"No. Not yet."

"What's to wait for?"

"Night. Coolness. Some rest. Now that we know where we're headed and don't need to scour the ground as we go," Firestick explained, "we can travel in the cool of the night and make up more of the time we lost today searchin' every crack and canyon we came to."

"This is mighty rugged ground to be coverin' at night, even if we ain't tryin' to follow sign," Moosejaw pointed out.

"The sky's clear and last night there was near a full moon once it peeked through," Firestick countered. "Should give us plenty of light to see by. And not bein' hammered by the sun and the heat, there's a good chance we'll make even better time. What's more, the farther north we go, the more the land will smooth out again."

Moosejaw continued to look dubious.

Then Firestick laid down the clincher. "If we give ourselves and the horses a good rest here, take on some grub and plenty of water, then stick to it hard when we do ride out, I can't see it not bein' in our favor. We'll keep goin' right on into tomorrow. Long as we take care not to ride right up on 'em, there's even a chance we could skirt around our quarry and get to the town first. Be waitin' there when they show up. The last thing they'll be ready for is us to have got in front of 'em."

Moosejaw's expression relaxed. "By damn, it just might work."

"That's the general idea," Firestick said. "Now let's get a fire goin' and cook some coffee and bacon before we grab a couple hours of shut-eye. I don't know about you, but I'm damn sick of gnawin' on nothing but jerky."

CHAPTER 43

Including himself, Beartooth picked six men for a posse. There was Oberon Hadley; Big Thomas Rivers, Kate's righthand man from the Mallory House; Gabe Hooper, a young stable hand from Roeback's Livery; and Russ Overstreet, one of the quarrelsome wranglers from the rodeo arena who hadn't yet left town. The sixth man would be Miguel Santros from the Double M, whom Beartooth intended to pick up by making a slight detour out to the ranch.

To look after things in Buffalo Peak during his absence, Beartooth deputized Sam Duvall, Frank Moorehouse, and Pete Roeback. All three were fair, tough minded, well respected in the community. And Duvall's previous history as a New York City constable before seeking the drier climes of the West for his health gave him added credentials when it came to law enforcement.

After making sure everybody was well

armed, had plenty of ammunition, and provisioned with three days' worth of food and water for himself and his horse, Beartooth led the posse out of town. They were already more than an hour behind their quarry and would lose more time making the swing to pick up Miguel.

Since the gang had fled due north, headed for the Vieja Mountains, they clearly intended to use the rugged, rocky terrain to mask their trail. It was their reliance on this notion that Beartooth figured to turn against them. He was confident his own tracking skills, supported by those of Miguel, would be up to the challenge of dogging their sign regardless. With this capability and being able to move fast with a small force of men, the former mountain man was counting on being able to catch up in time to not only retrieve the stolen money but hopefully also save Shaw before the robbers decided he was no longer an asset worth keeping around.

The stopover at the Double M was very brief. Miguel got ready in no time. Beartooth's time with Victoria was also very short. She had to absorb a lot of news in a big hurry — the robbery, the taking of Shaw as a hostage, and the posse headed by Beartooth going after them. The latter, since it included the calling off of the duel and the alliance of Beartooth and Hadley in its place, was a piece of good news wrapped within the rest. But Victoria took it all in like the tough frontier woman she had become — chin up, eyes bright, and a warm parting embrace and lingering kiss for her man.

As a result, Beartooth rode away wearing a lopsided grin that took a long time to fade from his face.

Angling north and east from the Double M, the posse picked up the trail of the fleeing robbers with little trouble. As anticipated by the way the gang had headed out of town, it led straight into the Viejas.

By the time the posse began its own ascent into the foothills, the sun was high and hot overhead and the horses were blowing hard from the pace Beartooth had set after leaving the Double M. The low, rolling hills of the prairie — turning lush and green as a result of the recent spring rains — began giving way to rocky, broken ground, ridges cut by twisting gullies, and upthrusts reaching steadily sharper and higher. The sun blasting against these stands of bare, bone-white rock reflected back like heat shimmering off a griddle.

When they reached a long slice of shade thrown across the deep bottom of a narrow canyon, Beartooth called a halt. "Water your horses good and saturate yourselves while you can," he advised everybody. "It's gonna keep gettin' hotter over the rest of the afternoon that's ahead of us. We'll be exposed through much of it, not in shaded cuts like this, with the sun bouncin' hot enough off some of the rocks to burn your skin. But you'll get your chance to cool off tonight because we'll be runnin' a cold camp."

"You got any more good news to cheer us up with?" Russ Overstreet asked wryly. He was a tall, lanky sort with a shock of blondish hair, prominent Adam's apple, quick smile, and pale blue eyes that always seemed to have a roguish twinkle in them. It was that twinkle and quick smile — often construed as being cocky — that tended to get him into scrapes like the one at the rodeo arena. Still, even though he'd ended up in the Buffalo Peak clink a few times for brawling, he always took his medicine and never tried to weasel out with some lame excuse, causing Beartooth to find him a likable sort.

"The good news," Beartooth responded to his question now, "is that the bunch ahead of us don't appear to be movin' particularly fast. Not even back when they had easier goin' out on the prairie. That tells me they're actin' kinda cocksure, thinkin' their hostage is ser vin' to keep at bay anybody like us intendin' to run 'em down. Which is why I don't want to advertise our presence with a campfire come nightfall. Let 'em keep bein' cocksure and not bein' in a rush. Then, tomorrow, we'll keep pushin' hard and fast and that'll give us a good chance to overtake 'em."

"Aye," said Hadley, leaning against the cool canyon wall beside Beartooth. "That's the part I've been thinking about — overtaking them, that is. What happens then? In regard to the captain?"

"I don't rightly know," Beartooth told him candidly. "That'll mostly depend on what the circumstances are when we *do* catch up with 'em. The lay of the land and so forth. If we're lucky enough to gain the high ground on 'em and then catch 'em by surprise . . . well, we'll have six crack shots against four targets. Do the cipherin'. We could wipe out the whole gang before they ever knew what hit 'em and before they had any chance to prop up Shaw as a shield to try and hold us off."

Hadley's heavy brows furled. "Ye would do that . . . such a cold-blooded strike . . .

411

to save the life of a man who has caused ye so much grief ?"

Beartooth shook his head. "That'd only be part of it. I'd also be doin' it to avoid a shoot-out and thereby minimize the risk to the lives of ourselves and these other men around us."

"Practical and efficient," proclaimed the big Englishman. "I like that."

"A minute ago you called it cold-blooded."

"Aye. And the hard truth is that being cold-blooded is sometimes the most efficient way."

Higher up in the Viejas, Pierce Torrence had also called a halt in the shade of some tall, outward-sloping rocks. Like the others, he was flushed and dripping sweat. The bandanna he pulled out of a pocket to mop his face was already sopping wet from previous use. Cursing, he wrung it as dry as he could, then poured some of the contents from his canteen over it and dragged it down over his face again.

Perched nearby on a flat-topped chunk of fallen boulder, Black Hills Buckner had removed his wide-brimmed hat and was also mopping his face with a hanky. Not too far from him, Romo Perlison was leaning against the rock wall with one hand and using the other to take frequent drinks from his canteen.

"Of all the lousy luck," Romo grumbled. "Only a few days ago we was nearly drownin' in cold-ass rain for days on end. Now, when we decide to pull a job, it's in the middle of a blazin' heat wave."

"Well, excuse me all to hell for not checking with the weather gods to arrange more pleasant conditions for you," snapped Torrence. "I'd like to see you find a job on your own where you could make anything close to the haul we just did and not have to break a sweat over it."

"Aw, take it easy, Pierce." Romo scowled. "I'm just sayin' it's damned hot, that's all. You ain't likin' it neither, are you?"

"Nobody is," said Black Hills. "But whinin' and bellyachin' about it don't help any."

Romo's eyebrows lifted. "Hey, Pierce. What you just said about the haul we made . . . You think it's a pretty good one, do you?"

"No way of knowing for sure until we count it after we make camp tonight," Torrence replied. "But it looked pretty good while we were raking it into those bags. Wouldn't you say so, Black Hills?"

"Seemed like, yeah," the big man agreed.

Romo smiled in anticipation. "Man, I hope so. That bank was a cracker box, just like you said, Pierce. To have it spill out a fat haul on top of bein' so easy, that'd be frosting on the cake!"

From behind a large, wedge-shaped section of rock that had split away from the taller mass, Leticia stepped into view. She had shed her yellow dress, which was now folded under one arm, and replaced it with a pair of snug jeans and a loose-fitting shirt with the sleeves rolled up past her elbows. Although the shirt was loose, it still didn't conceal the prominent thrust of her breasts, and the way she'd left the top buttons undone revealed another expanse of creamy, sweat-slick cleavage.

"While you're all complaining about the heat and spending money you haven't even counted yet," she said, "did anybody think to take care of the horses yet? They're kind of important to us, you know, and they've cooled down enough by now to get some water."

"I'll take care of 'em, Letty," Romo said, pushing away from the rock. He made no attempt not to stare at her breasts. "You want me to take your dress over and put it in your saddlebags?"

"Thanks, but I can take care of it myself."

Romo's eyes remained locked on her bosom for a long count before he finally turned and started in the direction of the horses.

"What about him?" Leticia said, jerking a thumb to indicate Rupert Shaw who lay sprawled on the ground a few yards from the other men, his hands still tied and his head and shoulders propped against a small mound of packed sand and gravel. "Anybody think to give him a drink?"

"Thought about it," Black Hills muttered. "Decided he wasn't worth the effort for me to get up and go over there to do it."

"Jesus!" Leticia spat in disgust.

She produced a canteen from within the folds of the dress under her arm, walked over, and knelt beside Shaw. Uncapping the canteen she held it to his mouth.

"Oh, God. Thank you, thank you," Shaw gasped between gulps.

"Just shut up and drink."

"Don't waste too much on him," Torrence called over. "We only need to keep him alive for a while, nothing says he has to be made comfortable. All he has to be is upright in case we have to show him off to a posse.

"Of course, could be that Mr. Fancy-pants might be worth something to somebody.

I've been sitting here studying him some. The cut of his clothes, the jewels glittering in those cuff links, the fine leather craftsmanship of his boots . . . I don't know how this British gent ended up in a flyspeck like Buffalo Peak, but I'm starting to get a hunch we may have latched on to somebody who has a lot more worth than merely as a shield against some posse bullets."

"You, sir, are more correct than you can imagine," said Shaw, his voice steadying, taking on a hopeful tone and a hint of shrewdness. "Furthermore, if you are willing to follow your hunch, along with also demonstrating a bit more of the civility being shown by this fetching lass, it could be that the 'haul,' as you put it, you took from that pitiful excuse for a bank a little while ago is only the beginning of how much you may stand to enrich yourselves."

CHAPTER 44

The Rurales found them just as dusk was settling.

In less than an hour, Firestick and Moose-jaw would have been on the move again, their senses at full alert. But in the lingering minutes of the vulnerable period while they remained at rest — their guard down, their horses still hobbled and unsaddled — the damn Rurales showed up and caught them by surprise.

Only the faintly echoing clack of a horse's shod hoof striking the rocky ground gave any warning. Both men reacted instantly, coming wide awake and snapping to sitting positions on their spread blankets as they reached for the guns that were close at hand. But it was too late. The Rurale patrol was already fanning out and forming a semicircle across the width of the cavern's mouth — twenty dark-faced men in dusty, sweat-streaked tan uniforms and gray, steeple-crowned *sombreros,* all heavily armed with rifles leveled on them.

In the center of the formation was the leader, a lieutenant by his uniform markings. He was lean, wide shouldered, with a mouth that was presently curved downward in a deep frown and beady, suspicious eyes that kept sweeping back and forth between the two former mountain men.

"Don't do nothing sudden-like," Firestick advised out of the corner of his mouth. "I think this jasper would just as soon kill us as look at us, and it wouldn't take much to give him an excuse."

"I'll do my best not to give him one," Moosejaw replied in a low voice. "Though I can't say I care much for that stink eye he's givin' us."

"Silencio!" the lieutenant barked. "Talk only to me. Tell to me your names and your business here." His English was quite good, which was convenient because neither Firestick nor Moosejaw had ever picked up much Spanish lingo.

Firestick cleared his throat. "We're *Americanos,* as you can see. My name's Elwood McQueen. My partner here is Jim Hendricks."

The lieutenant glared, waiting for the rest. Now Firestick adopted a frown of his own.

"We came down this way on the trail of a couple skunks we're lookin' to settle a personal score with," he said.

"To settle a score? With skunks?" The lieutenant repeated this, as if not quite understanding.

"Men who did us a bad turn. A grievance. They stole from us," Firestick said.

"So you are lawmen on the trail of these thieves?"

Firestick wagged his head. "No. We're not lawmen. We understand that law from north of the border has no say down here." Luckily, both he and Moosejaw had taken off their badges and stuffed them deep in their saddlebags before ever crossing the border, anticipating a possible encounter like this. "Like I said," Firestick continued, "this is a personal matter. All we want is to catch the men and make them return what they took from us."

"In our country," said the lieutenant rather stiffly, "it is the responsibility of the Rurales to handle such matters as theft. We do not condone the kind of vigilante ways we hear many reports of taking place up north. You should have immediately come seeking our help, not proceeded on your own."

Firestick thought fast, making up his tale

on the fly, trying to make it something plausible enough to keep him and Moosejaw from getting snarled up with these notoriously corrupt and brutal "rural policemen" who were supposed to maintain law in northern Mexico. "We sure would've done that, except for a couple problems. First off, you see, we didn't rightly know where to find you. Second, we was hot on the trail of those thievin' varmints and didn't want to let up for fear of losin' 'em. Until that blasted storm came along last night and wiped out all their sign.

"So we've spent most of the day tryin' to pick it up again. We sure would have welcomed some help from y'all, but like I said, we didn't know where to come lookin' for ya. And now — finally a piece of good luck — you've found us!"

"How lucky it is for you remains to be seen," the lieutenant said sternly.

Now Moosejaw responded. "What's that supposed to mean? You said just a minute ago that helpin' with thieves and robbers is supposed to be your responsibility."

"If indeed such crimes have occurred, yes," the lieutenant agreed. "Tell me . . . what is it that was stolen from you?"

There was an uneasy pause. Moosejaw glanced sideways over at Firestick.

Then, picking up his fabricated narrative again, Firestick said, "The thing is, er, this is sorta embarrassin'. You see, what got took was my friend's wife. She left him and ran off with some Mexican fella."

A number of the Rurale soldiers snickered. They seemed to find it amusing that one of their blood could lure away an *Americano*'s woman. Even the stern expression of the lieutenant faltered a bit.

Then, regaining his composure, he said to Firestick, "I can understand how the ox might have lost his woman. Escaping from under his great bulk might be reason enough for her to flee. But how is it that his size and apparent strength are not sufficient to find and deal with the wife stealer on his own? Why does he need you along?"

"Because," Firestick explained, "the wife stealer also has somebody else along with him. A fella known to be pretty good with his gun. So I came to even the odds as well as havin' a personal stake of my own. When they lit out, the lowdown dogs stole my horse for the woman to ride on."

The lieutenant smiled thinly. "Your tale of woe is very imaginative, I will give you that much. But of course, I do not believe a single word of it!"

"Believe it or don't. That's your prerogative," snarled Firestick. "But if you're callin' me a liar, mister, then that's a different story."

"Easy," muttered Moosejaw.

"With twenty guns against your two," replied the lieutenant, "I shall call it however I like. And your reaction proves that I am right in my assessment of who and what you two really are. Just another pair of hot-tempered *pistoleros* sneaking into my country, looking to sell your gun skills to the rebel pigs who are willing to pay money in the foolish belief your kind can help their cause!"

"I don't know a damn thing about what you're spoutin'," Firestick told him. "We don't know no rebels and we don't have no cause but our own."

The lieutenant bared his teeth in a wide sneer. "If you are no better with your guns than you are with your pathetic lies, then you would have been little use, anyway, to —"

His words stopped and what came out of his mouth instead was a thick, lumpy gout of blood as the report of a rifle cut the air and the bullet screaming in conjunction with it smashed into the back of the lieutenant's head. The officer's chin dropped onto his chest as his entire body went limp and began to sag from the back of his horse. At the same time, dozens more rifles roared in a ragged volley, and the resulting rain of lead ripped and hammered the curved row of Rurale soldiers savagely. Dust puffed from their jackets; spurts of blood and gore issuing from bullet holes turned the air around them into a scarlet mist. Horses screamed and either reared up on their hind legs or bolted in terror. Men dropped like stalks of corn cut down by invisible scythes.

With this carnage erupting before them, Firestick and Moosejaw scrambled as far back into the cavern as they could, bellying down low behind a rubble of broken boulders. Their handguns were in their fists and each had also snatched up his rifle. But amazingly, out of all the blazing gunfire ripping apart the air, not a single shot came near them.

As they continued to watch in stunned awe, the entire Rurale force was bullet riddled until every man in a tan uniform — increasingly streaked and splashed with blood — was crumpled and lifeless. It was over in a handful of minutes, and then there was only silence and slowly curling layers of gunsmoke hanging in the air.

At length, a voice called out from the jagged rocks not too far beyond the sprawl of

423

dead bodies. "Hey, *gringos*! Are you still alive?"

Firestick tried to pinpoint the spot where the voice came from. Though he was unable to, he went ahead and answered, "Yeah, we're still alive, thanks to you."

"*Sí*. It is good you recognize this. We will come out now and there will be no more shooting. Agreed?"

Firestick and Moosejaw exchanged looks. "Fine by us," Firestick called back.

"To help make sure of this, if you please, we ask that you leave your weapons on the ground and meet us with your hands held wide at your sides."

Again Firestick and Moosejaw exchanged looks. One corner of Firestick's mouth lifted wryly. "Not like we're really in any position to object, are we?"

"True. But a display of courtesy, whenever possible, is better than a harsh demand. Is it not so?"

"It sure is, *amigo*. Especially when we just saw how you handle things the harsh way."

With their guns left behind, Firestick and Moosejaw rose to their feet and walked slowly out of the cavern with their hands held wide at their sides. As they were doing this, a dozen hard-looking men — wiry, somber expressions on dark faces, clad in rope sandals, baggy pants, loose-fitting shirts hung heavily with cartridge belts or bandoleers — appeared out of the rocks and crevices just past where the dead Rurales lay. A few of them wore holstered pistols on their hips, most had machetes slipped through their belts, all were holding rifles at the ready. The guns on display — pistols and rifles alike — were predominately older models looking a bit worse for wear, but their effectiveness had just been proven pretty convincingly.

In the midst of this pack was a short, bandy-legged specimen with narrow shoulders, a bit of a paunch, an oversized nose somewhat offset by the long scar on his left cheek, and a prominent gold tooth displayed via an overbite thrusting out from under a stringy mustache. He was one of the pistol wearers — two of them, in fact, worn for the cross-draw on each hip. Neither were outdated models but rather a matched pair of very current Colt .45s with ivory grips.

"I," he announced, "am Ernesto Estarde — a colonel in the revolutionary army fighting to overthrow the corrupt government of our country, especially these vermin-ridden Rurale pigs of the northern reaches who answer to no god or no rule except the domination and butchery of innocents." He then spread his hands, indicating the men to either side of him. "And these are my brave comrades, fighting at my side for the same cause."

Firestick nodded. "My name's McQueen, and this" — he motioned to Moosejaw — "is Hendricks. The two of us are very much in debt to you and your men. I don't know what that Rurale lieutenant had in mind for us, but I'm pretty sure it wasn't anything good."

"He was convinced, as he said, that you are *pistoleros* come to join our revolution. Guns for hire. Mercenaries." Estarde eyed the two former mountain men. "Much as I hate to agree with any conclusion of that scum Lieutenant Ricardo, I must say that I, too, see the same when I look at you. Certainly something other than two men chasing a stolen wife and horse."

Once again, Firestick instinctively knew that leveling with these men, even though they'd saved the lives of him and Moosejaw, was not advisable. "If that's a question," he said measuredly, "then the short answer is no, we're not down here for the purpose I told the lieutenant."

Estarde merely regarded him. Waiting.

"As for the other," Firestick went on, "yeah, my friend and I have done gun work in the past and are open to doin' more of the same. When we heard there was need for such down this way and the pay was good . . . Well, here we are."

Now Estarde smiled. "This is good to hear. And while you feel indebted to me and my men, we also owe a certain debt to you. Though I have some concern about you being careless enough to allow the Rurales to corner you the way they did, it nevertheless resulted in them focusing so intently on you that it left them exposed for us to work close and strike unexpectedly, something we have been trying to do for days.

"So we have benefited each other. And all things considered, I feel we can do more of the same and each continue to get something useful from the other. Therefore, with night coming on, let us make camp here together and discuss further plans."

Then, gesturing animatedly, snapping his fingers and barking orders in rapid-fire Spanish, Estarde set the men about him scrambling into action. Several of them pounced on the Rurale bodies — stripping them of guns, ammunition, boots, money, anything of use or value — then dragging the carcasses out of sight off to some nearby gully. Others scattered to try and reclaim some of the horses that bolted away. The remaining handful disappeared back into the rocks out of which they'd only recently emerged and then appeared again leading their own horses. From these they produced supplies with which they began preparing a meal after they got a campfire going.

While this was going on, Estarde waved his arm at Firestick and Moosejaw, saying, "Go. Retrieve your weapons. Mingle freely. We are allies now and must learn to trust one another. Is it not so?"

CHAPTER 45

"Comin' in," announced Black Hills Buckner as he paused momentarily before entering the clearing Torrence had chosen for their camp. It was that gray, murky time between the last streaks of daylight and the descent of full night. Individual shadows cast from the higher rocks on all sides were merging into thickening, expanding pools of black.

Black Hills strode over to a low-burning campfire that had been built in a shallow natural depression and then surrounded by jagged chunks of stone. Pouring himself a cup of coffee from the pot that sat bubbling on the edge of the coals, the big man said, "I was able to catch glimpses of this fire from a couple different spots down the way. It ain't shielded near as good as you think."

Close on the other side of the fire, seated on the ground and leaning back against his saddle, Torrence replied, "More to the point, did you see any sign of anyone in pursuit of us?"

"Nary a one. Not even with these fancy goggles of yours," Black Hills reported as he held out Torrence's binoculars, returning them to him. "If a posse rode out after us, they must still be hangin' back quite a ways."

"Well, that's good, ain't it?" said Romo Perlison from where he also sat close to the fire.

"Indeed it is," confirmed Torrence.

"Almost seems too good, if you ask me," spoke up Leticia. She was seated between Torrence and Romo with a blanket draped over her shoulders.

"Why do you say that?" the gang leader asked.

Leticia shrugged. "Just seems like it is, that's all. We've taken hostages before and I don't recall it ever holding the posses at bay quite as thoroughly as it seems to be working this time. That's great if it's all on the up and up. But something about it just feels . . . well, fishy. At least it does to me."

"You suggestin' Black Hills missed something the times he checked our back trail?" Romo said, his eyes gleaming a little, as if he relished the idea of stirring up some hard feelings.

"Shut up, Romo," Black Hills growled.

"You know damn well I'm not saying anything against Black Hills. It's nothing like that at all." Leticia frowned. "Like I said, it's just a feeling I got. Nothing more, nothing less."

"Under different circumstances," said Torrence, "I might well share that skepticism, my dear. But the circumstances in this case, I'll remind you, are uniquely in our favor. First of all, as we've learned from our new friend Shaw here, those two idiots who came on ahead of us from Jepperd's Ford actually took our ridiculous advice and kidnapped two women from the town — apparently to make their brides. That pulled away two of the town's lawmen to chase them down, leaving only a single deputy on hand when we made our strike this morning.

"Combine that with the man we chose for our hostage, and I think it all falls into place. Any posse formed to pursue us — with only a marginally qualified lawman to lead it — would have to be very cautious considering Shaw's importance and the potential for repercussions that could be international in scope if they acted too hastily and contributed to harm befalling him."

Sitting on the opposite side of Torrence,

Rupert Shaw smiled disdainfully. "I think you may be giving too much credit to the capability of those back in Buffalo Peak to comprehend or care about international ramifications. But I assure you that my man Hadley — who thankfully remains behind and can be quite forceful at making himself heard — will *guarantee* they understand the legal and financial nightmare my family can cause to be visited on them if they act imprudently."

Black Hills twisted his mouth in a show of disdain not too dissimilar to the one Shaw had displayed when referring to the townsfolk. "He uses even bigger, fancier words than you do, Torrence, and I don't understand half of whatever the hell he's sayin'. I sure hope you do. And I hope this change of mind you got on how we're gonna get more use out of him ends up bein' worth it."

"Worth it?" echoed Torrence. His face showed a flush of irritation at having his leadership decision questioned. "We just took that Buffalo Peak bank for a little over forty thousand dollars. That splits out to ten grand-plus apiece. Not a bad morning's work, I would say.

"But if Shaw's family over in England is willing to pay an additional forty grand in ransom for his safe release, like he claims — how can that not be worth it? We've already got him in our custody, we're already clear of the bank holdup, so we stand to double our money with barely a sliver more of risk. I repeat: How can that not be worth it?"

"I swear to you my family's wealth can cover that amount. Nor will they hesitate to pay it for my safety," Shaw added with a sense of urgency. His hands were still tied in front of him but he'd been allowed to wash up earlier and to answer the call of nature with a measure of privacy before being allowed to eat and drink in the company of the others as they took their evening meal around the campfire. There was no mistaking the fact he was still very much a prisoner, but the deal he was trying to negotiate for himself and the fact Torrence was leaning in favor of it had at least gained him some improved treatment.

"All you have to do," he continued, "is get me to a town big enough to have a telegraph office that can connect to the transatlantic cable system and a bank big enough to cover the amount of money my family will wire, and it will be a victory for all of us. I get to keep my life and regain my freedom; you get to double your money with only a small amount of additional effort."

Leticia spoke again. "No matter what anybody says, that small amount of effort *does* come with some added risk. Whether a posse is hard on our trail or not, word is bound to spread about the Buffalo Peak holdup. And if Lord Almighty Shaw here is half the big shot he claims to be, that will only add to it. So if and when we go sashaying into a town somewhere down the line to do all this telegraphing and money wiring, won't there be a chance they likely got descriptions ahead of time and will be on the lookout for us?"

"I thought about that, too," Torrence said, tipping his head in a faint nod. "But that only applies if we're stupid enough not to make some adjustments to counter it. Like disguises. Going in at staggered intervals, not showing up in a town all at once . . . It could be worked out. And, for another forty grand, I'd say it sure as hell ought to be worth some amount of additional risk."

Nobody said anything for several minutes.

Until Torrence tapped the last of the coffee grounds out of his empty cup and announced, "But before we get the cart too far ahead of the horse, as the old saying goes, we need to take care of first things first. That means getting through this cold-ass night for starters. Then, tomorrow, we

434

start picking our way down out of these mountains and head for somewhere we can hole up and make double sure there's nobody close on our heels. Once we're certain of that, we'll go back to deciding on this ransom business and, if we go through it, where we'll be able to find a reasonable spot for the telegrams and wire transfers and the rest."

In the lower reaches of the Viejas, Beartooth and his posse were hunkered down in a small canyon whose floor provided some sparse graze for the horses.

"Well, you were right about one thing," Russ Overstreet said around a mouthful of biscuit. "The afternoon got hotter as we went along and now the night and this cold camp is plungin' us right back in the other direction."

"That's the way of it," Beartooth allowed. "But if you want to talk about cold, the chill we're gonna get here up in these piddly little hills, that don't even rightly deserve to be called mountains, ain't nothing. Why, I've seen times in the Rockies when me and Firestick and Moosejaw went weeks at a time where it stayed so cold you could spit and have it freeze before it hit the ground."

Overstreet rolled his eyes. "Watch out, fellas. We're about to hear some of those stories from mountain man days. I bet it was so cold you had to thaw out the fire each morning so's you could cook your coffee, right?"

Before Beartooth could respond, young Gabe Hooper groaned and said, "Oh, man, don't mention coffee, not even kiddin' around. That's pure torture. I'm already cravin' me a cup so bad it's got me achin' all over."

"Sorry to say you're gonna have to tough it out," Beartooth told him. "I think we closed the gap on those robbers more than we figured and more than they expect. Miguel scouted ahead and saw a glimmer of their campfire not too far up. So we ain't gonna oblige 'em with a fire of our own to let 'em know how close we are, not for coffee or no other reason."

"Sure. Sure, I understand that," Gabe said earnestly. "But you really think we're closin' in on 'em, eh?"

"I don't think, I know," said Miguel. "They are up there, and not that far ahead."

"In that case," spoke up Thomas Rivers, his dark face all but lost in the thickening shadows reaching in from the canyon walls, "what's to stop us from movin' up on 'em now? We could work in closer still, surround

436

'em, and hit 'em at first light."

"I like the sound of that," agreed Hadley. "It's a clear night. Once the moon comes out and our eyes adjust we should be able to make our way well enough."

Beartooth shook his head. "It's mighty temptin', but too risky. If we knew the terrain better — maybe. But we don't. And, even with a clear sky, there'll be other canyons and arroyos to pass through and deep pools of shadow cast by the taller rocks where you won't be able to see your hand in front of your face.

"Sound travels in the mountains in funny ways. A stumble, a stone kicked loose underfoot, that could give 'em all the warnin' they'd need. And, yeah, maybe we could still take 'em in a shoot-out — but what about Shaw? A stray bullet, or if the robbers decided to make good on their threat . . . You of all people, Hadley, should see where goin' at it with caution is the smarter way."

Hadley scowled. "Aye. Ye make good sense. I was being an over-eager ass on account of wanting to lay into those scoundrels so bad I didn't think it through."

"Don't worry," Beartooth told him. "There's every reason to expect you'll have a chance to get your licks in . . . when the time is right."

CHAPTER 46

Firestick could sense there had been a shift in mood as soon as he crawled out of his bedroll the next morning.

It hadn't been until late at night, in their bedrolls spread near each other with the rest of the camp asleep around them, that he and Moosejaw had been able to talk freely, though in low whispers. Even then, there was little they could come up with in the way of any ideas to solve their predicament. Unable to arrive at any feasible idea for getting out of their fix anytime soon left Firestick tossing restlessly all through the night.

And now, this morning, whatever was in the air suggested that their fix had somehow worsened.

At least Estarde didn't waste any time getting to it. As soon as he spotted the *Americanos* stirring and rising from their bedrolls he marched over to stand before them. Six of his men came with him, rifles held not in a directly threatening manner yet at the same time very much in evidence. Elsewhere in the camp, the eyes of others, even as they went about various tasks, glanced frequently in the direction of this meeting.

"Good morning, *amigos,*" Estarde greeted.

"Mornin'," Firestick replied.

"A good leader of men, especially a leader of fighting men," Estarde proceeded, "should know when to listen and pay attention to those who serve under him. I consider myself a good leader. In fact, for the purpose of this rebellion we are in the midst of, I choose to view it not as men serving under me but rather men serving beside me."

"Seems a decent way of lookin' at things," Firestick allowed, sensing Moosejaw looming up next to him.

"I explain this," Estarde continued, "because several of my men came to me during the night with concerns. Concerns about you and your large friend. I listened to them. They are of the opinion I was too quick to welcome you to our cause yesterday, too quick to take you simply at your word that you came seeking to join us and to fight with your guns against our hated oppressors."

"Did their concerns cause you to change your mind?"

Estarde's expression was stern, giving nothing away. "Let's just say I'm willing to admit that my acceptance of you was perhaps a bit hasty. The defeat of Ricardo and his entire force of men, and the part — though small — you and your friend played in it, had me feeling euphoric and more charitable than may have been wise."

"So where does that leave us?" Firestick said. "How can we convince you that we are what we say we are?"

"For starters, how do you explain that, as *pistoleros,* seasoned fighting men, you allowed the Rurales to trap you in the manner they did?"

Firestick considered before giving his response. "The simple truth, much as I hate to admit it, is that we let our guard down and got caught. We were weary, in strange territory without havin' seen tracks or any sign that anybody else was close around, and we damn near paid for it with our lives. No other way to say it."

A corner of the colonel's mouth lifted in what might have been a grudging smile. "To be honest in the face of error rather than to make sad excuses is a good thing. As long, of course, as making errors does not become a habit."

"Considerin' the places we've been and the things we've done," said Firestick, "if me or my friend made a habit of errors, we wouldn't be standin' here today."

"That implies a life of danger, in keeping with the image of fighting men and *pistoleros* as you present yourselves to be," Estarde said. "But one of your weapons raises another question about that. You see that most of my men are rather poorly armed, though hardly by choice. That is on the verge of soon changing, starting with what we took from the bodies of those we defeated yesterday. But if you are a fighting man by trade, and in spite of the more current weapons you *do* display — why do you also possess a relic even older than the oldest of our guns?"

With this, the colonel jabbed a finger to indicate the Hawken rifle lying next to Firestick's bedroll.

The former mountain man almost had to laugh. Of all the things to raise suspicion . . .

"If I may, let me correct you on something, Colonel," Firestick said. "First off, me and my partner never presented ourselves as *pistoleros* — or gunslingers, as we call them up north. Those kind are mostly fast with their pistols. That's fine for in-close fightin', in saloons and cantinas and the like. But while we *have* picked up some pistol skills along the way, our background is mostly with long guns. A true fightin' man ought to know how to use more than one kind of weapon.

"So while you're right in sayin' that rifle of mine is something of a relic, it still has value and very good use for certain situations. I first carried that gun as a hunter and trapper in the great mountains to the north. It shoots farther and hits harder than any other gun I've ever used. If you want, I can give you a demonstration of why I still sometimes carry it."

Estarde frowned. "A demonstration?"

"Pick a target. Make it as far or farther than your best marksman can hit."

Estarde turned to his men and a quick dialogue in Spanish ensued. While they were talking, Firestick calmly stepped back and retrieved the Hawken.

"How about," he said, "havin' one of your men take a tin coffee cup to one of those ridges out yonder? Set him to walkin', I'll tell him how far."

By now several of the men backing the colonel, having had it explained to them what was going on, were showing signs of increasingly eager interest. At Firestick's suggestion, Estarde ordered one of them to take a coffee cup and start walking out away from the cavern. While he was doing this, Firestick loaded and primed the Hawken. When the man with the cup had gone more than two hundred yards, Firestick said, "That oughta be pretty good right about there."

A shout was raised and the man with the cup stopped walking. He placed the cup on a hump of sand and gravel, then backed away. The cup picked up a faint glint from the morning sun.

"Amigo," said Estarde somewhat breathlessly, "that is an impossible shot to make. If not for the glimmer of the sun, I could not even see that cup."

Firestick grinned. "I don't need to see it. I just need to hit it."

With that, he planted his feet, raised the Hawken to his shoulder, and sighted. He set the first trigger, held his breath, and a moment later caressed the firing trigger. The Hawken roared . . . and a heartbeat later the .50-caliber slug sent the tin cup spinning and clattering out of sight.

All of Estarde's men reacted, some jerking their bodies as if experiencing the hit firsthand. A few even clapped their hands.

The colonel wagged his head in awe and

amazement. "Truly an incredible shot," he said.

"I can hit a man-sized target at twice that distance," Firestick said matter-of-factly. "Do you understand now why I keep this weapon at my disposal?"

"Without doubt," Estarde replied. Then, abruptly shifting his attention to Moosejaw, he said, "But what of your large friend? Can he also —"

"With all due respect, Colonel," Moosejaw interrupted him, "what I can do, among other things, is speak for myself."

Estarde's brows furled with a quick display of annoyance but then, just as quickly, relaxed. "Very well. That is reasonable," he said. "Tell me then, Large One, are you as good a shot as your friend?"

Moosejaw shook his head. "I'm pretty fair, but nobody shoots as good as my friend. As he said a minute ago, though, a good fightin' man should know how to fight a lot of different ways. Among 'em oughta be good old-fashioned rough-and-tumble."

Estarde frowned, not quite understanding.

Moosejaw held up his melon-sized fists. "With these — along with feet, teeth, elbows, whatever," he explained. "You call me large, but I notice that a couple of your men are also pretty sizable. Would either one of 'em be interested in tryin' to put me on my back and keepin' me there?"

Before Estarde could respond, one of the men behind him — a tall, ropey-muscled individual with a heavy brow and a jutting chin — apparently understood enough of what Moosejaw had said to show signs of wanting to accept his challenge.

But Estarde himself failed to look particularly keen about the idea. "We do not have such an abundance of men," he said, "that we can afford to lose one — or possibly two — due to injury from fighting with each other."

Moosejaw shrugged. "Set the rules to keep it from goin' too far then. No cripplin' or such, just straight slam and punch until somebody can't get back up."

More men were gathering around the colonel, all clamoring for the fight to take place. Among other things, this demonstrated that their understanding of English was much stronger than what they had let on earlier, and that the caution Firestick and Moosejaw had displayed last night when talking between themselves had been a wise choice.

"Very well," Estarde relented. "We will go ahead — but within the bounds of inflicting no serious or lasting injuries."

A space was quickly cleared. The two combatants stripped off their shirts, guns, and knives and then squared off, facing each other.

"Commence," Estarde said.

The big Mexican rushed forward in a slight crouch. Moosejaw stood his ground, feet planted, and met him with a perfectly timed, straight-from-the-shoulder right cross that stopped him cold in his tracks. The fist-to-face impact sounded like a slab of raw meat being slapped against a stone. The big Mexican's feet took a faltering half step past where his face and torso quit moving forward, and then his knees buckled and it was as if his entire body turned to pudding. He melted to the ground, limp and motionless with his eyes rolled back in his head, and the fight was over.

Jaws dropped open and a stunned silence gripped the onlookers.

For a long moment Estarde just stared down at his fallen man. Then, slowly, he lifted his gaze and fixed it on Moosejaw. At length, a smile spread across his face. "I think," he said, his eyes cutting back and forth between Firestick and Moosejaw, "I have done enough reconsidering and am ready to go back to my original decision to accept you two as fighting men worthy of joining our cause."

"Pleased to hear that," Firestick said, breathing a sigh of relief.

"Same here," agreed Moosejaw. "I hope I didn't hurt your man too bad."

"As soon as somebody throws a bucket of water on him and gets him back on his feet, he will be okay," the colonel declared. "Come, you two need to get some breakfast in you and then we must ride. We have lost enough time."

As they walked toward the campfire where meals were being prepared, he added, "Part of my men will be splitting away from us to take the guns, horses, and ammunition we confiscated from the Rurales for delivery to General Almarez. The rest, including you two, will stick with me for a very important rendezvous. It is where we were headed before the chance to ambush the Rurales presented itself. It may amuse you to know we will briefly be crossing over the border to the north. The rendezvous I speak of is to purchase a shipment of more guns and ammunition that is waiting for us there, in an abandoned old town by the name of Bright Rock."

CHAPTER 47

Near the end of another long, hot day in the Vieja Mountains, Beartooth and his posse came to a literal fork in the trail. The afternoon had brought a strong wind out of the north — a hot, dry, furnace-like blast that offered no relief, only particles of whipping, gritty dust and sand to sting the eyes and scrape exposed flesh raw. And also to erase even what minimal sign of their quarry had been discernible on the hard, rocky ground.

The fortunate thing was that by this point they were following a singular passage through the highest elevations, beginning a descent through the jagged peaks. For the past few hours it hadn't been so much a matter of following the robbers' trail as it was following the only way for them to have gone.

Until now.

Immediately ahead, the passage split and

angled downward on two different courses. One of them had to be a pass to the opposite base of the mountains; the other would most likely end in an impossible drop-off or narrow to an impenetrable wall. In addition to not knowing which was the through passage, there was also the question of which one their quarry had gone down.

"Even with this wind and the rocky surfaces," Beartooth told those gathered tight around him in a vertical crevice that provided a temporary respite from the howling gusts, "Miguel or I could pick up the robbers' trail again. But that would be bound to take some time. I don't know how much. But we've only got a couple hours of daylight left and I can't help but think we're very close on their heels. I'd hate to lose the distance they'd gain if we slowed to hunt for sign."

"So what are you saying?" Overstreet wanted to know.

"I think we should consider splittin' up," Beartooth said. "Half of us go down one fork, half the other. Whichever one happens to pick the way the robbers went, I think will have the chance to catch up before sundown. They have no idea we're back here, especially not so close. When they stop to make night camp, they should be prime for an ambush — either as it gets dark or just before first light when their guard will be the lowest."

"What about Captain Shaw?" Hadley said.

"If he's still alive — which I'm guessin' he is, since we ain't run across his corpse the way they would have dumped it if they'd decided they were done with him — then I expect he'll be apart some from the rest. Tied up and shoved to one side. That'll leave the others vulnerable for either gettin' the drop on 'em or, like we talked before, takin' 'em as targets."

Thomas Rivers said, "You've got it figured mighty fine . . . if they do everything the way they're supposed to."

"Nothing's a sure thing, Thomas. I know that," said Beartooth. "But if we let this play out until tomorrow and they make it down into the foothills on the other side where everything will open up again . . . It's gonna be a helluva lot harder to corner 'em. I'm sure of that much."

"This much is very true," said Miguel somberly.

"Aye. It sounds right to me, as well," seconded Hadley.

"I ain't sayin' nothing against what Mr. Beartooth laid out," Big Thomas said. "I'm just pointin' out that, in order for it to work, things got to fall a certain way."

"But if we hang back and play it safe, things could fall in a way that would make us worse off," Overstreet said, musing out loud.

"I say we let Beartooth make the call," spoke up young Gabe Hooper. "He got us this far and this close . . . well, him and Miguel . . . But we never started out just to play it safe, did we?"

There was a general mumbling of agreement. If not wholehearted, at least not strongly against.

Beartooth bared his teeth in either a grimace or a grin. "I say we go for it then. We split up and try to bring this thing to a close. Whichever of us takes the passage that somehow dead-ends, backtrack as soon as that much is clear and come around to the aid of the other. Okay. Now here are the groups we'll split into . . ."

Beartooth took Hadley and Gabe Hooper down one passage with him. Miguel, Overstreet, and Big Thomas went the other way.

Emerging once more from the crevice, the wind instantly tore at them again. Each man tugged his hat down tight and low above his eyes and pulled his neckerchief up over his nose and mouth. They plodded forward leading their horses, hugging close to the big bodies for a certain amount of wind blockage rather than sitting up in the saddles where they would have been lashed far worse.

The sun began to fade and the dimness of dusk was hurried all the more by the blowing gusts of dirt and grit.

Beartooth trudged in the lead of his group, straining to see around the next twist in the trail. The wind conveniently muffled the noise their progress made, but diminished visibility came with it.

Time blurred along with sight and sound. Beartooth tried to guess by the dimming light how long it had been since they'd parted from the others. Less than an hour, he judged.

He wished he had Firestick and Moosejaw along. In the old days, when it had been just the three of them and they'd faced dicey situations like this, they'd always done so with a spirit of rake-hell invincibility. They had complete confidence in one another and what the three of them could do. Together, they'd felt willing and able to spit in the eye of the Devil and jab him in the ass with his own pitchfork.

Now it was all different. The old days were

gone. Not only were the three of them often apart due to the demands of the ranch and from being lawmen, but there were so many more things — and people — also affected by their actions. The fact that some of these people were loved ones was a good thing for the most part — but with love, as Beartooth was finding out, came other concerns and responsibilities. He thought of Victoria waiting for his safe return. And of Daisy waiting for Moosejaw. And he couldn't begin to imagine what Firestick was going through, having the woman he loved stolen away . . .

Later, he would blame having been lost so deep in his ponderings for causing him to miss any warning sign that might have changed what happened next. Whatever the reasons, he got caught by surprise. From out of a blur of wind-whipped dust came another blur, and with it came a sharp blow to the side of his head. Something very hard crashed across his temple, stunning him, causing his knees to instantly buckle. His horse shrieked in alarm. He heard somebody shout and then what sounded like gunshots, distorted by the wind. As he clawed for his own pistol he found his fingers were suddenly floppy and useless, like an empty glove that could not grip or lift. And then another blow landed, to the back of his head this time, and he pitched forward into numbing blackness.

CHAPTER 48

When Beartooth opened his eyes again, he was no longer numb. Pain knifed through him, from his head on down his neck and into his shoulders. He held back a scream but could not suppress a loud groan.

A grinning face swam in front of him.

"What's the matter, Deputy? Regret now that you disregarded my simple warning? I never harmed a single soul in your stinking town, you ungrateful bastard, and all you had to do to keep it that way was to hold off your chase for a little while. Now a young life has been wasted and more are on the line, including yours. All because you insisted on playing the big, bold hero."

The face came into focus. A man with a long, thin nose and a pencil mustache. Angry eyes.

Beartooth could still hear the wind howling, though none was blowing against him. Overhead he could see a slice of the sky still holding some streaks of daylight. High, smooth stone walls all around. Not a cave, but a natural crevice cut into the side of the passage, out of the wind; similar to the one where he'd huddled with his posse not long ago, but much larger. A quick sweep of his eyes as he blinked them more into focus showed Oberon Hadley's bulk sprawled nearby him. No sign of Gabe Hooper. Straight ahead, on the other side of the man with the pencil mustache, was a dark-haired woman draped in a tan duster. She was holding a short-barreled pistol. Beside her, hunched forward with his hands tied in front of him, squatted Rupert Shaw.

The man with the pencil mustache reached out and cuffed Beartooth alongside the head. Not hard, just to get his attention. "How many more are trailing behind you?" he demanded. "Don't insult me by trying to make me believe you came after us with only a three-man posse."

Beartooth tried to lunge for the man, but all he managed was to shove himself up on one elbow before the pain streaked through him again and he fell back, gasping. The slice of sky overhead became smeared by another wave of dizziness.

"Not so tough now, are you, hero?" sneered Pencil Mustache. "You're going to die. You know that, don't you? The only question is whether or not you die quick and without more pain if you tell me what I need to know — or if you make us do it the hard way and you suffer greatly before telling me anyway."

"You go to hell," Beartooth snarled.

Pierce Torrence raised his hand to strike him again when Shaw blurted out from behind him. "There's an easier, quicker way!"

Torrence stayed his hand and spun around. "What are you talking about?"

Shaw inclined his head, indicating Hadley. "The big one there. Roust him back to consciousness and he'll reveal anything I tell him to. He's totally devoted to me. He'll talk for certain."

"And then what?" Torrence sneered. "I suppose you'll expect me to leave him alive in return."

"I don't care one way or the other. He will have served his purpose. All I want in return is one thing," Shaw said. He inclined his head again, this time toward Beartooth. "Him. I want that piece of backwoods trash dead. And I want to be the one to do it. You can add another five thousand dollars to the ransom money if you put a gun in my hand long enough to let me plant a bullet in his scurvy heart."

Leticia cast a startled glance in his direction.

Before Torrence could respond, two forms came ducking hurriedly out of the wind and into the chasm. Black Hills and Romo pulled the neckerchiefs down off their faces and inhaled some deep breaths of still air.

"We went back quite a ways without spotting anybody else," Black Hills reported. "If there's anybody back there, they're back a long way."

"I find it impossible to believe they sent only a posse of three!" Torrence insisted.

"Believe what you want," Black Hills said, scowling. "All I'm sayin' is that if there's more, they ain't close. I'm the one who spotted this bunch by scoutin' our back trail, ain't I? I think I know what I'm lookin' for."

"Yes, yes, Black Hills, no one is questioning your skill at that sort of thing. But it's a matter of practicality. It simply makes no sense to have sent such a small posse."

"Maybe there was a bigger posse but these three got separated from the others in that damn blinding wind," Leticia suggested.

"Or maybe," Romo said, "some of 'em went down that other fork back a ways."

"Yeah," said Black Hills, turning on him

with a hard frown, "and maybe they scattered farther back after hearing gunshots because you decided to start blastin' away at that third *hombre* instead of just clubbin' him like I did these two."

"Never mind that for right now. What's done is done," growled Torrence. "But thanks to our helpful Mr. Shaw, just before you two returned we were on the verge of finding out exactly how many posse members are back there. Black Hills, get that big fellow awake. Be careful, he's nearly the size of you. Romo, you stand ready with your gun drawn. Letty, my dear, eject all but one shell from your gun and have it ready for Shaw to use as his part of the bargain if he's able to get the information out of the ox."

Beartooth listened to all of this, his heart pounding, trying to keep his breathing under control. The dizziness seemed gone and his pain felt manageable. But he didn't know if he had the strength to rise up suddenly or if he'd collapse again as before. And even if he did make it up, what chance did he have against four armed varmints — plus that piece of scum Shaw — scattered across the width of the giant crevice?

He'd fallen back in such a way that his head was turned toward Hadley. He watched helplessly as they splashed some water on the big Englishman's face and then shook him and gave him some light slaps to bring him around. Hadley's eyes opened and he blinked several times, appearing at first disoriented, befuddled, then quickly forming into a glare . . . until they came to rest on Shaw.

"That's right, old chum," Shaw said with an encouraging smile. "I'm still okay. As are you. A bit roughed up perhaps, but nothing we can't handle, eh? We're going to get out of this. I promise. I've arranged everything."

Shaw rose rather awkwardly from his sitting position and moved forward in a low crouch until he was directly in front of Hadley. He dropped to his knees and leaned in close to the big man. "But in order to save ourselves, we're going to have to cooperate with these fellows. I'm afraid they've got the drop on us, as they say in those lurid thrillers you've been reading. It's the only way. You must reveal how many men started out in that posse with you and where are the rest? There must have been more than just you and two others, correct? Where are the rest?"

Hadley blinked rapidly some more. "Others? Posse?"

With his bound hands, Shaw grabbed him impatiently by his shirtfront. "Damn it, man, clear your head. Think! Our lives depend on it, can't you see? Where are the others?"

Hadley's blinking slowed, and then stopped. "Oh. You want to know where the other posse members are."

Every eye in the chamber was focused on the big man's gloriously battered face, waiting for the next words to come out of it.

Starting soft and low so that everyone had to lean closer to hear, Hadley said, "We . . . we left the rest of them . . . up your mother's bloomers, ye yellow wanker!"

The final sentence came out in a full-throated bellow, with Hadley's face jammed so close to that of his ex-captain's that it left the formerly pampered cheeks dotted with spittle. And as an exclamation point to the words, there came the muffled roar of a firearm. Shaw jerked backward. As he did so, his smoldering vest pocket was ripped away due to Hadley's hand being shoved in it. Gripped now in the former sergeant's big paw was a smoking over-under derringer.

With one chamber still to be discharged in the confiscated weapon, Hadley thrust his arm in the direction of Black Hills, whom he reckoned to be the most immediate remaining threat, and fired the second barrel. The slug slammed into the middle of the big outlaw, a few inches to the left of his belt buckle, and spun him partway around. It didn't knock him down but it did send him staggering into Romo and momentarily prevented the latter from aiming his already drawn gun.

That moment was all it took for more gun blasts to echo deafeningly in the stone-walled chamber. Bullets poured out of the deeper shadows toward the back of the crevice. A couple ricocheted in piercing whines, but far more thudded into meat and bone. Behind this burst of gunfire, the faces and shapes of Miguel, Big Thomas, and Russ Overstreet came charging out of the blackness. The bank robbers never stood a chance, never got off a shot. All three men went into lurching, spinning death dances that ended with them toppling to the ground. Only Leticia, whom the shooters swarmed over and nearly trampled, knocking her gun out of her hand, was spared a bullet.

"This crevice, this huge crack," Miguel explained after the shooting was over and everyone was trying to piece together exactly what had happened, "runs clear over to the other passage that forked off back up the trail. We discovered it just as that other way was narrowing to a dead end. We wouldn't have paid it much attention, not realizing how far in it reached, except when we were getting ready to turn around and go back, we heard voices coming through it. Like you said, Señor Beartooth, sound travels funny in the mountains."

"So, since we saw this big ol' crack was goin' toward the way you took and there was the voices comin' through and all, we started followin' it in," Overstreet said.

"It was mighty tight goin' in a couple places and dark as Hades part of the time, too," Big Thomas added. "But those yammerin' voices — not that we could rightly understand what they were sayin' — kept lurin' us on."

"Well, you'll get no complaints out of me that you allowed 'em to. That's for sure," said Beartooth. He was sitting up now. The dizziness and pain had mostly subsided and he felt like he could probably stand, but right at the present there was no need to hurry it.

"We came to the edge of the opening but still back in the shadows just as the hostage was presenting his idea for getting Señor Hadley to tell about other posse members," Miguel said, picking up the narrative again. "But then the other two came in and stood too close to Señor Hadley and you, one of them with his gun already drawn, so we could not make a rush right away for fear of one of you catching a bullet."

"But then ol' Hadley cut loose," said Overstreet, wagging his head partly in amazement and partly in admiration, "so all we could do was follow his lead and come blazin' out."

"I guess it was a bit of a reckless move," allowed Hadley, who was also in a sitting position next to Beartooth. "But after I heard the captain make a deal for himself to kill the deputy here while at the same time offering me up for sacrifice . . . well, I knew he had to die and I knew I should be the one to do it. I'd been laying there awake for quite a while, you see, listening and waiting for some kind of opening."

"How did you know about the derringer in his vest?" Beartooth asked.

"He *always* carries it there," Hadley answered. "I didn't know the robbers hadn't relieved him of it, though, until he came close and grabbed me by the shirtfront. I felt it against my arm. That's when I decided how I was going to use it, what I was going to do."

"If the robbers never found it and he had that hideaway gun all this while," said Overstreet, "why didn't he use it himself to try and escape? His hands were only tied in front — he could have got to it in that vest pocket if he'd wanted to."

"But he *didn't* want to. Because," Hadley said, a great sadness suddenly flooding his expression, "Captain Rupert Shaw was a coward. I refused to believe that for all these years, railed against the rumors and charges against him as the petty work of those who were merely jealous and seeking to get even. I guess I even looked away a time or two when I saw signs of it firsthand. Not wanting to admit it because, if I did, then I'd have to admit I'd been wrong in my judgment and maybe even that my defense of him was due to having gotten a taste of the finer things in life by being in his employ and not wanting to give that up."

Beartooth shook his head. "I think it was simply a matter of loyalty. Blind loyalty, maybe, but not for any reasons that were dishonorable. And one thing's for damn certain — you've proved beyond any doubt that none of Shaw's cowardice rubbed off on you."

Hadley met his eyes with a look of gratitude. "Once I made up my mind to try for that derringer, I would have gone through with it regardless, figuring neither you nor I had much chance anyway. But just as I was getting ready to make my grab, I looked past the captain's shoulder and caught a glimpse of Miguel back in the shadows. I didn't know why or how he got there, but I knew his presence meant we had a chance after all, if I just went ahead and set things in motion."

"And boy, did you ever do that," remarked Overstreet.

"The only thing that bothers me about it," muttered Miguel, "is that you were able to spot me. I must be slipping."

Beartooth's expression turned bleak. "You got no call to be bothered. I'm the one who walked into an ambush — got me and Hadley a couple busted skulls, got young Gabe killed."

"Don't do that to yourself, man," Big Thomas protested. "What with the poor visibility due to the wind and dusk comin' on —"

"Then if I wasn't up to dealin' with it," Beartooth cut him off, "I shouldn't have pushed so hard and insisted on catchin' up. We could have waited until tomorrow, and Gabe would have been alive to see it."

"Tomorrow comes with no promises for anyone," Hadley told him. "It never has and never will. And young Hooper knew the risks when he agreed to join this posse. In fact, he was bursting with pride over it. Don't diminish that by acting now as if you should have coddled him or not included him at all, just because he got caught by some bad luck."

Now it was Beartooth who reacted with a look of gratitude. Sighing raggedly, he said, "I guess it's like my pal Firestick is fond of sayin', what's written is written."

Nobody had a response to that.

After a minute, Beartooth pushed to his feet. Big Thomas reached to steady him. Glancing up through the open top of the crevice at the sky that had by now gone full dark, the lawman said, "I guess we'll be campin' here tonight. We'll need to gather up the bodies, wrap 'em in blankets, and put 'em off to one side in some decent way . . . especially Gabe's, which we'll find back down the trail. Then, first thing in the mornin', we'll tie 'em on horses and start back down the mountain to Buffalo Peak."

Overstreet and Big Thomas left to go get Gabe.

Beartooth stepped over to Leticia, who sat glaring silently in pretty much the same spot where she'd been nearly trampled when Miguel and the others charged over her. He took a pair of handcuffs from his belt and shook them loose. "And don't think I'm forgettin' you, sweetheart. You'll be goin' back down the mountain, too. In these." He tossed her the cuffs. "Clamp 'em on and start gettin' used to the idea of chains and bars. Because they're gonna be a part of your life for a long time to come."

CHAPTER 49

"Why not let me take care of it, Josh?" Charlie suggested in a low voice, his forehead deeply puckered. "You take the gals and walk a ways on ahead. Don't look back. I'll catch up when I've done what needs doin'."

Josh didn't lift his gaze at the words from his longtime partner. He just kept staring down at the gray mare who lay near where he stood with his rifle in his hands. The horse blew in a nervous, confused way.

"I'm obliged for the offer, Charlie," Josh said woodenly. "But it ought to be me. She's my horse. Been mine for nigh on to seven years. Ever since . . . well, you remember."

"Yeah, I remember. She's been an awful good horse to you."

"That she has. Never let me down. Not once. Not until she stepped wrong in that hole and busted her poor leg practically in two." Josh paused, swallowed hard. "Look at her, lying there in pain. She's gotta be hurtin' something fierce, but she's puttin' on a brave act. And if I asked her to, she'd do her darnedest to get back up again."

Cleo stepped up beside Josh, looking almost as forlorn as him. "Ain't there anything you can do to fix it — her leg, I mean?"

"Not really. Especially not way the heck out here." Josh's grip tightened reluctantly on his rifle. "Nothing for it but to put her out of her misery."

"That's so sad and awful," Cleo said, her voice now just a whisper.

"I know. But it's the only way." Josh sounded like he was reminding himself as well as trying to convince her. "Now go on over with Charlie and Miss Kate. Don't watch. It'll be quick and then she won't be sufferin' no more."

Cleo did as he suggested. She, Kate, and Charlie turned their backs and gazed off blankly. When Josh's rifle cracked they each winced involuntarily.

After a minute, Josh walked up level with them. He was carrying the saddle he'd stripped off the mare earlier. His rifle was shoved back in its scabbard. He took the saddle and swung it up on the packhorse, situating it so that it would ride secure on one of the bundles.

Without looking at anybody, he said in a thick voice, "We'd best get a move on. We're in Texas now, but the goin' is gonna be slower from here on since we're minus a horse and we still got a long stretch before we get to Bright Rock."

"That's too damn true," agreed Charlie. He squinted up at the early afternoon sun. "If we step to it, though, I think we still got a chance to make it by nightfall. We'll all walk for a ways. Then you gals can climb up double on my horse and me and Josh will keep wearin' down our boot heels."

They started out. Charlie took the front position, leading his horse; Josh fell to the rear, leading the packhorse. After a short ways, Cleo fell back and walked beside Josh. When she glanced over and saw that his eyes were shiny, she pulled a handkerchief from the waistband of her skirt and silently held it out to him. When he was done using it, he handed it back and she returned it to her waistband. After a few more steps, she slipped her hand in his and they walked like that for quite a ways.

Estarde split his force into two groups of seven. Those who separated from him were sent to General Almarez with the weapons and other goods that had been confiscated from the defeated Rurales. Along with them went a handwritten note from the colonel detailing the great success of the engagement and an assurance that Estarde, though somewhat delayed, would soon be returning from north of the border with even more weapons and ammunition purchased from the gunrunners in Bright Rock.

The groups parted and each went their individual way.

Estarde pushed those who rode with him at a hard, nonstop pace until they reached the Rio Grande. There he called a short halt to rest and water the horses, grab a bite to eat, and replenish their canteens. Some of the men took the opportunity to peel off their shirts and fling themselves into the river.

It was during this brief, raucous interlude that Firestick and Moosejaw got their first chance to talk alone for a few precious minutes. They sat on the riverbank, with their feet in the water, tipping their heads close together while the nearby splashing and whooping kept their words from traveling too far.

"I suppose," said Firestick, "we oughta look at this as a lucky break — gettin' swept up by these rebels and then findin' out they're headed straight for Bright Rock, right where we want to go."

"Yeah. A lucky break," Moosejaw muttered wryly. "Only question is whether it's all bad luck or we can manage to squeeze some good out of it."

"We've *got* to squeeze some good out of it," Firestick declared. "What we know for sure is that Estarde and his men are headed there and some gunrunners are waitin' for 'em. What we *think* we know is that the women and the skunks who took 'em are headed there, too. The real question is whether the skunks are somehow part of the rest or if they're on their way for reasons strictly their own."

"How are we supposed to find out?"

Firestick made a sour face. "I don't know. But it occurs to me if we could get two of the sides — don't matter which ones — fightin' against each other — either over the guns or over the women — we might have our chance to yank Kate and Cleo out of the middle of it."

Moosejaw regarded him. "Ain't sayin' it's a bad idea, mind you. But it's kinda light on details, don't you think?"

"Just be ready to follow my lead when I open the ball."

"Like I'm gonna have much choice," Moosejaw said under his breath.

CHAPTER 50

Three-quarters of the sun had sunk behind the western horizon when they started down the main street of Bright Rock. The old, sagging, partially dilapidated buildings cast long shadows, many of them oddly angled and grotesque in shape.

"I know it don't look like much, especially in the fadin' light," admitted Charlie as they paused to gaze down the empty, tumbleweed-strewn street. The air was still this evening, so even the freshest clump of sagebrush that had drifted in lay still and lifeless looking. "But we're bound to find some solid structures, and like we told you before, me and Josh will make some right nice dwellin's out of 'em."

"This place looks a million years old," Kate said dejectedly. "When was the last time anybody actually lived here?"

Halfway down the street, four men were

crouched behind the windows of the old hotel building, cautiously eyeing the approach of the new arrivals.

"Don't look like no ferocious, country-savin' Mexican revolutionaries to me," muttered Keefer Fleming.

"Who are they, then? And what in the world would cause 'em to show up here?" said Beaudine Jeffers, his young, sparsely whiskered face wearing an earnestly puzzled expression as he peered over Fleming's shoulder.

One window down, Lefty Gramlich said, "Judging by the fact they've only got one saddle horse and a packhorse, I'm guessing they had some trouble somewhere out on the trail and wandered this way looking for help."

"What kind of help would they expect to find in a ghost town?" Fleming sneered.

"I'm not saying they came here intentionally," Lefty snapped peevishly. "Did you hear me say they were wandering? Probably half-desperate."

"Well, worse luck for them, they ain't gonna find no help here," Vic Mason said with a flinty look in his eyes. "Estarde is due to be showin' up any time. He'll be expecting to see us — and only us. He spots a bunch of new faces, he's liable to get suspicious and back off. We didn't buck the damn army and lose Hawkins and sit here baking in this rotting pile of wood all this time to have it queered by some poor lost pilgrims!"

Beaudine made a distasteful face. "Jeez, Vic. We ain't gonna just . . . kill 'em. Are we?"

Mason glared up the street, not looking over at the younger man. "We're gonna get rid of 'em, Beaudine, whatever it takes."

"Here now, let's not get too hasty," said Fleming, who was continuing to study the approaching four. "I'm seein' me a couple women there amongst our visitors. And by the shape of 'em and the way they move, they ain't no fat old farm wives nor slat-thin, wore out ones, neither. That makes 'em something I'd say we ought not be in a big a hurry to get rid of."

"We get paid and finish what we came here for," Mason said out the side of his mouth, "there are plenty of women for you to chase down when our business is done."

"I tell you, I got me a wrong feelin'," Josh was saying as they walked slowly down the street. "We ain't alone here; we're bein' watched."

"Take it easy, pard," Charlie told him.

478

"You're just feelin' a little spooked by the old buildings and the sun goin' down and all. Just because they call it a ghost town don't mean it's got any ghosts."

"I know what Josh is talking about," spoke up Cleo. "I don't believe in ghosts, but I don't think we're alone here, either."

"See, Josh, now you're spookin' the women," said Charlie. "All of you just calm down. Ain't nobody came around this old place in years. Nobody but us showin' up here this evenin'."

"In that case," countered Kate, "what do you call that stepping out in the street up ahead?"

All eyes followed her words to the sight of Mason and Fleming emerging from the hotel and stepping off its sagging front porch.

The four new arrivals stopped walking. In a low voice, Charlie was quick to say, "You gals might see this as a chance to flee. But I'd think twice, was I you. Take a good look at the way those *hombres* are hung with guns and the way they're holdin' themselves."

"Plus there's a couple more still in that building," Josh added. "I seen 'em through the windows."

"I ain't going nowhere," said Cleo.

Kate said nothing. But neither did she flee. Her appraisal of the men up ahead, even without Charlie's advisement, told her they were trouble — even more trouble than she already had.

"Come on ahead, folks. We don't bite," said Mason, real friendly-like. His smile widened and he extended one hand, motioning them forward. "We're as surprised to see you as you are us."

Again in a low voice, Charlie said, "Come on. But, as we move ahead, ease on over toward the opposite side of the street in case we got to make a sudden dive for cover."

The four walked forward. Unhurriedly. Gradually edging toward the opposite side of the street from the hotel building.

Up ahead, Mason and Fleming stood waiting. The windows of the hotel looked on like lifeless, black eye sockets. But Josh knew better. There was life — and maybe sudden death — hiding in the darkness of those sockets.

They drew closer to the waiting men. As they did, Fleming's eyes hungrily devoured the women, feasting first on one and then the other. And then, as the four got closer still, his focus locked strictly on Cleo and he couldn't hold back a sudden exclamation. "Hey, I know you! From El Paso a few months back — you ain't no farm wife, you're nothing but a damn saloon whore!"

Josh took a lunging step and suddenly was standing in front of Cleo, his hand coming to rest on the grips of his Colt. "Take that back, you foul-mouthed son of a bitch! This woman is gonna be my bride!"

There was no holding it back then. Josh touching his sidearm triggered an involuntary response from both Fleming and Mason. Though both were experienced gun hands, neither made claim to being especially fast. Still, it came as a surprise to them, as well as Lefty and Beaudine observing from inside the hotel, that the simple cowboy-looking pair of Josh and Charlie cleared leather equally as fast as the hardcases.

Guns popped and spat flame frantically — too frantically for much accuracy to come into play. The closeness of the exchange meant that all four men were simultaneously and rather awkwardly trying to duck and dodge as they snapped off their shots. Fleming's hat went flying and he backpedaled wildly. Mason got his feet tangled and nearly fell as he crouched low and tried to shift sideways at the same time. Josh stood resolutely in front of Cleo and kept firing, barely shrugging as one of

Fleming's slugs punched through the meaty area of his left arm, just missing the biceps. Charlie yanked Kate around behind his horse and leaned out around the animal's heaving chest to trigger more shots. "Get in the building! Get inside to cover!" he shouted.

The others scrambled to follow his command. Josh pulled Cleo and himself around behind the packhorse, following Charlie's example and using the animal for a shield. Slugs coming from the hotel windows, now that Lefty and Beaudine finally had a clear field of fire without risking hitting their comrades, whapped into the bundles on the packhorse's back, kicking up mini geysers of dust.

The building Charlie was trying to get everybody into had the look of an old store. There was a walkthrough door in the middle of its front, with large windows to either side. These windows, of course, had long since been absent any glass. Charlie and Josh were trying to get their respective horses to plunge through these openings to make it inside. Bullets cut the air high and low, more of them striking the bundles on the back of the packhorse, others chewing into the weathered wood of the old store. Charlie had nearly succeeded in getting his horse to make the leap inside when the poor beast took simultaneous hits to the side of its neck and the back of its head and collapsed with a painful shriek. As the carcass went down, Charlie and Kate wheeled away and made their own dives over the low windowsill and rolled to relative safety inside. Moments later, Josh got the packhorse to make the leap through the window on the other side, and he and Cleo followed.

Switching now to their rifles, Josh and Charlie — the latter having managed to grab his from its saddle scabbard as his horse went down — quickly took up positions in the corners of the wide store windows and began returning more measured, more carefully aimed fire. Kate and Cleo hunkered close by and began reloading for them.

Only thanks to the shooters inside the hotel laying down a barrage of cover fire, also from repeating rifles, were Mason and Fleming able to desperately scramble in off the street without getting riddled to pieces.

CHAPTER 51

After the brief stop at the Rio Grande, Estarde pushed his men even harder to reach Bright Rock before sundown. Only after the shapes of the old buildings came into sight up ahead, with the last sliver of the sinking sun getting ready to slip behind the western horizon, did he signal a slowdown. Scarcely had the rebel group slowed to continue their approach at an easy canter, however, when the sound of gunfire suddenly erupted from somewhere within the gray husks they were riding toward.

Estarde reined his mount to a full stop. Firestick and Moosejaw pulled up on one side of him.

"What do you make of that?" Firestick said.

"I do not know. But I do not like it," said the colonel, aiming a deep frown toward their destination.

"Could it be your gunrunner friends are

484

fightin' amongst themselves? Or are they maybe doin' some target practice with the inventory?" said Moosejaw.

As abruptly as it had started, the shooting from up ahead stopped.

Estarde's frown deepened. "We did not come all this way to turn back at the mere hint of a skirmish," he said. "Let us proceed up the street. Cautiously. Fan out and keep a close watch on all sides."

From a side window of the old hotel, Beaudine glanced out and saw the group of men entering town at the far end of the street. He called out to Mason. "Vic — you'd better come see this! I think Estarde just arrived."

The gang leader hurried over to the window and looked out for himself. "Damn! Of all the lousy timing," he spat. Then, over his shoulder, he told the others, "Hold your fire! No more shooting at those peckerwoods across the way. Don't give 'em a target and don't give 'em a reason to fire back. If we can draw Estarde in close enough, I can call out to him and get him to join us on this side. Then we'll have those bastards over there outnumbered to a fare-thee-well and we can bring this to an end right quick!"

"We don't need no bunch of ragged-ass greasers to help us handle a couple no-account cowboys," protested Fleming.

He started to add on something more but Mason cut him short. "Shut up, Fleming! If your crudeness with women hadn't caused you to shoot off your mouth out there in the street, we could have had this over with already. But you couldn't hold your tongue then, so you'd damn well better do it now."

Estarde and his men proceeded slowly down the street, fanned out wide across most of its width. Firestick and Moosejaw rode off to the colonel's right. Seven sets of alert eyes swept ahead, darting from side to side, high and low, probing every window and doorway. As they drew closer, the carcass of Charlie's fallen horse became the focal point for many.

"Something more than target practice went on here," Moosejaw grated.

When they'd gone another half a block between the empty, weather-battered buildings, a voice suddenly called out from a side window of the old hotel up ahead on the left. Vic Mason appeared there for only a moment, waving his hat and shouting, "Estarde! Over here! Take cover and come around on the back!"

Estarde froze for a fraction of a second, trying to comprehend what he'd seen and heard and decide on what his reaction should be. In that half a heartbeat's hesitation, another voice cried out from up ahead, this time on the right. "Elwood!" Hearing that voice say that singularly meaningful name, Firestick's reaction was instantaneous. Jerking his horse hard to the right and simultaneously hollering "Moosejaw!" he spurred straight for a narrow alley strewn with heaps of drifted sand and broken bits of an old rain barrel, its curved gray staves poking up like broken stumps of teeth. Moosejaw came pounding right behind him.

Since the old store had no side windows, those inside hadn't had any awareness of the revolutionaries riding in until Mason shouted and drew attention to them. While Kate immediately recognized Firestick and could not hold back from calling his name, Josh and Charlie interpreted what happened next all as part of a single threat. Hearing Mason call in a familiar tone from across the street and then seeing two of those he'd called to suddenly break away down an alley on *their* side, the cowboy duo believed they were witnessing an attempt to get around behind their position. So they promptly opened fire on the two making the break, trying to stop them. This caused the rest of the men in the street — seeing two of their own being shot at — to open up on the store windows out of which the lead was pouring. And with all that busting loose, the men in the hotel, in spite of Mason's order to hold their fire, began shooting, as well.

The air suddenly filling with flying bullets caused Estarde's indecision to rapidly evaporate. Echoing Mason's words, he swept his arm in wild motions to his left and shouted, "Take to cover on this side of the street! Around back of the old hotel!"

The five remaining revolutionaries, including Estarde, spurred their horses hard to plunge between and behind the buildings on the left side of the street. Bullets from Josh and Charlie blistered the air around them and gouged chunks of rotted wood out of the structures they raced to get in back of for cover. Amazingly, no slugs scored a hit on any of the men.

But Charlie Gannon wasn't so lucky. In his desperation to stop the men he thought were attempting a flanking maneuver and then drive back the rest of those riding with them, he exposed himself too openly to the gunfire pouring out of the hotel. A bullet smashed high into the right side of his chest, just below the rifle he held raised and butted against his right shoulder. He flew back from the impact and hit the floor on his left side. His rifle fell clattering to the floor.

"I got one! I'm sure of it. I saw him go down!" crowed young Beaudine Jeffers from a front window of the hotel.

"Yeah, well keep quiet about it and get your own fool head down or somebody will damn sure return the favor," Lefty scolded him.

"Aw, let the kid crow a little bit," said Fleming. "Whatever he did, it looks like he took the fight out of 'em. They've stopped shooting again."

"That don't mean it's permanent — not permanent enough to start taking chances," argued Lefty.

"Lefty's right," interjected Mason. "Just go back to holdin' your fire and keepin' ducked down low. Estarde and his men will be comin' in through the back in a minute, and then we'll have the upper hand for sure."

"What about those two who skedaddled off to the other side of the street?" Lefty said. "What was that all about?"

"Yeah," said Fleming. "And it sounded like one of the women over across the way called something out to 'em. Who was that?"

"How the hell do I know?" growled Mason. "They're Estarde's men; he can explain what they're up to when he gets here."

Fleming scowled suspiciously. "Well, I don't like the idea of havin' some of 'em over there on that side — especially considerin' what else is over there."

"Seems to me that havin' 'em over there where they can work in behind those troublemakers in that old store could turn out to be a big advantage to us," Mason told him. "You ever think of that?"

Fleming still didn't look convinced. "Only as long as you're sure we can trust this greaser buddy of yours not to be playin' both sides against the middle."

In his peripheral vision, Josh had seen his longtime friend and partner go down. By the way Charlie flew back and as hard as he hit the floor, Josh knew it must be bad.

"Charlie?" He spoke the name as both a question and as a cry of alarm.

"Go to him," Cleo urged. She held out her hands. "Leave me the rifle. I know how to use it; I'll keep them pinned down across the way."

Josh hesitated. The thought crossed his mind that she might also turn it on him.

But locking gazes and peering deep into her eyes, even if only for a brief and intense moment, told him she wasn't prepared to do that.

Pushing the rifle into her hands, he said, "Stay low. Don't waste bullets."

A moment later, he was on his knees beside the fallen Charlie. Somewhat to Josh's surprise, Kate was already there, also on her knees, her hands tugging open Charlie's shirtfront, trying to get at the wound that was issuing thick spurts of blood.

Charlie's eyes were glassy and he was breathing in short, rapid gasps. "Aw hell, pard, they got me good. I . . . I think I'm a goner."

"Don't say that!" Josh insisted. "You hold on, you hear? You try to relax and let us get this bleedin' stopped and you'll be okay. You're gonna be okay, you hear?"

Kate had his shirt opened but was having trouble ripping away some of the already blood-soaked material that she intended to use as wadding to apply to the wound in order to try and stop the bleeding.

"I don't think the bullet went through," she said breathlessly. "If we can just put on enough pressure to close the front . . ."

Josh tore furiously at the shirt fabric, ripping away a long strip of it.

Charlie's eyes seemed to lose focus for a moment but then rolled to gaze up at Kate. In a thick-sounding voice, he said, "I sure am sorry I got you into this, Miss Kate. I . . . I really meant to protect you and treat you better than . . . I never figured . . . I . . ."

His words trailed off and his gasping ceased.

Leaning his full weight down on the wadded piece of shirt he was holding over the bullet hole, Josh felt his old friend's body go completely limp and still.

"Charlie! Damn you, don't you die on me!" Josh choked back a sob. "You can't give up. We got plans!"

Kate rocked back on her heels. Her shoulders sagged. After a moment she reached out and put one hand on Josh's shoulder as he continued to lean down and press hard with both hands on the wound that had now stopped pumping blood. "It's no use. He's gone," she said as gently as she could.

Josh's head continued to hang down for a long moment and Kate could feel a trembling in his shoulders. Suddenly his face lifted. Tears glittered in his eyes as they looked past her and swept in a wide arc over the shadowy rear area of the old store. In a voice revitalized by urgency, he said, "Those two that broke to this side of the street — we can't let them get in behind us or we'll all be done for!"

"The ones over in the hotel ain't doing nothing right now," Cleo called from the window. "I can hold them back if they try anything. You see to the back, Josh."

"No!" Kate immediately protested. "Those two men will help us. They came this way because I called. It's the marshal and one of his deputies from Buffalo Peak. They're here for Cleo and me, don't you see?"

"I see that don't make 'em good news for me," said Josh.

"Better than those hardcases across the way," Kate told him. "At the very least, I guarantee they won't try to gun you on sight. Not unless you give them no choice."

"Who *are* these skunks across the street?" Cleo said. "And who's the new bunch that just showed up? Somebody in that old hotel seemed to recognize them, almost be expecting them."

"I don't know any of that," Kate said, getting exasperated. "I just know the two men who broke to this side are Marshal McQueen and Deputy Hendricks from back home. And I know they'll fight to keep us safe from *whoever* the rest are."

Josh shook his head. "That don't wash. They rode in *with* that other bunch. And all the others scurried to join the men shooting against us — the men who killed Charlie!"

"You're a little late with your questions, *hombre,*" came a new voice, a strong, commanding one issued from the deepening shadows at the back of the room. Simultaneously, out of those same shadows, the face and form of Firestick stepped into view with his Winchester Yellowboy leveled on Josh's belly. "You should've found time to look for some answers before you got in such a hurry to start fillin' the street outside with lead. And you'd better hope I don't get to feelin' just as itchy."

Josh held motionless as this apparition came forward. He realized too late that, in his haste to come to Charlie's aid, he not only had handed his rifle to Cleo but had also left the Colt she'd reloaded for him lying on the floor by the window.

Behind Firestick, Moosejaw also appeared, moving with the same ghostly silence. He, too, held his rifle at the ready.

Kate rose to her feet with an uncertain smile. "Thank God you're here," she said. "But before anybody gets too itchy for more shooting, we need to have an understanding about some things."

CHAPTER 52

While Firestick and Moosejaw were joining up with those gathered in the old store, Estarde and his men had threaded their way in through the rear of the abandoned hotel and were being welcomed by Vic Mason.

The friendliness being exhibited by Mason, however, hardly cut both ways. "What the hell is this?" Estarde demanded to know. "You greet me and my men with bullets flying through the air and shout for us to duck around the back way like cowering thieves?"

"Please. Please accept my sincerest apologies," Mason pleaded. "This unexpected trouble broke out only moments before your arrival. I had no time to send word to warn you."

But Estarde was far from placated. "I am fighting a war in my own country. I did not come all this way to fight another in order to conduct a simple business transaction."

"I understand. Believe me, I do. If you'll

just let me explain the nature of this problem, then we can —"

Estarde made a slashing motion with his hand. "I do not need an explanation of your problem. I only need the guns you have promised. I am even willing to forget the fact that my men and I have been shot at." The colonel slapped the sash around his waist in which was wrapped a pouch containing silver coins. The coins clinked effectively. "I have the payment, you have the guns. We make a simple exchange and then my men and I ride away and leave you to your problem . . . as, I assure you, we will be returning to plenty of our own."

"Now wait just a minute, buster," Fleming tried to cut in. "I don't know who the hell you think —"

Mason fired him a scathing look. "Damn it, Fleming, shut up! I'm handling this."

"With *amigos* like this one," Estarde said, raking Fleming with his own hard look, "I am not surprised you have unexpected problems, Señor Mason. He is the kind who will always add such. The kind you should cut away like the poison from a snake bite — before he infects your entire crew."

Fleming started to take a step toward the colonel. "Aw, come on, Vic, you can't expect me to —"

This time it was Lefty who stopped him, clamping a hand on his shoulder and jerking him back. "Shut the hell up, you fool," he rasped. "Else I'll start carving on that poison myself."

Now Estarde's eyes bored directly into Mason. "Are you in charge here, or have I foolishly entered into a deal with a pack of snarling wolf pups lacking a true leader?" Behind him, his four flinty-eyed rebel fighters shifted into poised postures.

"Now just a damn minute!" Mason barked. He returned Estarde's hard glare. "Yes, I'm in charge of this outfit. I told you, we had an unexpected flare-up of trouble just minutes before you showed up. We've been waiting here for damn near a week. If you'd've gotten across the border when you were supposed to, then we all would have come and gone before those troublemakers across the street ever came into the picture. So, no matter who's in charge, by God, things don't always go according to plan!"

Estarde appeared to relent, but only slightly. "Very well. What is done is done. But we are both here now and your trouble — whatever its nature — seems temporarily quieted down. That means there is nothing preventing us from completing our transaction." He pulled the fat coin pouch from his sash and plopped it on the top of a gutted old desk that stood close by where the two men were facing one another. "There is your payment. Let me and my men examine some of the merchandise. If we are satisfied, you may take possession of this, we will take the guns, and then we will be on our way."

Mason licked his lips. His eyes fell to the bulging pouch, lingered there a long moment, then lifted slowly. "There's a slight problem," he said, much of the forcefulness that had been there only a minute ago now missing from his tone. "The crates containing your guns and ammunition, you see . . . are across the street in that old store where the men who shot at you are holed up."

"That's the pure craziest thing I ever heard tell," marveled Firestick. "Grabbin' a couple women off the streets of a town and haulin' 'em to some remote place, in the belief you could prove to be the husband of their dreams. Holy buckets of thunderation, not even the loneliest, looniest old mountain man removed from civilization for years at a time ever came up with anything wilder than that."

Josh remained seated beside Charlie's corpse, now covered by a tarp pulled from the packhorse. His head was hung low, and when he spoke it was in a barely audible mumble. "When you say it out loud like that, it sounds like an awful crazy notion. Pure crazy, like you said. But somehow it didn't seem so at the time, not when we first planned it out and set it in motion . . . But you don't need to rub it in any deeper. Charlie's dead and the women we meant to protect and impress we've put in bad danger. And me, at best, I'm headed for a long jail stretch. Makes it pretty clear how bad we messed up."

Still at the window, where she was continuing to keep an eye on things across the street, Cleo looked around and said softly, "You may have done some wrong things, but you never meant no harm. Not really."

"Maybe not," Firestick growled. "But that don't make a helluva lot of difference. Smack between gunrunners and Mexican revolutionaries ain't a healthy place to be."

"But you rode in with the revolutionaries . . . you had become friends with them," Kate pointed out. "Doesn't that count for something?"

"Maybe I need to make that whole thing a little clearer," Firestick said. "Yeah, me and Moosejaw made friends with the rebels . . . by lyin' to 'em about who we are and pretendin' we wanted to hire out our guns to their cause. So what that's gonna count for, I expect, is when they find out we were only stringin' 'em along, they'll likely be all the more pissed off."

"On the other hand," said Moosejaw from a shadowy corner at the rear of the store where he'd been doing some poking around before the light faded completely, "I might have come across a little something that *will* make a difference in dealing with Colonel Estarde."

He stepped forward into a band of pale light. In each hand he held a shiny repeating rifle. "I found these in a corner back there. Half a dozen crates of 'em — maybe a hundred rifles and plenty of cartridges to go with 'em."

"It was an easier spot to unload our pack animals," Mason was explaining defensively. "And the small, uncluttered old store was better for pushing the crates in toward the back, where they'd be in the shade and out of the dust for however long we were going to be here. Who the hell knew anybody else was going to show up like this?"

"Complication?" echoed Estarde. "You think 'complication' covers a mess such as this?"

"Look, there's only two rundown cowboys and a couple of women over there," Mason said. "It's not that big a deal. The guns are shoved toward the back; they probably don't even realize they're there."

"If it is not a 'big deal,' " said Estarde, sneering openly, "how is it that only two cowboys and women are holding off you and your men at all? Why are they not already gunned down like the interfering rabble they are?"

"They were a little quicker on the trigger than we expected and managed to make it to cover in that building before we could finish 'em," Mason answered.

"But I *did* finish one," spoke up Beaudine. "Leastways, I saw him fall back from the window and none of 'em have done any shooting since."

"And besides," added Lefty, "you've got two of your men somewhere over on that side of the street, Colonel. If they work in behind, we'll have those troublemakers in a box for sure. Like Mason says, then it ought not be a big deal to finish 'em off."

"Except it would mean putting some of my men at risk, involving them in your fight. As I said, we already have a fight — a war — on our hands. We did not come here for more conflict." Estarde scowled fiercely.

"Nevertheless, my men *are* over there . . ."

One of the colonel's men spoke up, making a quick remark in Spanish.

Estarde's scowl deepened. "*Sí.* Just before my men went to that side of the street, a woman called out. Did anyone hear what she said, understand what it meant?"

"No," said Mason with a shake of his head, "we've been wondering the same thing."

Sighing raggedly, Estarde edged forward toward one of the windows. "It appears I have no choice but to involve myself and my men." He paused and glared at Mason. "But it is going to cost you. If my men and I have to fight to take possession of the guns, it stands to reason that should affect the previously established price."

Mason tried to hold his eyes, but couldn't. He rasped, "Let's just get this the hell over with."

Chapter 53

"Hey, *amigos*! McQueen and Hendricks! Can you hear me?"

Firestick edged to a corner of the window previously occupied by Charlie. "We hear you just fine, Colonel. How y'all doin' over there?"

There was a long pause as Estarde, discerning that Firestick's voice was clearly coming from inside the store where the "troublemakers" were holed up, took time to try and process what that meant.

"*Amigos* . . . I do not understand. You are there *with* the men who shot at you?"

"Kind of a surprisin' development, I know. But yeah, that's pretty much what it amounts to," Firestick called back.

"Have you defeated them? Or are you saying you have joined them?"

"Neither one, exactly. But from your way of lookin' at it, you'd probably say we've joined 'em. It gets kinda complicated."

Estarde barked an epithet in Spanish.

"But let's quit nibblin' around the edges and get to the middle of the pie," Firestick went on. "What we got here is what a lot of folks call a Mexican standoff. No offense. In other words, you got something I want and I got something you want — without a clear way for either of us gettin' what it is we're after."

"I disagree, *amigo,*" came back Estarde. "I have nine men over here with me. You have four, maybe only three, and a couple of women. The way for me to get what I want seems *very* clear — although very costly to you, if you insist on making it difficult."

"Yeah, your outfit could no doubt overpower mine. But it'd damn well cost you, too, and you know it. And I don't mean just in lives." Firestick paused to let those listening wonder a minute before he hit them with the rest of it. "These rifles over here — your whole purpose for makin' this trip, the thing that's so important to your cause, your revolution — are sittin' in a weathered, dried-out old building that will go up like a tinderbox if flame was set to it . . . and that's exactly what I'm prepared to do at the first sign of an attack from any of your crew. This building will burn so fast and so hot those guns will melt like butter and the ammunition will explode uselessly."

"You wouldn't dare!" Estarde exclaimed. "It would gain you nothing — you would still end up dead, butchered, your women —"

"We'd be dead either way!" Firestick cut him off. "And you can bet we'd make certain our women didn't stay alive to end up in the hands of rapists and butchers. But the only thing you care about — the guns — they would be dead, too."

"The guns must live," Estarde insisted, his voice strained. "The freedom of my long-suffering people . . ."

"If you're willin' to make a deal," said Firestick, "there's a way for you to still get the rifles, at no risk to your men."

"How can this be?"

"You see, when I told you me and my friend did gun work, it wasn't a lie. I just neglected to mention that we did it from behind badges. So turn the gunrunners over to us. Let us take them — and the women — away from here. I'll see to it the gunrunners face charges and get a fair trial for the crimes they committed to get their hands on those rifles. While I'm busy with them, my back is bound to be turned. You should have all the time you need to grab the rifles and make it back across the border before I notice what you're up to or have any chance to try and stop you."

"You would do this? Even though you say you wear badges on this side of the border?"

There was a hurried and somewhat heated exchange of words from those over in the hotel. Firestick wasn't able to catch everything that was said, but it was evident the gunrunners were protesting against Estarde striking any kind of deal for the rifles.

When things quieted down, the colonel called again. "Were I not a man of my word, *amigo,* I might find your offer quite appealing. Unfortunately, a man must be able to live with himself or not be able to call himself a man at all, eh? Therefore, the deal I made first with these *hombres* over here I must honor. I cannot simply turn them over to you for the guns."

Firestick heard himself chuckle harshly. "I'd've been surprised and disappointed in you if you did, Colonel. I'd've still done the deal, mind you, but it would have been with some regret."

"You make less and less sense, *amigo.* But it matters not. The time for talking is through. I must have those rifles!"

"You'd better hope the time for talkin' ain't through, and you'd better listen tight or those guns are gonna go up in a puff of smoke. You push me, I guarantee we can hold off your bunch long enough for this building to become an inferno you'll never pull anything worthwhile out of."

"What more is there to say?"

"I got one more offer — a way we can work this out and both walk away with our honor intact. You need to listen and make up your mind pronto. It's gettin' darker right along and pretty soon it'll be easy for some of you from over there to slip across the street and flank us. I won't wait for that to happen. The torches will hit this building long before it does."

"Say your piece. What is your new offer?"

Firestick glanced around at Moosejaw, Kate, and Cleo. Then he turned back to the window and said, "It's real simple. The guns those runners claim to have for sale are over here. All they have to do is come get 'em. Me and my pal will meet 'em out in the street. Four on two. They get past us, they bring you the guns and you complete the deal you agreed to. We stop 'em, you no longer have any obligation to dead men. We ride away with the women we came after; you ride away with the guns you came after. You got five minutes to make up your mind."

■ ■ ■ ■

Inside the old hotel, Vic Mason was enraged. "You don't need five minutes; you don't need five stinkin' seconds," he said, thrusting his purpled face close to that of Estarde's. "Tell him to go to hell! He's in no position to bargain."

Estarde regarded him calmly. "He has the guns. He is *completely* in a position to bargain."

"He's bluffing! He won't torch that building. If he tries, we'll rush him. No matter what he says, the store ain't gonna go up in flames that fast."

"You have not seen this man shoot. I have. We try rushing him, he will cut down half our number or more before they ever make it across the street."

Fleming, who had been seething silently on the periphery of things for several minutes, could hold back no longer. "See, Vic?" he said, pushing forward. "I tried to warn you all along that you can't trust this greaser trash. First whiff of trouble, he's trying to sell you down the river. Hell, this so-called colonel and his 'amigo' across the street are probably in cahoots right down the line, have been all along. Are you too blind to see it?"

Estarde smiled. "Señor Mason, you may thank your friend Fleming for helping me to make up my mind. And then you may thank *me* for helping you to get rid of the poison within your ranks." At a very subtle signal from the colonel, one of the rebel soldiers standing behind Fleming glided up closer. The soldier's machete flashed dimly in the faded light and a thin arc of blood spurted up both in reality and in stark shadow.

CHAPTER 54

"You have your deal, *amigo.* You and your friend come out onto the street. We will send the gunrunners — now only three in number — to meet you."

Firestick released a breath he hadn't been aware he was holding. Looking around, his eyes fell first on Moosejaw. A corner of his mouth quirked upward. "Kinda late to be askin', I reckon, but you up for this?"

Moosejaw grunted. "If you really needed to ask, you'd have done it before now. Hell yeah, let's go clear the street and then get headed home."

Kate rushed into Firestick's arms. "Is there no other way?"

Firestick pressed her to him for a long moment, then held her back at arm's length. "You heard me lay out the options. This is our best chance. You also heard me and Estarde mention how you women might be treated. If neither Moosejaw nor me make it, you need to consider that."

Kate shook her head fiercely. "I won't contemplate such a thing. You will make it, and we will leave here together."

Suddenly Josh Stallworth was on his feet and crowded up close. "I'm goin' out there with you, Marshal. The only way you can stop me is to shoot me."

"Don't tempt me. You're the reason —"

"I know. That's why I've got to go. To hit a lick for the right side, to try and square at least a smidgen of what I helped mess up so bad."

"Let him come. We ain't got time to argue," said Moosejaw.

Firestick made an indifferent gesture and turned to the door.

Cleo came over and handed Josh his pistol. "Try not to get yourself killed," she said, gazing up at him. "You're lonely and you have some wrongheaded notions . . . but I'll always remember you saw me as an angel. Even though I'm anything but."

"That's the only thing I've ever seen when I look at you, Miss Cleo. From the first second I laid eyes on you."

Out in the street, the grotesque shadows thrown by the old buildings on all sides had pooled into patches of almost impenetrable darkness. But there was still enough gray half light to see sufficiently for what had to be done.

Firestick, Moosejaw, and Josh exited the old store and fanned out along the edge of the street.

A soft breeze had come with dusk, stirring the dust faintly, nudging some of the tumbleweeds so they shivered and rocked back and forth a bit.

Mason, Lefty, and Beaudine came down the steps of the hotel.

"Which one of you lowlifes killed my friend Charlie?" Josh demanded abruptly.

Beaudine swallowed. "I guess it was me. I didn't know if I kilt him or not. He's the first fella I ever straight up shot."

"I aim to make him your last," said Josh.

A single clocktick of time rolled by slowly.

And then it all broke loose. It started with young Beaudine, caving under the pressure of Josh's glare. The young man was fast, faster than Josh, and the bullet streaking from his gun hit its target square in the middle of the chest. Josh's torso jolted but he didn't go down, didn't even back up a step. And then his own gun was talking and it was shouting out revenge for his best friend. One slug and then another tore into Beaudine's spare frame. He jerked sideways, staggering, and his knees started to buckle. He squeezed off two more shots as he went down. One went high, the other pounded into Josh's chest. This time the cowboy was knocked backward and down but he, too, got off a final shot that drilled the final gasp of life out of Beaudine.

While that exchange was taking place, Mason drew on Firestick. He never came close. His gun failed to clear leather before the marshal's first slug punched through his guts and the next, a split second later, hammered his teeth out the back of his head.

Firing his Winchester from the hip, Moosejaw cut down Lefty also without him ever getting off a shot. Three rapid-fire rounds slammed in a tight pattern to the outlaw's chest, lifting him up on his toes and driving him backward until he collapsed on the hotel steps with his arms flung wide.

It was over in a matter of seconds.

The pools of shadow filling the street grew darker; only now, within them, were spreading patterns of scarlet.

CHAPTER 55

Two days later, they arrived back in Buffalo Peak.

A couple of wranglers from one of the outlying ranches spotted them on the way in and carried word ahead to the town. By the time Firestick, Moosejaw, Kate, and Cleo reached the outskirts, there was quite a throng waiting to welcome them.

Prominent among the greeters was Daisy, who wasted no time in literally dragging Moosejaw down out of his saddle so she could shower him with hugs and kisses until his face glowed as bright a red as one of the hot coals from her forge. Not far behind was Beartooth, ready with hearty handshakes and claps to the backs of his old friends and a chaste embrace for Kate. He and his posse had gotten similar treatment only the day before when they returned from running down the bank robbers.

A jubilant Victoria was present, too, having remained in town, staying at Kate's hotel until some kind of word was received on the fate of the abducted women. And Kate's loyal friends and employees — headed by a joyful Big Thomas Rivers and sobbing Marilu, who had kept the Mallory House running smoothly during her absence — were there, as well.

It was well into evening before the crowd of well-wishers thinned out and only a remaining handful retired to the Mallory House barroom to cap things off. By that point, the accounts of the abducted gals and their pursuers as well as details of the bank robbery and the successful rundown of the perpetrators had been exchanged and re-told a number of times. Oberon Hadley was among those gathered in the barroom, though it was revealed that he would be leaving the following day to accompany Rupert Shaw's body on its return to England.

In the end, during the ride back from the Viejas, the big Englishman's rage and disappointment in his former captain had subsided. He had asked the other posse members that the exact details of Shaw's cowardice and how he died be altered for the sake of his family and the proud Shaw legacy. "There's nothing to be gained by revealing the truth — only shame and deepened sorrow for his survivors. Let us merely say he stopped a bullet during the attempted rescue and retrieval of him and the bank money. Let him face eternity as the hero of Baba Wali Pass. A greater power will have the final say on his soul." The other posse members agreed to honor this request, and that's how it was told when they got back to town and how it was discussed still that evening there at the gathering.

Later, Beartooth would get around to telling Firestick and Moosejaw the truth; the bond between the three of them never allowed for anything less. In the telling, Beartooth would also speak of another bond, the rather unexpected one that had developed between him and Hadley. He genuinely hated to see the big Englishman go, yet his sense of Hadley's appreciation for the Western frontier and the American spirit left him with a strong hunch they just might be seeing him return one day.

All during the initial greeting in the street and then the smaller gathering that made its way to the Mallory House, Cleo had basically floated on the periphery of the talk and well wishes — uncomfortable looking, small and sad and mostly silent, an ill fit to the proceedings. Frenchy Fontaine and Earl

Sterling had welcomed her and embraced her, but then had faded back into the earlier throng and were no part of the group that eventually ended up at the Mallory House.

After a while, with the others hardly noticing her and darkness descending in the street outside, she slipped away from the barroom and started to leave the hotel. But as she was getting ready to step down off the boardwalk out front, a voice stopped her.

"Where are you going?"

Cleo turned to see Kate coming out behind her.

"I'm tired," Cleo said softly. "I . . . I thought I'd go on home."

"Home?"

Cleo gestured feebly toward the Lone Star Palace a short ways up the street. "The only place I got."

Kate frowned. "Is that how you want it to be?"

"Ain't a matter of want, Miss Kate," Cleo said with a somewhat bitter smile. "That's just the way it is."

"But it doesn't have to be."

"I'm afraid you're wrong. It's where I belong. I surely didn't belong in there" — she jabbed a finger toward the hotel behind Kate — "with you and your friends. Oh sure, everybody was polite and they all made sure not to say anything to offend me. But I could feel it every second. The message was clear. Every single person there was uncomfortable rubbing elbows with nothing but a dirty little who—" Cleo stopped short, checked herself from completing the word. And it wasn't because of anything Kate said or did or the way she was looking at her. It was because of a voice suddenly streaking through her head. Josh's voice, saying, *"Stop it! Don't call yourself that no more. You're better than that!"*

A strange smile spread across Kate's face. "He made you believe, didn't he?" she said softly.

"What are you talking about?"

"Josh. He convinced you that you were better than that. That you didn't *have* to be what you'd always been."

"Josh was crazy."

"Maybe. A little. But sometimes a little bit of craziness is what's needed to give us a kick in the bustle in order to keep us from being stuck in a rut. Being taken by Josh and Charlie proved to both of us that we are strong, smart, spirited women who are more durable than we might otherwise have ever thought. I know this because of what I felt in myself and what I saw in you. Neither

518

of us ever gave up, ever lost hope."

"It was easier for you. You knew Firestick would be coming for you."

"And you knew — or should have — that also meant he would be coming for you, too. But, in the meantime, you also realized . . . I know you did, I saw it in your eyes . . . that Josh was willing to lay down his life before letting any harm befall you."

"He did . . . lay down his life," Cleo said quietly.

"Yes. And do you think he did that so you could return to the Lone Star Palace?"

Suddenly Cleo fell into the older woman's arms and began sobbing raggedly. "I don't want to go back. I want to be something better. Like Josh believed I could. I know I can't be the angel he saw, but I want to try."

"If you really mean that and are willing to work hard," said Kate, "I'll find you a job here. It may only be maid service or kitchen help at first, but you're bright. I can see you learning the reception desk, maybe do some bartending. It won't pay a lot, but it will come with your own room and some of the best food in town out of Marilu's kitchen."

"That sounds like heaven," Cleo replied. Then, giving a little laugh through her sobs, she added, "Maybe I can come closer to being an angel than I thought."

"Just keep that in mind when some of your early jobs are apt to include mopping and cleaning spittoons," Kate told her.

"Don't worry. I've done worse," said Cleo. Then, abruptly, her body went rigid and she jerked partly away from Kate. "But what about my reputation, my past?" she gasped. "Folks all around town are gonna know. They'll talk and gossip . . . you know they will. Will that hurt your business? And what if some randy, half-drunk cowboys show up in town and won't want to believe I've changed my ways?"

"How about lettin' me worry about that?" said a new voice.

The women turned to watch Firestick ghost out of the shadows off to one side of the hotel's front door. "Excuse me for eavesdroppin' a bit, ladies. I came out to see where you two had slipped off to and stopped to listen a minute.

"I liked everything I heard except that last business about your worries, Cleo. First off, I think you'll find folks around town are more reasonable and forgivin' than you might expect. Second, any hardheads who *ain't* inclined toward such . . . well, me and my deputies, along with Big Thomas who looks after things around the Mallory House mighty tight, will see to it their attitudes get straightened out right quick."

Cleo wiped away a tear and regarded him with a lopsided grin. "I thought you were tired of cleaning up the trouble I seem to always end up in the middle of ?"

Firestick grunted. "Who says I ain't? But I've found out that when a body gets to be a certain age — and I ain't sayin' I'm old, mind you — you recognize you're stuck with certain habits. Some of 'em ain't especially good or even reasonable, but like I said, you might as well admit you're stuck with 'em. It's beginnin' to appear like you and your troubles have fallen in that category for me — especially if you're gonna be hangin' around Kate and the Mallory House from now on."

"That doesn't seem so unfair," said Kate. "After all, you've gotten to be a habit with me . . . and look at all the blasted trouble you keep throwing yourself at."

Firestick looked like he was going to try and defend himself. But then he changed his mind and instead spread his hands in a what-are-you-gonna-do gesture, saying, "You got me. Guilty as charged."

Six months later, ahead of winter's heavy snows, Cleo had saved up enough money to hire a pair of men with a buckboard to return to Bright Rock and dig up the remains of Josh and Charlie that had been buried there. She gave specific directions to make sure the right bodies were retrieved.

Back in Buffalo Peak, she had them reinterred in the town cemetery. She arranged stone markers for each.

Charlie's read: *Charlie Gannon — A Schemer and a Dreamer; He Died Bravely.*

Josh's read: *Josh Stallworth — A Kind-hearted Soul; May He Rest in the Arms of Angels.*

ABOUT THE AUTHORS

William W. Johnstone has written nearly three hundred novels of western adventure, military action, chilling suspense, and survival. His bestselling books include *The Family Jensen; The Mountain Man; Flintlock; MacCallister; Savage Texas; Luke Jensen, Bounty Hunter;* and the thrillers *Black Friday, The Doomsday Bunker,* and *Trigger Warning.*

J. A. Johnstone learned to write from the master himself, Uncle William W. Johnstone, with whom J. A. has co-written numerous bestselling series including The Mountain Man; Those Jensen Boys; and Preacher, The First Mountain Man.